HONOR 'N' DUTY

FEDERAL K-9 SERIES

TEE O'FALLON

This book is a work of fiction. Names, characters, places, and incidents are the product of the author's imagination or are used fictitiously. Any resemblance to actual events, locales, or persons, living or dead, is coincidental.

Copyright © 2022 by Tee O'Fallon. All rights reserved, including the right to reproduce, distribute, or transmit in any form or by any means. For information regarding subsidiary rights, please contact the Publisher.

Entangled Publishing
644 Shrewsbury Commons Ave
STE 181
Shrewsbury, PA 17361
rights@entangledpublishing.com

Amara is an imprint of Entangled Publishing.

Edited by Heather Howland
Cover design by LJ Anderson/Mayhem Cover Creations
Cover photography by MRBIG_PHOTOGRAPHY, Hirurg, Eric Metz, and HannaGottschalk/Getty Images

Manufactured in the United States of America

First Edition July 2022

HONOR 'N' DUTY

FEDERAL K-9 SERIES

At Entangled, we want our readers to be well-informed. If you would like to know if this book contains any elements that might be of concern for you, please check the book's webpage for details.

https://entangledpublishing.com/books/honor-n-duty

To my family—human and *canine. For being there. For loving me. For just being you!*

Prologue

Kade Sampson pulled into the Regional Bank & Trust's parking lot. The bank was hopping, forcing Kade to park in the back forty.

He turned off the engine, taking in the massive, two-story concrete and brick structure. With the never-ending bank of windows and the gold dome capping the second floor, it reminded him of the Emerald City in the *Wizard of Oz*. Kade's older brother had done good for himself. Better than good, actually.

Like their father, grandfather, and great-grandfather, they'd both been West Point grads. But where Kade had gone the Army Ranger–law enforcement route, Josh's expertise had taken him in an entirely different direction.

Now, as the newly promoted manager of RB&T's central branch in Marlboro, New Jersey, Josh supervised more than fifty people, plus another hundred or so at the bank's smaller branches scattered around North Jersey.

Not that Kade was surprised. He might have inherited their dad's athletic abilities, but it was Josh who'd inherited their old man's wizardry with numbers. No wonder he'd always kicked Kade's ass when their dad forced them to play board games that taught strategy, like chess and Monopoly. Kade and Josh had always been fiercely competitive, and those games had been a way for them to blow off steam without actually coming to blows. Most of the time, anyway. A shrink probably would have declared their sibling rivalry unhealthy.

The second Kade stepped outside, a strong gust of cool autumn wind whipped open his suit jacket, exposing his Glock to half a dozen video cameras. He pulled down the flap of the jacket, holding it in place as he walked to the entrance. No sense putting the bank's security team on red alert and tackling him the second he walked in the door.

He passed a brand-new silver Jaguar parked in the spot reserved for the bank manager. Knowing Josh, the Jag was probably the latest, top-of-the-line model. Kade could only imagine what his K-9's claws would do to all that buttery-soft leather upholstery.

He pushed through the heavy glass door and was hit by the low hum of customers waiting on one side of the lobby for a teller and more conversation at the dozen or so desks on the other side. He didn't know how Josh did it. Parking his butt at a desk all day would have killed Kade. Then again, his brother had a five-thousand-square-foot mansion overlooking the Navesink River in Rumson, one of the most exclusive neighborhoods in the state. The property boasted an enormous swimming pool and yard, plus a floating dock and a thirty-foot sailboat that he never used. The price tag on a place like that, let alone the taxes, made Kade's head hurt. Probably pocket change for Josh.

Heading for the elevators, Kade stuck his finger in the knot of his tie, loosening it and popping open the top button of his shirt. The damned thing was itching the hell out of his neck. Smoke had it made. Usually, the only thing his dog had to wear to work was the furry suit he'd been born with.

He pushed the up arrow, still curious about the unexpected call he'd received last night from his brother. Josh said he had news he wanted to share in person, then invited Kade to lunch. Kade didn't normally get down to Marlboro Township, but he'd been testifying in court for the local PD, and the courthouse was only minutes from the bank. The timing had worked out.

Half a minute later, the digital number above the elevator indicated the car was still on the second floor. He turned to look for the stairwell and promptly crashed into someone. "Sorry." He reached out to steady the woman he'd practically body-slammed.

Light-brown, almond-shaped eyes fringed by thick lashes looked up at him from the most beautiful face he'd ever seen. Long, straight, jet-black hair framed creamy skin with a hint of olive. High cheekbones gave the woman a regal bearing.

"Uh, you can let go, now." Rosy-pink gloss called attention to lips that lifted slightly as she looked up at him for a moment, then glanced warily at the open doors. "The elevator's here."

As she brushed past him, he inhaled her scent—subtle and sweet, like the honeysuckle vines that used to grow in his parents' backyard and…pears. He guessed she was about five-six, taller in those skyscraper heels. When she turned, his gaze dipped to the strand of pearls around her neck and the lacy top of a camisole peeking out from the open collar of her white blouse.

Kade's gut clenched at his unexpected reaction. Okay, so the woman was a knockout, but it was more than that.

Barracks bunnies always had a way of ferreting out the West Point grads and the Army Rangers, so he'd been with *lots* of knockouts. *This* woman did something to him.

Something basic and instinctive that made everything inside him jump to attention like a police cadet on his first day at the academy.

The elevator started to close, and she reached for the button panel, holding open the doors. "Are you coming?"

"Yeah," he managed after unswallowing his tongue, then joined her inside.

The doors closed and the elevator shimmied as it began to rise. A few seconds later, it lurched to an abrupt halt that had them both reaching for the handrails. A folder she'd been clutching fell to the floor.

"Oh, no." Her knuckles turned white where she gripped the rails, her chest rising and falling faster.

"Hey, it'll be okay. I promise."

She gave him a tight nod.

He peered through the narrow slit between the doors, not seeing any light, then pushed each button on the elevator one by one. Still, the elevator didn't budge. Next, he opened a small panel door beneath the buttons and pulled out the emergency phone. Seconds later, an operator answered.

"We're stuck between floors," Kade said, knowing the elevator company's twenty-four-hour monitoring service would automatically identify the elevator and the building's location.

"I understand, sir," the operator answered. "Is anyone hurt?"

Kade looked at the woman who'd begun to tremble. "Negative." *For now.* Although she looked ready to pass out. "How long?"

"Approximately thirty minutes."

"Make it faster." He reinserted the phone into the compartment, then took a chance and rested his hands on the woman's shoulders. "It really will be okay. They know exactly where we are, and they're sending someone to get us out."

Her inhalations were still coming too rapidly, and her hands fisted tighter on the rails.

Time for a little Sampson-charm distraction. "What's your name?"

"Laia," she whispered between breaths.

Even her name was pretty. "Mine's Kade. You okay?"

"Mm-hmm." She nodded, looking up and giving him an up-close-and-personal glimpse of those gorgeous eyes still brimming with banked fear.

"Claustrophobic, huh?"

"A little," she admitted, pressing her hand to her belly.

"You're not going to get sick on me, are you?" He'd said it in jest, but the more she kept touching her belly, the more he suspected she might really heave.

"Well, hopefully not *on* you," she answered, and he was rewarded with a hesitant smile. "I was actually thinking that corner would do nicely." Her face had flushed with what would normally be a pretty shade of pink. Except for the fact that she looked ready to lose her breakfast.

"Why don't we get comfortable? It'll help the time pass easier." He shrugged out of his suit jacket, spread it on the floor, then held out his hand. Her mouth fell open and her eyes widened as she caught sight of his holstered gun and badge. "I'm a Department of Homeland Security officer."

"Oh." Slim fingers clasped his, sending sharp tingles of awareness shooting up his arm. "But your jacket will get dirty."

"That's what dry cleaners are for." The floor of that elevator could have been coated with mud, grease, and oil, and he'd still sacrifice his jacket in a heartbeat.

That and his father *and* his grandfather would have smacked the back of his head with a book for ever allowing a lady to sit on a filthy elevator floor. Officers and gentlemen to the core, both of them. To a fault, actually.

"Thank you." Gracefully, she lowered to the floor, curling her legs beneath her and readjusting her beige skirt as she settled in the corner to face him. Her breathing seemed easier, although she still looked queasy.

"Better?" he asked, sitting and leaning against the adjacent wall.

"Yes, thank you." This time, the smile she gave him was genuine, but she swallowed hard as she took in the confined space they'd likely be stuck in for half an hour. More, probably.

"You work for this bank, right?" No jacket, purse, or briefcase, and the only thing she'd been carrying was that folder that now lay on the floor. She looked to be in her late twenties and wore no rings. His mind was quick to note that.

She nodded. "I'm an accounts manager."

"Where are you from, Laia?" Even if he hadn't been trying to keep her mind occupied, that was a question he would have asked anyway because he truly wanted to know more about her.

"Asbury Park, but my family is originally from Puerto Rico."

That explained the slight accent he'd detected that only made itself known when she spoke certain words. "I *love* Puerto Rico." He stretched out his legs, crossing them at the ankles. "I've been there a dozen times for work. I always tack on a few extra personal days to see the sights and have some fun."

"What's your favorite place?" She tucked a few strands of long, dark hair behind one ear, revealing a tiny pearl stud in her lobe.

"Hard to pick just one. The Bioluminescent Bay is one of the coolest places on earth."

"It is, isn't it?" This time she smiled fully. "Do you know what makes the water luminesce?"

"Dino flagellates. What else? They glow neon blue

whenever the water is disturbed."

"I'm impressed. Most tourists don't know."

"I've got a good memory for details." Something that had served him well in the Rangers and later in the DHS. "What's *your* favorite place?"

"Oh, that's easy." She sat up straighter, her eyes lighting with enthusiasm. "El Yunque, the rain forest. I loved looking at all the animals. The iridescent green and blue hummingbirds, the bats, geckos, and lizards. Once, I'm sure I spotted one of the most endangered animals in the world, the—"

"Puerto Rican Parrot," they both said at the same time.

"Exactly." She laughed, sending another jolt of awareness speeding through Kade's body, this one forcing him to adjust his legs. "There are less than thirty of them left in the wild, all living in El Yunque."

Laia's enthusiasm was totally contagious. "Have you ever gone ziplining at El Yunque? Gives you a better chance of seeing more birds."

"That I've never done," she said wistfully. "Mostly, that's a tourist thing. Maybe, someday."

"You should also go jet skiing at Isla Verde. Great way to see the coast." Kade still remembered that trip. Josh had joined him but never left the hotel, preferring to lounge by the pool rather than experiencing all the beauty, history, and adventure Puerto Rico had to offer. "But I'm guessing that's a tourist thing, too?"

"It is." She smiled. "There's so much more to the island than people know. Tourists only skim the surface and see what's in the travel brochures. To experience the true heartbeat of Puerto Rico you have to stray from the beaten path."

There was no missing the sadness brimming in her lovely eyes. "Sounds like you miss it."

"I do. Especially the food." She chuckled. "Puerto Ricans are as passionate about their food as the French."

"I didn't know that," he admitted. "Have you ever eaten at Casita Moreno? Their stuffed mofongo is awesome." The last time he'd gone there, he'd eaten two servings.

"I actually have eaten there." She nodded, almost reluctantly. "It's good, but the *best* mofongo I ever had was at a little hole-in-the-wall place down a side street you've probably never even heard of. You'd have to be a local to know it was even there. When I was little, we went there on my birthday for tres leches cake. It was my favorite."

He loved tres leches. "If you could celebrate your birthday anywhere in the world, where would you spend it?"

"Hawaii. I've never been there. What about you?"

"I think I'd like to go back to Puerto Rico again and see *your* version of the island, not the tourist version."

She blushed, and her eyes darted away, but not before he caught the little smile tugging at the corner of her lips. Here he was stuck in an elevator with a woman he'd known for less than ten minutes and he was already—

He glanced at his watch and *holy shit*. Forty minutes had passed.

The smooth skin on her forehead creased. "What is it?"

"Nothing." Nothing bad, anyway. Being stuck in this elevator with her for another forty minutes would be the best thing that had happened to him in a long time. But the frown on her face deepened. "Are you okay?"

She nodded. "I'm just late for a meeting. *Really* late."

"Do you want to call someone?" He dug into his pocket for his phone. "You can use my phone."

When he held out his cell, she reached for it but stopped. Rather than take the phone, she stared at him intently. When she smiled, his heart began slamming against his ribs. When they escaped from this elevator, there was no way he was saying goodbye. It was on the tip of his tongue to ask her to be his personal tour guide on a lengthy trip to Puerto Rico, which was ridiculous, considering they'd known each other less than an hour.

"Laia," he said, soaking up whatever this amazing connection bouncing between them was, "would you like to have dinner with me tonight?" The answer *had* to be yes. Judging by the electricity zapping between them, he sensed it would be. He held his breath, hoping she couldn't hear that muscle in his chest bouncing around like a beach ball.

Slowly, her smile faded, and her expression turned…sad. There was no other word for it. "Kade, I—"

The elevator jerked, then started to rise.

He grabbed the folder, handing it to Laia as he helped her to stand. The sorrow in her eyes had deepened, and she wouldn't even look at him.

"Laia?" He touched his fingers to her cheek. "What's wrong?"

Before she could answer, the elevator stopped, and the doors opened. Josh and a small crowd had gathered, including two elevator repairmen.

Kade dropped his hand, surprised to find a flare of annoyance in Josh's eyes. Okay, so he was late for their lunch, but it wasn't like his brother to get so bent out of shape over something so small.

"What the hell are you doing?" Josh asked him, then reached for Laia, tugging her into the hallway, then running his hands up and down her arms. "Are you all right? I was notified the elevator was stuck, but I had no idea *you* were in there."

"I'm fine," Laia said, trying to slip past Josh, but he didn't let her. Instead, he tucked her to his side, placing his hand protectively at her waist.

Josh refocused on Kade, his eyes still flashing with

annoyance, the source of which Kade didn't understand. Then he saw it, something else he'd long ago learned to decipher when his brother had managed to one-up him. *Satisfaction*.

His brother smirked. "Kade. This is my fiancé, Laia."

"*What*?" Kade remained in the elevator, looking from Josh to Laia, whose expression was anything but happy.

"Come to my office, bro." Josh's smirk deepened, then he leaned down to kiss Laia's cheek, never taking his eyes off Kade. "This was what I wanted to tell you. We got engaged last night."

The elevator could have dropped out from beneath Kade, sending him crashing into the basement, and he wouldn't have felt a thing. Laia blinked rapidly, as if she were about to cry.

Gut-sinking confusion rolled through him, pounding at him like a battering ram. This wasn't possible. The woman he'd stupidly envisioned taking to dinner, eating tres leches cake with, and, hell, even traveling to Puerto Rico with, and one day…

He couldn't even think it. Because she was engaged. To his *brother*.

Kade took in the pained, apologetic expression on her face, and his heart plummeted straight into his now-twisted guts.

He fisted his hands so hard his nails dug into his palms. *Shut it down*. Whatever emotional connection he had to his brother's fiancé had to end here, now, and…

Forever.

Chapter One

Nearly six years later

Kade gunned the SUV off Route 35 into the heart of Asbury Park. He and his new Belgian sheepdog K-9, Smoke, had been on the road for nearly four hours. Behind him on the bench seat of the mobile kennel, his dog sighed in his sleep.

Late June sunlight blared through the window as he serpentined in and out of shore traffic. Even with the AC blasting, his tuxedo jacket off, and his sleeves rolled up to his elbows, he was sweating his balls off.

He'd gotten Laia's call minutes before Cassidy Morgan had walked down the aisle and said "I do" to one of his best friends, Markus York. He'd let the call go to voicemail, listening to her frantic message an hour later at the reception. Her house had been broken into and ransacked. In an angry voice, she'd demanded to know if the Feds had served another search warrant.

Making his apologies to Markus and Cassidy, he and Smoke had raced north. Being stand-up people, his friends had understood the need for exigency.

At the next red light, he scrolled through his emails, double-checking in case he'd missed anything. During the drive from Maryland to Jersey, Kade had peppered his colleagues in the DHS and every contact he had in the DEA, IRS, FBI, and local police to verify there'd been no warrant. He already knew there hadn't been.

In Laia's message, there'd been no mention of a warrant left behind. Any federal or state agency or police department would have left a copy inside the house. Which meant this was either a random burglary...or something else. It was the *something else* that had a bucketful of agita roiling like bad sushi in his gut. Not once in the last few hours had Laia returned any of his calls.

When the light changed, he rolled through, then turned off Route 35 onto the local streets, heading unerringly for Laia's house. He knew exactly where she lived, had known it since the day she'd moved into the small rented duplex.

Long before his parents notified him of her new address, he'd checked up on her and his niece, Rosa. In fact, he'd been checking up on them since the moment Josh had been arrested. He'd seen Rosa at his parents' many times, but he hadn't seen Laia in two years. Since Josh's funeral. And before that, the last time he'd seen her had been three years earlier. At another wedding.

Hers.

Upholding his family's military legacy of bone-deep honor and duty, Kade had stood beside his brother that day as his best man. On the outside, he'd been the visual epitome of brotherly support, while on the inside, he'd been gut-punched and confused. He hadn't understood why Josh and Laia were getting married, hadn't glimpsed so much as a whisper of a real, honest-to-goodness connection between them.

That day still haunted him. The same lack of excitement—

no, *misery*—he'd been struggling with since Josh had announced his and Laia's engagement had been mirrored on Laia's face. At first, some part of him wondered if maybe it was because of him, because of their conversation that day.

As Josh had slid the ring on Laia's finger, she'd looked up at Kade, and for one brief moment her eyes shimmered but not from joy. When the officiant had pronounced them husband and wife, Kade could barely contain his frustration. His brother seemed content, but there was no spark between Josh and Laia, and she didn't seem remotely happy.

He braked for another red light, gripping the wheel tighter as he recalled their last conversation, so clear in his mind, as if it had happened an hour ago. He'd pulled her aside at the reception, guiding her to an isolated deck overlooking the Atlantic Ocean.

"Laia," he'd said, his heart squeezing at how beautiful she looked. And how sad. "Are you okay?"

"Of course." She held up her chin and mustered a patently false smile, the kind he'd been faking for the last two hours. "It's my wedding day. Why wouldn't I be?"

"You tell *me*." Gently, he cupped her face, and when she leaned into his hand, he nearly whisked her away on the spot because something about the whole wedding was totally off. Her hair was artfully arranged on the top of her head, with softly swirling curls framing her face. A light breeze blew one of them across her cheek, and he brushed it away. "I can tell something's wrong. Did *I* do something? Did I say something to you that—"

"No! Oh, God, no." She clasped his hand, the first time they'd touched since being stuck in the elevator three weeks earlier. "Don't *ever* think that."

"I don't know what to think. Didn't you feel something between us in that elevator?" When she didn't respond, he stared at their linked hands, completely at a loss. "I *know* you did because I felt it, too. Help me to understand what's happening here. Because it sure as hell looks like there's nothing between you and Josh."

She jerked her hand from his, the wall she'd been hiding behind slamming back up between them. "You're wrong. You might be his brother, but our relationship is *none* of your business, and you don't know *anything* about me. Whatever you think happened between us in that elevator didn't."

The absolute conviction in her eyes hit him harder than a baton strike to the stomach.

He'd been wrong. Kade didn't know how, but he'd made a horrible mistake in assuming there'd been something between them, something potentially amazing and—

In less time than it took for his heart to beat twice, that muscle froze into a solid block of ice. Accepting the truth went against every instinct he had, but there it was. No matter how much he hated it, Laia had something with Josh. For whatever the reason, she didn't want *him*.

He took a deep breath, reaching way down inside himself to find the strength he needed to get past this. "Fine. But don't hurt my brother." They may not have had the closest relationship, but they were still brothers, and Kade couldn't help but be protective. "Whatever's going on between you two, don't hurt him."

Her expression was a mixture of anger *and* pain, the same emotions tearing him up inside. "You don't know what you're talking about."

He leaned in. "Then *tell* me."

"Laia?" Josh strode toward them, shoving the two Champagne glasses he'd been carrying at a passing waiter and spilling some onto the guy's jacket. "What's wrong? What's going on here?"

"Good question," Kade had replied. "I was just saying goodbye."

Then he'd walked away.

Honking dragged him back to the present, and he looked up to see the light had changed. How could he have known then that his brother—not Laia—would be the one doing the hurting?

A psychoanalyst he wasn't, but in the years since, Kade had come to understand the undercurrents rolling off his brother the day he'd proudly declared Laia to be his fiancé. There was no doubting that Josh had planned on showing Laia off to Kade, but Josh had also seemed happy.

Which made having feelings for Laia that much worse.

He drove through the light, then hung a left onto Second Avenue and passed a funeral home. At the next intersection, he turned left onto Emory Street and parked behind two black-and-white Asbury Park PD units. Assuming Laia had called the police hours ago, he was relieved to see they were still there. Not every town's police department took burglaries as seriously as they should. Looked like Chief Hassan was making good on his promise.

Eight months ago, Kade and Smoke had assisted the Asbury Park PD on a drug bust and uncovered two kilos of hidden coke. The case had made headlines. Now Chief Hassan owed him a favor.

Laia's slightly beat-up, gray Ford Escape, one he knew she'd bought at a used car dealer, sat in the driveway she shared with the duplex's other tenant, Alvita Thomas, a Jamaican woman who'd moved in shortly before Laia and Rosa. Alvita's green minivan was parked behind the Escape and just in front of the six-foot-high wood fence leading to the backyard.

Alvita stood on the grass in front of her side of the duplex with her two children, five-year-old Coraline and seven-year-old Jaden, eying him suspiciously. Kade had never met the family but had surreptitiously checked up on them the day after Laia and Rosa had moved in.

Like Laia, Alvita was a hard-working single mother. Through his parents, he'd learned the two women had struck up a close friendship, sharing playdates with the kids and helping each other out with babysitting.

Smoke stuck his head through the kennel window, his tail thumping against the kennel when he caught sight of Coraline and Jaden. One thing Kade had learned quickly in the two years since he and Smoke had partnered up was that his dog loved children almost as much as bacon. Maybe more, and that was saying something.

"I know." He gave Smoke a quick scratch behind the ears, then dug his creds from the glove box. "You'll see Rosa in a few minutes."

Hearing Kade's niece's name, Smoke's head perked up, and he leaned farther through the opening, hoping to catch sight of Rosa.

He stuffed his creds in his back pocket, then hooked a leash onto Smoke's collar and let him out the side door. As they headed up the walkway, Kade noted the residual limp in Smoke's right front leg.

A week ago, they'd been racing after a mugging suspect at Newark Airport. The perp jumped off a wall, and Smoke took off after him, landing hard on the pavement. He'd taken Smoke to the vet for an X-ray. No broken bones, and the limp was considerably less now, to the point where most people probably wouldn't even notice it. But Kade did. He and Smoke were so attuned to each other, anything out of sorts with either of them…the other didn't miss it.

They maneuvered around a pink tricycle and a blue sandcastle mold set complete with two cylinders indented to form the outline of bricks, plus a sand scoop. Smoke's tail wagged furiously at Coraline and Jaden, who pointed to his K-9, *oohing* and *aahing*. Looking like a very large, pure-black cross between a shepherd and a collie, Smoke was an eye-catcher.

The duplex was, in reality, a small gray Victorian that had been renovated to accommodate two families. Not in the best part of town but not in the worst, either. If Laia had accepted the financial assistance his parents had offered or the checks Kade had mailed her, she and Rosa could have at least been living in a small house of their own. But she'd politely turned his parents down.

And never cashed a single one of my checks.

Something that still bugged him. She'd needed the money, but there was another reason he'd sent those checks.

Guilt.

For the role he'd played in all of this.

At the front door, he pulled his creds and damned if his hand wasn't shaking. His father would have berated him for that transgression, ramming down his throat what a sissy he was being because *a good soldier doesn't shake in their boots.* One of many military sayings his father had taken way too much joy in reminding him and Josh.

He was sweating again and this time not just from the heat. In seconds, he'd be face to face with the woman who'd haunted so many of his nights he'd lost count.

Rather than barge right in, Kade stuck to protocol and held up his badge to the cop who stood just inside the screen door. "Kade Sampson, Homeland Security. I'm Ms. Velez's brother-in-law." Shortly after Josh's death, she'd reverted to her maiden name.

The cop, who couldn't have been more than twenty-five, didn't hesitate to open the door, meaning Chief Hassan had made good on his promise and notified his people to cooperate. He could just make out two other cops standing in the kitchen doorway with their backs to him.

"Good-looking dog," Officer Padkin, according to his

nametag, said, giving Smoke a wide berth.

"Thanks." His K-9 weighed in at about sixty pounds, but with his thick furry coat, he looked even more massive. Beneath that coat was a lean, agile powerhouse body that could run down a perp in seconds.

As he and Smoke went inside Laia's house for the first time, Kade couldn't hold back a few muttered curses. The devastation was far worse than he'd expected.

An old brown sofa had been pulled from the wall and flipped over, its cushions sliced and diced, the filling strewn everywhere. The small wood coffee table that looked like it had seen better days *before* the break-in was overturned, two of the legs broken. Even Rosa's basket of toys hadn't survived. In between the balls of sofa filler were dolls and stuffed animals, including the pink sequined Rainbowcorn Kade had given her on her fifth birthday last year. The animal's gold feet and stumpy horn glinted in the sunlight streaming through the window. Resting on the carpet beside it was the Magic Bluetooth Karaoke Microphone he'd bought her for Christmas.

As he and Smoke moved deeper into the living room, past the broken table and toys, Kade shut off his cop brain long enough to absorb the unexpected decor.

Every wall was a different color. Pale yellow, turquoise blue, peach, and light purple. The large area rug echoed the same colors in a pattern that looked as if someone had dumped four cans of paint on the rug, started stirring, and just stopped. Through the living room windows he could see into the backyard to an old wood dinghy someone had painted pink and purple. Oddly, it went with the living room colors.

Pitched here and there on the floor were broken framed photos of Laia and Rosa, one showing them fishing at the end of a long pier, another of the two of them at the beach.

His dress shoes crunched on another broken frame, this one a photo of Laia and Rosa at a carnival. Their faces were painted with what he assumed were henna tattoos. In every photo, they were clearly laughing.

"Stay," he said to Smoke, not wanting him to step on any broken glass. His dog went completely still, arching his back with his head held high in a show dog–worthy pose.

All in all, the room was vibrant in color *and* spirit. If it weren't for the devastation, he would have smiled. He suspected every room in the house had suffered the same fate, and the panic that had him racing north to Asbury Park magnified by a thousand.

The police would go through the motions, but Kade's fifteen years on the job already told him this was no random burglary. This was cold, calculated, and thorough. Whoever did this was looking for something. If what he suspected was true, the remnants of black fingerprint powder the department's forensic unit had left behind wouldn't reveal any latent prints that didn't belong here.

Laia's house had been tossed by professionals.

Kade couldn't see her but heard her voice as she answered the other cops' questions. One of the officers, a tall, fit-looking Black man whose biceps threatened to bust open the seams of his gray uniform, sported three gold sergeant's stripes on his sleeve. The other cop was equally fit, with her blond hair braided and pinned tightly to the back of her head.

He signaled for Smoke, pointing to a narrow swath of the floor not littered with shards of glass. They followed a high-pitched voice to another room off to the side of the kitchen. This one, a small office, judging by the desk and filing cabinet, had also been tossed thoroughly. Every desk drawer hung open, the contents of which had been thrown on the floor. The filing cabinet lay on its side, its drawers also open and the contents decorating the carpet.

Thick textbooks—zoology, microbiology, organic chemistry, and others his brain cringed at the thought of reading—lay stacked in messy piles against the wall, along with open spiral notebooks filled with neat script.

Sitting in the only clear space on the floor was Rosa, wearing pink shorts with a matching pink sleeveless top and pushing buttons on an interactive world map.

Smoke snorted, his tail wagging as he strained at the leash, eager to give Rosa a proper, slobbery greeting.

Rosa looked up. "Smoke! Uncle Kade!" she squealed, jumping to her feet and running to Smoke just as Kade dropped the leash.

He honestly couldn't tell who was more excited to see who. Rosa flung her arms around Smoke's neck, hugging him tightly while Smoke twisted his neck to land lick after lick on Rosa's beaming face.

"Mommy called you." Next Rosa ran to Kade, holding up her arms so that he could lift her up. When she was at eye level, she planted a squeaking kiss on his cheek, then cocked her little head. "Why is Mommy mad at you? I heard her on the phone. Did you have a fight? Why doesn't she like you?"

Oh, boy. How to answer a five-year-old's loaded questions because there were too many reasons to pick from and all of them valid.

On Laia's wedding day, he'd all but flat-out accused her of not loving his brother. Yeah, that one had to be at the top of the list. Then he'd intentionally ghosted her and Josh. Every time he and Smoke had visited Rosa at his parents' house, he'd verified beforehand that neither of them would be there. He'd turned down every single one of her and Josh's invitations to join them at their house to celebrate family events. Including Rosa's birth. The icing on the asshole cake was that after Josh died, he hadn't taken any of Laia's calls.

Kade had never been able to forget that amazing

connection they'd shared, and seeing Laia with his brother would have dredged up things that shouldn't be dredged up. So he'd kept his feelings buried. Or at least, *thought* he had.

There was still one other possible reason she was pissed at him.

Because she knows the truth.

About how things had really gone down the day Josh was arrested.

Now he'd suck up the guilt and endure half a decade of Laia's pent-up anger and resentment to keep her and Rosa safe. He owed it to them.

He owed it to Josh.

Forcing down the burning grief in the back of his throat, he stared into Rosa's green eyes, so like his brother's. "I'll talk to her," he promised. "You don't have to worry about anything, Cream Puff." He kissed her cheek, smiling when she giggled at the nickname he'd been calling her since discovering their shared love of whipped cream squirted directly from the can—the only rebellious habit in his strict military upbringing and one that had gotten him paddled so many times as a kid it was a wonder the back of his ass wasn't as flat as a pancake.

"Kade." His heart skipped a beat, then another. He'd recognize that sultry voice anywhere. In his sleep. In his dreams. In the memories that would haunt him until the day he went Tango Uniform—tits up and buried on the wrong side of the grass.

With Rosa still hefted in his arms, he turned and his throat closed up tighter than a shell casing. He couldn't have uttered a single coherent word if his life depended on it. This wasn't a dream, and it wasn't a memory. Laia was really standing there less than three feet away. Vaguely, he registered the two cops who'd been in the kitchen now looming behind her.

"Laia," he managed in a voice so rough he didn't

recognize it as his own.

Her hair was pulled high and tight into a ponytail, emphasizing the beauty he remembered so vividly. Her lips glistened with pink lipstick a shade brighter than he remembered.

Yeah. Sap that he was, he remembered her lipstick.

Purple shorts—*short* being the operative word—revealed sleek legs. A white tank top that said: Greetings From Asbury Park scooped low enough to reveal the soft curves of her breasts. Hardly the conservative attire she'd always worn in family photos he'd seen of her with Josh. She could have been wearing a burlap sack, and he still would have been sucker-punched by the jumble of emotions that had instantly come rumbling to the surface the second he'd seen her.

"Mommy?" Rosa said. "Are you still mad at Uncle Kade? Smoke is here."

Rather than go to Laia, Smoke sat protectively at Kade's side. Smoke and Laia had never met, and with the two cops standing behind her, he wasn't budging from his protective position.

Over Rosa's head, Laia's eyes locked with his. Everything he'd buried and convinced himself that he'd moved past came rushing back in a flood of memories and emotions.

Laia Velez was not only more beautiful now than ever, but the mystical, magnetic effect she had on him was still imprinted on every cell in his body. If anything, the memory of her in his heart and in his head was etched deeper now than ever before.

And he was in big, *big* trouble.

Chapter Two

Laia's hands trembled, whether from rage or the thrill of seeing Kade again she couldn't be sure, but her heart thumped wildly nonetheless.

The years had been good to him. If anything, he was more handsome than she remembered. All high cheekbones and chiseled...everything. He seemed taller and bigger than she remembered, too. Broader shouldered, leaner, more powerful, and with the same commanding presence, something she learned he'd acquired in West Point and later in the Army Rangers. The only signs of age were the fine lines at the corners of his striking hazel eyes. A burst of fiery amber surrounded the dark pupils with golden green irises—

Stop it, Laia.

She shook the thoughts free and lifted her chin. She should *not* be ogling her brother-in-law. The words she and Kade had exchanged on her wedding day had left a permanent scar on her heart. She'd nearly broken down right then and there and fessed up. But she couldn't. The promise she'd made to Josh was one she couldn't have broken. Even now it didn't seem right to divulge their agreement. To anyone.

Since that day, she'd only seen Kade once. Three years after the wedding—at Josh's funeral—the only words he'd spoken to her were his condolences, a quick *I'm so sorry*, then a peck on the cheek and he was gone, never to be seen or heard from again. Until now. The only things that had driven her to call him again were desperation...and fear. Fear that Josh's past could put Rosa in danger.

"Officer Sampson?" Sergeant Braden boomed from behind her.

"Yes." Kade held out his free hand to Sergeant Braden first, then to Officer Garcia, the tall woman who'd responded first to Laia's 911 call.

How did they know who he was?

As Kade shook hands with the cops, the muscles in his forearms flexed below the rolled-up sleeves of his shirt—a *tuxedo* shirt. There could be many reasons why he'd be wearing a tuxedo. Surely, he wouldn't have left his own wedding to come to her aid. *Right?*

She looked at his hands. *No ring.* Besides, her in-laws would have mentioned if he was about to be married. His marital status was none of her business, and it probably would have been better if he *had* been married. Yet the breath she let out next was filled with relief.

"Chief Hassan notified us you were on your way," Sergeant Braden continued. "Anything you need, just let us know."

So Kade *did* have friends in high places. Just last week, the house across the street had been broken into, some cash and gold jewelry stolen. The police hadn't given the victims half the time they'd expended at her house.

"Thanks," he said. "Can you fill me in?"

As Sergeant Braden began rattling off the procedural steps the police had taken since their arrival, Officer Garcia laughed softly. Rosa had begun plucking at Kade's hair. Knowing her daughter and judging by the way her lips had twisted into an adorable pout, Rosa was clearly perplexed at how to braid a military-precision buzz cut.

Nothing about having his hair played with by a five-year-old while talking to the police diminished Kade's concentration, not even when Rosa pulled hard.

"According to Ms. Velez," Sergeant Braden continued, "nothing was taken, which is odd."

Odd, yes, but thank goodness she'd had her laptop in the car with her at the time of the break-in. Without it, she'd never be able to finish her vet school application for the January semester.

"As expected, forensics found lots of prints," Garcia said, "but we won't know until early next week whether they all belong to Ms. Velez, her daughter, her neighbors, or the burglars."

Rosa tugged harder on a strand of brown hair. "Ouch." Kade's hard, sensual lips lifted as he sent Rosa a mock scowl.

When his elusive dimples made a guest appearance, unwanted heat curled low in her belly. Despite her latent anger, watching him interact so naturally, so paternally with her daughter unleashed a yearning deep inside her, making her wish for things that could never be.

Long before Josh died, they'd ceased to be a family. But he'd taught her an important lesson that she'd never forgotten and never would.

That the only person she could truly rely on was herself.

And yet, despite all the resentment she'd built up over the years still shining brighter than the summer sun, when the shit had hit the fan, she'd thought of Kade. *Dammit.*

The second she'd opened the door and seen the mess, she'd been thrown back in time, two years ago to when federal agents had served a search warrant at their house in Rumson.

All the shock and fear she'd experienced then had come back today with a mighty roar.

She'd been petrified for Rosa's safety, so they'd run back to the car and driven around the corner to call the police. Then she'd reached out to the last man on earth she swore she ever would again.

Five minutes after making the call, she'd begun to regret her decision, doubting it had been the right thing to do. But Kade was a government agent in the drug world, and if this had anything to do with Josh, then she needed his help. Rosa's safety was the only thing that mattered.

Josh had warned her about his no-show brother, relating derogatory tidbits she never would have suspected. That Kade was self-centered and egotistical, only thinking about himself. Over the years, she'd come to believe it, since it was screamingly apparent that he couldn't be bothered with her. Yet today, he'd come when she'd called. When she'd finally heard Kade's voice inside her house, she'd been torn between rushing into his arms and slapping his face.

"The upstairs is in pretty bad shape, too," Officer Garcia added.

"Walk me through the house," Kade said, rather than asked, and the cops obeyed as if he were their commanding officer.

Coming from a long line of military officers, both Kade and Josh had that way about them. Kade more so than Josh, really. Kade had that special something. Charisma.

Sergeant Braden led the way, followed by Officer Garcia. Laia had expected Kade to set Rosa on the floor, but she'd plastered herself to his chest with her little arms around his neck. Laia and Smoke took up the rear.

"So you're the famous Smoke," she said, running her hand gently over the dog's thick black coat as he walked beside her. Rosa had always come back from her in-law's house beaming and talking nonstop about Kade's new dog and all the fun tricks she'd been teaching him. This was the first time Laia had actually seen Smoke. "Aren't you a handsome boy?"

Smoke paused to twist his neck and sniff her hand before pinning her with intelligent, chocolate-brown eyes. He licked her fingers. Whether it was a sign of affection or merely sensory exploration she couldn't be sure.

When he resumed walking, she couldn't stop analyzing his gait. Was he limping? It could have been all the canine physiology books she'd been reading on the side in her spare time, but at a minimum, he seemed to be slightly favoring his right front paw.

"They broke in through the back door." Sergeant Braden went into the kitchen, pointing to the damaged door. "Looks like they tried jimmying the lock, and when that didn't work, they probably used a crowbar."

Kade shifted Rosa to his other side but showed no signs that he was about to put her down. With Rosa growing faster than a weed, Laia couldn't hold her for more than a few minutes at a time. The family resemblance between Kade and Rosa was obvious. Her daughter had Josh and Kade's straight patrician nose and broad forehead, but her green eyes were all Josh's.

"Did any of the neighbors see or hear anything?" Kade eyed the dishware that had been removed from the cupboards and stacked neatly on the counter. "Looks like they were trying to be quiet."

Laia thanked God for that. Alvita was the only other person who had a key. If her friend had heard anything crashing to the floor, she might have come over to check and run straight into the burglars.

"I'd agree with that." Sergeant Braden nodded. "Nothing in the house that would have made much of a noise was broken."

Yet somehow, they'd managed to damage nearly every piece of furniture in the house. *Bastards.*

Officer Garcia glanced at her small spiral notebook. "Alvita Thomas, the next-door neighbor who lives in the adjacent side of the duplex, said she saw a cable company van driving away just as she was pulling up."

Kade turned to Laia. "Did you have a service appointment with the cable company?"

She shook her head. "No." *And certainly not to trash my house.*

"Anyone else see anything?" He looked through the kitchen window at the house visible across the tiny backyard on the other side of the picket fence.

Officer Garcia shook her head. "The Millers. Nobody there was home, and the neighbors across the street didn't see or hear anything, either."

Kade frowned. "Any neighbors have video cams or door cams?"

"One neighbor does." Sgt. Braden pointed in the direction of the front door. "Across the street and three houses down, but there's no one home. We'll check in with them later in the day or tomorrow, see if their camera records footage."

Smoke padded to Kade's side, and again Laia noted him favoring his right leg, stepping just a bit more gingerly with it than his left one. Could be he'd injured the soft tissue in his elbow joint—between the humerus and the radius and ulna. Or his knee, which equated to the human wrist. But Laia guessed it was an injury to the pastern, a dog's main shock absorber when running.

With his free hand, Kade absently stroked Smoke's head. The touch was gentle and affectionate, and Smoke leaned into it. Someday she and Rosa would get a dog. Sadly, that day was far off in the future.

She might have completed her prerequisite courses, but

if things went as planned, there'd be four years of veterinary school, followed by another year of specialty training as an intern. That was, of course, if she even got accepted to UPenn in the first place, and if she miraculously found the money to move to Philly, pay for her schooling *and* for Rosa's care while she attended classes. So many ifs stood between her and her dream. And now this.

The damage was bad, but material objects could be replaced. Someone had broken in and touched nearly everything that belonged to her and Rosa. Not for the first time since coming home to find her house ransacked, she fisted her hands, her emotions vacillating between anger and the undeniable sense of having been violated.

Kade tipped his head. "Let's go upstairs."

Again, Sergeant Braden led the way, leaving Officer Padkin guarding the door. Laia followed directly behind Kade, getting a view of his rock-hard ass as he climbed the stairs. Smoke's claws clipped on the bare wood steps as he took up the rear, his limp becoming even more pronounced.

The doctor-to-be in her wanted to help the dog and wondered if Kade had taken him to see a vet yet.

The tiny duplex was only a two-bedroom, with hers being at the top of the stairs. When they went in, her face heated more than it had earlier at the beach.

Like every room in the house, her bedroom had been thoroughly searched, including her bureau drawers. Satin and lace lingerie sat on the top of the pile, the only remaining pieces of her wardrobe that she actually wore anymore. Everything else she'd given to Goodwill. Since gaining her independence for essentially what was the first time in her life, she much preferred bright, colorful clothes and long, dangly earrings to conservative skirt suits and traditional pearls.

Having Officer Garcia and Sergeant Braden see

her undergarments hadn't bothered her, nor did it when the department's forensic unit had clinically tagged and photographed every inch of her room. Knowing Kade could see her undies was an entirely different matter.

He glanced at the pile of silk and satin, his gaze lingering a moment longer than necessary. The heat in her face blasted higher than the temperature inside the brick oven at Pizza Man, Rosa's favorite place to order pineapple pizza. Again, she questioned her decision to call Kade in the first place. But she'd had no choice.

"She might want to stay at a hotel tonight," Officer Garcia said, and it irked her that the comment seemed to have been directed to Kade, not her, as if *he* were making all the decisions here.

"Maybe," Kade muttered, his frown deepening as he took in the rest of the room, including the raspberry-red walls and colorful, modernistic prints she'd hung up right after painting the place.

"Mommy, I'm hungry," Rosa said, parking that adorable pout on her lips again.

When Rosa reached for her, Laia plucked her from Kade's arms. As she did, her hands grazed the sides of his broad chest, and she tried to ignore the warm, steely strength beneath his shirt and how the fabric stuck to his torso, outlining a defined set of abs.

She kissed the top of her daughter's head, then set her on her feet. "As soon as we're done here, we'll get something to eat." Given that the kitchen was a disaster zone, they'd have to grab something out.

Wordlessly, Kade went back into the hallway. Smoke followed him as he turned left in the direction of Rosa's bedroom. With his hands on his hips, he surveyed the damage, looking repeatedly from the floor to the ceiling, then to the pile of books and toys that had been emptied from a shelf onto the circular Peppa Pig rug.

He began stroking his chin, calling attention to the beginnings of a sexy five o'clock shadow gracing his square, chiseled jaw. His brows lowered so much they seemed on the verge of touching the fringes of his thick lashes.

"What is it?" she asked, automatically reaching for Rosa's hand.

"I don't know," he answered.

"Uncle Kade?" Rosa picked up her favorite book—*Cinderella*—one that Josh had given her and from which he'd occasionally read to her. "Can you read me this tonight before I go to bed?"

For a moment, he stared at the book in Rosa's hand, as if still in deep thought. Then the corners of his mouth lifted, revealing those devastating, deep-set dimples. "Sure thing, Cream Puff."

Rosa giggled, hugging the gently worn book to her chest.

Cream Puff?

Kade's expression sobered. "Has anything else unusual happened lately?"

The burglars had taken apart all the window air conditioners in the house, and the upstairs was quickly turning into a sauna. A bead of sweat trickled down Kade's temple. The clear-as-sin image of her licking it off his hot, wet skin flashed before her eyes.

Oh. My god. Stop it. Just...stop it.

"Laia?" Kade repeated. "Has anything else unusual happened lately? Strangers hanging around outside? Weird phone calls, anything like that?"

Huh? "Uh, maybe." Neither Braden nor Garcia had asked her those questions, so she hadn't thought about it until now. "Yesterday, after I left work to pick up Rosa at daycare, I could swear I was being followed."

"Is that the first time that's happened since...?" He let

the unspoken end of the sentence linger, but they both knew what he was referring to.

Since Josh was murdered in prison.

"No." She shook her head, which had begun to pound from mounting stress and anxiety over what might really be happening here. "Well, I don't know. I'm just not sure."

Kade's tone went hard. "What do you mean?"

"Sometimes I thought the same car—a gold Hyundai—was behind me in the morning on the way to daycare and the bank."

His eyes narrowed. "Did you get the license plate?"

"No." She should have. Her fear for Rosa's safety had pretty much obliterated everything else.

"That's okay," Kade reassured her. From the deepening creases on his forehead, she could tell it wasn't. "Did you get a look at the driver?"

"No, not really." God, she was terrible at the whole cop thing. "But one day when I came out of the daycare, a man was standing there, right outside the door."

Again, Kade's dark brows lowered. "Do you think he was waiting for you?"

"I'm not sure," she answered. At first, she hadn't noticed him, then as she'd walked away, a feeling she couldn't explain made her look over her shoulder to find him watching her, just a little bit too intently to be normal.

Kade rested his hands on her shoulders, then, as if realizing the gesture was too intimate, quickly dropped them. "Anything you remember could be helpful."

Yeah, right. With the imprint of his big, strong hands splayed over the shoulder straps of her tank top singed into her bare skin, remembering anything beyond her name was exceedingly difficult. "When I caught him looking at me, he looked away, as if he didn't want me to know he'd been watching."

"Do you remember what he looked like?"

Kade towered over her. The fiery amber sunburst surrounding his pupils seemed to glow as his eyes bored into her. "Um…" *Yes,* still *exceedingly difficult to remember anything.* "He was wearing blue jeans and a white T-shirt."

"Did you get a good look at his face?"

Come to think of it, she had. "He had brown hair and brown eyes. And really full lips. Oh, and a scar." Only now did she remember the scar arcing downward from his lower lip to his chin. "He was only standing about ten feet away when I came outside."

"Okay, that's good," Kade said. "We'll look at some mugshots tomorrow."

"Mugshots?" Officer Garcia looked skeptical. "How are you going to narrow down thousands of mugshots based on that description?"

"Are you thinking this has something to do with Ms. Velez's husband?" Sergeant Braden asked.

Instead of answering the sergeant, Kade looked at Laia, saying nothing for a moment, then, "Maybe."

Please, no. That was precisely why she'd called Kade for help, but even then, she hadn't actually believed it was true. *Hoped* it wasn't. Now she was starting to believe it was.

"The DHS has a collection of mugshots associated with that investigation," Kade said. "If this guy works for the same cartel, we might get lucky." He took a black wallet from his back pocket.

His gleaming gold Department of Homeland Security badge was a horrific reminder of the past, and she shuddered with silent fear *and* resentment. This was supposed to be over. Josh was gone. She'd buried him two years ago. Why would the cartel be following her and breaking into her home after all this time?

Kade tugged two business cards from his wallet, handing

one to Braden and the other to Garcia. "I'd like a copy of your report and anything forensics turns up. Let me know if this gets assigned to a detective."

"You got it." Braden likewise gave Kade his business card. To Laia, he said, "We'll do our best to find out who did this, but it happens more often than you think around here."

"Thank you." Having lived in Asbury Park for most of her adult life, she knew it was true. In fact, she suspected Kade had something to do with the fact that the police were treating her so kindly and had been there for hours.

"I'll walk you out." Kade accompanied the officers downstairs.

Laia sighed as she crouched on the floor where Rosa kept holding up her hand for Smoke to high five, which he did perfectly.

Smoke snorted, then lowered his paw, still holding it in the air at an unnatural angle, bending it right behind the metacarpal, the largest pad of a dog's paw. At first, Laia thought this was perhaps related to why he was limping. Then Rosa met the dog's paw with her closed fist.

"See what I taught him?" Rosa smiled, revealing a space where one of her lower teeth used to be. "It's a fist bump. Uncle Kade and I fist bump, so I taught Smoke to do it." Rosa giggled, fist bumped Smoke's paw again, then pulled her hand away, waggling her fingers in the air. "Boo-yah!"

Smoke cracked his jaws, uttering a half bark, half howl that sounded eerily like *boo-yah*.

"That's very impressive. You could be a dog trainer one day." Laia was only half kidding. Rosa possessed the same love of animals, dogs in particular, that Laia did.

The dog's dark-brown eyes watched Laia closely while she petted the top of his head. His thick hair was long and soft, his ears tall and pointed. There was no doubting his intelligence. It was in his eyes, in the proudly erect bearing with which he held his head. It was almost as if Smoke, too, had been influenced by generations of Sampson military men.

"Mommy, are you still mad at Uncle Kade?"

Yes. "No, of course, not." In a calm move that belied the frustration ready to burst from her head with more force than a shaken soda can, she brushed a silky-soft strand of hair from her daughter's cheek.

"I hope not." Kade had returned, crossing his arms as he leaned his shoulder against the doorjamb. "Because until we figure out what's really going on here, you're staying with me. At my house. For your safety and Rosa's."

"*What?*" Laia jumped to her feet. What he was suggesting was ludicrous. Impossible. "No. No way. There's not a chance in hell—"

"Heck," he said, his lips quirking as he raised his brows, tipping his head to Rosa and reminding her that she shouldn't be cursing.

She stepped closer, getting in his face and waggling a stiff finger at him. "Heck, Hades, purgatory, underworld... The only reason I called you was for my daughter's sake, to keep her safe from whatever's happening here. I appreciate you coming, but there's no way we're staying in the same house with you."

Kade pushed from the door to tower over her. A challenging gleam lit his eyes, making the amber halos in them burn like a ring of fire. "Wanna bet?"

He was so close, his heat washing over her, his nearness and clean, fresh scent so overwhelming she was forced to take a step back.

Renewed anger and fear stoked hotly up her spine. The anger she understood. The fear...she couldn't put into words as to why that was. One thing was for certain, though, and that was the neon sign blinking in her head, warning: *No, no, and just...no!*

Where Kade was concerned, her emotions were all mixed up, and she had to maintain a rational distance from him and keep reminding herself that for years, he couldn't be bothered with her. Now he wanted them to move in with him?

But he'd played on the one thing that could make her say and do things completely against her better judgment. *Rosa*.

Years ago, she'd married Josh, who'd turned her world upside down. Now, she was about to repeat history and live under the same roof with a man who would, she didn't doubt for one second, completely and utterly turn her world upside down, *then* inside out.

Chapter Three

Kade took the exit off Route 22 for North Plainfield. For what must have been the hundredth time since leaving Asbury Park, he glanced in the rearview mirror, relieved to see Laia's gray Ford Escape directly behind him.

He would have preferred they'd all driven in the same vehicle, but with the mobile computer, radios, and other gear obstructing most of the passenger seat, his Colt M4 rifle sticking up between the front seats, and Smoke's specially outfitted K-9 kennel taking up the entire bench seat behind him, there wasn't much room for anyone else.

Kade stopped for a traffic light and began tapping his fingers on the wheel, wondering if Laia had thrown any of that pretty lingerie into one of the bags she'd packed. Not that he had any designs on seeing her wear it, but how could he *not* wonder what she'd look like in it?

Amazing. No doubt about it.

The crotch of his tux pants tightened just thinking about running his fingers over that satin and lace while the warmth of Laia's soft skin seeped into his fingers and...

Reality. Gut. Check.

Laia had practically rammed it down his throat that she wasn't about to give him the time of day, personally, so how could he even think about a relationship, sexual or otherwise, with her? Because he couldn't help it. Just as he couldn't have helped it any time over the last six years. And lest he forget, there'd also be an adorably precocious little girl living under his roof. Laia and Rosa were staying with him for protection. Not so he could jump his sister-in-law's bones.

At seven p.m., it was still light out as they turned into his driveway. He clicked the garage door opener, then parked his SUV off to the side near the back of the house. As an added precaution, they'd prearranged for Laia to put her Escape inside the garage next to his POV—personally owned vehicle—a navy-blue Chevy Suburban. Considering he hadn't been in her or Rosa's life for...well, basically never, no one would ever suspect they'd stay here, but still.

As he watched Laia pull in, worry stuck to his brain like a giant burr. The police might think this was a typical burglary. Kade's gut said it was connected to Josh. When Laia talked about the man outside the daycare and being followed, he was sure of it. Laia knew it, too. He could see it in her eyes.

Kade unlocked the M4, then slung the strap over his shoulder. He grabbed his tuxedo jacket and overnight bag from the rear compartment and let Smoke out of the kennel. His dog trotted into the garage, circling Laia's Escape as he waited impatiently for them to get out.

While Laia unstrapped Rosa from the booster seat, he lifted the Escape's tailgate and retrieved their bags. Rosa scrambled off the seat, then crouched to throw her arms around Smoke's neck. His dog sat, happily enduring Rosa's attention and flicking his tail back and forth on the concrete. Where Rosa was concerned, Smoke's love of children went into major overdrive.

Holding Rosa's hand, Laia met him in the driveway, then looked up at his house. It wasn't much, a two-story white clapboard with brick facing and a pathetic flower bed planted with evergreen bushes and grasses, plants that didn't need much attention. Laia's lips twisted.

"There's really no need for us to stay here." With her free hand, she gestured to his house, frowning and looking as if the idea of staying with him was as repugnant to her as renting a room at a roach motel.

"Is there a problem?" he asked, staring at her lips because *yeah*...that was *definitely* a brighter shade of lipstick, and it looked good on her. Christ, he didn't want to still be so attracted to her. "My house may not be fancy, but it's clean."

"I didn't say it wasn't. I'm just surprised, that's all."

"At what? Did you think I lived in a tent?"

"No. I expected you to live in a condo or a townhouse, someplace that would have freed you up more to enjoy your bachelorhood."

"Meaning?"

"Meaning, if you didn't have a whole house and property to maintain, it would leave you more time to...to..." She arched a brow. "You know."

He narrowed his eyes as a spurt of annoyance shot through him. He understood what she meant but didn't want to verbalize it in front of Rosa. Laia assumed that he was a womanizer who spent his nights trolling the bars for action. Although just where she would have gotten that impression he didn't know, because he'd never been that kind of guy.

He tightened his jaw. "I enjoy my bachelorhood just fine, thanks. The house is mainly for Smoke. Before Smoke, it was for my K-9, Tango. Tango retired two years ago and spends most of his time with my parents."

"Well. We wouldn't want to be an imposition to you."

"An imposition?" She had to be kidding.

Or was she? By ghosting her all these years he'd given her that very impression.

The truth was that not only were she and Rosa family but Laia was... *What*? His ginormous guilt aside, she would always be his sister-in-law and the mother of his niece. Leaving them unprotected was out of the question. "You and Rosa are family. You could never be an imposition."

"No? You shut me out," she said, her voice low enough that Rosa wouldn't hear. "What kind of a man deserts his dead brother's wife when she has no one else?"

His jaw clenched. She had him dead to rights on that score. Not that he didn't want anything to do with her, quite the opposite actually. In fact, that was the *precise* reason he'd stayed away. He'd never forgotten those forty minutes in an elevator with her.

Sensing his roiling emotions, Smoke snorted, looking up at him with worried eyes.

Before he could respond, her gaze dipped down his tuxedo, then up. "Besides. Clearly we interrupted you in the middle of...something."

"I was at a friend's wedding in Maryland," he grumbled.

Her expression turned to one of shock. "You left a wedding and drove all the way up here because I called?"

"Yes," he said, irritated that she thought so little of him. He would have driven all the way from Alaska to get back here. Again, to protect her and Rosa. He had a familial obligation to them. There couldn't be more than that. Ever.

Keep telling yourself that.

As she followed him up the steps, he glanced back. The smooth skin over the bridge of her nose had creased. Whether it was from anger or confusion he couldn't be sure.

"I just thought that—" Her sexy pink lips pressed together in a firm line. "With everything that's happened... Frankly, I hesitated to call you at all because I never actually expected you to show up."

He exhaled a tight breath. There was no one to blame but himself for Laia's current state of TPO—totally pissed off. Between his parting shot at the wedding, then his disappearing act, he'd unintentionally created that monster, and there was no slaying it now.

If he could go back in time and do anything differently, would he?

Nope. There had only been one path to take, and it had led him on a straight line away from Laia.

He dug the keys from his pocket and opened the front door. Inviting her and Rosa to stay with him was the exact opposite of what he *should* do, but their safety came first, and this was the best option. For now. As soon as he figured out what was behind the burglary and the people following Laia, they'd go right back to where they were before.

Apart.

At the thought of never seeing her again, he curled his fingers tighter around the straps.

Smoke trotted past them, heading inside and going straight for his water bowl in the kitchen and taking noisy slurps.

Kade opened a closet and stowed his rifle in the gun safe, then headed up the stairs. "I'll show you to your rooms."

Behind him, Laia closed the front door. Kade paused on the landing, taking in a view he never expected to see. Laia Velez in his home. Evening sun backlit her hair, making it gleam like volcanic glass and casting shadows beneath her high cheekbones.

"I didn't realize Smoke needed an entire house," she said.

"He doesn't." Kade continued up the stairs and stopped in front of one of the bedrooms. "But he does need a fenced-in yard and room to exercise, and it's my duty to make sure he gets it. He might seem like my dog, but he's actually the property of the U.S. government, and Uncle Sam pays me a stipend to care for him."

"Well, isn't that thoughtful of the federal government." There was no mistaking the sarcasm in her tone, not that Kade could blame her for it. The Big G hadn't exactly been kind to her.

Still clutching one of Rosa's hands, she met him at the open doorway. "How many bedrooms are there?" she asked.

"Four." Guilt swamped him. He'd been living here alone for years while she and Rosa had been forced to live in a tiny two-bedroom duplex that had seen better days. And his actions were partly responsible for that. "Rosa, this can be your room if it's okay with your mom."

Rosa peered into the room, her eyes going wide as she uttered a tiny gasp.

The bedroom was the smallest of the four but painted lavender, with pink floor and ceiling molding. A glittery, enchanted castle scene took up an entire wall, complete with a prince and princess dancing in the courtyard. There wasn't much else in the room besides the double bed with a white bedspread, but it was definitely girly.

"Ooh, Mommy!" Rosa began jumping up and down, then Smoke joined in, pirouetting in place as he channeled her excitement. "Can I stay here? Please, please, pretty please?"

Kade couldn't help but smile at her enthusiastic response. When Laia's lips began to twitch, he took that as a yes and deposited Rosa's bag on the bed.

"Okay," Laia said finally.

"C'mon, Smoke!" Rosa ran to the enchanted wall where she ran her hands over the glittery castle and the princess's blue ballgown. Smoke went to the bed and began sniffing the bag. Whether he was searching it for food or automatically switching to narco-buster mode, Kade wasn't sure.

"I take it the previous owners had a little girl." Laia

followed him inside, inspecting the room.

"Yep." Kade gestured to the door. "C'mon. She'll be fine."

They left Rosa opening her bag and emptying her clothes and books on the bed. Smoke stayed behind to verify there was no bacon in the bag.

Kade went to the end of the hall and stood aside for Laia. Before crossing the threshold, she froze.

"I can't stay here." She looked up at him, so wide-eyed one would think there was a herd of cockroaches stampeding up the wall. "This is *your* bedroom. Did you really expect me to stay here with—"

He held up his hand, interrupting her as he lowered her bag to the floor beside the king-size bed. "No, I didn't. I'll stay in one of the other bedrooms." What kind of a presumptuous jackass did she think he was and why would she think that in the first place? "This bedroom's bigger, and you'll have your own bathroom."

He went to the master bath and flipped on the lights. When he'd bought the place, his realtor had told him this bathroom was the house's crowning glory. Judging from the look on Laia's face as she'd reluctantly followed him, the realtor hadn't been exaggerating.

Her jaw dropped. Slowly, she ran her hand over the silvery-gray, natural-stone wall tile that shimmered like diamonds, courtesy of the embedded shards of mica. Tiny mother-of-pearl accent tile ran in a three-inch wide swath around the entire wall. Equally glittery, light-gray granite countertops, shower and tub surrounds, and nickel faucets completed the look. But the icing on the cake was the crystal chandelier hanging over the giant soaker tub.

"Right?" He picked up a remote and pushed the button, lighting up the battery-operated, flickering candles on the chandelier. "This is a common tract house built in the seventies. Apparently, the last owners went all-out renovating the master bath."

"I can see that." Laia gazed lovingly at the tub. "I haven't seen a tub like this since—" She cleared her throat. "Well, it's been a while."

Yeah, he knew what she'd been about to say. That she hadn't seen a tub like his since the U.S. government had seized hers and Josh's house, along with virtually everything else they possessed.

"I can't stay here," she repeated, shaking her head. "This is your room and your bathroom. You should enjoy it."

"I don't take baths," he countered. "This tub is wasted on me. I bought the house for its location and the backyard." When she began backing away, he reached out and stopped her. "Please, stay here. I want you to enjoy it." *Because you deserve it, and it's the least I can do to make up for what happened.*

She thought for a moment, then took a deep breath and sighed. "Okay, but this is only temporary."

"Agreed," he said, holding out his hand to shake on the deal.

When she placed her hand in his, he was instantly thrown back in time, to another day when she'd taken his hand as he'd pulled her to her feet. Seconds after that, his world had imploded.

Their hands remained clasped, hers so small and delicate in his. The woman standing before him was the same, yet so different now. Stronger and more confident. Maybe being married and becoming a mother had done that. More than likely, it was a strength born of necessity after her husband was arrested.

Then murdered.

Living with Laia would bring back all the bad memories and the guilt he'd lived with for two years. But he had no choice. Laia and Rosa were now his responsibility. A responsibility that he fully embraced.

"They're searching for it, aren't they?" she asked as they returned to the bedroom.

Kade had been about to turn off the bathroom light, but his fingers froze on the switch plate. There was no need to verbalize what "it" was.

The ledger.

The critical piece of missing evidence that could have been Josh's get-out-of-jail-free card. Instead, it was the very reason he'd been murdered. That and his testimony.

He flipped off the lights. "I can't be certain, but yeah. I think so."

She sat on the bed. *His* bed. Another sight he'd never expected to see. "But why after all this time? The government looked for it. They searched our home, Josh's office, every computer he ever touched. I even looked for it. How do we know there ever *was* a ledger?"

Without thinking, he sat on the bed, too close to Laia's beautiful bare shoulders and sleek bare legs. All he had to do was reach out and he could caress all that soft, glowing skin. He swallowed, doing his best to focus on the wall over his bureau. "Every accountant keeps a ledger of some kind somewhere. Even money launderers have one. They answer to the person they're working for and have to keep track of all incoming and outgoing funds."

"I know that," she said. "I used to be an accounts manager. But why do they think *I* have the ledger?"

Kade followed the movement as she pressed a hand to the tops of her breasts. Clearing his throat, he forced himself to look away. "I don't know. Josh has been gone for two years. Fernando Colon has to know the government never found any trace of a ledger, or he would have been slammed with a significantly longer prison term."

"I never really understood something." She pivoted to face him, bending one leg on the mattress and giving him a tantalizing glimpse of her tanned, bare thigh. "Fernando Colon was already sent to prison. He was charged and convicted of many crimes. What does the ledger have to do with him getting sentenced to more time?"

"Jail time isn't determined solely by the crime itself. Other things factor in, such as laundering large amounts of money that was the proceeds of manufacturing, importing, or distributing narcotics. The more money involved, the more jail time. That's the way the federal sentencing guidelines work."

"Just how much money do you think Josh was laundering for the cartel?"

So much that even if his brother had lived and turned over his ledger to the U.S. Attorney's Office in exchange for leniency, he still might have received several years in jail himself. Or been forced to go into the Witness Security program.

But Laia didn't need to know that.

"Enough to send Colon away for over twenty years," he answered.

Her eyes widened. "No wonder he wants the ledger."

"Exactly." But why now, and why did Colon think she had it? Something must have happened, something to trigger that belief and push him to break into Laia's home and have her followed.

"I'd better go downstairs and feed Smoke." And put some distance between him and Laia. Kade pushed from the bed and went to the door, turning at the last second. "I'll figure out what's going on, and in the meantime, I'll keep you and Rosa safe. I promise."

Smoke met him in the kitchen, prancing and panting as he anxiously awaited his gourmet meal of kibble and ground beef. After setting his dog's dinner on the floor, Kade shoved his hands in his pockets and went into the hallway.

Staring back at him from the wall were family photos. Four generations of Sampson military men. Him and Josh on their graduation days at West Point. Their father during the Gulf War. Their grandfather in Vietnam. And their great-grandfather in World War II. Fighting for this country and doing the right thing was ingrained in him straight down to the cellular level.

Kade touched his fingers to the faded, graying image of his great-grandfather in the South Pacific during the war. Beneath the photo was the proverb: *A hundred years cannot repair one moment's loss of honor.*

Kade and Josh had never met their great-granddad, but that phrase had been kept alive by their grandfather and father. Their father, in particular, loved reminding them of those words every time they did something wrong. Which, when they were kids, seemed like pretty much all the time. Yet it had been Grandpa who'd turned out to be the most hardcore of them all.

Great-granddad fought directly under General Douglas MacArthur. Both Kade's great-grandfather and grandfather had attended MacArthur's retirement at West Point. *Duty. Honor. Country.* "Three hallowed words," as MacArthur had said in his speech that day, "that reverently dictate what you ought to be, what you can be, and what you will be."

Kade looked at the photo of the man he'd revered *and* feared. Grandpa Mike had taken the eye-for-an-eye thing to extremes, pitting one grandson against the other in fistfights meant to teach life lessons and that had often ended with Kade and Josh bruised and bloodied, lying on the ground while their grandfather towered over them spewing: *Never let your heart interfere with your honor or duty. If you do, you will fail.*

He rested his hands on the wall on either side of Grandpa Mike's photo and stared into the eyes of a man who'd died only last year at the age of eighty-seven. Seemed like Kade's whole life had been centered around honor and duty and still was.

As he had the day Laia had married his brother, Kade would continue doing the honorable thing and keep his confused feelings in check because there were more important things that took priority, and failing wasn't an option.

If he did, Laia and Rosa could get caught up in the same deadly game that killed his brother.

His heart pounded furiously in his chest.

They already *were* caught up in that game, and it was up to him to keep Laia and Rosa alive.

Chapter Four

After unpacking the meager clothes she'd brought with her, including her favorite green satin-and-lace nightie, Laia stacked her toiletries on the bathroom vanity's exquisite granite counter. She looked around at all the glistening, natural finishes. This bathroom was every bit as gorgeous as the one in hers and Josh's Rumson house. And the tub...

She sighed, closing her eyes and pinching the bridge of her nose. Prosecutors had concluded that Josh had comingled his equity in the house with drug cartel money he'd received in exchange for his "laundering" services. The beautiful house, along with everything in it, had been seized by the government. Worse, she'd made a critical error after marrying Josh—she'd comingled her own accounts with his, thereby tainting every cent she'd earned. As a banker, she should have known better.

In the end, she'd been left with virtually nothing. The only thing she'd been able to make a buck on was Josh's Jaguar, and the only belonging she'd kept from their house was the small wood dinghy he'd planted in the backyard for

Rosa to play on. The government hadn't wanted that. *Gee, go figure.*

The remote for the chandelier still sat on the tub surround, and she picked it up, watching the faux flames flicker back and forth. She might have to take Kade up on his offer to use the tub after all. Like the tub in her former Rumson home, this one could easily fit two people. But Josh had never once joined her in a sexy bubble bath. If he had, maybe their marriage wouldn't have crumbled, and maybe he wouldn't have made the dire choices he had.

Loud giggling came from downstairs, followed by Kade's deep laugh. Gratitude was what she ought to be feeling toward her husband's brother, and she did. After all, he'd given them a roof over their heads, and he'd left a friend's wedding—not his—to do it. She tugged her cell from her pocket and phoned Alvita, who answered on the first ring.

"Are you okay?" came Alvita's concerned voice.

"Yes, I'm fine. Rosa and I are staying with fa—" She'd almost said "family," but she'd never really considered Kade in that category. "We're staying with a friend," she corrected, realizing that was a misnomer, too. Kade had never been her friend, either. *Men and women can't be friends...* She'd heard that line in some famous movie with Billy Crystal.

"Do you mean that guy in the tuxedo? The one who looks like he just stepped off the cover of a magazine?" Alvita made a catcall whistle. "In that case, girl, I approve."

Laia smiled. Alvita had been trying to get her to start dating for over a year now. Not only couldn't Laia wrap her brain around dating again, but between Rosa, Laia's online courses, and attending the required in-person bio, organic chem, and zoology labs at night, there'd been no time for a man in her life.

Quickly, she recapped what the police said, leaving out hers and Kade's suspicions that this had something to do with

Josh. Alvita only knew Laia by her maiden name, and she'd never confided in her friend about what had really happened to her husband.

"When will you be back?" Alvita asked.

"I don't know." The thought scared her to death. Staying with Kade—in his bedroom, no less—made her so anxious and confused her belly had long ago twisted itself into a pretzel.

"I'll pick up your mail for you and hold it at my house. Call anytime if you need me to do something or if you just want to talk."

"Thank you, Alvita." Not only was Alvita the best next-door babysitter she could ask for, but she'd become a dear friend.

After ending the call, she turned to head downstairs but stopped and stared at the king-size bed. The second half of that Billy Crystal quote popped into her head. *...because the sex part always gets in the way.*

Laia rolled her eyes. Why even think in that direction? There was no chance there'd ever *be* a "sex part" between her and Kade.

She headed downstairs, following the giggling then an odd, squirting sound. Inside the kitchen and next to the stainless-steel refrigerator, Kade held a can with a nozzle to Rosa's open mouth. Beside them, with his tail swishing on the tile floor, Smoke licked his lips.

"Press harder," Kade said, and Rosa wrapped her tiny hands around his. The squirting sound grew louder, then Rosa's mouth filled with whipped cream.

"Mmm," Rosa mumbled, then licked her lips.

"Here you go, buddy." Kade held an identical can above Smoke's head, and he opened his jaws while Kade gave the can a squirt. A long strand dripped into the dog's mouth. Smoke chewed, then swallowed, licking his lips just as Rosa had.

Rosa began hopping up and down. "Again! Again!"

"No, not again!" Laia narrowed her eyes on Kade. "What in the world are you doing?"

"Having a little snack while we waited for you to come down." He put one of the cans to his mouth and pressed the nozzle. After swallowing, he held out the can to her. "Want some?"

"No, I don't *want* some." Though why she was so annoyed, she couldn't exactly say. It wasn't the whipped cream. Maybe it was seeing them together so naturally and having so much fun. Josh had loved Rosa but aside from reading to her had never actually taken the time to have fun with his daughter. He'd have to have been home for that to happen. A year after Rosa was born, he rarely was.

"Uh-oh." Rosa's tongue darted out to lick away a tiny gob of cream on her lower lip. "Mommy's mad at both of us."

"Is there a problem?" Kade arched a brow, but his attempt at being genuinely confused failed when a corner of his mouth lifted.

"Whipped cream?" She stared at him in disbelief. "You're feeding a five-year-old whipped cream directly from a *can*?" And right before dinner, no less.

"Yeah, I am," he answered with zero remorse, then threw Rosa a conspiratorial look that made her giggle again. "It's our thing."

"Your *thing*? What does that mean?" She grabbed the can in his hand, somewhat gratified to see this one had Smoke's name on it written in black marker. At least Kade hadn't been feeding Rosa from the same can.

"Relax." He held up his hands, palms facing her as he tried to calm her down. Instead, it only irritated her more. "Considering how the day started out, I thought Rosa could use a little fun. We've been doing this for years. Right, Cream

Puff?"

Rosa nodded emphatically. "Right, Uncle Kade. Smoke, too."

Smoke stared longingly at the can with his name on it.

She looked from her daughter to Kade, wondering what else they'd been doing at her in-law's house when she hadn't been there. Now she knew where the nickname he'd called Rosa earlier had come from. *Cream Puff.* Laia opened the refrigerator door. "Do you have anything *healthy* in here that we can cook for dinner?"

Ten minutes later, she was patting together ground beef for burgers and unwrapping a package of Coney Island's best dogs. Outside, Kade was heating the grill, keeping an eye on Rosa, who threw ball after ball for Smoke to retrieve. Laia could only imagine how sticky and wet with dog slobber her daughter's hands were.

Using a long-handled wire brush, Kade scraped the grill plates, and as he did, the gray T-shirt he'd changed into put his rippling biceps on full display. The man looked as good in jeans and a plain T-shirt as he did in a tuxedo. Still scraping, he pulled the phone clipped to his belt and held it to his ear.

If only she wasn't still attracted to him this strongly. Or better yet, not at all. Sure, when she'd seen him standing in front of that elevator it had been impossible not to notice how tall he was, or how he filled out his suit jacket, and when he'd turned around...*wow*. But it wasn't just his handsome face or his physique.

When the elevator had broken down between floors, he'd made her laugh, a tough thing to do, given the situation. Then it turned out they had so much in common, and she'd loved talking with him so much that she wished they could have been stuck there together for days. But she'd made a commitment, a promise she'd sworn to honor. She still remembered the emotional turmoil of her wedding day.

When she'd nearly faltered.

"Do you, Laia Maria Velez, take this man, Joshua Christopher Sampson, to be your husband? To love, honor, and cherish him for the rest of your days?" the officiant had asked.

First, Laia had glanced at her mother sitting in the first row. Her mom strongly supported the marriage, and when Laia had expressed her reluctance, her mother wouldn't hear of it. Given the secret she'd been keeping, marrying Josh was the financially prudent and Catholic thing to do, she'd said.

After Millie Velez had sent her a firmly encouraging nod, Laia had looked up and locked gazes with Kade's beautiful, pain-filled hazel eyes and in that split second imagined things differently.

A future with Kade, not Josh.

All she'd had to do was give in to the truth in her aching heart and walk off the altar, but that wouldn't have changed anything. There was no way she and Kade could ever have the future she'd dreamed about every night since they met right up to her wedding day.

So she'd said the words everyone expected her to say: *I do*.

As if that hadn't been difficult enough, later, Kade had taken her aside during the reception. He'd known something wasn't right, and he'd asked if he'd done something wrong.

"Don't *ever* think that," she'd said, making the fatal mistake of clasping his hand. Touching him again was like being connected to a wire that lit up her body so intensely she felt it right down to the very marrow of her bones.

When she didn't—no, *couldn't*—respond, not honestly, anyway, to Kade's question about feeling something for him, the tone of the conversation had changed. Drastically. Then Kade had warned her not to hurt his brother. Whatever emotions were whipping back and forth between them must have shown on their faces when Josh had caught them talking. When Kade stalked off, Josh glared at his receding back.

"Kade's just jealous because *I* have you." Josh's eyes softened as he faced her. "To love, honor, and cherish for the rest of our days." He took her into his arms, and she squeezed back the tears.

Laia stared at the hamburger patty in her hand, blinking back the unexpected sting behind her eyes. She had honored Josh. Since marrying him, she hadn't been with another man. In fact, she'd rarely been intimate with Josh after Rosa was born. But had she ever cherished him? Perhaps, but not in the way he needed or wanted her to. Had she ever loved him?

She swallowed the lump in her throat. Josh had been so incredibly in love with her, and she ought to have felt lucky. She'd tried, *really* tried, to love him back with the same passion and fervor. Eventually, she'd come to love him as the father of her child. That, at least, had been genuine, but the guilt haunted her.

Laia hung her head, wishing she'd been stronger back then, more independent. But there was no going back. On their wedding day, she'd done them both a disservice because she'd been unfaithful in her heart.

She lifted her head to see Kade, Rosa, and Smoke at the fence, talking to a very tall, very pretty woman with blond hair so long it grazed the top of her ass. She couldn't hear what they were saying, but the woman's body language spoke loudly enough for Laia to understand every word.

She wants him.

The woman touched Kade's forearm and laughed at something he said. He picked Rosa up and sat her on his shoulders. The woman had legs a mile long and wore a pair of red shorts that barely concealed the high, tight globes of her perfect backside. Again, she reached over the fence, this time dragging a finger down the center of Kade's chest.

Irrational jealousy speared her gut as she watched that finger go lower and lower... She picked up the plate of burgers and dogs, then went onto the deck, setting the plate down with more force than necessary. All heads turned in her direction.

"Laia." Kade waved her over.

Did she want to meet the woman Kade was sleeping with? Probably not. Not really. Make that an emphatic *never*. She had no illusions that he'd been celibate all these years, but meeting one of his harem was so not at the top of her list.

"Laia," Kade repeated, waving more emphatically.

"Mommy, come say hi." Rosa's face beamed. Already, her daughter was a social butterfly and not just with dogs.

Laia had lost count of how many times she'd caught Rosa answering her cell phone. Or how many times she'd tried calling Pizza Man herself to order pineapple pizza.

Here goes. Smoothing down her wrinkled shirt and shorts, she walked to the fence.

"This is my neighbor, Ashley," Kade said. "Ashley, this is my sister-in-law, Laia."

Good manners prevailed, and Laia extended her hand. "Hi. Nice to meet you." Ashley had to be pushing six feet tall, and Laia had to look up to meet the woman's perfect complexion, perfect eyebrows, and perfect nose. Norse princess, was all Laia could think. Along with how dowdy *she* must look in her filthy beach shorts and tank.

"Nice to meet you, as well." Ashley's smile broadened, revealing exceptionally straight white teeth. God, wasn't there anything *im*perfect about her? Not that Laia could see. The more she gawked, the more familiar the woman looked.

"Ashley's the best neighbor a guy could ask for. You might recognize her. She's been on the cover of *Vogue* and *Vanity Fair*."

Figures. Kade's neighbor just *had* to be a supermodel.

"Speaking of which," Ashley said, "I have to run off to an evening shoot. Catch you guys later. Bye, Rosa. Nice meeting you, Laia." With a long-fingered flourish, she waved and strode—no, make that *glided*—oh-so-gracefully back to her house, as if she were walking off a runway.

"Bye, Ashley." Rosa's hand waved back and forth like a metronome.

"Later, Ash," Kade called out, and Ashley threw him a sultry wink over her shoulder, leaving Laia wondering just how neighborly he was with her.

"Mommy, I like Ashley." Rosa tugged on Laia's hand. "Can we eat now?"

"Yes, baby. We just have to cook you a hot dog and wash your hands." They walked back to the deck where Kade began cooking the burgers and dogs. Smoke circled several times, then settled in a corner.

"Ashley seems very…nice." And, if Laia guessed correctly, had set her supermodel sights on Kade.

He closed the lid on the grill. "She *is* nice."

"She's really pretty," Rosa said, then took a slurp of juice from her cup.

"Your mommy's really pretty, too." Kade sat next to Rosa on the bench and picked up a pickle slice from the plate, shoving it into his mouth and watching Laia as he chewed.

"I know." Rosa mimicked Kade and picked up a pickle slice.

Under Kade's scrutiny, Laia's face started to heat. *Please stop looking at me.* The more he did, the more uncomfortable the bench she sat on became, making her shift and squirm.

Smoke seeped from beneath the grill lid, and Kade stood to attend to the burgers and dogs, then disappeared inside the house.

"Do you like Uncle Kade, Mommy?" Rosa popped the pickle slice into her mouth and chewed.

Laia opened her mouth and closed it, drowning in confusion at the many ways her mind tried and failed to answer that one simple question.

Yes, I like him. I more *than like him. I always have, but I'm still angry at him.* His words on her wedding day had stung and still did.

"Of course I do, sweetheart. He's your uncle." *And the man I lusted after before you were born.*

Lust was one thing. Letting herself get emotionally invested in him would be stupid. He'd already shown that he couldn't be trusted to be there when she needed him. He'd come this time, but that didn't mean he'd stick around or that he'd ever be in her life again. For him, this was all about the job.

Kade came back outside, carrying a small plastic container of sanitary wipes that he put on the table by Rosa and a bowl of water that he set on the deck. Smoke scrambled to his feet, again calling attention to his limp as he raced to the bowl and began lapping away.

He popped open the tub of wipes, plucked one out, and handed it to Rosa. "Clean your hands before we eat."

"Why?" Rosa asked, cocking her head.

"Because it's procedure," he answered in a clipped, military-type voice. "Every good little soldier cleans her hands before eating."

"Oh," Rosa answered simply and began using the wipe.

"Did you know he was limping?" Laia asked Kade, pointing to Smoke.

"Yes," Kade said. "You're very observant. I thought *I* was the only one who saw it."

"To me, it's pretty obvious. I noticed it back at my house." She waited for Smoke to finish drinking, then knelt in front of him and held out her hand. When he raised his paw, she took it, feeling around gently for swelling or tenderness, none of which she could detect. "He's what, about three years old?"

"Three years and one month."

"Too young for bone degeneration, and there's no swelling or tenderness. I think it's a ligament sprain in his knee, which equates to a human wrist. Did he have a hard landing recently?"

"Yeah, he did. How did you know that?"

She released Smoke's paw. "I'm studying to be a veterinarian." Pie in the sky though the dream was, her new motto was to live life to its fullest, even if she did, at times, fail in her endeavors and fall flat on her ass.

For a long moment, Kade didn't say a word. He just stood there, as if processing what she'd said and not knowing how to respond. "That explains the textbooks in your office. I'm impressed. But I thought banking and finance was your thing."

Hardly. "My mother channeled me down the path to finances, but it was never my passion." She went to the grill and lifted the lid, inhaling the meaty smells of burgers and hot dogs. She closed the lid. "Mom wanted me to have financial stability, and I did, but it never made me happy. Now that I'm on my own, I've decided to turn over a new leaf and pursue what makes me happy. What makes *Rosa* and me happy."

Kade leaned back against the deck railing and crossed his legs at the ankles. "Sounds like a good plan."

"It is." She leaned against the railing beside him. "But it's been a lot of work. It's taken me two years to make up all the prerequisite courses I need before I can even apply to vet school. I'm going to try for an internship with a vet at a local shelter first. My grades are good, but I need to do something extra to bolster my application to the University of Pennsylvania."

"That would be in Philly." Kade frowned. "You'd have to move." The creases on his forehead deepened, although why he'd care whether she moved to Philly or the moon, she didn't know. "Have you put out any feelers yet for an internship?"

"Not yet." Only because she hadn't had the time.

"Maybe I can help. I volunteer at a shelter in Westfield. That's where I found Smoke." He smiled down at his dog, who cracked his jaws, as if smiling back. "He was found wandering along the shoulder of Route 22, covered in mud, oil, grease, and enough ticks and fleas to start an army platoon of insects."

"He's beautiful and intelligent." Laia shook her head, astounded at how many animals were callously abused or discarded by people as easily if they were just taking out the trash. "Why anyone would want to give him up, I can't imagine."

"True that." Kade nodded. "Their loss is my gain. For a dog that wasn't bred and raised by a K-9 facility, he's got the best nose for narcotics I've ever seen, and he can take down a perp in seconds."

"If you like, I can put together an ice wrist wrap for him." Again, she knelt beside Smoke. "You apply it right here." She pointed to the impacted joint. "Fifteen to twenty minutes, several times a day."

"Thanks. I'll take you up on that."

The light stubble on his jaw that she'd noticed earlier in the day had thickened some, looking even sexier. Yet another of the man's physical attributes that she needed to stop ogling. And since when did a man's five o'clock shadow become a physical attribute?

The burgers took that moment to sizzle and pop. Kade lifted the barbecue lid and flipped them. "I asked Ashley to look after Rosa tomorrow while we go to the DHS office to look at mugshots."

"You *what*?" Laia shot to her feet. "Without asking me first? How do you expect me to leave my baby in the hands of a total stranger? I don't even know her." Other than the fact that she was an Amazonian blond bombshell.

"No, but I do." He opened the bags of buns and set them on the top rack inside the grill. "I would never leave Rosa with someone who wasn't completely reliable and trustworthy. Don't judge a book by its cover." He jabbed the spatula at her in an admonishing gesture. "Ashley has a PhD in psychology, and she's great with kids, so cut her some slack."

She crossed her arms. "Why can't we take Rosa with us?"

He took a step closer, towering over her as a gust of wind brought with it his cologne or whatever it was that made him smell so indecently good. "Do you really want your five-year-old daughter looking at mugshots?"

"What's a mugshot?" Rosa's face screwed up as she pulled out another sanitary wipe.

"A picture of someone who's done bad things," Kade supplied, making his point.

Neither of them wanted Rosa anywhere near this mess. "Fine."

"Good." He returned to the grill and plated up the dogs, burgers, and buns. He set the plate on the table, then helped Rosa pick out a hot dog. "You want this one, right?" He pointed to a hot dog that had golden brown grill marks.

Rosa nodded, and Laia's heart squeezed just a little. Most kids didn't want a hot dog with grill marks, but Rosa had always liked them that way. Somehow, Kade knew that. Not even Josh had known all of Rosa's food preferences. Especially the whipped cream thing.

When Kade began cutting up pickle slices for Rosa to put on her hot dog, Laia nearly choked on the lump in her throat. Rosa didn't like pickle relish, but she did love cut-up bread-and-butter pickles. How and when had Kade learned that?

He jabbed the hot dog with a fork and put it on the bun.

Whipped cream squirted from a can…grill marks on hot

dogs...chopped pickles...all the gifts Rosa had come home with after visiting her in-laws...

She'd known Kade had visited with his parents when she'd occasionally left Rosa with them for an overnight. To find out he knew this much about her daughter told Laia he'd spent a *lot* of time with Rosa. Just never when Laia was there. He wasn't an absentee uncle. Just an absentee brother-in-law.

"Here you go." He helped Rosa spoon chopped pickles on her hot dog.

The tightness in her chest eased, her heart softening as she wondered if Josh had painted an unjust picture of his brother, one of a selfish man so hung up on getting ahead in his career that he didn't have time to visit with his family. Speaking of family...

"After we go to your office, we need to pick Rosa up and visit with my mother." She selected a burger from the plate Kade held out to her. "She lives in East Brunswick at a senior-living community. We visit her every Sunday, and that's nonnegotiable."

"I didn't say it was." He held out a bottle of ketchup to her.

She shook her head. "No, thank you. I eat my burgers plain." The statement came out sounding like a reprimand. Probably because he knew her daughter's culinary preferences, and he didn't know a thing about hers.

"No need to bite my head off." He squirted a blob of ketchup onto his own burger.

Oh, crap. The man had taken them in, and she was coming off like a b-i-t-c-h. "Sorry, it's just that there's a lot you don't know about me." Including how awful her marriage had been, not that she was about to bring that up.

God, when would her life stop being a series of big, fat regrets? The only thing she didn't regret in her life was Rosa.

As they sat there eating dinner like a family, Laia couldn't prevent her mind from wandering into the land of make believe. In another lifetime—if things had gone differently—would this have been the way her life would have turned out?

Timing is everything.

And time had never been on her and Kade's side.

With Josh gone, she couldn't begin to guess at the direction life would take her next, but she was determined not to make the same mistakes again.

This time, she'd listen to her gut.

Chapter Five

Kade turned onto Frelinghuysen Avenue, checking the rearview mirror before turning into the Homeland Security Investigations parking lot. If Colon's people were following Laia and staking out Rosa's daycare, the situation could go from merely bad to the mother of all clusterfucks before anyone saw it coming.

Last night, he'd made a few calls and arranged for Laia to look at every mugshot in the HSI database that was associated with the Colon Drug Cartel. Specifically, he'd called the lead investigator on the Fernando Colon case, Special Agent Emanuel Dominguez. Unfortunately, Manny hadn't been available until later in the day, so now it was nearly four p.m.

For most of the day, Laia had been in his home office, glued to his computer and working on her vet school application. Between all the calls he'd made to the Asbury Park PD, the DHS, and his own chief to notify him of what was happening, he'd barely seen Laia all day.

"How'd you sleep last night?" He glanced at her in the passenger seat.

She yawned. "Very well, thanks."

Yeah, right.

Long, shiny dark hair cascaded perfectly down her back and shoulders, and she looked beyond pretty in a fire-engine red sundress, matching red sandals, and long, dangly yellow starfish earrings. But between the yawns and dark circles under her eyes, she appeared about as rested as he felt, which was totally not.

Her wardrobe may have gone from conservative banker-chic to bold and sexy, but she still wore the same delicate honeysuckle-pear fragrance. Yeah, he remembered that, too. Even now, her sweet scent filled the SUV and every breath he took.

Knowing that she'd been sleeping right down the hall—in his bed, no less—had him tossing and turning for hours before sleep had finally kicked in.

Although when he'd finally drifted off, it had been to images of one of her silky, satiny pieces of lingerie sliding over her bare skin.

"We're here." And thank God because he really needed some air that wasn't infused with her tantalizing scent.

He turned into the lot, then stopped at the gate and stuck his ID card into the card reader. The gate lifted and he drove through. Being Sunday, the lot was fairly empty, and he snagged a spot close to the building's front entrance and next to three other SUVs, all with Colorado tags.

"Ready?" he asked, shutting off the engine.

Laia began unclipping her seat belt. "As I'll ever be."

"Hey." He rested a hand on hers. "Rosa will be fine with Ashley. I promise. And Smoke is with them. He won't let anything happen to her, either. If you haven't noticed, Rosa and Smoke are pretty tight."

"I noticed." She blinked down at their hands for a long moment, then tugged hers away. "Let's go in and get this over with."

Before he could stop her, she'd finished unclipping her seat belt, then was out of the SUV and beelining for the building faster than an Olympic speed-walker.

Dammit. Kade yanked off his seat belt and raced to catch up to her. He shouldn't have touched her. For her sake and his.

As he passed the other three SUVs, he noted two of them had their engines running. Through one of the side windows, he glimpsed two pointed ears. Colorado tags? K-9 Interceptors?

When he caught up to Laia, she refused to look at him. He sighed and yanked out the same entry card he'd used to get into the parking lot and swiped into the building, holding the door open for her to enter first.

At the elevator, he slammed the up arrow with the heel of his hand. Mercifully, it opened right away. He followed her inside, and when the doors closed, he doubted the irony was lost on her. Here they were, alone in an elevator, yet this time the connection zapping between them was one of frustration. Neither of them spoke a word.

Man, he was really fucking this up. Whatever *this* was. More like, wasn't.

The doors opened, and he led the way through the zigzagging hallway, eventually swiping in again and holding open the heavy steel door used by employees.

Laia went in ahead of him, her head swiveling as she took in the maze of empty cubicles looming ahead. "Is this your office?"

"No." He waited for the door to click shut. "My office is at Newark Airport. This is where the agents work. I called ahead for one of them to meet us here. He's familiar with the Colon Cartel investigation and can help narrow down the database."

What Laia didn't know, and what he wasn't about to tell her, was that Manny Dominguez had been the one to transport Josh to this very office for processing before turning him over to the U.S. Marshals.

Most of the cubicles were empty, and he was grateful that even the agents generally took weekends off to be with their families. The last thing he wanted was for Laia to run into someone who might spill something that shouldn't be spilled.

Josh's face as he'd been put into the backseat of a patrol car, handcuffed, flashed before Kade's eyes. That was the last time he'd seen his brother. Alive, anyway.

Laughter rolled through the office. A familiar head poked out from behind the edge of the last cubicle by the window. *Thor?* Kade would recognize Adam Decker's K-9 anywhere.

The Belgian Malinois snorted, then galloped toward them, his powerful legs quickly eating up the distance.

"Uh, Kade?" Laia wrapped her fingers around his biceps.

Clearly, she wasn't afraid of dogs, but anyone *not* having a healthy concern for the giant K-9 charging at them would be foolish. Thor slowed, his tail wagging as Kade knelt to let the dog lick his face.

"Laia, this is Thor, the second-best narcotics K-9 in the country."

Thor sat and held up his paw for Laia to shake.

"Second-best my ass," a deep voice boomed.

DEA Special Agent Adam "Deck" Decker strode toward them, followed by ATF Special Agent Brett Tanner and FBI Agent Evan McGarry. All wore dark cargo pants and matching polo shirts with their respective agency's badges embroidered on their shirts.

"Kade Sampson, you sonofabitch." Deck grabbed him in a bear hug, practically lifting him off the ground as they slapped each other on the back.

"Been a long time." Kade shook the other man's hand, then did the same to Brett and Evan's. "You guys should have given me a heads-up you'd be here."

Brett extended his hand, giving Kade a closeup view of the nasty burn his friend had suffered last year. "We didn't know we'd be here until last night. We were on assignment in Delaware, then got detailed directly here to HSI."

Evan shook hands next. "Good to see you, Kade."

"You, too, Evan." Now the running engines and the Colorado tags made sense. "Blaze and Blue outside?" The ears he'd seen in one of the SUVs probably belonged to Evan's German Shepherd. Brett's arson dog, a hulking Chesapeake Bay Retriever, was probably sound asleep in the back of Brett's truck.

"Yeah," Evan said. "We're taking turns letting them have the run of the office."

Years ago, they'd all gone through advanced K-9 training together and had struck up a close friendship, although Kade hadn't seen any of them in the year since they'd returned to Colorado and joined Denver's Special Ops Task Force. "What are you in town for?"

Deck snapped his fingers, and Thor hustled to sit at Deck's left side. "Some of the big July Fourth events around the city. We just stopped in to pick up our assignments."

"Laia, this is Adam Decker. He's with the DEA's Denver office." While the two of them shook hands, Kade added, "Laia is my sister-in-law."

Still holding Laia's hand, Deck's head snapped back to Kade's faster than Linda Blair's in *The Exorcist*. His friend was one of the few who knew the truth. The *real* truth. Releasing her hand, Deck cleared his throat. "It's nice to meet you."

"You as well," Laia said, arching a brow at Kade, telling him she'd not only picked up on Deck's reaction but they'd be having a discussion about it on the way home. *His* home, anyway. Not hers.

This was exactly what Kade had wanted to avoid. Anything that could hurt Laia more by dredging up the past.

"This is ATF Agent Brett Tanner and FBI Agent Evan McGarry," he said, indicating his other friends.

"Nice to meet you." Brett's enormous hand engulfed Laia's as they shook.

"A pleasure," Evan said.

When Laia smiled, a spurt of unwanted jealousy shot up his spine. Not because he thought his friends would ever dare make a move on her, but because he had a feeling that he wouldn't be on the receiving end of one of her smiles for a very long time, if ever again.

"Yo, Sampson," another voice shouted from behind Deck. "You dragged my ass in here on a Sunday, so let's get to work. The day's not getting any longer."

Kade chuckled. The man was right. "Catch ya later, guys. Let's grab a few beers before you head back home." He touched his hand to the small of Laia's back, urging her further into the office.

As they brushed past, Deck, Brett, and Evan clapped Kade on the shoulder. "You got it."

"Why did your friend react that way when you told him I was your sister-in-law?" Laia asked as they walked away.

"Probably because he knows about Josh." A partial truth.

"Are you sure that's all it was?"

"Yeah," he lied, thankful that Manny wanted to get to work ASAP.

Manny uncrossed his arms and grinned stupidly at their approach. "You must be Laia." His grin widened and no wonder. Laia was a beautiful woman who had that effect on men. *Including me.*

"This is Special Agent Manny Dominguez," Kade said.

"Manny's been working cases on the Colon Drug Cartel for years."

Beside him, Laia stiffened. "I remember you."

Manny's expression sobered. "I'm sorry for your loss, Mrs. Sampson."

"Thank you," she said, then took a deep breath. This couldn't be easy for her. "And it's not Mrs. Sampson anymore. It's Velez. I go by my maiden name now."

"Okay. Have a seat." Manny shoved aside a black plastic tech box on his desk, then indicated she should sit in front of his computer. He plucked something from his ear about the size of a small button and placed it carefully in one of the slots inside the box.

"What is that?" Kade asked. "A receiver?"

Manny chuckled. "An experimental transmitter *and* receiver. We just got it in. I was testing it out, and it works like a charm. Undetectable by standard bug-detection equipment and good up to half a mile away. Even comes with digital recorder capacity."

"Not bad." As a DHS officer, he didn't normally get involved to any depth in investigations and rarely used covert equipment. Kade peered inside the box at the tiny gadget. "It's so small. Doesn't look big enough to hold a battery. What's the power source?"

"It's got a microscopic powerpack smaller than the head of a pin."

"No kidding. Won't it burn the inside of your ear?" One of the problems attributed to some wire transmitters was that they radiated a lot of heat, leaving behind nasty burns.

"It's coated with some kind of insulating gel." Manny snapped the box's lid shut, then addressed Laia. "Kade filled me in on what's been happening to you and that you might be able to ID one of the guys following you."

When Manny leaned over and hit the return button

on his keyboard, a mugshot photo populated the screen, along with the arrestee's physical identifiers. "I've narrowed down the database to those individuals with confirmed ties to Fernando Colon. There are around fifty. If you don't find who you're looking for here, I'll widen the database to include those with 'suspected' ties to the Colon Cartel. To scroll through the photos, just keep hitting the return button. Let me know if you recognize anyone."

"Thank you. I will." Laia rolled the chair closer to the screen and began scrolling through one image after the next.

Manny tipped his head to Kade, indicating they should talk privately.

"I'll be back in a minute," Kade said to Laia.

She nodded and resumed clicking through the images.

"I have news," Manny said when they were out of earshot. "You know Fernando Colon would have gotten more time in prison, but since we never found a ledger of any kind, we couldn't nail him with the heavier money laundering charges."

"And?" From the look on Manny's face, whatever he was about to say would be sucky news.

"Colon only received a three-year sentence, about twenty years less than what he would have gotten if we'd been able to tie him to more drug money." Manny shook his head, clearly disgusted. "Two weeks ago, Colon was released. Fucker shaved almost an entire year off his sentence for good behavior. *Good behavior.* You believe that?"

The timing coincided too closely with when Laia started feeling as if she were being followed, then her house getting tossed. Colon's release from prison had to be the trigger that set everything off. "Where's Colon now?" Like Josh and Laia's house, the fortified compound Colon had been living in had been seized by the government and sold off years ago.

"At his mother's house."

Kade snorted at the irony. One of the most powerful

domestic drug cartel kings was living in a cop's house.

Colon's father had been an undercover police officer, one of the best in the state police, before he'd committed suicide. Considering Colon had managed to operate right under their noses, untouchable for over a decade, it was widely speculated that, through his father, Colon had learned crucial details about how police departments and government agencies worked. Colon's father would be rolling over in his grave if he knew he'd unintentionally spawned a ruthless criminal.

Manny hitched his head to his cubicle. "If she really IDs one of Colon's guys, then I'd say they're after something, and we both know what it is."

"The ledger." Kade nodded, confirming the obvious. "But why now, and why right after Colon was released? His power base is still right here in New Jersey, always has been. Even in prison, he could have ordered his people to follow her and toss her new place years ago. We're missing something." Whatever it was, Laia and Rosa would remain in the line of fire until they figured it out.

"If she *can* ID one of Colon's goons, I can get authorization to put some money on the street to try and come up with the answer."

"I'll do the same." Even if the cash came from his own pocket.

He turned to head back to Laia when Manny stopped him.

"Hey, man. I know we searched the house, and we must have asked her ten times and ten different ways if she knew anything about a ledger, and she always said no. Is there any chance she was lying?"

Kade glanced at Manny's cubicle. With his height, he could make out the top of her head as she focused on the monitor. In many ways, most in fact, they hardly knew each other. But his gut said she was telling the truth about this.

"No. If she knew, she would have said so."

"Are you sure?" Manny asked quietly. "Josh told his lawyer that he had a ledger, but he refused to say where it was. Then he requested to see his wife."

"That doesn't automatically mean she knew about it back then." Kade crossed his arms. Manny was a top-notch investigator, but he was on the wrong track. "That ledger was Josh's only chance of working out a deal with the U.S. Attorney's Office. He might not have trusted his own attorney enough to make sure it made it into the right hands."

Kade had learned after the fact that between the time when his brother had placed that call to Laia and her arrival at the jail, Josh had been murdered. To keep him from doing exactly what he'd planned on doing—squealing on Fernando Colon. It was the only chance Josh had of receiving a get-out-of-jail-free card. The only reason anyone knew about the ledger at all was because that lawyer had mentioned it to the prosecutor. Even after Josh was dead, they'd all looked for it.

As it had when he'd gotten word from the Marshals that his brother was dead, Kade's breath caught in his throat, and he could barely breathe. He'd been the first of his family to view the body. It had been surreal. He half expected Josh to jump up from that cold steel gurney, then grin and call him by the same word he always had when he'd fooled Kade. *Sucker.*

"Okay," Manny said. "But she's here, and you know I gotta ask her again."

"I know." And it killed him. He'd known bringing her to the HSI office would be hard enough. Having to answer questions again would reopen jagged, painful wounds that he suspected had taken years to heal. If they ever really had.

"Anything?" Manny asked Laia in a casual tone when they'd returned to his cubicle.

Kade suspected she'd see right through Manny's bland demeanor.

"Not yet." She didn't turn around, just kept pecking away at the return button.

Manny sat on the edge of his desk. "I have to ask you something again."

Her shoulders stiffened, and her fingers stilled on the keyboard. Slowly, she swiveled the chair, then crossed her arms. Fire might as well have been shooting from her eyes. She'd been grilled too many times by Manny and other federal agents not to know when the questioning was about to kickstart all over again.

Kade braced himself for the explosion about to level the building.

Chapter Six

"How many times do I have to answer the same question?" Laia ground her teeth as she glared at Agent Dominguez, knowing with unerring certainty what he was about to ask. "I don't know anything about any ledger. Josh didn't tell me about one, and if you recall, my husband was murdered—in *your* care, I might add."

"I'm sorry." Dominguez held out his hands in a placating gesture. "We're just trying to understand why Colon's people would start harassing you after all this time."

"*We're* just trying to understand?" This time she turned her deadly glare on Kade. "Is this why you really brought me here? You didn't believe me when I said I don't know anything about the ledger?" She grabbed the armrests, resisting the urge to commit bodily assault on two federal officers.

"That's not it, and you know it." Kade moved closer. "*I* believe you."

She let loose with both barrels. "You people," she began, looking alternately from Kade to Dominguez, intentionally including Kade in what she was about to say, "searched my house, served subpoenas on our bank accounts, then froze all our assets. When that wasn't enough, you seized my house, then kicked me and my three-year-old daughter out on the street."

Kade's brow furrowed, and his eyes shone with sympathy that only served to enrage her further. "While you were all gloating about taking down a drug cartel," she snapped, "*I* was barely able to pay the bills and put a roof over my daughter's head."

Laia paused to take a breath, but she was only just getting started, and it occurred to her that she'd been holding in all this rage for a very long time. "The second the bank Josh and I worked for found out he'd been arrested, he was fired. A week after that, I was politely informed that my accounts manager position was being eliminated, a not-too-subtle way of shit-canning me, too. I was an embarrassment they couldn't afford to have around. I had to revert to my maiden name just to get a job, and the only one I could get was as a bank teller, earning a fraction of the salary I'd been pulling in before."

Unable to look into Kade's softening eyes, filled with so much apology it gutted her, she spun the chair around to face the monitor and resume viewing images. Embarrassingly, her hand trembled over the keyboard.

"Laia, please—"

For what seemed like the fiftieth time, she hit the return button. Then gasped. The face staring back at her was young, no more than twenty-five. He had brown hair, brown, wide-set eyes, full lips, and a mustache. Curving down from his lower lip and continuing to his chin was a scar.

"That's him." She pointed at the monitor. "That's the man who was waiting outside Rosa's daycare."

When Kade rested his hand on her shoulder, leaning over her to get a better look, this time she didn't flinch.

Agent Dominguez peered over her other shoulder, then made a *hmphing* sound. "Jesus Montoya. He's a low-level guy in the Colon Cartel. I arrested him myself less than a month ago. The little punk's still on parole." He pulled the keyboard closer and clicked the print button. "I'll grab another agent and go talk to him. Don't worry. We'll find out why he was outside your daughter's daycare."

"Thank you, Agent Dominguez." Laia breathed a little easier.

"Call ya later, Kade." He grabbed what looked like a fishing vest from a hangar. "Yo, Cisneros," he shouted over the top of his cubicle. "You're with me."

A moment later, he was gone, leaving her alone with Kade. She stared at the man's image on the monitor. Why had this man been watching her? Was Rosa really in danger?

How could Josh have done this to us?

"I didn't know you lost your job," Kade said softly, watching her from where he sat on the far side of the desk. "My parents never told me."

"That's because I never told them. I didn't want to add to their grief." Finding out their son was a criminal had been enough of a brutal, ugly shock to her in-laws. Even Josh's father, a stern military man, had wept alongside his wife at hearing the news.

"A lot of years have passed. Couldn't you apply for another management position at a bank under your maiden name?"

"I thought about that, but to start over would mean long hours. Contrary to the phrase 'banker's hours,' it takes time, long days to build up a good reputation and a solid resume. As a teller, I *do* have banker's hours. That's better for maintaining Rosa's schedule, and it allows me to spend more time with her and still squeeze in my online courses at night."

She stifled another yawn, inwardly cursing Kade and his generous offer to give her his room. Sleeping in his bed with his personal belongings and his scent everywhere had left her tossing and turning, imagining his powerful, naked body doing all kinds of erotic things to hers.

Ending this was the only thing that would save her from shoving aside her latent feelings of resentment and doing something stupid. Like acting on her lustful urges. *Like throwing myself into his arms.* But she'd stay with him for the next ten years if that's what it took to keep Rosa safe. "Even if they offered me my old job back tomorrow, I'd turn it down."

"All the more reason why you should have taken my parents up on their offer to come live with them. They love you, and they love Rosa."

She shook her head, wishing life were that simple. "They were planning on retiring and moving to Delaware. We couldn't be the reason for them changing their life plans. After Josh died, it was too painful for them to stay. Besides, I've only just learned to stand on my own two feet. I relied too much on my mother, then I did the same thing with Josh. It wouldn't have been fair to transfer that responsibility to your parents." And it only would have prevented her from pursuing her own dreams.

"Is that why you never cashed the checks I sent you?" Kade asked.

She looked at him, again desperately wishing time could have been their ally, but it hadn't been and never would be. "I couldn't accept your charity any more than I could have accepted your parents'. And I know that when they started sending me checks, you were giving them the cash."

His voice took on a hard edge. "You should have cashed them. I told you that you're family, and family takes care of each other."

"Do they?" she shot back. "Do I really have to remind you of how many voicemail messages I left that you never returned? *That's* why I didn't cash your checks. It wasn't because I didn't need the money. God knows I did. You thought you could pay off family obligations with money. What I really needed back then was a friend, a shoulder to lean on, someone to talk to, and *you* weren't there. You said we had a connection in that elevator. Apparently, that was bullshit."

"It *wasn't* bullshit. If you believe nothing else, believe that." He drew in a deep breath, then dragged a hand down his face. "I meant what I said then, and I mean what I'm saying now. Family takes care of family."

Josh had been her family. Had he really taken care of her and Rosa in the end? No. He'd let them down in the worst way possible. Then again, it had been the continual disintegration of their marriage that had paved Josh's way to the cartel. Perhaps she was as much to blame as he was. She never should have let her mother talk her into—

Mother.

She jumped from the chair. "Do you think my mother is in danger? I need to call her. We need to go to her place and check on her."

"No, we don't. At least, not right now."

"Why not? How do you know that?" She began digging in her purse for her phone.

The relationship she had with her mother had been a rough road, especially where her marriage was concerned, but other than Rosa, she was Laia's only living blood relative, and she loved her nonetheless.

"Because," he said, resting his hands on her shoulders, "this morning before we left to come here, I spoke with the director of security at your mom's community. I told him what's going on, and he agreed to keep an eye on things."

"What does that mean? Is this guy a trained bodyguard or a Navy SEAL?" She was sputtering and didn't care how ridiculous she sounded. "I doubt he can watch over her twenty-four hours a day."

"You're right, he can't. But the rotating private guards I hired started their first shift at eight this morning. These people *are* trained."

Her jaw dropped as she absorbed all that Kade had been doing for her, and she hadn't even known. "How did you even know where she lives? I never told you."

A corner of his mouth lifted. "There's a lot you don't know about me," he said, echoing the exact same words she'd thrown in his face last night.

"I-I..." The sputtering had returned. She didn't know what to say at his thoughtful generosity except, "I'll pay you back."

His hands slipped from her shoulders down her arms, sending goose bumps barreling across her skin. "I won't take your money. If it makes you feel better, I'll consider those checks cashed. Okay?" When he touched two fingers to her cheek, those goose bumps prickled every hair on her body as if she'd been playing footsie with a live wire.

"Okay," she whispered.

Releasing her other arm, he cupped her face. As if having a mind of their own, her lips parted. She and Kade had never kissed, never even—

He took a step back, then tugged his phone from the clip on his belt. He stared for a moment at the screen, then swiped to take the call. "Ashley, is everything all right?" He listened a moment longer. "No, I didn't. Stay inside and lock the doors. We're on our way."

Laia's heart began tripping in her chest. "What is it?"

He ground his jaws, every muscle in his sculpted face flexing. "Ashley said there's a cable repair company at my house."

"Oh, no." This was the absolute worst news. "Alvita said there was a cable company at *my* house the day it was broken into."

"Yeah." His eyes narrowed dangerously. "And I don't *have* cable."

Chapter Seven

Kade punched it, slamming his foot on the accelerator and pushing the SUV as fast as he dared.

Beside him, one of Laia's hands rested on her thigh, curled into a tight fist. Her other hand gripped the phone he'd given her so that she could call Ashley and speak to Rosa directly. Hearing her daughter's voice had been the only thing having a calming effect on her.

That still didn't alleviate the rising fear in his gut. Colon's release had triggered a sequence of events that he suspected was about to spiral at light speed into the deadly zone.

"We'll be there in ten minutes," he said, trying to reassure her and knowing there was nothing he could say at the moment that could possibly come close to accomplishing that.

"What if they find Rosa before we get there?" Her voice was tight, filled with the depth of fear only a parent could have for her child, yet he felt it, too. "What will they do with her?"

"Nothing, because they don't know she's next door with

Ashley." He hoped and prayed that was true. He pushed the air horn button three successive times, scattering the traffic ahead of them. "The police are on their way. They'll probably get there before we do."

He risked a quick glance at Laia, then jerked his eyes back to the highway. Her chest was heaving as she took in a series of short breaths. He wanted to hold her hand, to reassure her that everything would be fine, but he couldn't do that. Not only was he driving, but he couldn't be absolutely sure everything *would* be okay.

With the exit to North Plainfield coming on fast, he serpentined through the thickening Sunday traffic, hitting the off-ramp way too fast, then pushing the air horn button again as he slowed to maneuver around another vehicle stopped at the top of the rise.

Minutes later, he braked to a screeching stop in front of his house. Two patrol cars were already on scene. The Somerset Cable Company van Ashley had described was nowhere in sight, and they hadn't passed one on the way in.

An officer walked along the north side of his house, her hand at the ready, resting on her holstered weapon. Another cop tried the front door, then peered through a window.

Laia tore off her seat belt.

"Wait!" He grabbed her arm. "Stay here. I want to check things out first."

Her eyes widened. "You've got to be kidding. My daughter—your niece—could be in danger, and you want me to sit here on my ass?"

"Laia, please. Between me and the police, there are four armed officers on scene, and Smoke is with Ashley and Rosa. We can't do our jobs if we have to worry about you, too." Her lips tightened, revealing tiny white lines etched at the corners of her mouth.

"The windows on this vehicle are tinted. As long as you

stay inside, no one can identify you, and I'd like to keep it that way. Talk to Rosa on the phone again if you want to, but do not go outside. Trust me on this, okay?"

Now her lips trembled with the effort it was obviously taking her not to lose it. "Okay, but hurry."

He went out to meet the officer waiting for him by his patrol car. The cop said something into the microphone clipped to his shoulder strap.

"Kade Sampson," he said as he approached, shifting aside his overshirt to clearly display the badge and holstered Glock. "I called this in."

"Sergeant Morales. All windows and doors are intact," the cop said. "Do you have an alarm system? We didn't get any notifications."

"Yeah, me, either." Which didn't mean much. Standard domestic alarm systems were meant to prevent break-ins by run-of-the-mill burglars with no skills. The Colon Cartel had people with skills on their payroll. "I'm going in. Back me up."

"Copy that." Morales fell in step as they went to the front door, clicking his mic. "We're going inside."

Kade caught movement at one of the windows on Ashley's house. She'd pulled back the curtain and gave him a reassuring wave. Smoke's ears were visible over the top of the window ledge.

He pulled out his keys, unlocking the door, then unholstering his weapon. He turned the knob and pushed the door open. The system began beeping. With the muzzle of his gun, Kade did a quick sweep of the interior of the house, then punched in his code. The system went silent.

Both he and Morales remained in the hallway, listening, but the house was quiet. Kade led the way through the ground floor, then up the stairs and into the bedrooms and bathrooms. There were no signs that anyone had breached the security system. He holstered, as did Morales.

"Let's go talk to my neighbor." Kade led the way downstairs, then out the door. "Give me a second."

Kade headed to his SUV to let Laia know everything was secure. He opened the door. "Laia—" The passenger seat was empty.

He looked up just in time to see Laia going in the front door of Ashley's house and the door closing behind her. He pressed his lips together, more annoyed than he thought possible that she didn't trust him enough to heed his warning. He hitched his head to the cop, indicating he should follow. Knowing it was locked, he rapped twice on the door. "Ashley, it's Kade. Open up."

The door opened. Laia sat in a chair, holding Rosa in her lap as the child yawned. Smoke raced to his side, his tail wagging, ears alert. "Good boy, Smoke." He scratched his dog behind the ears and was rewarded with a soft groan, telling him he'd hit the right spot at the base of his ears that Smoke loved.

"Everything okay at your house?" Ashley asked as Morales shut the door.

Kade nodded. "Tell us what you saw."

"I can do better than that." Ashley picked up her phone from a small table next to where Laia rocked Rosa and handed it to Kade. "I took photos."

Kade held the phone for Morales to watch as he began scrolling through the photos. The first few shots were of a white van with the words Somerset Cable Company in green lettering. The next showed two men wearing ball caps tugged low enough to cover their faces as they went first to the front door, then headed around to the backyard.

"Sorry," Ashley said. "I couldn't get any shots of the license plate without going outside, but if you keep scrolling, there's a fun little video."

He swiped again, then hit play and watched one of the men creeping around the side of the house while the other remained at the front door holding a clipboard in one hand and a toolbox in the other. Naturally, the guy wore gloves. The wail of sirens came from the phone. As the sirens grew louder, the guy at the door shouted something, then ran to the van and got in. As soon as the other guy jumped in the passenger seat, the van raced off.

Kade scrolled back to the photo. "Somerset Cable Company. Ever heard of them?" he asked the sergeant because Kade hadn't.

Morales shook his head. "Nope. I can put out a BOLO for the van. We might get lucky before they ditch it."

"Maybe." He seriously doubted it. Colon's people weren't stupid.

Laia continued rocking a sleeping Rosa in her arms, the same way she'd held her daughter at the cemetery while Josh's coffin was lowered into the ground.

Jesus Christ, Josh.

Kade had loved his brother, but if he were still alive, he'd punch Josh's lights out. The legacy he had left behind in the wake of his death was snowballing into something ugly.

Smoke nudged his hand, snorting as he looked up at Kade. Even his dog knew something was about to go down.

"Sergeant." He turned to Morales, who'd already taken out a pad and was making notes. "Can you finish documenting this incident? My place has been compromised, and I need to get them out of here."

"No problem." Morales turned to Ashley. "Ma'am, can I get your name?"

As the sergeant spoke to Ashley, Kade knelt beside Laia. "We can't stay at my place anymore."

She nodded. "Where can we go?"

"I know a place. Wait here while I get our bags." He stood

and didn't stick around for a response.

He went back outside and swapped his DHS SUV for his Suburban in the garage where Laia's car was parked, then headed for the door to the house to pack their bags.

Colon knew he was Josh's brother, and it probably wouldn't be too difficult to find out where Kade lived. But how would Colon have known that Laia was staying with him? She'd only moved in yesterday. If cartel goons had been skulking around his neighborhood, he would have noticed.

Kade reached for the doorknob but stopped and turned to stare at Laia's Escape.

I never checked her vehicle.

He grabbed a flashlight hanging on the garage wall, then searched beneath the Escape. Just when he'd begun to think he was wrong, he saw it. A tracker. Kade grabbed the black box, set it on the concrete, then slammed the heel of his boot down hard. The cover cracked. Pieces of tracker guts skittered across the floor.

Kade hurled the flashlight against the wall. He should have seen that coming. Instead, he'd been distracted enough by Laia and Rosa's presence that he'd let his heart interfere with his duty.

Shake it off and focus.

He charged back into the house to pack. Rosa had taken most of her toys to Ashley's. What little she'd left behind he stuffed into Laia's overnight bag, along with Laia's toiletries, clothes, and an emerald-green silk slip of a nightie she'd left draped over a chair. As he crammed the shimmery lingerie into her bag, he shoved aside all thoughts of her wearing it.

And of me stripping it off her with my teeth.

He stowed their bags in the Suburban's rear compartment, then gave the sergeant his business card and requested he be notified of any investigative findings. After transferring the booster seat from the Escape to the Suburban, he closed the garage doors.

No more than ten minutes had passed before he returned to Ashley's house. "Thanks, Ashley. We're heading out. I don't know when we'll be back."

"I figured that," she said. "Let me know if I can do anything to help."

"Will do. Let's go," he said to Laia, pausing at the threshold to look both ways down the street. With Sergeant Morales on their six and two other cops on the street, he didn't really think anyone would try something but still... "Stick close."

Kade turned to see Laia heft Rosa in her arms. "I've got her." He slipped a now-fully sleeping Rosa from Laia's arms to his. "Thanks, Sergeant," he threw over his shoulder.

"You got it."

"Smoke." He hitched his head for Smoke to go first, and his K-9 bounded down the stairs, loping to the Suburban.

"Wait!" Laia said. "I need to get a—"

"Booster seat? Already done." He glanced behind him to see a surprised look on her face, one mixed with gratitude.

When she opened the rear door, he gently placed Rosa in the seat, leaving Laia to buckle her in while he rounded the hood and opened the other side door for Smoke to hop in. Seconds later, they were speeding east on I-78.

Every mile or so he glanced in the rear- and side-view mirrors, mentally tagging every make, model, and color of the cars behind them and continually varying his speed. Anyone who sped up to stay with them was suspect, and anyone who slowed so as not to pass them was suspect, too.

With every mile, Kade's heart rate slowed, and he breathed a little easier. None of the vehicles behind them pinged his radar.

He cued up Manny Dominguez's number, continually glancing in the rearview as he waited for Manny to pick up.

"Dominguez."

"Manny, it's Kade. They tracked us to my house. We're okay, but we'll be staying…someplace else." Not that he didn't trust Manny, but the smaller the circle of people who knew where Laia and Rosa were the better. "Did you find Jesus Montoya?"

"He's in the wind. I'll find him."

Kade had a bad feeling it could take a while to pin anything on Fernando Colon. "Keep me posted."

"Ten-four."

Kade set the phone in the console. Risking the likelihood that she'd only pull away, he rested his hand on Laia's. Surprisingly, she not only didn't resist but actually clasped his hand tightly. "You okay?" he asked.

"Not really," she answered in a shaky voice.

He took another chance and laced his fingers with hers. As the warmth of her soft skin seeped into his, his entire body gave an inward sigh. For years, he'd thought about holding her hand, but not like this. Not when their lives could very well be in his hands. "I'm sorry about all this."

"Why would you say that?" she asked. "It's not your fault. None of this is."

A big fat lump of guilt rose in his throat, nearly choking off his oxygen supply.

Isn't it?

He could have let Josh go. In fact, Kade's brother had begged him to do just that, but Kade hadn't. If given a second chance to do things differently, would he?

He tugged his hand away, returning it to the wheel where his knuckles cracked. Again, he checked the rearview mirror, looking at the vehicles behind them, including a white sedan. He shifted his focus to the sleeping child behind them, furious with his brother and wondering if he'd made the right decision.

Laia didn't know the whole story, what really went down between him and Josh the day he'd been arrested. If she did know, she'd hate him until he took his last breath.

He looked at both mirrors again. The white sedan was still there, maintaining the same ten car lengths back.

Kade depressed the accelerator, gunning the Suburban twenty miles past the limit. For a few seconds, the distance between the sedan grew. Then it shortened, confirming his fears.

"Smoke, sit," he called to his dog, who'd been standing. To Laia, he said, "Hold on," then slammed his foot down on the accelerator, and the Suburban's 8.1 liter, 340-horsepower engine kicked in, blasting them down the highway.

"Kade?" came Laia's worried voice. "Something I should know?"

Lots, actually, but now wasn't the time. "We've got a tail."

Chapter Eight

"A tail? As in we're being followed?" Laia twisted her neck to look behind them. Sure enough, a small white sedan was zigzagging through traffic, clearly trying to keep up with them.

"Yeah." Kade maneuvered around a car in front of them, smoothly shifting into the center lane, then back into the left lane. His gaze flicked back and forth between the highway ahead and the rearview mirror. Other than the clenching of his jaw, the man looked as cool as a proverbial cucumber, like he'd been a professional racecar driver his entire life.

She turned to Rosa, but her daughter was sleeping peacefully, one tiny hand curled into a fist around Smoke's fur. Oddly, Smoke had draped one front leg across her lap, as if he was trying to protect Rosa from being thrown forward.

"Can you lose them?" She sure hoped so. If he couldn't…

"Working on it. Hang on, and this time I mean it. Grab onto something."

Laia gasped, her eyes widening at the traffic jam a hundred yards ahead and completely blocking all lanes. She grabbed onto the armrest and held her breath because Kade wasn't slowing down.

"Smoke, down!"

She hazarded a glance to the seat behind her. Smoke lay down, still maintaining a protective leg across Rosa's lap. *Amazing.* How did he know to do that?

Kade slowed the SUV, slightly, anyway, then jerked the wheel to the right and gunned the vehicle up the shoulder and past the unmoving cars. An exit ramp loomed ahead. Some of the cars stuck in the right lane crossed into the shoulder, forcing Kade to slow down.

She glanced behind them again. The white sedan was still doing its best to follow them.

Kade punched the SUV up the ramp, riding the tail of the car ahead of them until they made it to the stop sign. At the top of the ramp, he cranked the wheel and passed the line of cars, looking both ways at the intersection, then gunning onto the road.

Several minutes passed before he slowed the vehicle on the rural, twisting street. A short distance ahead, he took the entrance to the Garden State Parkway south, casting more looks into the rear- and side-view mirrors before taking a deep breath. "I think we lost them."

"How did they find us so quickly?"

"They must have left someone nearby on a side street to watch for us." He glanced over his shoulder at Rosa and Smoke. "That, and there was a tracker under your car."

"A tracker?" *Oh God.* How long had it been there? Days? Weeks?

"Yeah, but I destroyed it."

Laia's heart jackhammered and her knuckles were white where she had the armrest in a death grip. She really hadn't imagined it. They *had* been following her all this time. "Where are we going?"

"A friend's house." He tugged his phone from his belt and cued up a number. "Jamie," he said. "Mind if I stay at the shack for a few days? I'll explain later. Call me back." He ended the call, then dropped the phone into the center console.

"The shack?" That didn't sound particularly inviting, more like an outhouse in the middle of the woods. "Do we need to stop for sleeping bags, bug spray, and bear repellant?"

Kade snorted, and she glimpsed his right-side dimple. "Nah. We're good. But we do need to get some food. Jamie hasn't been around for six months. Probably won't show up for another six. Whatever food he's got in the shack is probably covered with three shades of green mold by now."

Yum. Though Kade couldn't see it, Laia wrinkled her nose. "Where is this place, exactly?"

"Manasquan."

"*Manasquan*? That must be some 'shack' your friend has." That part of New Jersey was right on the water. Like Rumson, the cost of houses there was through the roof.

"It's not bad." While still keeping one eye on the road, Kade picked up his phone again and placed another call. "Jose," he said when a voice answered, then, "Yeah, I know it's been a few years. I need your help." Laia heard another man's voice but couldn't make out the words. "Fernando Colon was released two weeks ago. I want to know what he's been up to. Someone's been watching my brother's wife, and her house was broken into. We already know this has something to do with Colon, and I want to know what he's after. I'm willing to pay for it. Whatever it takes."

A moment later, he ended the call and began tapping his fingers on the wheel. Silence filled the passenger compartment, as if neither of them wanted to address the hulking white elephant taking up most of the space and hogging all the air.

"Who was that?" Laia asked, looking at Kade's hard

profile.

"An informant."

Bile rose in the back of her throat. Her house had been broken into. They'd just escaped a "tail" by racing down the highway at breakneck speed. Now Kade was calling informants. This was all becoming far too real. Her world was about to fly apart all over again.

"Don't worry. We'll figure this out." Again he rested his hand on hers, squeezing it and casting her a quick glance.

She looked down at his hand, so big and strong. So reassuring and—

Don't even think it.

As the exit numbers went down, she began chewing on one of her nails. Manasquan was only twenty minutes or so from Asbury Park and her job, but how in the world could she possibly return to work with everything that was happening? She couldn't, and there was no way she'd drop her daughter off at daycare.

"What's wrong?" Kade asked, tacking on, "Other than the obvious."

The enormity of the situation was suddenly overwhelming. "I have to call work and tell them I won't be in tomorrow."

"Can you take the week off?"

Not really. Given the short notice, her boss would blow a fuse. Then there was that pesky little issue of not getting paid. Between her week-long vacation with Rosa and taking care of her mother when she'd come down with the flu earlier in the year, she'd used up every last one of her vacation days. "I'll have to."

She dug around in her bag for her phone and called her boss, Bill Weiss. "Hi, Bill," she said when he picked up after three rings. "Sorry to bother you on a Sunday, but I, uh, have to take the week off. I have a—" Bill's expectedly annoyed reaction came through clear as a bell. "I'm sorry, but it's a family emergency." As Bill rattled on about her job obligations and how difficult it would be for him to find a replacement on such short notice, she stupidly imagined telling him the truth: *A drug cartel is after me.* The only thing that would get her was unemployed.

"I'm sorry," she continued. "And yes, I know I won't get paid. Believe me, I don't have a choice. Again, I apologize for the short notice."

When she'd stowed her phone back in her purse, she leaned back and couldn't stop the groan from escaping her lips.

"Don't worry about the money," Kade said. "Jamie's place is free, and I'll take care of buying groceries and any other expenses that come up."

She shook her head. "That's very generous of you, but you've already done enough for us by helping with the police and giving us a place to stay. I'll find a way to pay you back."

"No, you won't."

A flash of indignation had her lifting her chin. "Yes. I—"

"Forget it," he snapped, clenching his jaw.

What did *he* have to be angry about? "Look"—she shifted in the seat to face him—"I appreciate you driving all the way from Maryland to my house. I didn't really expect you to do that, and I probably shouldn't have called you in the first place."

"Why not?" When he looked at her, he was frowning. "I should *always* be the first person you call for help."

"Are you *kidding*?" She widened her eyes, staring—no, make that *glaring*—at him. "In the last six years, how many times have you bothered to show up in my life? Twice. On my wedding day and for Josh's funeral. Your complete and utter absence made it crystal clear to me that whatever you *think* we felt for each other in that elevator is null and void." If not completely dead and buried. "So why should I call you first?

For anything?"

"It wasn't like that. It was—" He smacked his palm on the wheel. "Christ," he muttered half under his breath, then his chest expanded as he took a deep breath. "Let's just concentrate on getting you and Rosa somewhere safe, then we'll talk more about what's next."

His voice might be calmer now, but judging by the continual flexing of his fingers and a tic in his jaw, he was anything but calm. The same could be said for her. So many emotions screamed inside her head to get out, confusion being at the tippy-top of the list.

This man—the one who'd raced to her house yesterday, taken total charge with the police on two occasions, and was now rescuing her and Rosa from God knew what—wasn't the same selfish, self-centered man she'd come to expect. This man was more like the person she'd met in that elevator. Kind. Caring. Charming. And who'd gotten her blood pumping with excitement the same way it was doing now. Even having an argument with him was more passionate than anything she'd experienced with Josh. Or any other man.

And that was the most dangerous revelation of all.

Two hours later, and after a quick stop for groceries, Laia's jaw dropped when Kade parked the Suburban inside the attached garage of Jamie's so-called *shack*.

The garage alone was bigger than the entire ground floor of her duplex rental. The house itself was an enormous structure on stilts and situated at the end of a road on the beach. As in... On. The. Beach. As in, uber-pricy beachfront real estate. The kind she and Josh used to live in before...

Before everything bad that could have happened actually *did* happen.

"Mommy, can we go to the beach?" Rosa kicked her legs up and down, a sign that she'd been in the booster seat for too long.

"No, sweetie." Laia got out of the Suburban and opened Rosa's door. "It's dinnertime."

The moment Kade let Smoke out, the dog ran right to a short stairway and stood in front of another door, acting as if he'd been here many times before. "I've got her." Kade had opened up his side and was now reaching over to unbuckle Rosa.

As Rosa scrambled into his arms, once again Laia was struck by sheer and utter confusion. This uber-helpful, unselfish side of Kade was still difficult to wrap her brain around. Had Josh been lying to her about him all these years? Either that or Kade had been body-snatched and replaced by an alien.

"C'mon, Cream Puff." He winked at Rosa. "I think you're going to like your room. Leave the groceries," he ordered Laia, using the same commanding tone he'd used when ordering Rosa to wipe her hands before eating. "I'll come back for them, then fix dinner." The shock must have shown on her face because he frowned over Rosa's head. "What? I *can* cook."

"It's not that I—" Just assumed *she'd* be the one doing things like carrying Rosa inside and cooking. The same as her life had been with Josh. "I figured I'd do the cooking."

"Nope. I've got that covered." He grinned, leaving her standing there, stupefied as to how such a masculine face could have such adorable dimples.

After Kade had punched in a code on the security box by the connecting door, they followed him and Smoke inside, through an enormous dining room with a table so shiny she could see her reflection in it. Mahogany. She and Josh used to own a pricy dining table made of rosewood. Funny how none of that seemed to matter anymore.

Next, he led her through a kitchen that was as equally jaw-dropping as the rest of the house. The Sub-Zero appliances alone were worth more than a year's rent at her duplex, and the living room view was spectacular.

Floor-to-ceiling windows ran the lengths of the east- and north-facing living room–great room, providing unobstructed views of the Atlantic Ocean. There was only one full wall, and it housed the biggest big screen TV she'd ever seen. It had to be close to eighty inches.

"Wow."

"Yup." Kade turned so Rosa could look through the windows. "See?" He pointed. "There's a lotta sand out there with your name on it. Maybe tomorrow, if your mommy says it's okay, we can all go to the beach."

"Really?" Her face lit up, then fell. "But I forgot my sandcastle buckets."

Kade sobered. "I'm sure I can dig one up around here somewhere." Then he grinned.

Rosa giggled. Looked like even five-year-old girls weren't immune to his killer dimples. "Can Smoke come?"

Hearing his name, Smoke barked.

"Yes. Smoke can come."

Smoke barked again, and Laia could swear the dog had actually followed the entire conversation.

Rosa pressed her nose and hands against the window. "Can I go on the Ferris wheel?" Through the window Laia saw that a small carnival had been set up on the shoreline about half a mile down the beach. "Pleeeze?"

Laia could only shake her head. Already, Rosa was a master manipulator when it came to getting something she wanted. "We'll see."

"No, you won't," Kade interjected. "You both need to keep a low profile."

She opened her mouth to object, but he was right. They had to remain hidden. Rather than being annoyed with him for making parental decisions for her, she ought to be grateful for him taking charge, not just with the police but of their safety.

"Let's go look at your room." Kade led them up the stairs to the second floor.

Rosa's room was small but had an ocean view and a twin bed with a pretty yellow flowered quilt. Against one wall was an antique oak bureau. The other wall was taken up by a matching bookcase that, to Laia's astonishment, held several children's books. On the bottom shelf was a stack of board games, including Trouble, Operation, and Monopoly.

"You like it, Cream Puff?" With Rosa still clinging to his neck, Kade went to the bookcase, then set her on the floor.

"Mm-hmm." She nodded, reaching for a worn copy of *Sleeping Beauty* on the lowest shelf.

"You can have the master bedroom," Kade said to Laia.

She followed him down the hall and into another bedroom, this one huge, with cream-colored carpeting and a king-size scroll-top bed with a matching chest and bureau.

He flipped on the bathroom lights. "This one has a soaker tub even bigger than mine."

Laia peered around the doorjamb. "You aren't kidding. It's big enough for a school of dolphins."

"Two of them, anyway."

The heated look Kade gave her made her breath catch. And when he continued staring, a sudden flush of warmth spread steadily from her neck downward.

Were they still talking about dolphins?

He shook his head, as if to clear it. "I'll get our bags and the groceries. Make yourself at home." Kade and Smoke left, leaving her alone in the master suite.

With rubbery legs, Laia sat on the edge of the bed. No

matter how much she tried, it was impossible to banish the image of the two of them in that tub, naked and—

"Mommy, can I watch TV?" Rosa asked, skipping into the room.

"Come here, sweetie. Mommy needs a hug." *And a change of subject.*

Laia held out her arms, then picked Rosa up, hugging her tightly. She nuzzled her daughter's head, inhaling her sweet little-girl smell. Josh used to do that as he'd read to Rosa. Eventually, he started working late, not getting home until after Rosa had gone to sleep. Then came the frequent business trips. Long before Josh was gone, Laia had effectively become a single parent.

Rosa wriggled her way from Laia's lap. "Mommy, *now* can I watch TV?"

"I think that's a good idea." That would give her and Kade time to unpack and get dinner ready. Easing off the bed, she followed Rosa downstairs. In the four years they'd been married, she and Josh had never done such simple things together, like preparing a meal or taking Rosa to the beach.

Melancholia dampened her already dismal mood. Things should have been different. Josh should have been helping her raise their daughter, not disappearing on weekends. How had things gone so horribly wrong?

The slow disintegration of their relationship had been subtle, at first. After Rosa was born, it had spiraled quickly into nonexistent.

But if she were honest with herself, it had started the day she'd said *I do.*

Chapter Nine

Outside, the sun was low on the horizon, and the temperature had cooled off some. Inside the house, Kade had the AC cranked up, yet the kitchen was hot. *Equator*-hot.

After unpacking the groceries, Laia got Rosa and Smoke settled in front of Jamie's mega monster-size TV, watching *The Nanny*, which Rosa got a kick out of. Something about Fran Drescher's New Yawk accent had Rosa rolling with laughter.

Through the opening to the living room, Rosa held up her hand to Smoke, turning her head away from the dog. "Tawk to the paw."

He chuckled when Smoke raised his paw to Rosa's hand.

"You have to turn your head around, too," she said to Smoke, repeating, "Tawk to the paw."

Smoke had the paw thing down but hadn't quite grasped the concept of twisting his neck around the way Fran Drescher did with her talk-to-the-hand thing.

The kitchen wasn't small, but it might as well have been a four-by-four-foot square box. The woman of his dreams—

some clean, some X-rated—was standing on the other side of the kitchen chopping ingredients for the salad. If he stuck a thermometer in his mouth, he was more than certain his temperature had soared well into the triple digits. If he'd been in a doctor's office right then, they probably would have called an ambulance to truck him off to a hospital and throw him in a tub of ice.

Kade grabbed yet another sheet of paper towel from the roll and wiped his brow. Then he made the mistake of looking again at the subject of his thoughts. Laia had showered and changed into a lavender sundress with thin little spaghetti straps. Her hair was still wet, leaving a damp spot on the back of the dress, and every time a bead of water rolled down her smooth shoulders, he had to clamp down the urge to lick it off.

Didn't help any that she was barefoot, revealing sparkly purple polish on her pretty toes. And damned if she wasn't wearing a silver toe ring with a tiny jewel that flickered every time she moved. He'd never thought much about toes or toe rings before. Now it was *all* he thought about. *Laia's* anyway, and sucking her toes into his mouth right before letting his lips do the walking directly north to the satiny curves of her calves and thighs.

The zipper over his crotch protested at the sudden pressure. *Yeah, bad idea.*

He turned back to the tortillas, sprinkling shredded cheese and cut-up vegetables he'd sautéed over one tortilla, then topping it with another.

"You really *can* cook." A hint of a smile curved Laia's lips, the first smile she'd graced him with since he'd shown up at her place yesterday.

"Told ya." His head was playing major games with him. Seeing her smile turned his insides to mush. *Soft, squishy mush.* Which only exacerbated his dilemma.

She was still the same woman he'd been crazy-attracted to in that elevator. Now he was seeing that she was also a caring, sensitive woman who loved her daughter—Josh's child—to distraction.

With superhuman effort, he refocused on the quesadillas. It didn't matter that his brother was gone. Laia had chosen Josh over him, and he had to remember that.

"How long do you think that tracker has been under my car?" she asked, then set down the knife she'd been using to slice cherry tomatoes.

Kade leaned back against the counter, grateful for the distraction. The skin over the bridge of her nose was wrinkled in concern. She was worried, and she had every right to be. "There's no way to know that. The battery wouldn't have lasted for more than five days. Your Escape is parked in your driveway at night, so they could have been replacing it every time the battery died. Do you know anything about Colon's background?" She shook her head. "He thinks like a cop. His father was a cop, one of the best undercover officers the New Jersey State Police ever had."

Her brows shot up. "You're kidding."

"Nope." He shook his head. "He grew up in a police family and learned all the tricks from stories his father told him. Including knowing everything about a target, in this case you. He knows who I am and what I do for a living. He'd know that if I had the ledger, I'd turn it over to the U.S. Attorney's Office so they could indict him all over again."

"I can't believe his father was a cop. That must have been difficult to live with, knowing his son had become a drug dealer." She turned to open one of the overhead cupboards, then stood on her tiptoes to try and grab one of the large bowls.

"I'll get that." He reached over her shoulder for the bowl, and in the process, his chest and arm grazed her shoulder, and he felt her body tensing. As he set the bowl on the counter, she averted her eyes but not before he caught her cheeks pinking.

Maybe she's not immune to me after all.

He sure wasn't immune to *her*. Being in the same room with her made him hot. *Touching* her—even inadvertently—made his skin flame like the inside of a volcano.

He set the bowl on the counter in front of her, then returned to his side of the kitchen. "I'm sure it would have been hard on Colon's father if he'd lived. He committed suicide when Colon was just a teenager. How such a good cop could have spawned a monster like Colon, we'll never know."

Laia began chopping lettuce. "What about his mother?"

Kade remembered Cecilia Colon from court. Her son showed absolutely no remorse for his crimes, while his mother sat weeping silently in the back of the courtroom. "I don't think she ever condoned what he did. She was a cop's wife and from what I heard was active in the police community for a long time after her husband died."

"Watching her child get sent to prison couldn't have been easy on her." Laia looked into the living room where Rosa had climbed off the sofa and was settling against Smoke's body, using him for a pillow.

"You're a good mother," he said, thinking she was looking at her daughter for reassurance.

Laia stiffened. "How would *you* know? You've only seen us together for less than two whole days." She turned her back to him and resumed cutting tomatoes like she wanted to kill them. Or maybe she was imagining his neck on the cutting board.

Rather than respond, he clamped his mouth shut because she was right. He'd made damn sure to stay out of her life, and he deserved her irritation when he reminded her of the fact.

Kade's phone blared from the kitchen table. Manny

Dominguez's name lit the screen. "I have to take this. Manny, how'd it go?" he said after answering.

"Jesus Montoya confirmed it," Manny said. "He didn't participate in the burglary and doesn't know who did, but he was ordered to put a tracker under your sister-in-law's car and to follow her around and see where she goes."

"Did he confirm they're looking for the ledger?" He glanced up when Laia moved closer.

"Yeah," Manny said, "but that's not *all* they're looking for. Get this…they're searching for a large amount of cash Josh stole from Colon."

Now it was Kade's turn to frown. Before he was murdered, Josh had already admitted to the AUSA that his cut was 3 percent of any amount he laundered, which was enough that the government had seized most of his and Laia's property and holdings. "How much are we talking about?" Because if Colon was looking for it two years after the fact, it had to be a ton of cash that he only now discovered was missing.

"Somewhere around two million. I cut Montoya loose and sent him back out there to get more information in exchange for not locking his ass up."

"Thanks, Manny. Keep me posted, and I'll do the same."

"Well?" Laia asked when he'd ended the call.

"The man you ID'd—Jesus Montoya—said Josh stole two million dollars from Colon."

Laia's jaw dropped. "Two *million*?"

"Yeah. He also admitted he was following you and that Colon's people broke into your house."

Her expression brightened. "That's good. Now you can arrest Colon, right?"

If only it were that simple. "It's more complicated than that. Jesus Montoya wasn't part of the burglary, so that's all hearsay, not probable cause to arrest anyone. Manny cut Montoya loose to get us more intel. He can be more valuable that way."

High-pitched giggling came from the living room where Rosa was busy high-fiving Smoke and still trying to get him to "tawk to the paw."

Her brows drew together. "I don't have any of Colon's money. Why does he think I do?"

"I don't know." What he did know was that stepping closer to Laia was a bad, bad idea, and idiotic sap that he was, he did it anyway.

"And why would Josh have to steal from Colon in the first place? Wasn't he already getting paid for laundering his money?"

"I can't answer that. For Colon, getting back any money Josh skimmed off the top would be a matter of principle. No one steals from him and gets away with it." Kade had once thought there wasn't anything else his brother could have done to make things worse. He'd been wrong. "Did Josh give you any money that you forgot about?"

"No!" She looked at him as if he had two heads. "Don't you think I'd remember if he handed me two million dollars? Why don't you ask your friends? Anything Josh gave me the government took away. Or did you conveniently forget that?" She covered her face with her hands and began shaking her head. "I can't believe this is happening again."

When her shoulders began trembling, Kade's resistance crumbled faster than a house of cards in an earthquake. He pulled Laia into his arms, and she let him. Her body was slim, soft, curvy. Her soft hair tickled his chin, and he couldn't keep from nuzzling the top of her head.

She sighed, a grief-filled, gut-wrenching sound that made everything in him want to protect Laia and her daughter from all the evils of the world. *Starting with Fernando Colon.* He tensed when her arms crept around his rib cage and wrapped around his back. God, she felt good. He'd never actually held her before, only dreamed about it. More specifically, dreamed about holding her lithe body as he drove deep inside her.

"We'll figure this out," he whispered. "I'll be here with you every step of the way until we do."

She lifted her head. "Why are you doing this?"

"Doing what?"

Her arms around his back loosened. "Being so...helpful. So attentive."

"You called me for help, and that's what I'm trying to do. Help you."

She pushed at his chest, forcing him to release her. "I did call you, to help me at the house with the burglary and to talk to the police. I knew they wouldn't do anything unless you were there. But that's over and done with. Why are you *still* helping us? Whatever's going on here isn't your problem. We," she added, gesturing to the living room to include Rosa, "are not your problem."

Now it was his turn to be confused. "Did you really think I'd just abandon you?" He could no sooner have done that than he could have cut off his own foot.

"That's exactly what I expected from you." She lowered her voice as she cast a quick glance to Rosa. "Not to belabor the issue, but you've made a distinct point of staying away all this time, so why would I ever think you'd actually stick around now?"

Jesus, she had no idea how much it had hurt, how much it had scaled his heart to keep his distance from her. He shook his head at the incredulity of what was happening and just how very wrong she was. About *everything*.

He ground his jaw, vividly remembered every single invitation he'd turned down because he couldn't put himself through any more pain. "Don't you get it? Once you married Josh, I couldn't be near you."

"Why not?" She parked her fists on her hips. "You were

part of the family, yet you did an awesome job of being a selfish, self-absorbed, absentee brother-in-law. You could have joined us for Christmas, Thanksgiving, all kinds of family gatherings that for some reason you couldn't manage to drag yourself to."

"You're right, and you're wrong. I couldn't have been there for any of those occasions, but not for the reasons you obviously think."

"At the risk of repeating myself, why not?"

She was killing him, slowly, by painful degrees. Telling her the truth would be opening up a can of soup and turning the can upside down. Everything would spill out, and there'd be no putting it back.

"Kade, for God's sake! Will you just talk to me?" When she took a step closer, he stepped back. "What in the world is going on with you?"

He squeezed his eyes shut, willing his heart not to burst from his throat and divulge how it felt. Then she reached for him, gently touching his forearm, and his eyes snapped open.

Something inside his chest lit, then exploded with the force of a hand grenade, and he couldn't tamp it down a second longer. And what did it matter anymore? He still couldn't have her.

He ground his jaw harder. "Since the moment I first saw you, I've never stopped thinking about you. Wanting you. Just because you said *I do* to my brother didn't make that stop."

Laia's arms dropped to her sides. Her mouth opened, but no words came out. She stared at him, her brown eyes as wide as chocolate Moon Pies.

Christ, his skin was on fire. He had to get out of the kitchen, the walls of which were closing in on him, squeezing the life from his body and suffocating him. If he didn't get a cold shower now, he'd die of heatstroke.

Chapter Ten

To say she was shocked was an understatement of monolithic proportions. Laia couldn't move, could barely breathe even though her heart pounded fast and loud in her ears.

He had to be kidding if he thought he could drop a bomb like that and just walk away. He'd never stopped thinking about her. He wanted her. He'd always wanted her. *Oh my God*. How was that even possible?

They'd spent a grand total of about forty minutes in an elevator plus a few angry words at her wedding reception, followed by one sentence of condolences at Josh's funeral.

Somehow the signal from her brain finally made it to her feet, and she raced after him through the living room, but he was already climbing the stairs. "Kade, wait."

"Mommy," Rosa said as she draped an arm over Smoke's back. "We're hungry. When can we eat?"

"Soon, sweetie," she mumbled, staring at Kade's back. "Kade, stop. We need to talk."

His back stiffened. "I know you can hear me." At the top of the stairs, he turned and disappeared. *Damn him. Damn* all *men*. The Sampson brothers anyway.

Numbly, and with her heart slowing only fractionally, she headed back to the kitchen.

"Mo-meee, I'm hungry," Rosa wailed. She and Smoke were still cuddled up on the floor. The best thing to do would be to get her daughter fed and up to bed before she had a real crank-fest.

"Dinner will be ready in ten minutes," Laia called out.

She went back into the kitchen. For a full minute, she stared at the three perfectly constructed quesadillas waiting to be heated.

Just because you said I do *to my brother didn't make that stop.*

A man with Kade's looks and personality could have any woman he wanted, and she'd assumed that once he found out she was engaged, he'd moved on. Had she known on the day of her wedding what she knew now, would she have done anything differently?

Perhaps not. Probably not. No. Admitting it sucked, but back then she'd been a different person, one incapable of standing alone on her own two feet.

Weeks before she'd ever met Kade, the wheels of fate had already been set in motion. Two pink lines on the pregnancy test wand and her life changed forever. More importantly, her life was no longer her own. From that moment on, she, and only she, was responsible for another human being—the tiny life growing inside her.

She turned on the faucet, splashed cold water on her face, then dried herself off with a towel.

Minutes before walking down the aisle, she'd nearly taken off and escaped down the beach. All because she'd looked into Kade's eyes. Kade had said he'd wanted her. But would he have wanted Rosa, too? Rosa was another man's child. His *brother's* child. She couldn't have taken that chance. Securing a future for her child was the only thing that had mattered. So she'd sacrificed her own happiness, her dreams, and agreed to a marriage that wound up failing miserably in so many ways she could never have imagined in her worst nightmares.

She drizzled oil into a pan and, when the oil was hot enough, placed one of the quesadillas in to heat. As she chopped the rest of the tomatoes and lettuce, she did a mental rewind, trying to remember everything Kade had said and done in the last twenty-four hours. *Since coming to my rescue*, which was exactly what he'd done, no questions asked.

In truth, over the last twenty-four hours, Kade had been nothing but kind and had behaved more like a father to Rosa than Josh ever had. It was almost as if Josh had been in love with the idea of having a family, but when it came down to the practical realities of it had become disappointed. And there was no way the picture Josh had painted of his brother was accurate.

It had all started at the wedding reception. Kade had just warned her not to hurt Josh.

"What's going on here?" Josh had asked.

"Good question," Kade snapped. "I was just saying goodbye." Then he'd walked away, leaving her upset and confused by his hurtful words.

Josh had cupped her face. "Laia, did he hurt you?"

"No, of course not. Why would you say that?" She stared at Kade's receding form, wondering how she could feel something so strongly for a man she barely knew.

When she turned back, Josh's expression had gone hard. "There are things you don't know about Kade. He can be a real selfish bastard."

Now she understood Josh's harsh words stemmed from sibling rivalry. She'd often wondered if Josh had been envious of Kade. Maybe he'd sensed something between them.

Laia dumped the chopped lettuce into the bowl Kade

had taken down for her. Despite his words to her that day, and the fact he'd avoided her entirely since then, she'd never stopped thinking about Kade, either, which made her partly responsible for her marriage spiraling downhill.

Josh had hoped she'd eventually come to love him the same way he'd been in love with her. She'd honestly tried to love him back in the same way, but it just wasn't there. Eventually, he'd realized that and given up on their marriage.

Sizzling drew her back to the stove where she flipped the quesadilla, pressing down on it once more with a spatula. Now for the big question: *How do I feel about Kade?*

Honestly, she didn't know. In fact, she knew next to nothing about him. She placed the salad on the table, wondering what kind of dressing he preferred, then transferred the quesadilla to a large platter, rolling a pizza cutter through it to form wedges.

Voices drew her attention to the living room, and she turned, about to announce that dinner was ready. The sight that greeted her instantly dried up every saliva gland in her mouth.

Kade sat on the sofa, his long, tanned, muscular calves and thighs on full display stretched out on the coffee table. He'd changed into khaki cargo shorts and a snug black T-shirt that hugged his broad chest, but that wasn't what made every saliva gland in her mouth instantly dry up. *Oh, no siree.* Well, okay, maybe it did, but it wasn't the only thing.

Smoke now lay on the sofa, his big furry head resting in the crook of one of Kade's arms. Rosa sat in his lap as he read to her from a large book. Still remaining in the kitchen, she crept closer until she could read the book's title. *Encyclopedia of Dog Breeds.*

The tightening in her chest was almost unbearable.

Had she made a terrible mistake all those years ago?

And more importantly, why did the answer scare her

almost as much as Colon coming after the ledger?

...

An hour after dinner, Kade carried Rosa up the stairs. Smoke padded silently ahead, still limping slightly.

"Once we put Rosa down, I'll help you ice his paw," Laia said from behind him.

"Thanks," he whispered over his shoulder.

Rosa's head lolled against his shoulder, and tiny little snores came from her open mouth. Moonlight lit the interior of the bedroom, so there was no need to turn on the lights.

"Give me a second." As Laia edged past, she brushed against his back, instantly cranking up his body temp all over again and making his abdominal muscles tighten. She pulled back the covers, then stepped aside for him to lower Rosa gently to the bed. Smoke sniffed her little hand, which she'd fisted against her mouth.

Kade backtracked to the open door, watching as Laia tugged the covers over her daughter, then leaned in to brush a lock of hair from her forehead and kiss her softly. At this point in his life, he wondered if he'd ever have a child of his own, let alone one as sweet and beautiful as Rosa.

When he'd first heard the news from his parents that Laia was pregnant, he'd done the honorable thing, smiling and expressing his joy. It had occurred to him then that they sure hadn't wasted any time starting a family. If Rosa hadn't been a bit premature, she would have been born about nine months after the wedding.

All the more reason to have kept his distance.

"Mommy," Rosa mumbled, half asleep. "Can Uncle Kade and Smoke kiss me good night?"

Laia winked at him. "I'm sure they'd love to."

He pushed from the door and leaned over to kiss Rosa

on the forehead. "Smoke, give Rosa a kiss." His dog stretched his neck over the edge of the mattress. When he gently licked Rosa's chin, she giggled. "'Night, Cream Puff."

"'Night, Uncle Kade."

For a moment, he couldn't move, could only stare down at the adorable little face. His niece—the best thing Josh ever did in his entire life.

Moonlight streamed in behind Laia, backlighting her hair. She looked like an ocean goddess. The only thing missing was a scallop shell.

"Help me with Smoke's paw," she whispered. "Then we need to talk."

Oh boy. He nodded, then followed her from the room.

After blurting out his guts, having a deep-dive conversation was inevitable. He'd never regretted saying something so much in his life.

A tactical retreat was in order, and he knew precisely how to execute his withdrawal. Thinking about her as his brother's widow was all it took to re-erect the barrier he'd so skillfully built between them and so stupidly and carelessly bulldozed to the ground.

Smoke led the way downstairs, then curled up on the living room rug. After Kade had set the alarm code by the front door, Laia came in from the kitchen with a plastic bag filled with ice and a colorful scarf.

"Give me a hand?" she asked, then knelt on the floor to stroke Smoke's ears. "This is going to be a little cold, and he probably won't like it."

Kade knelt next to Laia, doing his best not to stare at the gentle curves of her breasts just visible beneath the top of her dress.

"This will make you feel better. I promise." Smoke's ears flicked as she continued talking to him in a soothing voice. "You'll be back to chasing bad guys in no time."

The moment the ice pack hit the pads on the bottom of his paw, Smoke jerked his leg away.

"Easy, boy." Kade rested his hand on Smoke's belly, rubbing it in slow circles, distracting him while Laia applied the icepack.

"Here. Let's try this." She picked up Smoke's paw and held it on the ice for a few seconds, then removed it, repeating the process and adding in a few seconds each time. By the time she'd gotten to the fifth round, Smoke allowed her to wrap her scarf around his paw and secure the icepack to his injured joint. "See?" She pet his head, smiling. "That wasn't so bad, was it?"

When Smoke gave her an answering snort and a quick lick to her chin, she smiled. "Thank you. That's all the payment I needed. Now," she added, pointing a finger at his dog, "I want you to ice your paw at least three times a day, fifteen to twenty minutes each time."

The directions were, Kade knew, for him more than Smoke. He continued rubbing Smoke's belly, wanting to make sure he remained still and didn't dislodge the icepack. "You're as gentle with animals as you are with children. You'll make a great vet." She'd make a great *anything*.

"I hope so."

For a few more seconds, she continued petting Smoke, then she looked at Kade, and he knew his momentary reprieve had come to an end.

"Stay," he ordered Smoke, and when Laia sat on one side of the long sofa, he took up position on the other end. As far from her as he could get. He rested his arm over the back of the sofa, doing his best to look relaxed. Inside he was tied up in knots, his muscles coiled tighter than a muzzle spring.

The corners of her mouth lifted. "I won't bite you."

I can only wish.

"Tell me something." She scooted to the center of the

sofa, halving the distance between them. "Josh has been gone for over two years. If you never stopped thinking about me, why did you stay away? Why didn't you take any of my calls?"

He struggled to find the right words that wouldn't land his sorry ass in a world of hurt. "I wanted to." He took a deep breath, then stared for a moment at the ceiling. "I just... couldn't."

"Why not?" she repeated.

Kade dragged a hand down his face. Josh might as well have been sitting on the sofa between them, pushing them apart with his bare hands. "I stayed away all this time because if I heard your voice, let alone saw you in person, I wouldn't be able to walk away again. It was better if I just didn't show up at all."

What he *should* do was get up and walk away. *Now*. Sitting right there, not three feet away, she was his worst nightmare *and* his hottest dream. "You were in mourning." They'd all been in mourning. Especially his parents.

"Exactly." She pointed to her chest. "I *was* in mourning. Part of me will always miss Josh. He's the father of my child, and nothing will change that. But I don't intend to wear black for the rest of my life or enter a convent. Six years ago, you said there was something between us, so don't even try to deny it."

She was right. He couldn't deny it. But it didn't change a thing.

"It's more complicated than that. I can't just move in on my brother's widow." To this day, he'd never told his parents how he felt about their daughter-in-law. They'd been blissfully ignorant, celebrating their oldest son's wedding, then the birth of their first grandchild. He couldn't take away their bad memories of what happened to Josh, but he could still preserve the good ones.

Laia's brows drew together. "When this is over with

Colon, you'll walk away and leave all over again. Won't you?"

His throat closed in so tightly he could barely choke out the word he hated saying. "Yes." Because the guilt eating him up inside was still there like an immovable steel barricade that not even a missile could penetrate. But he couldn't tell her that. *Ever.*

She took a deep breath, then shut her eyes. When she opened them, they were soft, calm, drawing him into their beautiful depths as they always had. "Since we're being honest here, tell me...what would you have done if I hadn't married your brother?"

Moved heaven and earth to make you mine. "I'd have asked for your phone number."

"And then?" She inched closer on the cushion, sending up warning flags in Kade's brain.

"Then..." *Don't do it.* The last thing he should be doing was playing this dangerous game with her because he was weak and getting more so by the second. "I'd have asked you out to dinner."

Her tongue darted out to lick her lips, not a seductive move, just nervousness, judging by the white-knuckled way she twisted her hands together.

"Where would you have taken me?" she asked.

That was an easy one. It was a scenario he'd gone over and over in his head hundreds of times. "Mandino's in Long Branch." His favorite restaurant, one he'd been certain she would have loved.

She smiled. "I know that place. It's on the water. I've never been there, but I've heard it's beautiful. And romantic."

Yeah, there is that. He'd never taken a date there before for just that reason, but it was exactly why he would have taken Laia there.

Laia stood, then smoothed her hands down her dress. She sat down again, this time parking her pretty little butt right next to him. The air conditioner took that untimely moment to kick on, sending her intoxicating and sweetly flowered scent directly into his nose. At least he had Smoke there to—

But his dog's snout now rested between his paws. His eyes had closed, and his chest rose and fell evenly.

Way to abandon your partner. He'd been hoping Smoke would have wedged himself between them the way he usually did when someone got into Kade's personal space.

She rested her hand on his forearm, lightly swirling her fingers across his skin. It was like being stroked by warm satin and velvet. His skin erupted in goose bumps and his heart hammered faster. "Laia, don't do this." He reached for her hand, intending to remove it when she clasped it, threading their fingers.

Sweat trickled between his shoulder blades. She had him in a corner—literally—and he was powerless to move.

"Don't do what, touch you?" She skimmed her hand up his biceps, over his shoulder to his neck, caressing him there with lightly stroking fingers.

Oh, boy. He swallowed again, then had to open his mouth to get enough air to breathe. And that hammering in his chest was now a loud and constant pounding at every one of his pulse points. Including the one he could swear was in his dick.

Wasn't this what he'd always wanted, what he'd dreamed about during so many hot, sleepless, sweaty nights?

"What would we have done after dinner?" Again, she licked her lower lip, only this time there was no doubting her intent.

"I, uh..." *Christ.* Soon he'd be out of religious expletives.

He'd participated in countless high-risk warrants involving drug dealers, gun smugglers, and violent terrorists without sweating a drop and with his heart rate barely in the sixty-beats-a-minute range. Now he was sweating bullets and his pulse had to be soaring into the nineties.

She cupped the side of his face, and before he knew what was happening, he was leaning into her palm. "Well? What would we have done?"

"I'd have taken you down to the beach."

"Would you have held my hand?"

"Uh-huh." *To start with.*

"Would you have kissed me?" She leaned in, placing her hand on his hip, way too close to his groin. "Would you?"

Yeah. This was what he'd always wanted. She'd been a craving he'd never been able to eradicate, never been able to erase with anyone else. So what was he waiting for?

Don't do it, the rational part of his mind screamed again.

Once he had the taste of her mouth and skin on his tongue, there'd be no stopping him.

Laia leaned in closer until her soft breasts pressed against his chest.

"Laia—" He clamped his jaw together. If she were any closer, she'd be under his skin.

So much for religion because she was *already* under his skin.

"Kade," she whispered, his name warm and gentle across his lips, the way he imagined a butterfly's wings would feel.

Her teasing gentleness was the spark, the emotional catalyst that set off a nuclear chain reaction.

His head grew hot. His blood started to boil. Then an explosion rocked his heart, releasing everything inside him that yearned to take full possession of the woman he'd wanted for so long he couldn't remember.

With a loud groan, he cupped the back of her head, then slanted his mouth across hers. She answered with a throaty moan, throwing her arms around his neck.

Her taste was nectar on his tongue, and he wanted more. Deeper, hotter…he wanted to take all she was offering.

With a hungry, feral growl, he pushed his tongue inside her mouth. Molded to him as she was, with no space between their bodies, hers was warm, soft, and infinitely perfect.

He crushed her against him, wrapping his arms around her back, skimming his hands over her bare shoulders as he deepened the kiss. How he thought he could ever manage walking on this earth without her, without kissing her, touching her, breathing in her very essence, he didn't know.

"God, Laia," he rasped against her lips, pulling away only long enough to get more air. He began kissing his way to her ear, then down her neck. Finally, he pulled away, breathing hard.

Her chest heaved as hard as his. "Kade, don't stop. *Please*, don't stop." As she eased backward, she pulled him down on top of her, spreading her legs for his body to settle between her thighs.

The second his straining erection contacted her panty-clad pussy, he nearly came in his shorts. He'd always known this was how it would be—sparks, fire, total combustion because she was always meant to be his.

He pressed his lips to her breastbone, kissing and lightly licking her skin, loving the taste of flowers and woman and... *heaven* was the word that came to mind. When her hips surged against his raging erection, he groaned and slid one hand beneath her ass, cupping her bottom.

Chee-rist. He was in way over his head, and he didn't care anymore. Whatever was happening between them might very well be a mistake, but at this point there was no turning back.

Vaguely, through the haze of lust overtaking his body and every thought in his head, he heard Smoke snort. Then something clicked. The front door.

Someone was coming inside the house.

Kade bolted from the sofa, getting a quick glimpse of Laia's glazed eyes and her kiss-swollen lips before he shot across the room and reached to the top of a bookshelf where he'd stashed his gun out of Rosa's reach.

Smoke leaped to his feet, his tail down and his head hung low. The ice pack wrapped around his foot slipped off.

Whoever was about to come through that door was in for a nasty surprise.

The muzzle of my Glock jammed in their face.

He slipped his gun from its holster and inched toward the door. Slowly, it swung open. A large black boot appeared first. Then Kade aimed in.

Chapter Eleven

What the—?

With her heart skipping and her libido about to drag her lust-crazed body clear into the next county, Laia snapped open her eyes.

Kade held a gun, aiming the muzzle at a tall, darkly bearded man who'd just come through the front door. Smoke faced down the man with his ears erect and growling low in his throat, sounding like a muted jet engine.

Laia jumped from the sofa and raced to the bottom of the stairs, resting one hand on the railing and the other on the wall, blocking the stairway. *Right.* Given that this guy had to be at least six-foot-three, maybe more, and built like a decathlete, she'd be no match for him. But if he so much as twitched in the direction of the stairs leading to Rosa's room, she'd launch onto him and do as much bodily harm as she possibly could.

The security system beeped, but instead of turning tail as she expected him to do, the bearded guy's dark brows rose. The large black duffle over his shoulder dropped to the floor with a solid thump, then he slowly raised his hands in the air like a burglar who'd been caught red-handed opening a safe loaded with family jewels.

"Shit, Jamie." Kade jerked the muzzle away from the man, aiming it at the floor. "You could have called." To Smoke, he said, "Easy, boy. Sit. He's okay."

At the realization that Kade knew the dark-haired, dark-eyed stranger she'd thought had been about to whip a machine gun from his duffle and kill them all, Laia's heart finally began to slow. As did her libido.

Talk about coitus interruptus. Was there such a thing for women? She supposed so.

Smoke sat, licked his lips, then yawned. Apparently, the excitement was over.

The man-now-known-as-Jamie lowered his hands, then went to the still-beeping control panel next to the door. He punched in a code, then glanced at Laia before turning back to Kade.

Jamie's face twisted in confusion, calling attention to his mustache and the pointed beard that hung at least three inches below his chin. "Why would I have called? It's *my* house."

"Oh, I don't know," Kade said, now *his* face twisting in annoyance as he stashed his gun back onto the shelf, "maybe because I left you a message that we'd be here *and* to call me back."

"I lost my phone." Jamie's face darkened for a moment, then he walked to Kade and narrowed his eyes. "New one's getting delivered here tomorrow."

Laia watched the two men, fascinated by the testosterone-charged confrontation as they stared each other down for several seconds, then grabbed each other in a bear hug that would have crushed a brick.

"Good to see ya, buddy," Kade said.

"You, too." Jamie clapped Kade's back. "Your new K-9?"

"Yep. Smoke, meet Jamie."

Smoke walked to the other man, then sniffed his size-thirteen-or-so boots. "Shake hands with Jamie." The dog lifted its paw, holding it in the air until Jamie leaned down and shook it.

"Nice to meet ya, furball." Jamie grinned, revealing a set of even white teeth that contrasted sharply with his olive skin and dark beard.

The man's accent was either classic New Jersey á la *The Sopranos* or classic Long Island, an equally distinctive New York version. The man could be of Hispanic, Middle Eastern, or Italian descent. Whatever it was, any woman could see that beneath all that facial hair he was sinfully handsome.

When Smoke wagged his tail, Jamie crouched and stroked the dog's head. A few sniffs later, and they must have become best buds because Smoke proceeded to lick every inch of Jamie's face that he could find, mustache and beard notwithstanding.

Jamie sifted his hands through Smoke's thick black coat. "Does he shed?"

Kade chuckled. "Yeah."

"That's a lotta hair. Damn."

"Hey, there's a lady present." Kade gave a quick nod at Laia.

"So there is." Jamie rose, then went to where Laia still stood at the bottom of the stairs. "My apologies. Jamie Pataglio, at your service." He held out his hand.

"Oh, brother," Kade muttered, subtly shaking his head. "Here we go."

The second Laia slipped her hand into Jamie's, he brought her fingers to his lips, kissing them gently.

"Always a pleasure to be in the presence of a beautiful woman." He smiled, the corners of his eyes crinkling, and yet, the smile never quite made it to his eyes.

"Okay, Romeo. You can let go of her hand now."

He did, stepping back and bending at the waist and mimicking a formal bow. "You must be Laia. I'm sorry about your husband."

"Thank you."

He stepped back. "You probably don't remember me. I attended his funeral."

Jamie was right. But as she scrutinized his bearded face, she had a vague recollection of six giant men she didn't recognize, first at the church, then at the cemetery. The memory was fleeting at this point, but what struck her was that whoever these men were, they had seemed to be there to support Kade, rallying around him as if they, too, were family.

"Must be the beard," she said, also vaguely recalling that none of those men wore one.

"You might be right." He stroked his very tan, very large hand down that devilish beard. "Time to shave it off, though. It's too fu—" He broke off, again bowing slightly at the waist. "Pardon me. It's too *hot* around here for comfort. So," he added, turning to Kade, "you wanna fill me in?"

Kade's eyes narrowed to slits. "Do *you*?"

Something silent passed between the men. Laia was unsure whether it was suspicion or a warning. She looked from Kade to Jamie then back to Kade in time to understand the true underlying message: Kade was worried about Jamie. The hard, unyielding expression on his face softened with obvious concern.

"Where's Jax?" Kade asked.

Jax?

Roughly, Jamie shoved a hand through his hair. "Not here."

Kade dropped a hand on his shoulder. "Do we need to

talk?"

"No." Jamie shook his head. "I'm dealing with it."

"Is Jax...*dead*?"

Again, Jamie shook his head, more adamantly this time. "No. At least, I don't think so."

"Jesus," Kade muttered.

Whoever Jax was he must be pretty important. To both of them.

"Yeah. Later." Jamie glanced down at his duffle, then addressed Laia. "Is Rosa here, too?"

Laia was impressed and shocked that he seemed to know a lot about her family.

She nodded. "She's upstairs."

"Well, then." Jamie unzipped the duffle, then pulled out two handguns and a curved, sheathed knife, the blade of which had to be close to ten inches long. He went into the living room and secured the weapons on the same shelf where Kade had hidden his gun. *Must be the go-to spot for deadly weapons.*

"Thank you." It was impossible not to appreciate the men's thoughtfulness.

"No problem," Jamie said. "I've got ten nieces and nephews, and they all like to play cops and robbers. Anyone else want a beer while you fill me in?" Without waiting for an answer, he went into the kitchen, leaving her alone with Kade and Smoke.

Lingering heat from their near-sexual encounter shot across the five feet separating them. His touch, the feel of his hands on her bare skin was so memorable, she might as well have been standing too close to a barbeque grill or a campfire. Even now, the sizzling look from those hazel eyes singed her skin.

Jamie popped the tops off three beer bottles sitting on the kitchen island. Anyone else would surely have tried watching and listening in, but he didn't. Jamie actually seemed to be going out of his way not to.

Smoke sat on the floor in between them, swinging his head back and forth as if sensing the invisible heat wave rolling through the room.

What would have happened if Jamie hadn't interrupted them?

We would have made love on the sofa. Hot, crazy, no-holds-barred love until they both screamed.

Well, maybe not screamed. Not with a five-year-old upstairs.

They wanted each other, and there was no stopping what was to come. For her it was a foregone conclusion. No other man had ever touched that part of her, made her want to crawl under their skin and breathe the same air molecules he breathed.

Kade stepped closer, then reached out, but instead of kissing her as she'd expected—as she'd *wanted* him to—he hooked his pinkie around the spaghetti strap of her dress. In all the excitement, the darned thing had slipped down her arm.

For a long moment, he stood there, staring at her bare shoulder. Then he slowly, tantalizingly, began dragging the strap up her arm, caressing her skin with his knuckles. He licked his lips, swallowing again, and holy moly. She was fully clothed yet this was, quite possibly, the hottest, most sensual foreplay she'd ever experienced.

His eyes tracked the strap's journey up her arm. The pulse in his neck ticked faster, mimicking her own racing heartbeat. If Jamie weren't in the kitchen not ten feet away, she would have yanked the dress off and thrown herself into Kade's arms.

By the time he had the strap over her shoulder, her entire body was shaking. If this was what the barest touch of his knuckles did to her, she could only imagine what would happen if—no, *when*, what with the foregone conclusion and all—they made love.

Smoke whined then, as if someone had flipped a switch, Kade stepped away and cleared his throat. When he spoke, his voice was gravelly, sexy. "I have to take Smoke out. Back in a few."

Only when he and Smoke had disappeared out a door from the living room that led to the beach did she take a breath.

"Beer?"

"Huh?" Laia had no idea how long she'd been staring at the door.

A corner of Jamie's mouth lifted, and he really did look like the devil. A very *handsome* devil. In fact, *all* Kade's friends—Deck, Brett, Evan—were hot by any woman's standards. He held up a bottle. "Come on in and have a beer."

An ice-cold beer might be just the right antidote to cool her absurdly hot libido.

Laia went into the kitchen and accepted the bottle Jamie offered, then sat on one of the counter stools. She tipped the beer and took a long sip, allowing the tasty ale to trickle down her throat. When she set the bottle down, Jamie's dark eyes bored into hers. Behind the beard and mustache, the man was frowning.

The tender skin around her mouth and along the parts of her neck where Kade's stubbly five o'clock shadow had left their mark, naturally, took that moment to tingle. Her lips had to be swollen and her skin red from their frenzied kissing.

"Kade's a good friend." Jamie began peeling the label from the bottle. "He's family to me. It's none of my business but…"

"But what?" she asked.

Dark eyes grew darker, staring at her with an intensity that was unnerving and made her heart beat faster. "Whatever's going on between you two, don't hurt him."

The exact same words Kade had said to her on her wedding day. She parked the beer bottle on the counter harder than intended and a resounding crack rent the air. "Why does everyone think I'm going to hurt the Sampson brothers?"

Jamie's eyes flashed. "Because you already did."

"What?" The only time they'd been in the same room together for more than forty minutes was on her wedding day. "When?"

"The day you married Kade's brother."

She shook her head, still finding this revelation difficult to swallow. Even after his confession that he'd never stopped thinking about her, she hadn't realized how much she'd actually hurt him. "He barely knew me then. We spent forty minutes in an elevator."

"For some guys, forty minutes is enough."

The door leading down to the beach had opened, letting warm air swirl inside. A moment later, Smoke trotted into the kitchen.

"Enough for what?" Kade asked.

"Enough time to fill me in on what's going on." Jamie handed Kade a beer. "I'm pretty beat, so let's get to it."

Kade's gaze darted from Jamie's to hers, as if he knew they'd been on a totally different conversational track. He pulled out another stool. "How long you sticking around this time?"

Jamie shrugged. "Not sure. For now, I'm in a holding pattern."

Kade narrowed his eyes on his friend. "What are you waiting for?"

"A phone call. As soon as my new phone gets here." Jamie took a long slug of beer, then swallowed. "But I don't expect to hear anything for at least a week."

Laia suspected Kade wanted to shout *bull*, but the only indication he wasn't buying into what Jamie had just related was the subtle tapping of his finger against the side of his beer. "What about the Port Authority?"

"I've been on loan to another agency for a while now. Until they call, I'm all yours."

"Okay then," was all Kade said. But from his darkening expression, she understood that whatever kind of work Jamie did, it was covert. And *dangerous*. "The Colon Cartel has been following Laia. They broke into her house when she wasn't home and tossed it. Then they tracked her to my house. This time it's not just about the missing ledger."

"Ah, the missing ledger," Jamie said. "You always figured Josh kept one."

"Yeah, and now word on the street is that Josh also stole money from Fernando Colon. Two million dollars."

Jamie's brows shot to his hairline. "What's the plan?"

"Manny Dominguez is working on it. I'm putting money on the street with some old informants. In the meantime, we'll go back to her house and poke around." He turned to her. "Is it okay if Jamie watches Rosa for us?"

Laia took a harder look across the island at this man who so obviously harbored dark, dangerous secrets, wishing she could read his mind. It was on the tip of her tongue to object and suggest they take her daughter with them, but that would be stupid.

The cartel didn't know about this beach house, so Rosa was safer here. What's more, whoever Jamie really was and whoever he worked for, she surmised that, like Kade, he had skills. Skills she suspected involved mortal combat. Judging by his heavily muscled physique and the deadly weapons he'd stored on top of that shelf she had no doubt he could protect Rosa from any*thing* or any*one*.

"Okay." She nodded, still uncomfortable with the idea of leaving her precious daughter with yet another total stranger. But if a supermodel could keep Rosa safe, this enigmatic man definitely could.

She yawned and covered her mouth. "If you'll excuse me, I'm going to bed."

As she left the kitchen, Laia felt both men watching her. Jamie obviously knew something about how she and Kade met. For that matter, Kade's friend, Deck, also apparently knew something. She hadn't missed his whiplash reaction when Kade had introduced them.

She climbed the stairs, opening Rosa's door to find her daughter snoring lightly. After quietly closing the door, she went down the hall to her bedroom. Rather than go through her nightly ritual involving more toiletries than she could count, she slipped into her favorite green nightie and fell into bed.

Another yawn had her touching her fingers to her mouth. *That kiss.* Her body shivered just thinking about it. Somehow, she'd always known Kade would be a good kisser. And she could only imagine how skilled he'd be at lovemaking. He'd be the kind of man who would put her needs first because of how unselfish she now knew him to be.

Despite what Josh had told her.

She ought to have been angry about his deception but wasn't. That hardly seemed fair. Because *she* was lying to Kade about something, too.

Chances were he also had secrets. Everyone did.

Including her. *About Rosa.*

The only difference was how many people would be hurt if hers was ever revealed. She'd been keeping it for six years but had a feeling it would come out soon.

Whether she liked it or not.

Chapter Twelve

Kade headed north on Route 71 toward Laia's house in Asbury Park. Luckily, Monday morning traffic in the summer wasn't that bad.

At ten a.m., the sun was shining, the temperature already near eighty, and the humidity was as thick as a stick of butter. Laia sat beside him, but neither of them had spoken a word about the "sofa incident."

He never should have let her get under his skin. He never should have let her get *on* his skin, but when she'd crawled onto his lap, every ounce of gray matter in his brain dove directly south. To his *other* brain.

He cranked the AC higher.

Smoke stuck his head through the opening between their shoulders, providing a barrier between him and Laia. That didn't stop Kade from remembering more things he wished he wouldn't.

Last night he'd been on fire, his skin seared with every light touch of Laia's fingertips, every whisper of her sweet, soft breath on his face. Sex with Laia would have been—

No, not sex. He had a feeling that sex with Laia would be…something more, because where Laia was concerned, *both* his heads were in deep.

Again, he shifted in his seat, staring straight ahead and gripping the wheel tighter. Looked like his dick was directly connected to his thoughts because he was on the verge of a giant, embarrassing boner.

"Kade, are you all right?" Laia asked. "You haven't said a word since we left the shack."

"I'm fine," he managed. About as fine as a horny, blue-balled teenager with no place to bury his raging hard-on.

"You don't *look* fine."

Yeah, well… But a quick glance told him she wasn't staring at the uncomfortable bulge in his crotch.

She rubbed Smoke's ears, peering around his furry head. "Is everything okay with your boss?"

"Yeah." He cleared his throat, trying to swallow the sandpaper that had taken up position in between his tonsils. "We're good. He gave me a week to figure this out." Although initially, they *hadn't* been good.

Before leaving Rosa playing piggyback with Jamie, Kade had called his boss and requested he be taken off shift at the airport. He could practically feel heat from the steam that had to be shooting from the man's ears.

"Are you sure everything's okay?" When she leaned around Smoke, all he could think was: *Don't. Look. Down.*

He adjusted one of the vents, angling the air directly at his crotch.

"You seem awfully quiet."

"I have a lot on my mind." Not just about sex.

Not telling her the truth about Josh was eating away at his insides like acid. If they'd had sex, it would only make things worse when she found out. *If* she found out. Part of him wanted to get it over with and just tell her.

"Something's up with Jamie," he said instead. Aside from kissing Laia's hand, nothing his friend had said or done last night was the Jamie Pataglio he knew. And there were still lingering questions about Jamie's frequent and extended disappearances over the last two years.

"Did you talk to him after I went upstairs?"

"Kind of." He braked for a red light. "He wouldn't even tell me where Jax was."

"Who's Jax?"

"Jamie's K-9."

Smoke pulled his head back, giving Kade an unobstructed view of Laia's bright-green sundress, the color of which really brought out the green flecks in her eyes. Another set of long earrings dangled from her ears. Arborist he wasn't, but even he could identify them as palm trees.

"He's not at a kennel?"

"No. We take our dogs home every night. They live with us just like family." Kade couldn't imagine being without Smoke. It would be like having his right arm torn off.

And Jax was Jamie's family in every sense of the word. They had one of the closest bonds Kade had ever seen in the K-9 world. Making Jax's absence that much more disturbing. That alone would be enough to screw with Jamie's head.

"Who exactly does Jamie work for?" She angled her body to face him more, and God help him. That cute little dress hiked up, exposing her sleek, tanned thigh.

"Honestly, I'm not sure anymore." The light turned green, and Kade resumed their trek north. "He's a K-9 sergeant with the Port Authority at JFK Airport, but I have a feeling he jumped ship and has been working for another agency." Which one he didn't know. That in itself was a red flag the size of a football field. Whatever Jamie was involved in had to be black ops and clandestine as hell.

Twenty minutes later, he turned onto Laia's street, not

stopping when they arrived at her house but slowing enough for him to look inside every parked vehicle on the block.

"Hey, aren't you going to stop?" she asked.

"Yeah, but first I want to see if anyone's watching your house." He continued to the intersection, then turned right. After he'd squared the block, he finally pulled into an empty spot at the curb and shut off the engine.

"You're very cautious, aren't you?" Laia asked in a tone laced with a touch of humor.

He grabbed Smoke's leash from the console. "Caution's my middle name." Something that had kept him from getting blown up or taking a round of lead while he was in the Army Rangers and now in the DHS.

He'd been about to grab Smoke's leash when his phone buzzed. Before answering, he looked at the screen. *Chico.* Another informant, one he didn't use often but whose information had always proven reliable. "Sampson," he said.

"I got something for you," Chico said. "You wanted anything about Fernando Colon and the book he's looking for."

"Talk to me." Kade reached for a small pad and pen he kept in the console.

"Right before Colon got out, someone inside told him about a conversation he heard a couple of years ago between another guy and that guy's lawyer. They were talking about a *ledger*."

"What *about* a ledger?"

"That's it, man. That's all I got for you."

"Wait." Kade tried processing Chico's info but wasn't certain that it had relevance.

Two years ago, the day Josh had been arrested, he'd met briefly with his lawyer and said he had a ledger. They knew that because after Josh's death the lawyer had told the prosecutor about it.

"Are you saying that another inmate overheard a conversation between *another* prisoner and *that* prisoner's lawyer?" Had Josh's lawyer been arrested? What other lawyer could they be talking about?

"Yeah, man. That's what I'm sayin'."

"And this was two years ago?"

"Yeah."

"When did Colon hear about this?"

"Two *weeks* ago."

That was it. The trigger.

Now Kade understood why Colon had started searching for the ledger after all this time. Since the federal government hadn't found it, Colon must have thought he was in the clear, and that maybe there *was* no ledger. But two *weeks* ago, just before he'd been released from prison, he'd gotten information that the ledger truly existed.

He couldn't figure out how another inmate could have overheard a confidential conversation between Josh and his attorney, but maybe he'd also overheard Josh insisting that he wanted to talk to his wife. *Laia.*

"Thanks, Chico." He stuffed the phone back into his pocket, then grabbed Smoke's leash. "Let's do this."

Outside, Smoke led the way, his nose to the ground, his tail swishing back and forth as he pulled in smells from the walkway, the grass, then the front steps right up to the door.

"Ready?" he asked when Laia didn't immediately unlock it. Instead, she held her keys in her hand and stared at the knob. "Why don't you let Smoke and me go in first?"

Her big brown eyes were slightly watery, and he about melted right there on the porch. All she had to do was look at him, and he'd do just about anything for her.

He took the keys from her and opened the door. As soon as Smoke stepped over the threshold, he unhooked the leash and let his dog do his thing, searching and scenting for any hidden dangers.

"C'mon." He held out his hand, and when she took it, he gently urged her inside. With Cartel goons following her, standing on the front porch, visible to anyone driving by, was something he wanted to avoid.

Her expression was identical to one he'd seen on many a victim's face. This wasn't blood and carnage, but it was her home, and it had been invaded for the second time. The first had been by federal agents executing a search warrant. The second time had been by a drug cartel's henchmen.

"What now?" she breathed.

"Stay here while Smoke and I clear the house."

Moving swiftly, he and Smoke went through the rest of the downstairs, then headed to the second floor. After reassuring himself that there were no uninvited guests in the duplex, they rejoined Laia in the living room. "Now we go room to room. I'll ask you some questions as we go."

She nodded. "Okay."

"Take a look around the living room." If he'd ever had the balls to paint his bedroom walls in different colors like this, his father or grandpa would have forced a can of castor oil down his throat.

Sighing, she picked up one of the framed photos, shaking off the broken glass. It was the photo of her and Rosa at the beach.

Crouching, he picked up another photo, the one of Laia and Rosa fishing. "I didn't realize you were such an adventuress."

She smiled at the photo in his hand. "You seem surprised."

Was he?

The woman he'd spent forty minutes with in an elevator had such a conservative air about her. So yeah, he *was* surprised. Then again, he'd never really gotten to know her.

"Are you?" she prodded. "Surprised?"

"No." He shook his head, then, "Yeah. Maybe a little." Try a *lot* more than a little.

He'd seriously liked her when they'd met, but this unexpected side to her personality was a breath of fresh air in his own by-the-book, play-only-by-the-rules lifestyle.

"I wasn't always this way." With care, she leaned the broken frame against the wall. "After Josh died, I decided to stop trying to be what everyone—Josh, my mother—expected me to be and live my life the way *I* want to. And I'm trying to instill that in Rosa, too, so she won't make the same mistakes I made."

He wanted to ask what mistakes she was referring to but didn't. "It takes courage to go against people's expectations." He admired that in her and wondered if his life would have turned out differently if he'd had the same guts, if he'd rebelled against his family's military legacy filled with rules, structure, and duty above all else. "Is there anything Josh left you in this room?"

She turned slowly in a one-eighty. "Nothing."

He put his hand at the small of her back, urging her into the kitchen where every drawer had been pulled out and every cabinet door opened. The contents of the space beneath the sink sat on her kitchen table, along with dishes, pots, and pans.

A choked gurgle came from the back of her throat. "Josh didn't cook. He couldn't even boil an egg."

He chuckled. "You know, you're right. He couldn't." A memory blasted his consciousness—the two of them cooking in their mom's kitchen or, at least, trying to. Josh's hard-boiled eggs had turned out more like cement eggs, cooked about twice as long as necessary and hard as a brick.

Next they moved into the little office adjacent to the kitchen. He pointed, indicating Smoke should search not for people but for narcotics. If there was so much as a dust-size speck of cocaine or heroin in the room, Smoke would hit on it and sit in front of the location. Smoke finished circling the room, then trotted out into the living room.

"What about in here?" Kade asked. "Were any of Josh's files or papers stored in the desk or filing cabinet?"

"No. You, I mean your agency, took all of Josh's papers. In the end, the only document of any importance to me after he died was Rosa's birth certificate. Not even his will did us any good. Anything he might have left to us was seized by Uncle Sam."

"I know." He *did* know because he'd been told after the fact that the evidence custodian had driven off with an entire cargo van full of boxes. He'd also heard that Josh's office at the bank had been searched, but no ledger was ever found, hardcopy or digital.

Laia began stacking her textbooks and spiral notebooks in a neat pile against the wall. "This will take forever to straighten up."

Smoke came back into the room and sat beside Laia. His ingrained canine response was to offer sympathy the only way he knew how. Smoke let out a soft, commiserating whine, as if sensing her sadness, and rested his snout on her shoulder. She put her arm around the dog's back, leaning into his body for comfort.

Kade gritted his teeth. It should be him offering her his body to lean on, but he couldn't risk it, couldn't so much as touch her. What had almost happened last night on the sofa couldn't almost happen again. *Stick to business.*

"Is there anything here that Josh left you? Something you might have forgotten about, no matter how small?"

"No." He couldn't see her face, but she shook her head.

"Did he have a storage facility?"

"No."

"Did *you* have a storage facility?"

Irritation bubbled to the surface. "No, dammit! There's nothing! Josh left me *nothing.* I know you're just doing your job, but *please* stop interrogating me." She stood, then swept her arm around the room. "All this…everything in this house is mine and Rosa's. There's nothing here that belonged to Josh."

Laia rolled her lips inward, and this time, no amount of blinking in the world could stem the flow. Tears streamed unchecked down her cheeks. "Even when I do clean this mess up, I don't think I'll ever feel safe here again."

When she covered her face with her hands, muffled sobs filtered through her fingers and straight to his heart where they pried that beating organ in two.

Ah hell.

Kade jerked her into his arms, holding her tightly while she cried. There was nothing he could say or do except hold her. So much for his resolve to never touch her again. So much for his resolve to never let her under his skin again.

Damn you, Josh, for whatever made you do it.

If his brother weren't already six feet under, Kade would have decked him, thrown him to the ground, then *kept* hitting him until he *was* six feet under.

Her arms crept around his waist, and his muscles involuntarily shuddered. He shouldn't have been thinking how good she felt, snugged up against his body from her pretty head to equally pretty toes, but he was.

He breathed in her scent, knowing it was the worst possible thing he could draw into his lungs because it did all kinds of things to his body. Like make him want to kiss her again, then lay her down on the floor, strip off her clothes, and make her forget for just one moment that a violent drug cartel was tracking her movements.

"I can't believe this is happening," she sobbed, her tears wetting his shirt.

He couldn't quite believe it, either. Or the fact that he could easily fall for Laia all over again. Harder this time. If he didn't find a way to cushion his fall, there'd be hell to pay soon.

And *he'd* be the one paying it.

Chapter Thirteen

The old elm tree in the backyard kept Laia cool while she and Smoke sat in Rosa's pink and purple dinghy watching Kade rummage through the small storage shed in the backyard.

It also gave her a place from which to watch all those thick muscles bunch, flex, ripple, and send her wayward thoughts directly into the bedroom.

After her embarrassing emotional meltdown, they'd finished the walkthrough of the first floor, then gone upstairs. Through Rosa's bedroom window he'd noticed the storage shed, and even though she'd been adamant that everything in the shed belonged to her and her alone, he'd insisted on poking through it all himself.

At first, she'd been annoyed, thinking he didn't trust her, but maybe he could find something she'd missed. Then when he'd taken off his shirt and began hauling bins from the shed...*oh my*. Any lingering annoyance disappeared in less time than it took for Smoke to swish his tail.

Wearing khaki cargo shorts, sneakers, and a gun strapped to his side, all the glory that was Kade Sampson's finely honed and chiseled body was on full display.

Okay. Technically not all of it.

No fair that all a man like him had to do was haphazardly throw on shorts and a T-shirt to look fabulous, while most women had to primp and preen for an hour in the bathroom, then agonize over what to wear. When she'd chosen this sundress, she'd wanted to look pretty for Kade. He hadn't seemed to notice.

As he carried another plastic bin from the shed and set it on the grass, his thick biceps, powerful shoulders, and back muscles bunched. Last night, in the throes of what she could only call a moment of pent-up, libido-driven lunacy, she'd dug her fingers into some of those hard muscles. And felt his arousal against her abdomen. Hard to miss that.

Smoke yawned, then licked his lips. Laia leaned down to where the dog lay at her feet with his snout covering the tips of her toes peeking out from her sandals and reexamined his injured paw. Still no swelling and no tenderness, all good signs that the sprain wasn't a bad one and would eventually heal on its own.

As more and more bins stacked up on the grass, the hope of finding the ledger and turning it over to the prosecutor began fading faster than a rainbow.

Smoke lifted his head, uttering a quick snort before leaping from the dinghy and trotting to the picket fence separating hers and her neighbor's tiny backyards. He rose up on his hind legs, resting his front paws on the picket rail to greet Alvita.

"Is this the dog Rosa's always talking about?" Alvita called out as she gave Smoke a good scratch behind his ears. "Enjoying the view?" she whispered at Laia's approach, dipping her head in Kade's direction, then waving to him.

Kade waved back, then returned to prying the lid off another bin.

"I know *I* am." Alvita giggled. "Who is he? He looks familiar."

Kade wiped his brow before tossing the lid on the grass.

"He's Josh's brother." Alvita had never met Josh, but she'd seen family photos of him on Laia's living room wall. "He's helping me deal with the police and the burglary." The less Alvita knew, the better off she and her kids would be.

"Wow. So that's Uncle Kade, huh? And you said he was only a friend." Alvita's grin broadened. "Rosa talks about him all the time, too. How come you never do? That man is *fine*."

Laia could only nod in total agreement. *He sure is.* "Because—" How to answer that question? Better not to answer it at all. Airing the Sampson family secrets, let alone hers...*nope*.

On the rare occasions when Kade's name had come up in conversation over the years, she'd done her best to shove all thoughts of him aside. The tactic had never been terribly effective. She'd often wondered where he was, what he was doing, what woman he was with at that exact moment. There had to have been plenty of them. "He's just a busy man." *But he's here now. For how long, though?*

Kade began carrying the bins back into the shed.

"Ookay." Alvita eyed her with unconcealed suspicion, but as a friend, she knew well enough when to move on to another topic. "What's he doing?"

"We're looking for some things of Josh's." When Alvita opened her mouth to say something, Laia quickly added, "Don't ask."

"Okay, I won't." Alvita threw up her hands, then looked over Laia's shoulder. "You know he's watching you. He's *been* watching you since the moment we started talking, like a wolf tracking a little doe-eyed deer. Is there something going on with you and him?"

"There's *nothing* going on between us." So why was her face heating at the thought of what *had* almost happened between them?

As he came over, more memories washed over her. Not twenty-four hours ago they'd had their tongues down each other's throats, their hands on each other's bare skin, and she'd been seconds from tearing off his shirt and shorts and begging him to get inside her aching body.

"Hi," Kade said, extending his hand to Alvita. "I'm Kade Sampson."

"Nice to meet you." As they shook, Alvita threw Laia a knowing look that she barely caught because Alvita was right.

Wow.

Every square inch of Kade's chest and arms glistened gloriously with sweat, rivulets running down his temples, more trickling between his thick pectorals to the sexy channel separating one half of his six-pack from the other.

"Where are your kids?" Kade asked.

"They're at summer day camp, which reminds me." Alvita tossed Laia another sly look. "I'd better be getting to work myself. Have fun, you two. See ya around, Kade."

Alvita disappeared inside her half of the duplex.

"I'll just be a few more minutes." Kade picked up another bin and headed for the shed.

She gestured with her hand. "C'mon, Smoke."

Smoke followed her back to the dinghy and hopped in. She sat on one of the wooden bench seats while the dog resettled at her feet. Together they watched Kade load the last bin in the shed, then close the door. He grabbed his shirt from where he'd draped it on a corner of the dinghy and put it on.

So that was that. No ledger and no money. "They'll never stop coming for us, will they? I have no way to keep Rosa safe from them."

Having no other release for her fears or the helpless fury bubbling up inside her at the thought of something happening to Rosa, she began rocking back and forth. It didn't matter that she didn't know where the ledger or the money Josh stole was. Fernando Colon would keep assuming she did because it would be the only thing that would make sense to him.

Kade stepped into the boat and sat beside her. He clasped her chin in his big fingers, forcing her to look at him. "You're wrong about that. *Dead* wrong. You and Rosa have *me*." From where he lay on the floor of the dinghy, Smoke woofed. A corner of Kade's mouth lifted. "And you have Smoke."

Kade's eyes darkened and his jaw clenched tighter than she thought possible. The next thing she knew, his arms were around her and he was kissing the top of her head. "I won't leave you," he whispered against her ear. "No matter what you think, I won't leave you alone to deal with this."

But he *would* leave, eventually. That's what he'd said last night. Right now, she needed him, needed his comfort, and he was here for her.

She leaned into him, sliding her hands to his waist and not caring that he was sweaty. He was turning out to be so much more than she ever expected or could have hoped for. In the safety of his arms, he made it seem as if everything really would be all right.

Laia shifted to look into his eyes with their unique starbursts, and her belly did a little flip flop. "I believe you."

"You should." He tucked a lock of her hair behind her ear, sending a tiny shiver down her neck and spine. "I'll never lie to you."

Somehow, she knew that. "I'm sorry about the angry words I said to you last night in the kitchen. I've been on my own for so long now, it's become easier to think the worst of people."

"That way you're less likely to be disappointed by them. Or hurt," Kade tacked on.

"Exactly." He really did understand her, and it felt good to know they were so in sync.

"You've been through a lot. Raising a child all alone can't be easy," he said. "And you're right. I should have been there for you." When he cupped the side of her face, it was all she could do not to melt into him, to absorb his strength and the safety that came with it. "But I'm here now."

He brushed his lips across hers. Unlike their frenzied make-out session on the sofa the night before, this kiss was soft, exquisitely gentle, and yet so full of emotion and unspoken words that she dared to think—

Kade pulled away, then tugged his ringing cell phone from his pocket to take a call. "Sampson." His brows lowered, and for the next few minutes, all he did was listen. "Thanks, Chief. Let me know if you turn up anything else." He stuffed the phone back into his pocket. "That was the chief of the Asbury Park PD. He put a rush on the prints pulled from your house."

"And?" she asked hopefully, but her hope died when Kade gave a grim shake of his head.

"The adult prints match yours and the sample taken from Alvita. The others were small, probably Rosa's and Alvita's kids."

Her heart sank with disappointment. "So that's a dead end. We have no way of connecting Fernando Colon with whoever broke into my house."

"Maybe not. But I have another idea. The cartel didn't find what they were looking for at your house. Otherwise they wouldn't have tracked you to my house with the intention of breaking in." He pointed to the duplex. "But Josh never lived in this house. So it makes sense that the ledger and the cash aren't here."

"What's your idea?"

"Federal agents searched your Rumson house, but we should go back there anyway."

"Why? If the ledger or the cash was there, wouldn't they have found it?"

"Maybe. But they didn't have what I have."

"What's that?"

"Smoke."

Chapter Fourteen

During the drive to Rumson, they barely exchanged three sentences, and that was okeydokey with Kade. His brain was on overload.

Executing a search warrant inside Laia's mouth hadn't been the plan, but when she'd looked up at him, so forlorn and at her wits' end, his heart had cracked wide open, and his lips had taken a walk all by themselves and unerringly found the way to her mouth.

At the time, he'd told himself he'd done it because he didn't have any response that could possibly alleviate her fears. Colon would keep coming until he found what he was after. If he didn't find it, Kade had no doubt the powerful drug lord would mow over anyone who either got in his way or was useless to him and had to be discarded. Including Laia and Rosa.

But if Kade was truthful with himself, that wasn't the only reason he'd kissed her.

Where Laia was concerned, he was weak. He'd successfully managed to avoid her for two years. In the span of less than three days, all his efforts went down the drain faster than flushing the toilet. The brain inside his skull kept reminding him in no uncertain terms to keep his distance. His other brain was failing him. Bigtime.

He took the turn onto Laia's former street, at the end of which was her former house—the one she'd lived in with his brother.

The SUV's tires crunched on the sparkling white stone driveway that had to be a hundred yards long. That was more than enough white marble stone to fill an Olympic-size swimming pool.

He continued past the neatly pruned boxwoods, the perfectly manicured lawn dotted with pine trees and decorative Japanese maples, to the circular parking area in front of the house, then parked behind a shiny red Mercedes AMG GT Roadster. The last issue of *Road & Track* he'd flipped through listed the starting price of that car at a mere $130K.

Laia peered out the window at the massive three-story gray stucco house. Unbeknownst to her, Kade had driven by many times after Josh died and before she'd been forced to move. Just checking up on her, he'd told himself at the time. He'd sat at the end of the driveway in his vehicle under the cover of darkness, much like a criminal would, ironically, but he'd never driven up to the house. Never had the balls to knock on the door.

She took a deep breath, as if to fortify herself. Laia had been forced out of this beautiful mansion most people would never have the opportunity to live in. Now she was living in one half of a rented duplex. Coming back here after all this time had to be difficult, but the expression of sadness and longing he'd expected wasn't there. Something else was, although he couldn't put his finger on precisely what.

"Are you anxious about going inside?" If she was, he and

Smoke could do this alone.

"Yes. And no." She continued staring out the window, taking in the long porch with its dozen or so white square columns, the second-story balcony with its arched windows, and finally, to the enormous twin chimneys.

"It must have been something to live in a place like this." Behind the house, he could just make out the Navesink River and the long wood dock where Josh had tied up his sailboat. "There have to be some good memories here to go along with the bad." Standing by helplessly while federal agents tossed your house couldn't have been easy.

"Some." Her brow creased. "Life here with Josh...wasn't easy."

Huh?

Aside from that one little flicker of doubt he'd seen on her face the day of her wedding—one he'd ultimately attributed to wedding-day jitters—he'd always assumed Josh and Laia had a marriage that books were written about. Perfect couple. Perfect home. Perfect little girl.

Although in truth, he'd never really understood that term—wedding-day jitters—because if he ever proposed to someone, there'd be no doubt in his mind about spending the rest of his life with that person.

Especially if that person was Laia.

"What do you mean life with Josh wasn't easy?" he asked because he couldn't *not* ask.

"At first things were okay, I guess. I suppose every couple has issues." The crease on her forehead deepened. "Ours were just...different." She cleared her throat and smiled, although it most definitely never made it to her eyes. "Let's go in."

Without waiting, she unbuckled her seat belt and opened the door.

Ookay. Conversation over, clearly, although his curiosity

was pinging like crazy.

He grabbed Smoke's leash, then stepped outside. The hot, humid air slammed into him. Rosa's idea of heading to the beach later was a no-brainer.

Kade popped Smoke's door, then hooked on the leash. He wagged his tail as Laia approached, then wagged it faster when she bent to stroke his ears. She really would make a great vet. He wasn't kidding when he'd said that.

"I'm not sure the Sandersons will appreciate a dog in their home," Laia said.

Before leaving Asbury Park, Kade had a run a quick check to see who owned the house now. Mr. Bryan Sanderson and his wife, Jennifer.

"Then I'll have to convince them," Kade said. "I want Smoke to check the inside for hidden currency."

"Currency? I thought he was a drug dog."

"He is, but very often currency associated with drug transactions has drug particles on it, the odor of which can be detected by a trained narcotics K-9. I'm sure the house was thoroughly searched during the warrant. Like I said, they didn't have Smoke."

Hearing his name, Smoke woofed softly.

Kade went to the door and pushed the doorbell button. Twenty seconds later, the door opened but not all the way. A middle-aged woman with short blond hair and wearing a sleek blue top and matching pants stood there, her face somewhat distraught.

"Can I help you?" the woman asked.

He flashed his badge. "Mrs. Sanderson, I'm Officer Sampson. I'm with the Department of Homeland Security. May we come in and speak with you?"

The woman looked from Kade to Laia, then her eyes dipped to Smoke sitting at his side. "I don't understand. What interest could the Department of Homeland Security have in this? I already told the police everything I know."

He glanced at Laia, then back to Mrs. Sanderson. "Know about *what*?"

"This." The woman opened the door the rest of the way and stepped aside.

Laia sucked in a breath. Kade catalogued the interior of the vestibule and what he could see of the adjoining two rooms. Papers were strewn everywhere, furniture pillows lay on the floor, their stuffing littering the expensive-looking rugs and marble tile. Other pieces of furniture lay overturned. Lamps and sculptures lay broken on the floor.

"We came home Friday night to *this*." Jennifer Sanderson's voice shook as she swept her arm, encompassing the room, then indicated the wide stairway. "It's the same upstairs. Every single room is in shambles. I just couldn't stand being here, so we've been staying at a hotel for the last few days."

Laia went to her and rested a hand on the woman's shoulder. "I understand exactly how you feel, Mrs. Sanderson. Not too long ago, *my* house was burglarized. To say it was upsetting is an understatement."

Jennifer sniffled. "I feel like my privacy was invaded and I'll never feel safe here again."

"I know." Laia nodded, meeting Kade's gaze and conveying it all. She really *did* know.

He appreciated Laia's discretion in not expanding on the fact that she used to live in the Sanderson's house, although the implications were screaming in his head like a banshee.

The Sandersons' house had been burglarized the day *before* Laia's, suggesting that Fernando Colon had sent his goons here first, and when they didn't find the ledger or Josh's cash, they moved on to Laia's duplex, then tracked her to Kade's house. He also had to consider that they could have found the cash *or* the ledger but probably not both. Otherwise they wouldn't have broken into the duplex or followed her to his place.

"I'm sorry this happened to you," Kade said, taking in what he could see of the dining room with its overturned table and broken legs—the room where Josh and Laia once ate together as a family.

Feeling like a voyeur, he swallowed the rising growl of disgust in his throat. "Mrs. Sanderson, was anyone hurt during the break-in?"

"No, thank God." She shook her head, her relief a palpable thing. "My husband was at work, and I was out shopping. Our children are both home from college for the summer but were out working at their summer jobs."

That, at least, was good news.

From personal experience, Kade knew the Colon Cartel was comprised of a variety of people with a multitude of specialties. Some had no criminal record at all. Yet. Others had been imprisoned for violent crimes that had left a river of blood and a trail of bodies in their wake.

"What did the police have to say?" He planned to speak with the Rumson PD's chief himself, not only to hear it directly from her but to inform the department of the likely connection between the two burglaries.

"Not much, really." She pointed to a tiny camera on the wall over the door. "We have a complete security system with cameras that were supposed to activate any time the alarm is triggered. The police think the burglars knew exactly where the feed wires were and cut them before they broke in. The only thing retained in the video memory of any use is what was recorded before they cut the wire."

"And what was that?" Kade asked.

"A cable company van pulling up outside."

No shock there.

The cable company van was the common thread

connecting this burglary to the one at Laia's duplex *and* to the attempted break-in at his own house. "May I see the video?"

"Of course. Come in."

After they'd gone inside, Kade closed the door behind them. Mrs. Sanderson hadn't so much as twitched at Smoke setting foot in the house. An enormous crystal chandelier hung over their heads, the light from which made the tiny specks in the pure white floor tile—Italian marble, Josh had once told him—glitter like shards of ice.

Mrs. Sanderson went to a table in the vestibule, one of the only pieces of furniture that wasn't broken or still upside down. She pulled a cell phone from her purse, then began scrolling through it. "Here it is. The camera outside the door was triggered when the van pulled up." She handed the phone to Kade, who held it out for Laia to watch, too.

A white van with a rectangular green sign attached to the passenger door parked by the front stoop. Somerset Cable Company, the same company name on the photos and video that Ashley took outside his house. Only this time, the entire license plate was legible. C90 EMZ.

Kade pulled out his own phone and tapped the tag into a note page. He assumed the Rumson PD had already run the plate, but he'd do it again anyway.

The remainder of the thirty-second video showed two men wearing jeans and matching green shirts with the Somerset Cable logo getting out of the van. Both wore ball caps pulled down low so their faces were almost completely obscured from the cameras, telling Kade they'd cased the house and knew precisely where the cameras were. And they wore gloves. Even if the PD had dusted for prints, he had no doubt that would be a dead end.

One of the men pushed the doorbell. After about twenty seconds, he pushed the doorbell again and knocked. The other man stood guard with his back to the camera and looking out at the driveway. Eventually, when no one came to the door, they both went to the corner of the house behind the bushes.

Kade pointed to the same corner. "Is that where your utility lines come into the house?"

Jennifer nodded. "Yes. The police said that even if we had locked the electrical box, they probably just would have broken off the lock or found some other way to get the cover off."

"They're probably right," Kade agreed. If a burglar had the skills and wanted to break in, there was no stopping them.

Jennifer's voice trembled. "I don't understand why they had to destroy practically everything in the house. They made such a mess that I can't even tell if they took anything."

He handed the phone back. "Would you mind if we took a look around?"

"What are you looking for, exactly?" she asked.

Kade exchanged a quick look at Laia.

Drugs. Cash. The missing ledger that could put a dangerous drug lord in prison for the rest of his life. "Anything that might give us some leads on who these people really are." Not a total lie, but hardly the truth, either.

"I suppose it's all right."

"Do you mind if my partner comes with us? He's a trained K-9."

Mrs. Sanderson looked longingly at Smoke. "May I pet him?" When he nodded, she did. "Our Daisy, a Golden Retriever mix, passed away two years ago. We were about to get another dog. I'm so glad we didn't yet. He or she would have been home when the burglars broke in."

Kade could only nod in sympathy. "Smoke." His dog perked up his ears. "Search."

Smoke put his nose to the expensive marble tile, sniffing and circling, then moving into the dining room. Laia and

Mrs. Sanderson followed closely behind.

"This is fascinating," Mrs. Sanderson said. "I've never seen a police dog at work." She uttered a sad laugh. "And I certainly never expected to see one in my own house. He might smell Daisy. We're still finding her gold hairs tucked away here and there."

"That's okay," Kade answered over his shoulder. "Smoke can work around that."

He allowed Smoke the full length of his leash and followed his dog into the massive kitchen, with its black granite center island, pricy Thermador appliances, and another crystal chandelier, this one smaller than the VW-size one in the vestibule. Smoke circled the entire room, sniffing, his tail whipping back and forth as he processed scents.

Kade allowed Smoke to set the pace, following him back through the dining room, the vestibule, two smaller rooms, then into a large study with an antique oak desk, dark red leather furniture, and high shelving crammed with books.

A lump formed in the back of his throat. This had been Josh's office. He could imagine his brother sitting at a similarly impressive desk, working on papers, reviewing bank documents and…

Laundering money for a drug cartel.

Laia's face was a blank mask, and it was so obviously not normal for her, since he'd figured out that she generally wore her emotions on her sleeve. The only indication she was struggling being back in this house was her tightly clenched hands.

"May we go upstairs?" Kade asked.

"Yes, of course." Mrs. Sampson led them back into the vestibule, waiting for them to head up the long spiral staircase first.

Smoke's nails clicked as he went up the stairs, sniffing each one before moving on. At the top of the stairs, he pulled harder and led them into what had to be the master bedroom.

A king-size sleigh bed made of some unidentifiable yet expensive-looking light-colored wood sat against one wall. The beige bedspread and matching rug completed the creamy, soothing ambiance, but all Kade could think about was that this was where Josh and Laia had made love and conceived a beautiful little girl.

Through the bedroom window, the clear aqua water in the swimming pool shimmered in the late morning sun. Beyond that were the Navesink River and the Atlantic Ocean, a view that few could afford.

Smoke's breathing grew louder. He strained harder at the leash until Kade gave him free rein. Smoke kept his nose to the ground, tracking directly to a brass HVAC vent in a corner of the wood floor.

Smoke sat and looked at Kade. His dog had just hit on something.

Kade knelt in front of the vent, trying unsuccessfully to peer through the slats to see whatever his dog had detected. "May I take this vent cover off?"

Normally, he'd need a search warrant, but since Mrs. Sanderson had agreed to them looking around, he was on solid legal footing. If what he hoped was down there actually was down there, he'd have her sign a consent form.

"I suppose so," she answered. Not exactly a yes, but definitely not a no. He'd take that. "What kind of police dog did you say Smoke was?"

I didn't.

Feeling as if they were about to overstay their welcome, Kade quickly slipped a folding knife from the pocket of his shorts and began prying off the cover, doing his best not to scratch the wood floor. "Don't worry, Mrs. Sanderson." He winked at the woman, sensing she needed reassurance that he wouldn't drag her away in cuffs. "It's probably just something of Daisy's that fell through the slats."

Not likely. Smoke loved bones and toys as much as the next dog, but when he was in work mode, he didn't hit on them, and there was barely enough space between the vent's slats for a piece of kibble to fall through. He knew his dog's body language like he knew his own. Whatever was down there fell into one of two categories.

Narcotics or something tainted with narcotics.

He tugged off the brass cover. Two inches down and taped to the side of the vent tubing was a plastic baggie.

Jennifer Sanderson gasped. "Oh my God. What *is* that?"

Though she'd remained silent, Laia's lips had compressed into a tight line.

"My guess," he answered, holding the baggie up to the light. "Cocaine."

Chapter Fifteen

For the entire drive back to the shack, Laia had stewed over what Smoke had discovered in her former house. In hers and *Josh's* former house. By the time they turned onto Jamie's street, the temperature of her blood had reached the boiling point.

Beneath her crossed arms, her hands were tightly fisted. If her mother hadn't brought her up with strict rules of decorum, she seriously would have considered punching out the SUV's window.

"How could he have done that? How could Josh have brought illegal drugs into our home?" Both rhetorical questions, but recklessness was unforgivable. "What if Rosa had found that cocaine? I don't know who was more horrified when you pulled out that baggie, Jennifer Sanderson or *me*."

Kade slowed before turning into the driveway. "I know it's a shock, but it doesn't mean he was using in the sense of being an addict, and I don't think there's any way Rosa could have pried off that grating. I had to use a knife to do it."

"That's not the point," she snapped, then realized he was

only trying to make her feel better. "I'm sorry, I'm just so... so...*pissed*." And with no possible way to vent her fury on the man responsible because he was dead. "What will you do with that baggie?"

"Incinerate it." He put the gear shift in park but didn't shut off the engine.

After using a test kit he had in the back of the SUV to confirm the drugs were indeed cocaine, Kade had assured Jennifer Sanderson that the baggie had probably been hidden there long ago by one of the previous owners. *Josh.*

Smoke shoved his head through the opening between them, and Laia absently began stroking his ears, letting the soothing comfort of petting a dog ease some of the tension and anger that had been whipping up inside her head. "I feel like an ignorant idiot. A wife who didn't know a thing about her own husband until it was too late."

Kade unbuckled his seat belt and turned to face her. "My brother was one of the smartest people I've ever known. If I had a dime for every secret he kept from our parents, I'd be a rich man. Trust me, if Josh didn't want you to know what he was doing, there was no way you would ever find out. Don't beat yourself up over it." His expression darkened. "Everyone has secrets."

Laia had to look away, so great was the mammoth-size lump in her throat. Everyone did have secrets. The only question was what would happen when hers was revealed.

"C'mon." He shut off the engine. "We've got company, and I want to log in and run the tag on the cable company van."

Another SUV sat in the driveway, one with a Colorado license plate. She'd been so thoroughly distracted she hadn't even noticed it until now. "Who's here?"

"Deck, the DEA agent you met yesterday. He and Thor must have some down time on their schedule."

"Oh, right." The tall, handsome agent with the warm brown eyes, and his huge Belgian Malinois.

Laia followed Kade and Smoke to the front door. As soon as he pushed it open, the alarm began beeping. Smoke bounded inside while Kade punched in the code.

"Why would they set the alarm if they're home?" she asked. A sliver of apprehension crept up her spine as Kade's brows bunched. Aside from Smoke slurping water in the kitchen, the house was eerily silent. No TV blaring. No music from Rosa's karaoke microphone. For that matter, no Rosa and no Jamie.

Her worry ratcheted up tenfold. "Kade?" She grabbed his forearm, the muscles of which were as taut as a bowstring.

"Stay behind me," he whispered and pulled his gun from the holster hidden beneath his shirt.

Oh God, no. How could they have found them again? And how could they have gotten past Jamie and Deck?

Even the slurping sounds from the kitchen had stopped.

With the muzzle of his gun aimed at the floor, Kade moved through the kitchen. Smoke wasn't there.

Laia put her hand at the small of his back, then his shirt, twisting the fabric in her fingers—the only way she could think to keep from screaming her panic at the top of her lungs because neither Rosa, Jamie, nor Deck were anywhere in sight.

Slowly, step by step, they moved into the living room to find Smoke standing at the door leading to the beach, his thick black tail whipping back and forth.

To her shock, Kade chuckled. Actually *chuckled*. Then he tugged the holster from his belt and stuffed the gun inside before placing it on top of the high shelf.

"There they are." He pointed at one of the large picture windows.

Laia rushed to the window, the breath whooshing from

her lungs in a giant gust of relief. Jamie and Rosa stood next to a seriously complex-looking sandcastle compound, but their attention was focused on the water.

She squinted, trying to understand what she was seeing. A man was bodysurfing and next to him, doing the same, was Thor.

Kade fist-pumped. "Surf's up." Grinning, he tugged a black wallet from his back pocket and tossed it on the TV console. He whipped off his shirt, giving her a look at his gloriously wide, magnificently male, and muscled bare back. "C'mon, Laia. It'll put you in a better mood. Smoke! Let's do this!"

Smoke barked and danced in circles as Kade opened the door. The two of them charged down the steps onto the beach with Smoke barking the entire time. They tore at break-neck speed into the surf, then dove in.

Laia kicked off her sandals, then made her way down to the beach where Jamie and Rosa stood cheering on the men and dogs as they swam out to catch a wave. The dogs paddled furiously to hit the crest like trained surfers. In the distance, the bells and whistles from the nearby carnival carried over on the wind.

When she reached Rosa and Jamie, Jamie hitched his head to the water. "Do you mind?"

"Go for it."

"Yesss." Jamie, who already had his shirt off, revealing more cut muscles than she could count, raced into the surf and dove in.

For the first time all day, Laia smiled. And what was it with these K-9 guys? She guessed being gorgeous, well-mannered, and hunky must be a prerequisite for the job.

"Mommy, Mommy! Did you see Smoke and Thor body surfing?" Rosa continued jumping up and down in the sand, clapping her little hands together. "Can I go body surfing, too?"

"How about you give me a big hug first?" Because she sorely needed it, and because even though Rosa could swim, she wasn't quite sure she was ready to see her five-year-old baby girl "catching a wave." She knelt on the warm sand, then held open her arms. Rosa flew into her embrace, and Laia inhaled the scents of sand, salt, and ocean air in her daughter's hair.

Rosa wriggled from Laia's arms. "I want to go body surfing with Smoke and Thor and Uncle Kade and Jamie and Deck."

Holding on to Rosa's hand, Laia eyed the sizable waves rolling onto the beach. Kade and Smoke had just "surfed" in and were running toward them. There was no way she'd let Rosa out in that surf. Wading in the shallows, sure.

Smoke loped up the beach, then shook, sending water droplets flying in every direction.

Laia covered her face in the nick of time. When she dropped her hand, Rosa threw her arms around the wet dog, smiling and giggling and letting Smoke drown her in slobber.

Again, Laia smiled. Kade was right. This *had* put her in a better mood.

There was no doubting her problems were still out there, lurking and waiting to be dealt with, but for now this was an oasis in the midst of the storm she felt certain was yet to come.

At Kade's approach, Rosa ran to him and held up her arms. "Up. Up!"

As if she weighed no more than a seagull feather, he easily lifted her up and onto his shoulders. "Did you bring a bathing suit?"

"Uh," was the only word Laia could manage.

Every square inch of Kade's body glistened with water, his muscles flexing as he held her daughter securely on his shoulders. Wet khaki shorts stuck to his body, revealing a sizeable mound at the juncture of his thighs.

So much for cold water shrinkage.

Quickly, she hid her eyes by pretending to shield them from the blazing afternoon sun. "No, but I have shorts and a tank top."

"Go ahead and change." Kade began bouncing Rosa on his shoulders. "I'll watch Rosa for you."

"*Mo-mmeee.* I want to go in the water." Rosa's face scrunched up in the most adorable little frown it was all Laia could do not to laugh.

But mommies didn't laugh when doling out orders. "Wait here. I'll be back in a few minutes." She turned to head into the house to change when laughter and barking drew her attention back to the water. "You know what, sweetie?" She looked at her daughter. "You're absolutely right. Let's do this!"

Without waiting, and without returning to the house to change, she charged down the beach to the water. Because this was all part of the new and improved Laia Velez, the one who embraced life to its fullest and didn't let anyone tell her what to wear or how to just...*be.*

"Hot damn!" she heard Kade exclaim.

"Hot damn!" Rosa squealed, loudly enough for Laia to hear.

Apparently, Kade had forgotten that children excelled at parroting taboo adult phrases. Chastising him for that transgression would have to wait.

Smoke loped past, running into the water ahead of her. Rosa's giggling grew louder as Kade caught up to them.

Laia dove in, sundress and all. Cool ocean water hit her skin, enveloping her body and instantly washing away the tension faster than someone snapping their fingers. Until that moment, she hadn't realized just how tight her muscles had been. Since discovering Josh's hidden stash of coke, she'd been wound tighter than a yo-yo.

When she surfaced, she saw Smoke wade into the shallows next to Kade, who leaned over to set Rosa on her feet. When he looked up, he grinned. As his gaze dipped, the grin faded and his jaw went hard.

There was no need for her to look to understand what he was staring at. The cool Atlantic Ocean hadn't had any effect on *him*, but her nipples had hardened into tight little buds. She could feel them pressing against the wet fabric of her dress.

The intensity of Kade's scrutiny stole the air from her lungs. Finally, she released the pent-up breath she'd been holding. "I think I'll go inside and change after all." Crossing her arms over her chest, she headed back to the beach. "Only body surfing in the shallow water," she warned both of them.

Rosa giggled. "Okay, Mommy."

Kade merely arched a brow.

As she trudged up the sand to the shack, she noticed two small red boats beneath the deck, one a kayak and the other a canoe. At the top of the stairs, she pulled open the door, unable to keep from checking again on Rosa, but she needn't have worried.

Kade hovered protectively at Rosa's side while she dog paddled in the shallows, kicking and splashing like a future Olympic freestyler. Smoke dutifully took up position on Rosa's other side, allowing her to periodically rest her hand on his back for balance.

Not wanting to drip all over the house, she twisted the hem of her dress, squeezing out as much water as possible. The hot sun had already dried most of her skin. After grabbing a towel someone had left hanging over the deck railing, she went in, then closed the door behind her.

This was how it should have been with Josh, enjoying time together with family and friends. It was on the tip of her tongue to once again blame Josh for everything. For how he'd slowly but surely detached from her and Rosa as a family.

For laundering money for a drug cartel.

And for getting murdered.

But as she stood there, watching Kade with Rosa, the truth was a painful pill to swallow. There'd never been a chance of them being a real family because *she'd* never given their marriage a chance. Not really, and that made her just as responsible for all that had taken place since then.

She'd gone into the marriage with good intentions, but that spark—that elusive chemistry between two people needed to make a marriage work from the day they said *I do* right up to their golden wedding anniversary and, hopefully, beyond—had never existed between them, and she'd known that from the start.

Jamie, Deck, and Thor joined Kade, Rosa, and Smoke, and she snorted when all of them began doggie paddling side by side. That was another thing Josh hadn't been there to do. Teach Rosa how to swim. Having been born in Puerto Rico, Laia had loved the sparkling blue Caribbean water and had insisted that Rosa learn to swim at an early age. Someday she'd take Rosa to Puerto Rico to experience the beauty and culture of the island.

Laia had never doubted Josh's love for Rosa, but he'd never even taken her to the beach. He'd never had the time. As soon as the full impact of marrying for the wrong reasons had finally sunk in, his ardor had dwindled like an ebbing tide and he'd begun working late, traveling nearly every week to God knew where.

If she'd made a different decision six years ago, Kade could have been in her life. Kade and the children they might have had. Then again, she could never know for sure if things would even have worked out between them.

Her heart squeezed painfully at all the mistakes she'd

made, the mounting pile of regrets.

And that's my fault.

No matter how much she blamed Josh, it wasn't fair to lay it all at his feet. It was finally time to grow up and take responsibility for contributing to who and what Josh had become. By cowing to her mother's pressure, she'd done them both a disservice. She should have been stronger, should have stood up to Millie's unwavering belief that marrying Josh was the right thing to do.

A phone beeped from somewhere inside the house. Laia turned from the door and dug her phone from her handbag where she'd left it on the kitchen counter. Three calls and two voicemail messages from her mother. Millie didn't believe in texting.

She cued up the messages, the gist of which were all pretty much the same.

When are you and Rosa coming to see me? was the message that kept repeating in her mother's perfectly enunciated English.

They'd left Puerto Rico over twenty years ago, and while her mother's voice still retained its beautiful Spanish inflection, Laia's had long ago disappeared.

She took a fortifying breath, then draped the towel over one of the kitchen stools and sat down to return Millie's call. She loved her mother to tears, she really did, but Millie had been raised a strict Catholic and had tried to raise Laia the same way, which, to Millie's eternal chagrin, hadn't gone exactly to plan. Another reason why her mother had been so adamant that she marry Josh.

"Laia, where have you been? Why haven't you answered my calls?" came her mother's worried voice.

"I'm sorry, Mama. I've been busy." What with evading a drug cartel and all.

"When are you and Rosa coming to see me? You didn't

come yesterday after church, and you know I don't like my schedule being disrupted."

Laia did know that. In fact, being a total micromanager, anything that didn't fit into Millie's perfectly executed plans drove her mother completely nuts. "I think we can come—"

"I made flan for you, and Rosa's favorite—quesito—and it will all go to waste if it's not eaten soon."

Millie's flan was restaurant quality, and Rosa's favorite sweet was quesito, puff pastry filled with cream cheese and guava. "We can try to come—"

"I miss it when Rosa doesn't read to me," her mother interrupted, *yet again*. "You have to keep up with her reading skills, you know that."

"Yes, Mama. I know." That was the last thing in her daughter's life her mother needed to worry about. Rosa *loved* reading.

Laia breathed a frustrated sigh, then plunked her elbow on the counter and her chin in her hand while her mother proceeded to tell her how to live not only *her* life, but how to micromanage Rosa's life, too.

Before she knew it, fifteen minutes had gone by, and the hand holding the phone was cramped. "Mama," she tried breaking in.

"Maybe you should enroll Rosa in one of those private summer daycare places where they teach children at a very young age all about history, art, and—"

"Mama."

"—politics."

"Mama, *please!*" Laia let her head fall back, then stared at the light fixture over the kitchen island. "Rosa is *five* years old. Trust me, she can wait a few more years before worrying about politics." Before Millie cut her off again, Laia blurted, "I have to go now, but we'll come and see you soon. I promise. And I look forward to your flan."

"But—"

"I'm sorry, but I really have to go. Have a good evening." She ended the call, then groaned. Was there anything stronger in the house than beer?

She went into the living room and looked out the enormous picture window to see Kade toweling off Rosa. At the bottom of the stairs, Deck and Jamie were hosing off the dogs. She returned to the kitchen, then opened the refrigerator door. One of the door racks had been replenished with River Horse Ale. She reached for one, then stopped.

On the lower shelf was a tall metal can. Whipped cream. *Well, why not?*

She lifted the can from the rack and was about to grab a spoon, but as she began shaking the can up and down, she found it was nearly empty. After popping off the red cap, she tilted the can, put the nozzle to her mouth, and pressed it with her finger.

Gurgling came from the can as the sweet cream shot into her mouth. She swallowed, then uttered a moan of satisfaction. Kade and Rosa were on to something.

Tilting the can again, she pressed the nozzle, emptying the can and continuing to apply pressure to eke out what little cream remained. But all that came out was air.

"Did you just do a whippet?"

Laia spun to find Kade and his friends, along with Rosa and the two dogs, staring at her. She swallowed, then hiccupped. Humming from the refrigerator sounded like a foghorn, and she had to reach out to the counter to steady herself.

Kade grinned. The other men chuckled.

Rosa scrunched up her face. "Uncle Kade, what's a whippet?"

"Uh." His expression quickly morphed from one of humor to seriousness. "It's a dog. Remember, we read about them in the dog encyclopedia."

Rosa's tiny brows met over her nose before she smiled. "Oh, yeah." Then she sauntered back into the living room with the dogs in tow.

Deck chuckled. "Nice save."

Oh. My. God. She'd inadvertently given herself a high from the residual nitrous oxide in the can of whipped cream, and all in front of three federal agents and her five-year-old daughter.

Wonderful.

Chapter Sixteen

"Quickly the King beck—" Rosa wrinkled her nose as she struggled to pronounce the word. "Beckoned to the musicians, and they struck up a dre-dreamy waltz."

"You're really good at this," Kade said, amazed at Rosa's level of reading, although since the pages were worn, and the binding already coming apart, he suspected she'd read this book a hundred times. Maybe more.

While Rosa turned the page, Kade tucked a lock of hair behind her ear, marveling at its softness and her adorable, freshly-bathed little girl scent. He grinned when she clambered higher on the bed to snuggle against his chest.

Smoke had curled up on the foot of the bed. He'd closed his eyes, but every now and then his ears flicked, telling Kade he was still awake and listening to every word Rosa recited.

"Go on," he urged when she yawned. She was the one getting sleepy, but he was enjoying this too much for it to end so soon.

While she found her place again on the page, he wondered if he had a child whether his or her hair would be as soft as

Rosa's. Would they have his eyes or...*Laia's*?

Jesus, he had to stop thinking like that.

Without warning, Rosa landed a wet kiss on his stubbly jaw. "Uncle Kade, I'm glad Mommy's not mad at you anymore."

"Me, too." Although how long that would last was anyone's guess. "Keep reading." He pointed to where she'd left off.

"The Prince and Cinderella swirled off in the dance. Uncle Kade, can you be my prince?"

Okay, that got him. That one little question had the equivalent effect of parting his heart down the center while she jumped in and took up permanent residence. Right in the middle of the ooey-gooey center.

Rosa cocked her head. "Or maybe you can be Mommy's prince. Mommy needs a new prince since Daddy died."

Oh boy. How many months after Laia had married his brother in a fairytale wedding had he lain awake in bed torturing himself by thinking of the two of them together?

Rather than answer Rosa's question, he kissed her forehead. "Keep reading."

"And the King, chuck-chuckling over the suck-success of his plan to find a bride for the Prince, went happily off to bed."

"Just as you should do, young lady," a voice said from the doorway.

Laia leaned against the doorjamb, her eyes glowing with a soft, gentle light that took his breath away.

"How long have you been standing there?" What he really wanted to ask was how many of Rosa's questions she'd overheard.

"Long enough." She came to the bed, sidestepping the open Monopoly box and the little game pieces strewn about the floor. Laia took the book from Rosa's hands.

Long enough for what?

When Kade slipped from the mattress, she leaned down and kissed Rosa. "Say good night to Uncle Kade."

"G'night, Uncle Kade. Can you teach me to play Monopoly tomorrow?" Rosa asked on a yawn. Looked like an afternoon at the beach had finally tuckered her out.

"Sure thing, Cream Puff." He knelt and began packing the game back into its box.

"Isn't she a little young for Monopoly?" Laia whispered, kneeling beside him to help.

"Josh and I used to play this game when we were kids," he whispered back. "I think she inherited his gift for banking." Kade's chest tightened as he recalled those rare, quieter moments with his brother.

Smoke took that moment to yawn, too, cracking his jaws, then licking his lips before returning his snout to where it had been between his front paws. Body surfing had tuckered Smoke out, too.

"Deck and Thor are getting ready to leave." Laia went to the bedside table and turned out the lamp.

"Mommy, can I kiss Thor g'night, too?"

"No, baby." Laia pulled the covers higher. "Thor has to leave, and it's time for you to go to sleep."

"Okay." She yawned again. "But can we go see Mima tomorrow?"

Laia shot him a questioning look.

Kade hitched his head to the hallway. "Let's talk downstairs," he whispered, then handed her a cell phone. "This is yours, right? Rosa was playing with it."

"Thanks." She laughed softly. "Only five years old, and she already wants one for her birthday."

He'd been about to indicate Smoke should follow, but his dog had shifted positions and now lay on his side, looking thoroughly content at the foot of Rosa's bed. Smoke seemed very protective of Rosa, and with all the threats lurking, that wasn't a bad thing. Before they'd even left Rosa's room, gentle snores came to his ears.

Laia looked at the book, whispering, "This was the one thing Josh always did with Rosa. Read to her. I remember when he gave her this book. He told her that it was a very special book and to keep it with her always."

A very special book?

Kade took the book from her hands. "*Josh* gave this to her?"

"Yes. She couldn't even read yet. He—" She stared at the book. "You don't think…"

He *didn't* think. He *hoped*.

Laia had said Josh didn't leave *her* anything. But he'd given this book to Rosa.

They went out into the hallway. Kade opened the book, running his fingers along the end paper glued to the inside of the cover. No bulges that he could feel, and no sign that the paper had ever been removed and glued back down again.

He flipped to the end of the book and examined the end paper there, too. Again, no signs it had ever been tampered with, and the spine appeared to be intact. He pulled a folding knife from his pocket. "Do you mind?"

She shook her head.

Doing his best not to unduly damage the book, he slipped the tip of the knife between the front cover and the end paper, separating the two until he could peel the paper away. *Nothing.* He did the same with the back cover with the same results. *Nada.* Too bad. Kade had thought they were on to something.

Over the book, their eyes met, hers looking as disappointed as he felt.

"It was worth a shot." She took the book from his hands. "I'll see if Jamie has any glue."

As he followed her down the stairs, Kade couldn't help but notice her delicate calves or the gentle sway of her hips.

"Midnight shift?" Kade asked, taking in Deck's change of clothes—black cargo pants, a matching black polo with the DEA badge embroidered on the left side of his chest, and a pair of heavy-duty, shit-kicking boots.

"Yep. Ready to rock 'n' roll." Thor's big body quivered with a typical K-9's excitement at the prospect of going to work. To Jamie, he said, "Thanks, man. It was a good day." Jamie and Deck fist bumped.

Thor nuzzled Laia's hand, then she leaned over to pet his head. "Goodbye, Thor." She gave the dog one final pat. "Will we see you again before you leave?" she asked Deck.

"Depends." He pulled a set of keys from his pocket, and Thor trotted over and sat in front of Deck, his tail whipping back and forth on the tile floor. "In case you haven't heard, the opioid crisis is at an all-time high, pardon the pun, in Denver. I might even get pulled off this detail early." He opened the front door. To Laia, he said, "Kiss Rosa for me and Thor."

She smiled. "I will."

"Later, guys." Then Deck and Thor were gone.

Jamie crossed his massive arms over his chest. "So what's next for you two?"

"I'll fill you in." Kade hitched his head to the living room. Jamie joined him and sat in an overstuffed armchair, resting his forearms on his knees. Laia sat on the opposite side of the sofa from Kade, tucking her legs beneath her.

"I ran the tag we got off the Somerset Cable van," Kade began. After dinner, he'd updated Jamie on the burglary at the Rumson house. "Comes back to a nonexistent company using a vacant lot smack dab in the middle of Newark as their address."

Jamie grunted. Neither of them had actually expected that lead to pan out.

"I also called the Rumson PD and let them know there could be a connection to the Colon Cartel and the burglary in their jurisdiction. The chief said they had no leads."

"What can I do to help?" Laia asked.

"Nothing." Mainly because he wanted to keep her as far as possible from whatever went down next.

"What do you mean *nothing*?" She swung her legs out from under her. "I can't just sit around and wait for the cartel to make their next move."

Now probably wasn't a particularly wise moment to tell her how beautiful she looked when she was angry. Or happy. Or sad. Or... To him, she was beautiful *all* the time.

"You're not doing nothing," he countered. "As far as I'm concerned, you've got the most important job of all—being Rosa's mother."

He could tell the instant his voice of reason struck home. Laia sat back, crossing her arms, but the wind seemed to have been taken out of her sails and she visibly deflated.

"We won't stop working on this until we find what the cartel is after and turn it over to the U.S. Attorney's Office."

"What if we never find anything?" she asked. "Does that mean we can never go home? We can't just keep running from house to house."

"The lady has a point," Jamie said. "What's your backup plan?"

Leave it to Jamie to get to the heart of the shitstorm. Kade *did* have a backup plan, but it was risky, and he needed to give it light-years more consideration. Too bad he didn't *have* light-years.

"Working on it."

"Can you at least enlighten us?" Laia asked. "I'd really like to feel as if we're getting somewhere."

"Like I said. Working on it. Everything needs to be done by the book." He understood her impatience, but the fewer people who knew what he was planning the better.

Jamie arched a brow but remained silent. Initially, Kade had planned on recruiting Jamie to back up his backup plan, but his idea was so monumentally insane that he wasn't sure involving his friend was a good idea. No sense both of them getting their asses handed to them. Or killed. Because, yeah, on the risk factor scale, ten being the riskiest, this hairbrained plan ranked a solid twenty.

"I don't mean to sound ungrateful, but how long exactly might it take for you to finalize this plan?" Laia looked skeptical. "If I have to take more than a week off, I'll probably lose my job."

"I'll do my best." And pray his best was good enough.

Jamie cleared his throat, then stood and went to a credenza. He opened the biggest drawer and pulled out a blanket. "Why don't you two go down to the beach and talk some more? It's a warm night, and I've always found there's something about the sand, the water, and all that fresh ocean air to help clear the mind. It's a calm night. Take one of the boats out if you want."

A boat ride *would* help to ease the tension. If only Laia didn't look ready to punch Kade's lights out.

"Thank you, but I can't ask you to watch Rosa for me again," she said to Jamie.

For the first time since he'd returned from wherever he'd disappeared to, Jamie smiled, revealing the same lady-killer pearly whites that had landed him the nickname Romeo so many years ago. "Smoke and I've got this. We'll watch Rosa for you, and as for asking me to… Any family of Kade's is family of mine."

Kade sent Jamie a grateful look, one that said, *Thanks, bro.* Whether it was dire circumstances or moral support, one thing he never doubted was that his friends would always be there for him. Anytime. Anyplace.

Laia opened her mouth, clearly ready to object again when Kade stood and held out his hand to her. "C'mon. He's right. A little fresh air might do us some good." And God knew they needed to talk.

She took a deep breath, then placed her hand in his. His rough, callused fingers closed around her smooth slim ones, making him realize once again just how delicate she was. In body, that was. Her spirit was the size of a dragon.

When Kade opened the door, the warm, humid night air settled around them. He led the way down the stairs, pausing at the boats.

"Boat ride?" he asked.

When Laia shook her head, they began walking in silence and didn't stop until they'd reached an isolated section of beach about a hundred yards from the shack. No houses. No roads. No lights. Sand dunes and tall grasses concealed their location from the street and the park behind them. The only sounds were from the gentle waves rolling onto the beach, and the only witnesses were the twinkling stars in the night sky.

He unfolded the blanket and laid it on the sand. When they sat, it was with a good two feet between them, as if they were both afraid of the potent emotions that, apparently, were so strong that Jamie had orchestrated this little beach blanket bingo.

Now that they were finally alone, fear kept Kade from forming a single coherent sentence. What if he said the wrong thing?

She'd go running for the hills, which was probably the best thing for them both. The reasons he'd stayed away all these years were still valid. Besides, after marrying his brother, she probably hadn't given Kade a second thought. Maybe the only thing hovering in the air between them was physical chemistry.

Even as he thought the words, he knew there was so much more between them.

Laia made a soft *hmpf*ing sound. "I never told you this, but when we met in the elevator that day, I felt...happy."

"Because you were about to get married." His tone sounded bitter, even to himself.

"No. Because I'd met *you*."

He stopped breathing. Had she really just said that?

"For that brief moment, I let myself believe that I actually *could* be happy. All we did was talk, but we connected in a way I haven't connected with anyone. Before *or* since. I just didn't want to admit it then. Afterward, it was too hurtful to think about."

"Hurtful?" The one thing he'd never meant to do was hurt her.

"I should have said something before I married Josh. I should have said something sooner, but I didn't. I—"

"I'm sorry," he interrupted. "I never should have said anything to you that day. You were right, it was none of my business why you were marrying him."

"Perhaps. I guess I can understand why you backed off and never visited us."

He couldn't see her face clearly but heard the sadness in her voice.

"Yeah." When Josh had ruined all his fantasies by dropping the bomb that Laia was his, he'd backed off, all right. Straight into a deep, dark hole that he was beginning to realize he still hadn't managed to crawl out of.

The selfish side of him wanted to grill her about why, if she felt such a strong connection to him, she'd still married his brother. Just as it had been then, it still wasn't his business.

"I worried then that I was making a mistake." In the near-darkness, she turned to face him. "At the time, I felt I had no choice."

"No choice?" Again, he couldn't contain the bitterness in his voice. "About marrying someone?"

She sighed. A deep, heavy, emotion-laden sigh. "There were other things to consider."

"There's only one reason to consider marrying someone, and that's whether you love them and want to spend the rest of your life with them." Fool that he was, he truly believed that, which was why he'd never once considered marriage. Stupidly, after spending forty minutes on his ass in an elevator, the only person he'd ever imagined he might marry was her.

"Sometimes," she continued, "there are other reasons. At least, I thought so at the time."

"Did you love him?" He honestly didn't know if he wanted to hear the answer.

For a long moment, she said nothing. "I cared for him. I wouldn't have gone out with him in the first place if I hadn't."

"If you didn't love him, why in the world did you marry him?"

Ignoring his anger-laced question, she sighed. "We dated for several months, and when I realized I didn't love him, I broke it off. And then—" Her voice wavered.

"Then what?" Now he had part of the answer. Whatever reason she'd married him for, it wasn't love.

"Then I found out I was...pregnant."

Kade's heart stopped beating, then pumped so hard he could hear it over the waves. *Jesus.*

In the elevator that day, she'd been holding her hand to her belly, and he'd assumed she was claustrophobic. *She* hadn't actually said that word. *He* had. He'd made that assumption because she'd looked ready to puke at the time. Because she'd probably had morning sickness.

"So Rosa wasn't premature, after all." That was what Josh had told his parents and what they, in turn, had told him.

The moon broke free of the clouds, illuminating the

despair on Laia's face as she shook her head. "A month before I found out I was pregnant, I broke it off with him. He was upset. He said he was in love with me. I cared about him, really, I did, but I just couldn't stay with him. It would only have made things worse if I'd dragged it out."

Kade ran a hand down his face. More things were starting to make sense now.

"Then I missed a period, which was a total shock since I was on birth control pills. My cycle had been irregular for years, and my doctor had just switched up my prescription." She uttered a bitter laugh. "I guess something went wrong with the new meds and…"

"Rosa," Kade finished for her.

"Yes, Rosa. The most wonderful thing that ever happened to me." Her expression of despair changed to one of absolute love. "I didn't go to Josh for money or anything else. I just thought he deserved to know the child was his and to have an opportunity to be part of her life."

That much he understood. If it had been Kade who'd fathered a child, not only would he want to know but he'd definitely want to be a father to him or her. "If you didn't love him, and you only told him so he'd know he fathered a child, why did you marry him?"

"Because he offered," she answered simply. "He said he'd take care of us. The only thing he asked for in return was that I keep the pregnancy a secret at first. He didn't want his family, friends, or colleagues thinking that Rosa was the only reason we got married. It was important to him that everyone believe we were in love."

Kade tilted back his head to stare at the stars. How could he not have known this?

Because Josh didn't want me to. His brother really *had* been good at keeping secrets. That trait ran deep in their family.

Unlike Kade, dating and meeting women had never come easily for Josh. Deep down, he'd always known this. His brother had been born with a financial intellect Kade could never hope to achieve, but where the fairer sex was concerned, he'd always struggled. Landing someone as perfect as Laia must have been a dream come true.

All these years, he'd wished a thousand times that Laia hadn't married his brother. Even if she hadn't, it wouldn't have changed anything. They could never have been together, and she knew it, too.

Because she'd been pregnant with his brother's child.

That would have been an insurmountable problem, a mountain so high that should they have even attempted to scale it, they never would have reached the top.

"Kade?" She touched his arm, and he felt her warmth clear down to his toes. "Say something."

He opened his mouth to do just that but… What *could* he say?

The only words that came to mind wouldn't do a bit of good. He could practically see his brother looking down on them, shaking his finger, and warning Kade to back away from his wife. And he was sick and tired of it.

If he kept sitting on his ass, letting his guilt and his dead brother stand in the way, he'd let the best thing that could ever happen to him slip from his grasp before he ever reached for it.

Laia.

He wanted her with every beat of his heart. But did she feel the same?

It was finally time to quit being a chickenshit and find out.

Before it was too late and he lost her all over again.

Chapter Seventeen

"Laia." When Kade touched her cheek, she wanted nothing more than to give in, to lean into his embrace and let go of the past. But there were things she had to get off her chest first.

"It's my fault," she whispered, staring at the waves she couldn't see but heard rolling on shore.

"What is?" Kade asked softly, shifting on the blanket to face her and move closer.

"What happened to Josh. I'm at least partly to blame, and I have to take responsibility for that." A little late, though.

"What exactly is it you think you're responsible for?"

"It was selfish of me to marry him. I don't think I ever gave our marriage a chance, and that's what drove him out the door seeking thrills he could only get from working for a drug cartel."

"Laia, don't." In the dim light, she could just make out Kade's handsome face, the lines of his strong jaw. "Don't blame yourself for the choices my brother made. Those were his and his alone to make."

"If I hadn't been weak. If I hadn't listened to my mother...

Oh, God." She covered her face with her hands. She could still remember her mother's firm words, urging her to follow her faith and do the right thing by giving her unborn child a last name and a secure future. But it hadn't been *her* faith, it had been her mother's. For too long, she'd depended on her mother's emotional support, and the day of her wedding, it had failed her. Miserably.

"On my wedding day," she continued, letting her hands fall to her lap as she recalled the abject misery strumming through every cell in her body in the moments before Josh slid the ring on her finger, "I looked at you, and I knew in my heart that it was wrong to marry one man when I felt so strongly about another. I almost ran away. Not doing so was the biggest, most cowardly mistake of my life. I don't want to make any more mistakes."

After Josh died, and everything that had happened in the aftermath, she'd sworn that whatever came next, she'd face it headlong and do it alone, without any outside influence.

"Tell me something." He cupped her face and began gliding his thumb back and forth across her skin, sending delicious tendrils of sensation down her neck to her breasts. "What mistakes are you worried about making?"

The moment of truth had come. Time to make good on the promise she'd made to herself.

She swallowed. "Not telling you how I felt in that elevator and not telling you how I feel now." Like how her heart was ready to beat right out of her chest, and how frightened she was of the admissions on the tip of her tongue.

He leaned in close, brushing his lips against her ear. "Tell me now," he whispered, then his lips burned a hot trail down her jaw.

Tears backed up behind her eyes. All the feelings and emotions she'd kept a rein on all these years burst forth from the tightly sealed box she'd stowed them in. "I felt as if I'd known you my entire life. The connection we had then is still there."

Kade pulled back, gazing down at her with a blank expression she couldn't decipher. Then a corner of his mouth lifted. "I've waited a long time to hear you say that."

"Then what are you waiting for?"

"Absolutely nothing." Kade captured her mouth in a kiss so deep, so hot, and so full of desire and promise that her bones seemed to liquefy right there on the blanket.

As his tongue swept her mouth, he tasted of mint and chocolate from the ice cream they'd had after dinner. With every breath, she inhaled his seductive combination of spice and leather tinged with...gun oil? Whatever it was, it sparked every one of her nerve endings to life.

His broad palm—hot and cool at the same time—stroked up her thigh beneath the hem of her dress, creating a trail of goose bumps that left her trembling in his arms.

His lips moved down her neck to her collarbone, nipping gently and eliciting tiny little moans from the back of her throat.

"I've wanted this for so long," his deep voice rumbled between her breasts. "You have no idea what you do to me."

Maybe not, but what he was doing to her was unbelievably and impossibly awesome.

Her skin was hot, yet her body shivered, as if she were sitting on a giant ice cube. Her panties were soaked as she imagined what might come next. Kade, settling himself long and deep within her.

Waves of heat rolled off his body. "Tell me you want this," he said. "Tell me you want *me*."

Impossible, but the way he'd said the words led her to believe he doubted just how *much* she wanted him.

"I want this. I want *you*!" she cried, then clasped the sides of his face and pulled his mouth back to hers.

Suddenly, her back was slammed down on the blanket.

Kade's big body covered hers. His tongue delved deeper, swirling, tasting, and sending her on a one-way trip to Lustville. The bone-liquifying sensation she'd experienced moments ago was magnified by a factor of a thousand, and all she could do now was hang on for the ride.

Kade's rough fingers tugged down the thin spaghetti straps of her dress, baring her breasts. Warm air blew across her nipples, tightening them to hard nubs. His hand closed over one breast, massaging and squeezing gently before capturing it between his thumb and forefinger.

Thankfully, his mouth was still firmly over hers, because the moan she heard next—hers—would have been loud enough to summon the dead.

He tugged the straps of her dress down to her waist. She lifted her hips, urging him to tear the garment from her body. Anything to get them skin-to-skin faster. Her tiny little thong was the next to go.

She reached for his shirt, yanking it up his arms and over his head. Next she fumbled with the snap of his jeans, somehow managing to pop it open, but her fingers were so shaky she couldn't manage the zipper over his erection.

"I've got this." He stood, then shucked his shorts and underwear.

A shaft of moonlight took that moment to peek through the clouds, bathing Kade's glorious body in an ethereal light and giving her a glimpse of...wow.

Gently, he lowered himself on top of her, nudging her hips wider and nestling between her thighs. He fastened his mouth on her breast, sucking her nipple into his mouth, then gently catching it with his teeth and tongue in a hot, teasing tug.

Laia hooked her legs over the backs of his thighs, undulating her hips and urging him to get inside her before she screamed.

Speaking of screaming... They were in an isolated, fairly

concealed area, but this beach was still public. The muscles in her lower belly quivered. There was something so deliciously dangerous at the prospect that they could be seen by anyone who happened to be walking by.

As Kade afforded her other nipple the same attention, he rocked his body against hers, nudging his stiff erection against her wetness.

"Baby, I need to get inside you. I don't have a condom. You still on that birth control?"

"Yes." If for some reason her birth control failed her again, she didn't care. This child would be made with...love? *Don't think about that now. Just enjoy.*

And then he was there, kneeling between her outstretched thighs as he rubbed the throbbing tip of him against her slick folds, teasing and torturing and making her squirm to get closer.

"Kade." His name left her mouth on a breathy sigh. "Now. For God's sake, now!"

With every ripped muscle in his torso glistening with sweat in the moonlight, he pushed inside her tight channel.

"Ahh," she gasped, gripping his forearms, though they were so thick she could barely close her fingers around them. She hadn't had sex in so long the intrusion of his body was both welcome and frightening.

In stark contrast to her racing pulse, she forced herself to breathe slowly, rhythmically, the way she'd been taught to do when giving birth.

He must have sensed her discomfort because he slowed his penetration, stopping before burying himself completely inside her. "You okay?"

His deep, rumbling voice, so full of concern, did what no amount of carefully orchestrated natal birth breathing technique could possibly accomplish. Her inner muscles relaxed.

"That's it. Just *feel*, Laia." He rubbed the palm of his hand on her lower belly in slow circles above her pubic bone. His thumb dipped lower, pushing between the top of her folds and teasing the hard little nub while he pushed deeper inside her.

The stimulation from his touch was so intense, her body vibrated with need, and she bucked against his hand.

"Laia," he whispered against her parted lips. "What do you want?"

"You," she whispered back, her mind as clear as crystal, with no other thoughts except the two of them and what they were about to do. *Make love.* Finally, after all this time. "Ju*s*t you. *All* of you."

He froze. In the near darkness, she could just make out the glittery amber of his eyes as he held himself above her. "You *have* me." He kissed her again, his lips hot, his tongue wet as he surged the rest of the way inside her core.

His body was hard and warm, his hips pistoning as he thrust faster. There was something so wonderfully possessive about how his magnificent body covered hers from head to toe. *Like I belong to him.* Did she want that?

Yes. Totally. Utterly. Completely.

She grabbed his buttocks and pulled him deeper inside her. With every powerful thrust, every surge of his hips, her breath came faster, in tiny gasps. As her body started to fly apart, she curled her fingers around his biceps. A scream rose in her throat, then Kade covered her lips with his. A second later, his body tensed. Together, they groaned their release, chest to chest, breathing as one.

Laia floated back down to earth, shattered, sated, and feeling more alive than she'd ever been in her life. A smile formed on her lips.

Even in her orgasm-induced haze, the reason for that was patently obvious.

She was falling in love.

Chapter Eighteen

This was how Kade always imagined it would be between them.

Life-altering.

As were the all-consuming, possessive, and protective urges taking hold. He rolled onto his side, taking Laia with him so that she lay next to him. Their chests still rose and fell rapidly, a testament to the intensity of what had just happened.

Before they went back inside, he had to have her again. Slower, though, so he could worship her body the way she deserved and like he'd always dreamed about.

Looking back, what he'd experienced with Laia six years ago was an instantaneous attraction, intense physical chemistry—a major crush. Granted, one that had haunted him ever since, but whatever this was between them now was so much deeper and more meaningful.

"You okay?" he asked.

"Mmm." The mumbled word vibrated against his throat, tickling his skin. "You?"

He chuckled. "Oh yeah." Better than okay, actually. He had enough energy buzzing through him to swim clear across the Atlantic. He skimmed his hand down the curve of her spine, loving the feel of her soft skin beneath his roughened fingertips.

She shifted, allowing him to curve his arm around her shoulder as they looked up at the sliver of moon and the stars twinkling overhead. "Did you ever dream we'd wind up here, like this?"

Again, he chuckled. "You mean naked on a beach?"

"No." She laughed. "I meant the two of us, together."

He began stroking her cheek with the backs of his knuckles. "I *have* dreamed about it, so many times I've lost count."

"Really?" She giggled. "That's nice to hear. You know, I dreamt about you, too."

"I didn't know that." But he was damned glad to hear it. He turned to see a beatific smile on her lips and moonlight glinting in her eyes.

"I dreamed we were making love. Not necessarily buck naked on a public beach. Although now that we've done that, I think I want to do it again sometime."

How about in five minutes? As soon as he was ready to rock 'n' roll again.

She sighed, and he tucked her closer. "So, where do we go from here?" she asked.

"Anywhere we want to." And he meant that. With her, he *would* go anywhere. He knew that as surely as he knew the sun would rise in the morning. "It doesn't matter where as long as we go there together. You. Me. Rosa. And Smoke."

She smiled. "I like the sound of that."

He twisted a lock of her hair around his finger. "I may not have the right to say this, but I will anyway. I'm proud of who and what you've become."

Laia levered up on her elbow to look down at him. "What makes you say that?"

"You're strong. Protective. A loving mother." And so much more, but the words got clogged in his throat.

"Sometimes I feel selfish."

"Why? The last six years of your life have revolved around Rosa. How is that selfish?"

"I spend my days working, then—"

"Yeah, to put food on the table and a roof over your heads."

"Right, but at night I've been studying and taking online courses so that I can apply to vet school."

Yet another thing he admired about her. Her love of animals, and the desire to devote herself to healing them. All the road blocks she'd had to hurdle, yet she still managed to find time for her daughter and to pursue a life for herself.

"You're amazing," he said. "There's nothing wrong with having personal goals. Happiness comes from many places."

"Are you happy?" she asked.

For most of his adult life, job satisfaction had been the source of his happiness. Now he knew how much he'd been missing. "I am now." He rolled onto his back, pulling her on top of him for a deep kiss, trying to pour his very soul into hers.

When she sighed, the sound shot directly south, and he could feel his balls tightening and his dick sparking to life all over again.

Slowly, she pushed from his chest, spreading her fingers over his nipples. Straddling his hips, she began rocking back and forth against him, and he went more vertical than a flagpole.

A shaft of moonlight illuminated the loveliest breasts in the world. He palmed them, rubbing his thumbs across the tight little buds.

"Mmm." She arched her back, thrusting her breasts into his hands as she began rocking against him. "Wait!" Her eyes flew open. "I have a better idea. A *much* better idea."

She wriggled, which naturally made him even harder, then to his horror, she climbed off him and stood. "I've never gone skinny dipping in the ocean. Have you?"

"Uh, no." *But why not?* This wild-woman side of her was completely and utterly intoxicating. And ten shades beyond sexy.

Two seconds later, they were holding hands like teenagers and running into the waves, naked and laughing their asses off.

When the water was deep enough, he dove in, coming up for air a few seconds later beside Laia, who'd begun breast-stroking through the rolling surf. Moonlight reflecting off the water illuminated the smile on her face.

Kade dove under again, breaking the surface directly in front of her this time and making her squeal.

"Don't *do* that." She laughed, then splashed water in his face and began swimming away faster than he expected.

"Oh no, you don't." Kade took off after her, admiring the graceful way her arms cut through the water. Eventually, he managed to snag her ankle, pulling her backward and into his arms. "You swim faster than a marlin."

She laughed. "One of my hidden talents."

Kade grinned. "I'll bet you have a *lot* of hidden talents, and I'm looking forward to learning what they are." All of them. In fact, every day he spent with her made him want to know everything there was to know about Laia Velez. Even if it took the rest of their lives.

For a moment, he froze. Specifically, his brain did.

He'd been fantasizing about her for years but had convinced himself that it couldn't possibly have been love at first sight. That was the only way he'd managed to keep his feelings buried. But now he wanted more, and the word *forever* flashed brightly in his mind.

He pulled her closer for a deep, heart-zinging kiss that should have made the surrounding water sizzle from the heat of their bodies.

Unable to stand, she clung to his shoulders, then wrapped her legs around his hips. With her pressed against him and the sensual slide of warm ocean water lapping against his skin, his semi-hard erection responded by turning to granite and lengthening to the point of pain.

He hauled her tighter and brought himself snugly into intimate contact at the juncture of her thighs.

She maneuvered her hand between them, stroking her palm down his erection. "No shrinkage here." She giggled, a sound that lit him up like a firecracker and had his dick pulsing with the need to bury himself inside her warm, wet body.

"You know, you're right." He skimmed his hand over her hard nipples, then leaned down to suck one into his mouth.

She let her head fall back while he administered the same treatment to her other breast. "One would think, living on an island for half my life, I would have gone skinny dipping before, but this is a first for me."

"Me, too." He kissed his way to the smooth curve of her neck and from there to her enticing earlobe. He could practically hear his grandpa's words of warning in his ears: *an officer doesn't do anything unbecoming.*

Like making love on a public beach. Or in the ocean.

Only Laia could make him toss aside the lifetime of rigid code and conduct that had been drilled into him.

She shuddered in his arms.

"Cold?" he asked.

"Not at all." She looked up at the inky sky, dotted with twinkling stars. "Don't you think there's something so sensual and erotic about being naked in the ocean?"

"Uh-huh," he breathed into her ear, snugging her tighter against his raging hard-on.

"This is entirely against my mother's strict behavioral code." Again, she giggled. "Breaking the rules is fun. I should have done this years ago."

No, you shouldn't have, he thought to himself as he stroked his hand between her breasts, continuing to her flat belly, then began rubbing the tip of his thumb against the hard little nub between her wet folds. She hissed in a breath.

Because if she'd done this years ago, it meant she wouldn't have been doing it with him.

The thought of her doing this—or any *other* sexual act—with anyone else from this point forward had him gnashing his teeth.

She reached between them, nudging his hand aside, then curling her fingers around him. Now it was his turn to suck in a breath and groan like a wild animal. "You're a mermaid, you know that? A seductress. I'd do anything for you. *Anything.*"

Her eyes glittered. "I believe you." Then she gave him the sweetest, hottest kiss he'd ever experienced and began stroking him, her hand so warm and tight he nearly released right there in the water.

His abdominal muscles clenched and bunched against her fist as she continued stroking him, pausing occasionally to gently touch his ball sack.

"Holy mother of—" He pushed her away.

"You don't want to come?" she asked.

"Of course I do." He uttered a laugh. Coming was most definitely on his bucket list within the next five minutes. "But first I want to taste you. Float on your back."

When she'd done as he commanded, he closed his fingers around her ankles and pulled her out to deeper water until his head was even with the surface. He spread her legs wide enough to stand between her outstretched thighs, then draped her legs over his shoulders.

"Kade, what are you—"

"Shh. Just relax." He spread her folds and thrust his tongue inside her.

"Oh. *Ohhh.*"

Yeah, oh.

This was the hottest thing he'd ever done in his entire life. Pulling her tighter to his mouth, he speared his tongue deeper, fastening his lips on her warm, slippery folds.

Laia bucked against him, gasping and arching her back. She tasted of sweetness and sex. Passion and need.

Her chest rose and fell faster. Water sloshed over her breasts. She was close, so close he could feel her body start to vibrate, her inner walls contracting and squeezing around his tongue.

He shifted his hands beneath the water to cup her ass, hiking her higher into his mouth, enabling him to flick at and nibble on her most sensitive spot.

She moaned, turning her head from side to side, but he didn't let up, wanting to draw out her pleasure as long as possible.

"Kade!" she cried, her glistening breasts pushing skyward as her body bowed.

When he was certain she'd fully climaxed, he tugged her against him, letting her slide down his chest. Along the way, his erection bumped against her belly, and she wrapped her legs around his waist, sinking fully on him and not stopping until he was buried inside her still trembling body.

"Oh, Jesus." He threw back his head, staring at the heavens and feeling like he was already there. *In heaven.*

Holding her ass, he pulled out, then thrust deep again, already feeling the pulsing sensation at the base of his cock. Soon, the force of his thrusts whipped the water around them into a frenzied whirlpool of motion.

She clung to his back and shoulders, digging her fingers into his skin as he thrust faster. It wasn't long before his balls began tightening. "Oh yeah, baby." He gritted his teeth. "That's it. Jesus, I'm going to come so hard inside you."

"Do it. Do *it*," she cried.

Her words were the spark that set off his fuse like a cannon.

A bolt of energy surged from his balls straight to the tip of his cock. He growled as the explosive orgasm took over, leaving him shaking and curling his toes into the soft sand beneath his feet.

The only sounds were their harsh breathing and the gently lapping water against their bodies. If it weren't for the water's buoyancy, he would have fallen to his knees and drowned. Although he already was drowning.

In her.

Laia pulled his head down and fastened her lips on his. They remained that way for several seconds longer. Her breath was his. His breath was hers.

"Wow." She laughed softly.

"Yeah. Wow." He chuckled, remembering Jamie's offer for them to take the boat out. "No need for a boat."

Laia snapped her head up. "Oh my God!"

"What is it? What's wrong?" He turned them, twisting his head in every direction. If he'd missed a threat and Laia got hurt because he'd been so crazed by his need for her, he'd never forgive himself.

"The boat!"

"Where?" He kept looking around them but didn't hear an engine and didn't see anything.

"No, not *here*." She clasped his face. "Josh *did* leave us something."

"What?"

"The dinghy. *Rosa's* dinghy."

Chapter Nineteen

In the dim light cast by the SUV's dashboard, Laia glimpsed the five o'clock shadow on Kade's hard profile. Bristle that had left the skin around her lips burning from the last kiss he'd given her before they'd gone back inside the shack to update Jamie on where they were going and why.

She'd felt stupid for not having thought of the dinghy sooner. Josh had given it to Rosa when she was only three, then painted it in her favorite colors. Rosa had adored it from the moment she'd seen it.

Rosa was still blissfully asleep in her bed, but they'd taken Smoke for backup and Jamie's police-issued K-9 SUV.

"We've got company." Kade shot past her house without stopping.

"Who?" Laia twisted in the seat to look back at front porch of the duplex, but it was nearly midnight, and the porch was dark. "What did you see?"

"Two men in a car parked directly across from your house. One of them just lit up a cigarette." Kade made two more right turns, then parked at the curb in front of the

Millers' house, her neighbors directly behind the duplex.

"Then how do we get in the front door without them seeing us?" They were so close to finding the missing evidence she could barely sit still.

"We don't." He shut off the engine. "Not through the front door, anyway. We need a distraction." He picked up his phone and punched in a number. The numbers 911 soon lit the screen. When the dispatcher answered, Kade said, "I want to report a suspicious vehicle parked across the street from 241 2nd Avenue in Asbury Park. I'd appreciate it if you'd send someone to check it out."

"What's your name, sir?" Laia heard the dispatcher ask, but instead of answering, Kade hung up.

He leaned across her legs and pulled a small black flashlight from the glovebox. "Let's go," he said, opening his door and adding, "Try not to slam the door."

Laia got out and quietly nudged the door shut with a soft *click*. The Millers' fence ran the entire length of the duplex's divided yard that she shared with Alvita. No lights shined inside or outside of the house.

Kade and Smoke waited for her on the curb. Her heart beat a little faster at the prospect of finding the ledger, but she couldn't afford to get her hopes up. Kade lifted the rear door of the SUV, searched for a minute before pulling out a crowbar, then nudged the door shut.

He led the way up the Millers' driveway to the six-foot-high wood gate that led to their backyard. "Wait," he whispered.

A car turned onto the road and drove past but kept going. Kade flipped open the gate latch, hesitating when it squealed. Laia winced, then glanced up at the house, half expecting every light inside to come on, and the Millers' cute but excessively yappy beagle puppy to wake up and start barking its adorable head off.

He eased the gate open enough for them to squeeze through. "Stay close."

The only sound came from Smoke as he sniffed the dewy grass and stopped to inspect the swing set, seesaw, and other kids' toys strewn about the lawn.

Laia's feet were already soaked. Had she known they'd be trespassing then sneaking through her neighbor's back lawn, she would have changed from her sundress and sandals into something more sensible. Like boots, face paint, and black camo.

Clouds had begun filling up the night sky. The only light in her backyard was a gentle glow from the partially obscured moon. She could just barely make out Rosa's dinghy on the other side of the fence.

Unlike the driveway gate, the fence between hers and the Millers' backyard was only four feet high. Kade quietly dropped the crowbar over the fence onto the grass. "Smoke," he whispered, pointing over the fence.

Smoke charged to the fence and leaped. The dog was a dark, graceful shadow as he easily cleared the fence, then landed with a soft huff on the grass beside the dinghy.

"Now you." Kade's breath was warm against her ear. She'd been so enthralled by Smoke's Olympic-style hurdle, she hadn't even heard him come up beside her.

He slipped one arm around her waist and the other beneath her legs, lifting her then holding her over the fence and releasing her so she could stand. The next thing she knew, he landed beside her.

Kade flicked on the flashlight. Unlike the yellow she'd expected, the flashlight's beam was red.

"Smoke, guard." He pointed to the gate that led to Laia's driveway, then swung the beam along the interior of the dinghy. Next, he reached under the boat and flipped it over, exposing the hull. He looked in the direction of the road behind the duplex. The air was quiet, too quiet for him to start tearing the dinghy apart without making some kind of sound. They could have waited until daylight, but Kade had wanted to get to the dinghy ASAP, saying the longer they waited, the more time there was for the evidence to disappear.

"Here we go," he whispered. Blue-and-red strobes flickered from the other side of the duplex and driveway gate. Less than a minute later, muted voices drifted their way. "Keep an eye out on your neighbors' houses."

He began prying off the boards, which, to her immense worry, squealed in protest as the rusty nails reluctantly released their hold. With every squeal, she glanced at her driveway gate, worrying that the police or whoever was sitting in that car not a hundred yards away would hear the sounds and come running. She could just make out Smoke's profile as he stood by the gate, his body stiff and alert.

Kade set the crowbar on the grass. Keeping his voice low, he said, "Come over here and shine the light inside." He handed her the flashlight. She knelt beside him and shined the beam into the now-open bow section of the hull. Kade peered inside. "There's something in there." He reached into the hull.

A car door slammed, and Laia whipped her head around. The blue-and-red strobes that had been on abruptly shut off. The police car was leaving.

"Kade, hurry! The police are leaving."

His shoulder was obscured as he fished around in the hull of the boat. When he pulled out his arm, he held a clear, yet dirty, plastic bag. Inside the bag was a black-and-brown leather ledger book. A few tiny spiders dropped off the bag and scurried away.

"Jackpot." Kade grinned.

Laia's heart raced faster than a greyhound's at the track. This was what the cartel had been searching for, and she'd had it the entire time. She ran her fingers down the cover, still not quite believing what she was seeing.

Behind them, Smoke growled. The driveway gate rattled.

Kade grabbed her around the waist, then pulled her down to the grass behind the overturned dinghy and covered her body with his.

A thin beam of light struck the picket fence directly behind them, as if someone was aiming a flashlight through the small space between the driveway gate's doors.

Again, Smoke growled, a low, fear-instilling sound that should make any burglar think twice about opening the gate.

"Shh," he said against her ear.

Her heart raced even faster, and with the weight of Kade's body on hers, she could barely breathe. When he'd come down on top of her, she'd automatically spread her legs to accommodate his hips, vividly reminding her of what they'd been doing just over an hour ago.

So here she was, in mortal danger, hiding out from a drug cartel, and all she could think about was making love again with the man lying on top of her.

The pounding she heard was definitely her own heart pounding but also Kade's. Pressed together as they were, she heard and felt a double heartbeat. Almost like the proverbial two hearts beating as one.

In the darkness, she rolled her eyes. Living her life to its fullest was one thing. Getting hornier than she'd ever been in her life because she could die any second... What an aphrodisiac.

The light on the fence disappeared.

Kade shifted his head, whispering across her lips, "Don't move."

"Okay," she whispered back, then clasped his face, intending to pull his mouth to hers. If they were going to get shot full of holes any second, what better way to go than to be kissing the man that she—

"Let's go." He pushed off her, interrupting her thought before she could finish it.

Kade pulled her to her feet, then lifted her up and over the fence. He snapped his fingers softly, and Smoke sailed over and landed next to Laia.

With the ledger in one hand, Kade did a one-arm hurdle, heaving himself onto the Millers' grass. Then they were running.

Chapter Twenty

Kade checked the rearview mirror again. They'd driven out of Laia's neighborhood and were now flying south on Route 71 back to Manasquan.

Smoke had long since lain down in his kennel and gone to sleep. Beside him, Laia fidgeted with the book in her hands. She'd wanted to read it right then and there, but he'd insisted on putting some space between them and the duplex ASAP.

"Pull over, *please*."

"We'll be home in fifteen minutes."

"I can't wait a minute longer. I get sick reading in a car, and I need to see what's in this book that's so important it got my husband killed."

How could a guy say no to that?

Kade took the next exit and turned off the highway onto a side road, not stopping until he found what he was looking for—a dark, deserted linen supply warehouse. Before parking, he drove around to the backside of the building to the employee parking lot.

"Can't you just park anywhere?"

"I want to make sure there's no overnight skeleton crew." All the rear doors to the building were closed. No signs of employee vehicles, only company vans and trucks.

He parked in the farthest corner, in the darkest section of the lot but with the front bumper facing out so he could see anyone coming. They both unbuckled their seat belts. To avoid night blindness, he clicked on the same flashlight with the red filter he'd used earlier.

Laia tore off the plastic bag and dropped it to the floor at her feet. When she opened the cover, he aimed the light on the first page. It wasn't what he expected. The only numbers he could identify with any degree of certainty were the deposit dates and dollar amounts. "This is your expertise. Tell me what I'm looking at." Because most of the entries looked like undecipherable code.

She flipped to the next page, then the next. In all, he counted at least twenty pages of entries, each filled with his brother's borderline illegible scrawl.

"See these?" She ran her finger down a column filled with numbers. "These are account numbers." She did the same with the next column over. "These are country codes, most of which are in the United States. I don't recognize any of the company names."

Neither did he. No surprise there. "Probably shell companies. Drug dealers use them to mask their identities and to hide their money. What about these letters?" He pointed to another column and one line in particular with the letters VA.

Laia shook her head. "I don't know. They don't look like country codes or any bank code I've ever seen before." She turned the page. "There are more of them. BA, KA, IA, SCP. They all have check marks next to them. I don't know what that means, either."

With each flip of the page, she ran her finger down the

column with the running tally. "My god," she breathed. "Josh laundered over a hundred million dollars for these people." She flipped to the last page and dragged her finger down to the date column of the final entry.

Over the ledger, their eyes met. The last entry—for $20 million—was made the day before Josh was murdered. There was no checkmark beside the number, but there was a two-letter code: OA.

Kade swallowed the lump in his throat. Looking at his brother's handwriting was weird enough. He still had difficulty believing Josh had gotten so neck-deep in with a drug cartel, but there it was in black and white.

Laia flipped through the rest of the ledger, the remaining pages of which were blank. But sticking out from a pocket on the inside of the back cover was an envelope. He tugged it out, again staring at his brother's jagged scrawl. The letter was addressed to Laia.

Their gazes met as he handed her the letter. Technically, it was evidence, but he had a feeling whatever was inside was personal.

She took the envelope but didn't open it right away. For several seconds, she stared at it. Finally, she slid her finger beneath the flap and pulled out a folded sheet of paper. Slowly, she unfolded it. In the blood-red glow of the flashlight, more of Josh's handwriting stared up at them.

"Laia," she began reading out loud. "If you're reading this, I'm either in really big trouble…" Her voice trembled, and she blinked rapidly. "Or dead." She covered her mouth with her hand, shaking her head. Letting her hand drop, she handed him the letter. Her eyes glistened. "I can't. You read it. *Please.*"

As he took the letter, his throat threatened to close up on him. This was a letter from the grave. Josh had known something might happen to him, and he'd been right. He focused the flashlight on the letter.

"I'm sorry for what happened between us," Kade began. "I never should have asked you to marry me. I see that now. You were never in love with me, but I was so in love with you that I didn't care. I used our unborn child to keep you, and it was wrong."

A sob from Laia had Kade stopping, and he looked up to see tears leaking from her eyes and streaming unchecked down her face.

"Give this ledger to Kade," he continued. "He'll know what to do with it, and he'll take care of you and Rosa. Maybe he's what you need—what you've *always* needed. Deep down I knew that. I just didn't want to admit it to anyone, especially myself. Kade's a good man, the best man I've ever known, and I never should have said otherwise."

A big, fat, burning tear rolled down his cheek. He hadn't known Josh had felt that way about him. Hearing it now, this way—in a letter written by a dead man—had the equivalent effect of cracking open his chest, tearing out his heart, and squeezing it until there was no blood left inside.

He leaned his head back and closed his eyes, not knowing if he could keep reading.

Laia's soft touch on his cheek opened up the floodgates. At no time in his entire life had this ever happened. Tears rolled freely down his face. Mercifully, she took back the letter and the flashlight.

"The key is to a bank box at our bank," she read.

Key?

He snapped open his eyes and grabbed the envelope. When Laia shined the light inside, the beam reflected off a long, slim brass key.

A safe deposit box key.

"Keep reading," he said in a hoarse voice.

"The box is registered in your maiden name. What's in it

is for you and Rosa. It's the least I could do. Please know that despite everything that happened between us, I-I will..." She began sobbing openly. "Oh God, I can't."

Together, they read Josh's last words in silence.

Thank you for staying with me all these years. I will always love you and Rosa. Josh.

Kade didn't know what to think or what to say. All he felt now was a desperate and numbing sadness. For all that had passed between him and his brother during the last five years of Josh's life. For everything Laia and Rosa had been through. It never should have gone down that way, and it was too late to fix it. *Any* of it.

Laia clasped her arms around her shoulders, weeping, her body shaking. Kade wanted nothing more than to pull her into his arms, but he couldn't.

He set the letter on the seat between them. Though he and Laia were only inches apart, it might as well have been a mile.

Frustration rolled through him faster than an Army Thunderbolt jetfighter because even in death, Josh would always come between them.

• • •

Laia lost track of how long they sat there, saying nothing, each of them with their guts twisting in grief and guilt. It could have been seconds, minutes, or even an hour, so great was the overwhelming pain in her chest.

Kade cleared his throat. "I'll turn the ledger over to Manny in the morning. He'll get forensic accountants working on it. Maybe they can figure out the code. On the way to the office, we can stop by the bank."

Whatever was in that box, Josh had intended for her to have. Assuming it was money, it was probably dirty. Drug money. "If there really is money in that box, then maybe this can all be over soon."

"Maybe." Oddly, he didn't sound as enthusiastic as she'd expected.

"What do you mean *maybe*? You said that if we found the ledger, Fernando Colon could be charged with more crimes and be sent to prison again. Once he knows the government has the ledger, he'll stop coming after me for it. And if we find money in the bank box, it has to be what Josh was skimming from Colon, right? We can turn that over, too. Won't that eliminate all Colon's reasons for following me?"

"I hope so." In the dim light, she couldn't miss his skeptical frown. "I think so, but it's a little more complicated than that. He still thinks you have the ledger and the money. We need to work fast and turn everything over to the prosecutor, then make sure Colon's attorney knows that you had nothing to do with it."

"Then there's hope. Right?" Hope for a future.

With Kade.

She refused to let anything from the past keep her from finally finding the joy and—dare she say it, *love*?—that she wanted. *No, dammit.*

Love that she deserved.

Sure, they'd have to find a way of keeping the past where it belonged. In the past.

If she could snap her fingers and bring Josh back to life, she would without hesitation. But his death was a glaring sign, blinking in bright neon colors and telling her that life was too short and too precious to screw up twice.

Emotions so strong and fierce raced through her blood. What she needed most right at this moment was reaffirmation of life. Finally, this was her chance, and she was taking it by the horns and never letting go.

Laia refolded the letter, then tossed it and the ledger on

the dashboard. She shimmied across the seat, clasped Kade's face, and drew his mouth down to hers.

"No, Laia. Not like this. Not *now*." He tried pulling away, but she refused to release him.

"*Yes*, like this and *definitely* now. Don't you want me?" She certainly wanted him, and it wasn't just about the sex. Heavy, heart-wrenching emotions fueled the need to make love with him. Right here. Right now.

"Of course I do. I never wanted anyone more in my life."

"Then kiss me." When he didn't, she began peppering his closed mouth with kisses, urging him to give in. She knew the exact moment that he did.

A low groan came from his throat, and he dragged her the rest of the way over the seat and on top of him so she was straddling his thighs.

The abrupt movement woke Smoke, who rose to his feet and tried sticking his head through the kennel opening.

"Sorry, buddy." Kade closed the solid divider between the passenger compartment and the kennel. A sharp whine came from the other side of the divider.

He slid his hands along her thighs beneath her dress, then tugged aside her panties and plunged two fingers between her wet folds.

"Oh, yesss." She rocked her hips forward and back in tandem with the thrust of his fingers. Her muscles were wound so tight, she forced herself to relax.

"That's it. Relax," Kade said against her open mouth just before pushing his tongue inside.

The taste of him—hot, minty, and all man—made her body throb with more need than she thought possible. She reached between them to unbuckle his belt and pull down the zipper of his shorts. Beneath the soft cotton of his undershorts, he was hard and pulsing as she cupped him, reveling in the steely strength of his erection.

Hooking the waistband of his underwear with her fingers, she freed him, stroking his hard length and rubbing her thumb over the tip. He cupped her ass, lifting her, then slowly lowering her onto him.

Her inner walls, though still sore from the intensity of what they'd done on the beach and again in the ocean, quickly moistened, taking all of him in a deep, slick, sensual slide. She moaned as he lifted her again. Slowly. *Too* slowly.

"Faster," she whispered. Already, waves of sensation were building in her core.

Kade tugged down the straps of her dress, baring her breasts. He sucked one nipple into her mouth, holding her at the waist now as he surged upward inside her.

He released her nipple. "Look at me," he commanded, his face harsh in the dim light. He was close. She could feel him holding back, waiting for her to come.

Her body trembled, then she grabbed his shoulders as the powerful orgasm ripped through her. "Kade!"

He pressed his face to the hollow of her neck as he came on a loud groan.

Still breathing hard, Laia smiled against the top of Kade's head. She'd wanted a reaffirmation of life, and she'd gotten it.

The route to get here had been long and difficult, fraught with so much pain and anguish she'd never expected. The light at the end of her tunnel was now warm and bright, filled with possibilities.

It had taken a lifetime to get here. There was no doubt in her mind now.

She'd fallen hard for Kade Sampson.

Chapter Twenty-One

"Manny," Kade said, keeping an eye on the front doors of the Regional Bank & Trust as he put the call on speaker. "Laia Velez is with me. We found the ledger."

Beside him, she squeezed his thigh, the first time she'd touched him since they'd returned to the shack after finding the ledger. Laia had insisted they maintain separate bedrooms. *For Rosa's sake*, she'd said.

"No shit," came Manny's excited response. "Where was it?"

"You remember that old pink and purple dinghy?"

"Yeah?"

"It was hidden inside the hull."

Manny's curse was mingled with laughter. "It was right under our noses this whole time."

"We'll bring it to the office in about an hour." A bank employee unlocked the glass doors to the bank, then several other people exited their cars and went inside. "We also found something else." Wanting to get to the box ASAP, he quickly recapped what they knew about the key and the safe deposit box in Laia's name. "We're heading inside now. I'll let you know what we find."

"Ten-four," Manny said. "I love it when a case starts coming together."

"You and me both." But for entirely different reasons. He could give a rat's ass about the investigation as long as it got Laia and Rosa off Fernando Colon's radar. Kade ended the call. "Let's go in."

She turned to his dog. "Be back soon, Smoke." When Smoke licked her cheek, she laughed, a sound he hoped to hear a lot more of once they turned over all the evidence.

Leaving the engine running and the AC on for Smoke, he locked the vehicle. A minute later, they were standing inside the bank, the first customers of the day.

Laia had brought a light-purple sweater that she put on over her purple tank top. "It was always cold inside here, even first thing in the morning." She rubbed her hands over her arms, but Kade suspected it was more nerves and excitement than an actual chill in the air.

By the end of the day, the government might have all that was needed to put Fernando Colon away for twenty more years.

"Laia! My goodness, it's been ages since you've been here." A short, smiling Chinese woman of about forty and wearing a navy-blue pants suit strode toward them, then gave Laia a big hug. "It's good to see you again. And I'm so sorry. About Josh, I mean."

"Thank you, Li-Mei." Laia smiled, but this one was perfunctory. The tension in her posture told Kade it must be incredibly difficult being back in Josh's bank.

After quick introductions, the other woman asked, "What can I do for you? Did you want to open a new account?"

"Actually," Laia said, pulling the key from the pocket of her khaki slacks, "I'd like to access my bank box."

"Oh." The woman's brows rose. "I didn't even know you had one here."

It occurred to Kade that no one had accessed the box since at least before Josh's death—two years ago. Payments on the box must have been made years in advance, otherwise Laia would have been notified of a delinquent account.

"I haven't accessed it in quite a while." Keeping with the plan they'd discussed, Laia made a dismissive gesture with her hand. "I completely forgot I even had one here."

"That shouldn't be a problem." Li-Mei used a similar hand gesture. "Follow me."

The woman's high heels clip-clopped on the granite floor as they followed her to the back of the bank where the vaults were located.

Li-Mei stopped next to a small shelf just inside the first vault. Several small metal boxes sat on the shelf. "What's the number?"

"Two thirty-nine," Laia answered.

Li-Mei began flipping through the signature cards in one of the boxes. "Here it is. Oh, you've got one of the *big* boxes." When she pulled out the signatory card, Kade noticed Laia's name printed on the top. Every line below it contained a signature. Li-Mei flipped over the card. Half of that side was filled with more signatures. "You know the drill."

"I certainly do." Laia handed her key to Li-Mei, then accepted the pen and signed her name, which looked reasonably like all the other signatures.

Kade's phone buzzed, and he tugged it from his pocket. "Excuse me," he said to the women. "I have to take this." He stepped back outside the heavy iron vault door. "What's up, Manny?"

"Did you open the box yet?" he asked in a somewhat worried voice.

Kade frowned. "No. We're about to."

"We've got a slight problem. The AUSA wants to get a search warrant for the box."

"Why? We can get in there right now. Laia is the signatory."

"The AUSA wants to play it safe and be conservative. She doesn't want to risk whatever's in that box being thrown out on a technicality."

As soon as Manny said the word technicality, Kade realized his eagerness to get inside the box for personal reasons had clouded his professional judgment.

"On paper," Manny continued, "the box is in Laia's name, and since she's in possession of the key, obviously she can access the contents."

"But," Kade interrupted, realizing his mistake, "since she admitted that she didn't set this box up, defense counsel could argue that she has no legal right to what's inside."

"Exactly. But it's not like the contents are going anywhere. AUSA Parcells is in trial for two more days, so we'll have to wait to get the warrant. She said you and I should start drafting the affidavit. That way she can review it as soon as she's freed up and get it before the judge as soon as possible."

"Fine." *Not really. Not by a long stretch.* "We're on our way to you right now." For a day that had started out with such promise, it was already going down the crapper faster than a mudslide.

He went back into the vault where Li-Mei was inserting the bank's master key into the brass outer door of one of the largest safe deposit boxes in the vault.

"Laia, wait."

Li-Mei opened the outer door, revealing a large green metal box inside.

"Something's come up. We have to leave. *Now*," he added, wanting to emphasize the point but not get into it front of Li-Mei.

"Okay." Laia rolled her lips inward, trying not to let her disappointment show, but he saw it. "I'm sorry, Li-Mei, but we'll have to come back another time."

"All right. No worries. We'll be here when you're ready." Li-Mei closed the brass outer door, turned both the keys, then handed Laia her key back.

"Thank you," Laia said in a strained voice.

"We'll be back in a few days. Thanks." Kade touched his hand to the small of Laia's back, urging her from the vault ahead of him.

"What just happened in there?" she practically growled as he held open the glass door.

"The prosecutor said we need a search warrant."

"Why?" she asked in a quiet voice that was screaming with exasperation. "I have the key, and the box is in my name. I just want this to be over with."

When he'd unlocked the vehicle, she yanked open the passenger door and got in. When they were both inside, Kade explained the AUSA's rationale behind obtaining a warrant, ending with, "It wasn't my call to make. There's a protocol for this, and we have to follow it. To the letter."

"Seems like there's a protocol for just about everything in your world." She busied her hands, petting Smoke, and he could see Hurricane Laia was about to whip into a frenzy.

"Laia." He turned to her. "There's nothing I want more than for this to be over with so we can go back to our lives." No, that was a lie. He didn't want to go back to his old life. He wanted to start a new one. With her and Rosa. "So we can see where this thing between us takes us."

She closed her eyes, took a deep breath. "I'd like that."

Those three little words were all it took. The thundercloud that had been hovering over their heads broke open, and a warm ray of sunshine seemed to burst from his chest. Maybe they really could make things work between them.

He started the engine. Just before driving from the lot, he glanced in the rearview mirror at the bank Josh had been so proud to manage. And just like that, warning bells began clanging in his head.

Along with the nagging gut feeling that cutting the cord between Laia and the cartel wouldn't be easy.

...

Manny was waiting for them when they arrived at the DHS office. "Hey, Smoke." Smoke wagged his tail and presented Manny with his paw.

If only Laia could feel so happy to see the man. He'd effectively slammed the brakes on what she'd been hoping would be a day of celebration.

"Well?" Manny stood from where he'd been playing footsie with Smoke. "Let's see it."

Kade unslung the backpack from his shoulder, pulled out the ledger, then handed it to Manny.

"And the key?" he asked. "I want to get these booked into evidence right away, then get the money geeks looking at the ledger."

Reluctantly, Laia pulled the safe deposit box key from her pocket and turned it over.

"Thank you," he said. "I know this is difficult for you, and we appreciate your help. Let's go to my desk and you can sign the paperwork."

"Me?" Laia asked as she followed the agent down the long corridor to his cubicle. "Why do *I* have to sign anything?"

"Because the ledger and the key were found on your property," Kade answered from behind her. "The chain of custody has to reflect from whom the government receives anything that gets used as evidence."

"Oh." *More protocol.* And yet another trail leading

directly back to her doorstep.

"Manny is going to sign you up as a CI—a confidential informant. Anything with your name on it, and anything you actually sign, will be locked up in a safe. The chain of custody will only have your CI number on it. Have a seat, and I'll walk you through this."

Manny indicated for her to sit in his chair. On the desk in front of her were various forms with red *X*s telling her where to sign.

One document was a Background Questionnaire and the other a Confidential Informant Registration. As she took the pen Manny handed her, her mind began to go numb. None of this seemed real, but it was. *Horribly real.*

This wasn't over. Not even close.

A strong hand came to rest on her shoulder—Kade's.

"You've got this," he said, then leaned in to whisper, "And you've got *me*."

Smoke rested his head on her thigh, looking up at her.

"And Smoke," he added, smiling down at her with concern and something else. Something more. Dare she hope it was the same thing blooming inside her own heart? Was it love?

"Thanks, Smoke." She petted the top of his head, running her fingers through his thick black fur and letting his innate calming presence do its thing.

"There's a fresh pot of coffee in the break room," Manny said. "You both look like you could use a jolt." He pointed to the forms on his desk. "I'll be back in a minute, and we'll fill them out."

"Laia?" Kade's brows rose. "Coffee?"

"Thanks. Cream, no sugar."

"Smoke, stay." Kade pointed to the floor inside the cubicle, then he and Manny went to get coffee.

Laia picked up the Confidential Informant Registration

form and looked it over. A chill snaked up her spine, and she felt as if she were sinking in quicksand with no way out. In minutes, she'd be a confidential informant, nothing more than a number. This was unbelievable. Her life was turning into a living, breathing episode of *Law and Order*. *Dun dun.*

She tossed the form back onto the desk where it landed next to a thick folder. On the folder's tab, written in black magic marker, was a name: SAMPSON, Joshua C.

She glanced over her shoulder to verify no one was nearby. Satisfied there wasn't, she opened the folder, and the bottom of her stomach sank to the floor.

The top page was an arrest sheet. Clipped to it was a photo of Josh. His eyes looked tired, his hair was askew, and his normally pressed shirt was completely rumpled.

Was this what he'd looked like on the last day of his life?

Beneath the photo was his physical description. Six-foot-one, brown hair, green eyes. After that came a list of charges, Title 18 codes for several crimes, including money laundering, and beneath that—

Laia gasped. Right below the list of charges was the name of the arresting officer.

Kade Sampson.

For a moment, she stopped breathing. It had to be a mistake.

After Josh had been arrested, she'd received word from his attorney that Josh wanted her to come to the prison. By the time she'd arrived, he was already dead. The more she thought about it now, the more cryptic DHS officials had been regarding the circumstances of his arrest. The only thing they'd told her was that he'd been discovered during a raid at Fernando Colon's compound in South Jersey.

Had Kade really arrested his own brother? Was that what Josh had wanted to tell her? Or had he wanted to divulge the location of the ledger? She stared, still not believing it could possibly be true.

Manny returned, holding a mug. His lips pursed as he took in the open folder.

"Is it true?" she asked.

Kade now stood behind Manny, holding a mug of coffee in each hand and wearing a murderous expression as he glared at the other man. Surely he'd confirm that this was a mistake.

He didn't.

Instead, taking a deep breath, Kade momentarily shut his eyes. When he opened them, they were filled with abject misery.

"No," she whispered, more to herself than anyone else. "*You* were the one who arrested Josh?"

Kade's jaw clenched, and a muscle ticked furiously in his jaw.

Abruptly, she stood, sending the chair rolling backward and whacking into the desk.

Smoke lifted his head from the floor.

"Is it true?" It couldn't be. Kade would never have arrested his own brother. Would he?

That would make him partly responsible. For *everything*. *Please, no.*

Her heart pounded faster than she thought possible. "Answer me!"

His chest expanded, and just when she thought he'd deny it, she saw the truth in his eyes.

"Yes," he confirmed in a low voice. "I arrested Josh."

Chapter Twenty-Two

Kade hadn't wanted Laia to find out—*ever*—if he could help it. Then again, if there was any chance of them winding up together, their relationship couldn't be based on secrets or lies. Sooner or later, the crap would have flowed over the bowl, but he hadn't wanted it to go down this way.

"Laia, I—" *What*? What could he really say? Sorry didn't come remotely close to cutting it.

Wordlessly, she glared up at him with her chest heaving and her hands clenched into tight fists.

Regret and self-loathing pounded him from all sides. The pain etched in her features was his doing, *not* his brother's. He'd made a serious tactical error, and now he'd never have the chance to tell her the truth in his own way and at a time of his own choosing. The only question now was how bad the fallout would be.

Kade set the mugs of coffee on a table in the corridor and held his hand out. "Let's talk about this in private." Before every agent in the office got a ringside seat to Kade's guts getting splayed out on the floor.

She looked at his hand but didn't take it. "Fine."

Without needing to be told, Smoke followed them down the corridor until Kade found an empty office with a door that he could close. A desk took up most of the office, along with two small upholstered armchairs.

Laia's complexion had paled considerably. He indicated she should sit. When she didn't, he thought she might clock him in the kisser with one of her clenched fists. He'd deserve it. And so much more.

"How *could* you?" Her words had come out through clenched teeth. "Josh died in prison because you put him there. He wouldn't have been there in the first place if you hadn't *arrested* him!"

"Laia—"

She lifted her hand. "I'm not done! Rosa didn't deserve to have her father die. And my marriage might have been in shambles by then, but Rosa and I didn't deserve to have our lives turned upside down. Neither of us deserves to be on the run, but we are because my husband was arrested—and murdered—before Colon could get his filthy hands on that goddamn ledger. *You* did that."

She was killing him. But everything she'd just thrown in his face was true. *Balls-on accurate.*

Laia's chest heaved and her knuckles had turned white from fisting her hands harder. Seeing her pain, her rage, and her suffering...he wished he could absorb it from her body and take it into his own.

What he'd done to Josh that day had set something in motion that he'd always known would come back to haunt him. Hell, it already had. For two years, he'd been drowning in guilt. That was the real reason he'd stayed away, not because he'd secretly lusted after his sister-in-law. In his own way, he was just as guilty as Josh had been.

Finally, she sat, her shoulders slumping. Smoke

whimpered, then circled three times and lay down on the floor at her feet.

"*Why?*" she asked, looking up at him with shimmering eyes. "Why did you do it?"

He shoved his hands in his pockets and paced a full circuit of the tiny office before leaning back against the edge of the desk. How to begin? He honestly didn't know.

Finding the right tactical approach had always come as easily and naturally to him as breathing. Knowing the appropriate thing to say to the men he'd served with had never been an issue. Right now, he couldn't put together a single coherent sentence, and his tongue felt like rubber. But there was no putting this off any longer.

He cleared his throat and dove in. "I was requested to participate in the raid at the Colon compound," he began. "There had to be fifty agents and cops there that day. We went in on initial entry to help clear the main building and subdue anyone who tried to run. We had arrest warrants for some and were told to cuff anyone else and hold them until they were identified and questioned. As soon as the main building was cleared, we went outside to assist with the outbuildings."

Unable to look into Laia's face, Kade stared at Smoke, recalling with vivid clarity every single godforsaken thing that had happened next.

"Tango, my K-9 at the time, led me to an outbuilding, one of the cabanas by the swimming pool. I opened the door and—"

He swallowed. What he was about to say would hurt Laia all over again, and that was the last thing he wanted to do.

"Tell me," she whispered, as if inherently knowing what he'd been about to describe would be ugly and hurtful.

Picking up on her distress, Smoke rose and sat close enough for her to pet his ears.

He took a deep breath, wishing there was another way.

"I opened the door, and the cabana was empty." Or so he'd thought. "There was a mirrored table with lines of coke and two straws. Tango picked up on something else and led me to the closet door. I pulled my gun, aimed in, and opened it."

To this day, what he remembered most about that moment was the shock. On *both* their faces.

Kade dragged a hand down his face, feeling as if he'd aged twenty years, not two since that god-awful day. "Josh was hiding in the closet." The drugs were bad enough. He really, *really* didn't want to tell her the rest of it.

"You said there were two straws." Her fingers on Smoke's ears stilled. "Was there someone else there with him?"

Damn.

"A woman. They were both naked. She was a prostitute."

When Laia hung her head and sighed, Kade fought his instinctive urge to haul her into his arms. He had a feeling that wouldn't go over big right about now.

"You know," she began, her eyes glistening with sadness, as he'd expected, "after Rosa was born, I thought she would bring Josh and me closer. As a family, I suppose she did. The three of us went everywhere together, and he seemed to be embracing fatherhood. But as a couple...as husband and wife..."

Did he really want to hear this? Yes. And no.

"Not too long after we brought Rosa home," she continued, "the business trips started. At first, Josh would only be gone for a couple of days during the week. Then a couple of days turned into full weeks at a time and occasionally weekends, too. At some point, I knew. Then it was as if we both realized marrying had been a mistake, and we both stopped trying."

Again she sighed, heavier this time, and she averted her eyes and began stroking Smoke's ears faster. "We were civil enough to each other, privately and in front of company, but we hadn't had sex for a very long time before he died, so I can't really blame him for seeking it elsewhere."

A selfish part of him had always wanted to hear something like that, but there was no joy in finally hearing it now.

She lifted her head, pinning him with her beautiful, almond-shaped eyes. "What happened next?"

The worst moment of my life. That's what happened next. *Suck it up and tell her. She deserves to hear it. All of it.*

"I told them to get dressed, then handed the woman over to a uniform to cuff her."

"And Josh?"

Kade shook his head, his eyes glued to Laia's fingers on Smoke's head. As he began reliving every horrible second in his mind, his guts twisted in agony.

"Well?" Josh had said from the wicker sofa Kade had directed his brother to sit in. His brother's eyes had been filled with a mix of fear and rage. "What are you going to do?"

Christ, he didn't know. There was no protocol for catching your brother naked, with a hooker, snorting coke in a drug lord's compound.

"What are you doing here?" he'd asked, then realized the stupidity of his question.

"I think that's pretty obvious," Josh answered, then pursed his lips.

He gripped Tango's leash tighter. "I mean, what are you doing *here*? In Fernando Colon's compound?"

Wisely, Josh didn't answer the question. Even if he did, anything he said would be inadmissible. Any half-assed lawyer a day out of law school would successfully be able to argue that Josh was in custody and hadn't been read his Constitutional rights.

No, this was a conversation between brother and brother, and they both knew it. But somehow, the personal and professional lines had crossed, and for the first time in his life, Kade was utterly and completely frozen into immobility.

Josh stood, then grabbed his slacks from a chair and began dressing. "I'm in deep shit here, aren't I?"

"You're damned right you are. The place is swarming with police and federal agents. If you didn't have your head so full of coke and your dick so far up—" He drew in what was meant to be a calming breath. "How could you do this to Laia and Rosa? They'll be devastated."

Josh grimaced and began massaging his temples. "You're right. I have to leave." He snagged his shirt from the floor, then made a move for the door.

Kade grabbed his arm. "You can't just walk out of here." Much as he would have liked to allow it. For a split second, he nearly did and loosened his hold on his brother's arm.

"Sure I can. Watch me." Josh shrugged from Kade's grasp and took another step toward the door, but Kade blocked him. Tango backed him up, lowering his head and uttering a low growl. Josh's face twisted with disbelief. "Seriously?"

"I'm a federal agent, Josh, and you're sitting right in the middle of a major takedown operation. Everyone on the premises is getting arrested and questioned. I can't just let you go. You know that."

They'd both been raised in a military family and both attended West Point. His brother, of all people, should understand the requirements that came with duty.

"You're my brother, for God's sake," Josh countered, getting in Kade's face. "Are you really going to arrest me?"

His brain struggled for the answer, but all he could think was: *This can't be happening.* Of all the weird, twisted things he'd expected to find when he'd opened the door to the cabana, this wasn't it. Worse, he couldn't believe what he was about to do. What he *had* to do.

He dropped Tango's leash and drew a set of handcuffs from his belt. "Turn around."

Josh scoffed. "You're kidding."

"I'm not." He clenched his jaw, still finding the entire situation surreal, as if he were watching the scene go down but it wasn't really him about to cuff his own brother. "I'll do everything I can to help you. I'll talk to the AUSA. I'll make them understand. I'll find the best criminal defense attorney in the state and get you out of this."

"Kade—"

With his heart pumping so hard it felt like it would leap straight from his chest into the swimming pool not fifteen feet away, he took his brother's arm and spun him. He snapped on the cuffs before Josh could utter another word.

He loved his brother, but how could he possibly have compromised everything he'd been led to believe his entire life...everything he'd lived and fought for?

A hundred years cannot repair one moment's loss of honor.

Over his shoulder, Josh speared him with a pained look of shock so fierce he might as well have stabbed him in the heart.

That was the last time he'd seen his brother alive.

Tears leaked from Laia's eyes, and he'd put them there. "I'm sorry," he said. "At the time, I didn't know if I was doing the right thing." Had he known the devastation that would rain down on Laia's head in the aftermath of his decision, would he have done things differently? "I should have told you sooner. I just—" Was a coward. A chicken-shit of immeasurable proportions.

Instead of railing at him some more, she stared up at him with sympathetic eyes. "You were just doing your job. He was my husband, but he was also a criminal, and I have to accept that. I did accept it, a long time ago. Hearing the details now... It's a lot. I'm going to need some time to process it. Now there's a certain reality to it that I didn't comprehend before. I can't begin to understand how hard that must have been for you."

He didn't deserve the kindness she was showing him. He didn't deserve anything at all from her. One of the many reasons he'd stayed away all these years. The guilt. The grief. He'd been consumed with it and in many ways still was. Looking back, he owed his brother and would never be able to fix it.

Laia stood, and when she palmed the side of his face, his heart squeezed and he nearly lost it.

In a shaky voice, she said, "You're not to blame."

"Aren't I?" he croaked. How in the world could he make her understand?

"You had an obligation, a duty. To let Josh go would have compromised everything that you are."

Well, hell. She did understand, but it didn't change anything, and it didn't make him feel a whit better. In fact, it made him feel worse, guiltier, and more like he was the very last man on the planet she should wind up with because he didn't deserve her.

When Laia dropped her hand, he tried clasping it to his chest, but she pulled away. "I just need time to…process all this. Would you take me back to the shack, please?"

"Of course."

He and Smoke followed her from the room, down the long corridor, and outside to his SUV. The sorrow he'd felt moments ago worsened, becoming an agonizing pain dead center in his chest.

She'd said she understood, but that didn't stop him from worrying that whatever foundation had existed between them was on the verge of cracking down the center.

Chapter Twenty-Three

Experiencing so many emotions in one day—shock, anger, sadness, grief—the very same ones Laia had lived through after learning who and what Josh had become, had sapped the strength out of her. The moment the front door of the shack closed behind her, she nearly sank to the floor in a boneless heap of jelly.

She pulled her phone from her purse and flipped the side switch, taking it off silent mode, then set it on the counter. In the living room she found Rosa and Jamie watching *The Little Mermaid*. How many times had she forced him to watch that movie or more reruns of *The Nanny*? Poor Jamie.

During the drive from the DHS office, Kade had called ahead to notify Jamie they were on their way. Other than that, he hadn't said a word. Neither had she. Now he was on his way back to the office to work with Manny on the search warrant affidavit for the safe deposit box.

After getting over the shock of what Kade had admitted to, she'd wanted to hate him but couldn't. He really had only been doing his job. Despite what he'd revealed, she missed him, missed not being with him. In such a short time, he'd become part of their lives.

"Mommy!" Rosa squealed, jumping from the sofa to run over and wrap her arms around Laia's legs.

She knelt to give her daughter a big hug. "I missed you *so* much." Holding Rosa in her arms was almost enough to wash away all the ugly truths she'd learned today. *Almost.*

"I missed you, too, Mommy. Can we order pineapple pizza from Pizza Man?"

She laughed. "We're too far away from home to order from Pizza Man, but maybe we can get pineapple pizza from somewhere else."

"Ooh." Rosa stomped her foot. "I. Want. Pizza Man."

She sighed. One day she'd remember recalcitrant days like this fondly. Today was not that day. "I promise we'll find you pizza you like even better than Pizza Man."

"Can we go to the beach?" Rosa asked, happily veering off on a completely different track. "I want to swim with Ariel and go on the Ferris wheel."

Laia chucked Rosa under the chin. "Let's start with the beach. Just give me a few minutes to unwind." *Try a few hours.* Even a few days might not be long enough to absorb all the recent revelations.

"You okay?" Jamie asked.

"Peachy keeno." She'd never really understood that fruit analogy.

After Rosa had scooted back onto the sofa beside Jamie, Laia went into the kitchen for a glass of water, then decided on something else. She opened the refrigerator, then took out a can of whipped cream and popped off the cap. She upended it and squirted a long blast directly into her mouth. The cool, soothing cream slithered down her throat as she swallowed.

"Bad day?" Jamie's broad shoulders filled the doorway, his dark eyes probing.

"I could easily get addicted to this stuff." She held up the can, jiggling it before replacing it on the door and closing the refrigerator. When she turned around, Jamie was still there, watching her silently.

"Did you know?" she asked.

"Know about—" His eyes narrowed. "Oh. Know about *that*. Josh."

She nodded, not really surprised. Kade seemed pretty close with Jamie and Deck.

"Yeah, I knew." Jamie came into the kitchen and leaned his hip on the counter. "He's been carrying the weight of that with him every day. It's been tearing him up inside. After Josh died, he drowned himself in expensive scotch for three days straight."

"I didn't know that." How *could* she have? He'd disappeared again right after the funeral.

"He cares about you. He's *always* cared about you. A lot."

"It's not that simple," she said, shaking her head and wishing it was otherwise.

"Why can't it be?"

"There's been so much dishonesty. So many secrets." Both brothers had kept secrets from her. *Big* ones. Both different, and in their own ways, both just as devastating. "Must be something that runs in the family."

Jamie shrugged. "Every family has secrets. Guess it boils down to whether or not you can live with them."

When his expression darkened, Laia was no longer sure whose family they were talking about. Kade's…or Jamie's.

"Mommy?" Rosa called from the living room. "The movie's over. Can we go to the beach now?"

"Duty calls." The second the words had flown from her mouth, it struck her that *everyone* had duties and obligations that overruled everything else in their lives. For her, it was her daughter and all the responsibility that came with motherhood. For Kade, it was his duty to the job, some of which stemmed from his family's military background.

"I need to grab a shower and run some errands." Jamie pushed from the doorway. "Make sure you turn on the alarm after I leave."

"I will. And Jamie?" Gently, she touched his arm. "Thanks for the talk."

"Any time." He winked, then bounded up the stairs.

As Laia watched Rosa upend the bucket to make the first of what would become sandcastle turrets, she lay back on the blanket to finish drying off.

They'd walked to the end of the beach where the ocean meandered inland, then gone in the water for a quick swim. The hot, late afternoon sun was quickly drying her bright orange two-piece bathing suit and any remaining droplets on her skin. With the sun beating down on her and a light breeze to keep the air from being oppressively hot, she finally began to relax.

When they were both dry enough, she rubbed sunscreen on Rosa's face, arms, and legs, then did the same for herself. She put on her sunglasses and closed her eyes, going back over everything that happened since the moment she'd called Kade four days ago.

There'd been numerous times when she'd questioned the wisdom of calling him in the first place because of who she'd thought he was. Then she'd gotten to know him, *really* gotten to know him, and stopped judging him by the preconceived notions she'd had of an aloof, selfish person. Now she and Rosa had started to fall in love with him.

"Mommy, can we order pizza now?" Rosa continued shoveling sand into the bucket.

"Yes, we can order pizza." She smiled as Rosa turned over the bucket, creating another perfect turret. Her daughter's culinary inclinations tended to go in one direction and one direction only: pizza.

In the distance, the town's July Fourth kiddie carnival was in full swing, the Ferris wheel spinning round and round, the occasional bell ringing as someone won a prize at one of the many game vendors. Perhaps, if the carnival was still there when things were safer for her and Rosa to go out in public, she'd take Rosa on the Ferris wheel. Maybe Kade could come with them. If they were talking again by then.

A brief vision of them crammed into a Ferris wheel seat, Rosa plunked between them, popped into her mind. "Maybe," she whispered to herself, smiling.

Rosa looked up. "Maybe *what*, Mommy?"

"Nothing, sweetie." She smiled, then leaned back on the blanket and propped herself up to watch a young couple strolling along the water's edge a hundred yards away. They were too far away to hear what they were saying, but there was no mistaking their body language. Hand in hand, turning every so often to look at each other. They were in love.

As she watched Rosa construct the walls of her sandcastle, a tiny seed of regret rooted itself in her belly. Not for having Rosa, never that.

The person Laia was now would never marry any man just because she was pregnant. *That* woman was strong. *That* woman would have made things work and found the security and financial stability to raise her daughter on her own. And waited for love.

Did she have that with Kade?

Her heart did a little flip flop. Despite all the hurdles yet to climb, she *did* have that with him. At least, she hoped she did. With all their secrets out in the open, now they could start building a relationship, the one she'd always dreamed of having.

Raised voices drew her attention back to the couple. They'd

stopped walking and seemed to be arguing. The woman had her hands planted on her hips and the man jabbed a finger in her direction as he shouted something Laia couldn't hear. Then he grabbed the woman's shoulders and began shaking her.

Laia bolted upright just as the woman began screaming.

"Let go of me!" She struggled in the man's grasp. "Somebody, help me. *Please*!" Catching sight of Laia, she screamed again. "*Please*, help me!"

"Mommy, why are they yelling?" Rosa asked.

She rummaged in the pocket of her sundress, then in her shoulder bag, searching for her cell phone to call the police, then realized she'd left her phone on the kitchen counter. She got to her feet, looking around the beach for someone to assist, but this part of the beach truly was deserted.

"Rosa, you stay here. Do you understand me?"

"Yes, Mommy."

"I mean it." She pointed to the blanket. "Right here. You do *not* go anywhere near the water without me."

"Okay."

Leaving Rosa, even for a minute, didn't sit well, but neither did leaving a woman alone to be beaten.

She pounded over the sand, running as fast as she could. As she neared the couple, the man caught sight of her and released the woman's shoulders.

"I'm sorry," he shouted. "I didn't mean to hurt you, I swear it."

"Well, you did." The woman rubbed her shoulders.

"Are you all right?" Laia asked, breathing heavily. "Do you want me to call the police?" Without a cell phone, it was an empty threat, but the guy didn't know that.

"No!" The woman's eyes widened. "Please don't do that. But would you stay here with me for a minute?"

The guy hung his head. "I really am sorry. This won't happen again. You just made me so angry."

Laia looked at the other woman, noting her heaving chest and trembling lips. The man held out his hand. "Can we just go somewhere and talk about this?"

The woman sighed. "Fine." Then she placed her hand in his. To Laia, she said, "Thank you for rushing over, but we're fine."

Laia cast a suspicious sideways glance at the woman's companion. "Are you sure?"

She nodded. "Yes. Thank you."

Laia watched the couple walk back in the direction they'd come from. They weren't holding hands, but neither were they arguing. Just to be sure, she continued watching, not understanding how a couple could be so clearly enthralled with each other one minute then nearly coming to blows the next.

She turned and started walking back to the blanket. No matter how bad things had gotten between her and Josh, they'd never—

The temperature had to be over ninety, but Laia froze like an ice cube.

Rosa was gone. Her partially constructed sandcastle was still there, along with the beach blanket, but her daughter was nowhere in sight.

Laia's heart raced as she spun to look at the water. Surely, she would have seen Rosa in her peripheral vision if she'd gone into the surf. *No.* Rosa wouldn't have done that. Living on the Jersey shore as they had for Rosa's entire life, they'd established hard and nonnegotiable rules about swimming that her daughter had never once disobeyed. Not *once*.

She ran to the blanket, her heart pounding, then turned in every direction, sucking in deep breaths, trying to curb the rising panic. "Rosa!" she cried. "Rosa!"

When she sucked in quick breaths through her nose and mouth, she vaguely registered the lingering scent of...pizza.

Footprints in the sand and leading away from the blanket

toward the sand dunes caught her eye. Had they been there before? She couldn't be sure.

She ran to the dunes, scrambling over the top, then searching the empty road. "Rosa!" Her daughter didn't answer.

Laia climbed back over the dune to the beach and raced to the small boats stored beneath the shack. "Rosa, answer me!"

Again, she ran to the water's edge, racing up and down the shallows, searching for her daughter's body and praying she didn't find her little girl face down in the water, not breathing.

Realizing this was futile, and still not really believing Rosa would have disobeyed the cardinal rule and gone swimming alone, she raced back up the beach.

By the time she reached the stairs to the shack, her body was shaking and she felt as if she was about to throw up. She took the stairs two at a time, then flung open the door to the living room. "Rosa! Answer me, *please*!"

Footsteps pounded down the stairs, too heavy to be Rosa's. Jamie appeared at the bottom of the stairs, his hair dripping and a towel tied around his waist.

"Laia, what's wrong?"

"Rosa!" she screamed, racing past Jamie and up the stairs to her daughter's bedroom. The room was empty. "Rosa?" she cried again, searching every other room on the second floor, then returning to Rosa's room. She turned to find Jamie had followed her.

"Laia, talk to me."

As she stood there in the middle of Rosa's room, gasping for air, the horrible reality slammed home. "She's gone. Rosa is *gone*."

Chapter Twenty-Four

Kade took the final turn onto Jamie's street faster than was safe. When he hit the straightaway, he pounded his fist on the wheel.

From what Jamie had related during their brief phone conversation, the police didn't know with any certainty that Rosa had really been kidnapped, but Kade knew. Every fiber of his being *knew* Fernando Colon was behind Rosa's disappearance. Killing Josh was one thing but taking a five-year-old girl…

The man had just signed his own death warrant.

Kade cranked the wheel hard and came to a screeching stop in the driveway. Two Manasquan PD cars were parked on the street outside the shack. He hit the remote on his belt, popping open Smoke's door and not bothering to leash him. With Smoke leading the way, he raced to the door and flung it open.

In the living room, Laia ran to him, flinging herself into his arms. "Kade, she's gone," she said between sobs. "She's just…*gone*."

Every sob was a knife strike to his heart. "We'll find her. I promise."

"I don't know what h-happened," she muttered against his chest. "One minute she was there and the next..." Her voice drifted off, ending with more gut-wrenching sobs.

"Honey, look at me." When she didn't, he pulled away enough that he could tip up her chin. "We *will* find her. Do you hear me? I'll do everything in my power to find her, and I won't stop looking until I do."

Over her head, he took in Jamie's grim expression. Slipping into Army Ranger mode, he locked eyes with Jamie first, then the Manasquan sergeant. "What do we know?"

"I was in the shower when this happened." Jamie shook his head. "I'm sorry, man."

"Not your fault," Kade reassured him.

The sergeant, whose name tag said K. Malloy, looked at his pad. "Ms. Velez and her daughter were on the beach when Ms. Velez went to the aid of another woman who was being roughed up by her boyfriend. When Ms. Velez turned around, her daughter was gone."

"I searched the house, the garage, and my next-door neighbor's property," Jamie said, again shaking his head.

Kade hated what he had to ask next, but there was no getting around it. "Laia, is there any chance Rosa went into the water without you?" No matter how hard he tried not to imagine it, awful images of Rosa's little body floating somewhere out there in the ocean or sinking to the sandy bottom only to be found days later came to him.

"No!" She shook her head adamantly. "Rosa wouldn't do that, she wouldn't! We come to the beach all the time, and we have strict rules about not going in the water alone. She's a good swimmer. Besides, I would have seen her. I was standing right at the water's edge. If she had gone into the water, I would have seen her. I *would* have."

"Okay, okay." Which brought them full circle back to the only remaining possibility. Rosa really had been taken.

"Ms. Velez told us her daughter has never run off before and has no history of disappearances," Sergeant Malloy said. "We have officers searching the beach and the Coast Guard's been notified. We secured the girl's last known location for forensics to process the scene. I also have a request in for a county search dog."

"We can help with that." Kade tipped his head to Smoke. "He knows Rosa. If she's out there, he'll find her." To Laia, he said, "Tell me about that couple."

"They were arguing. I thought he was going to hit her, so I ran over to help. As soon as I got there, things seemed to have calmed down. When I turned around, that's when I couldn't find Rosa."

"What did that couple have to say? Did they see anything?" he asked Sergeant Malloy.

Malloy shook his head. "We couldn't find them."

"I looked for them, too," Jamie said. "No sign of them anywhere. I don't have any cameras facing the beach. Neither do most of my neighbors. Most cameras are aimed at the road in front of the houses."

Kade clenched his jaw. "They were a decoy."

"A *decoy*?" Laia's voice cracked. "You mean they set me up so someone could take Rosa?"

"Looks that way. Did you see where they went?"

She pressed her lips together, looking more distraught by the second. "Back down the beach in the other direction, but I didn't see where. When I ran back to the water to look for Rosa, I wasn't paying attention to anything else but finding her."

"That's okay, honey." He stroked her hair. "You were distracted. That was their intention."

Through the windows facing the beach, Kade saw half

a dozen uniformed officers combing the beach. Beyond, the kiddie carnival Ferris wheel spun round and round.

Kade looked at Jamie, then nodded to Sergeant Malloy. "Did you tell them *everything*?"

Jamie shook his head. "That's your call."

While he'd planned on keeping Laia and Rosa's location a secret from everyone, including the local PD, the plan had changed. Drastically. "We don't know for certain," he said to Malloy, "but we have reason to believe that Rosa Velez was kidnapped by Fernando Colon."

Malloy had been taking notes, but at the mention of Colon's name, his pen froze over his pad. "*The* Fernando Colon?"

"Yeah." Sonofabitch. "The only question is how he found them here."

"You want me to call in the FBI?" Malloy asked. "If it's a kidnapping, they've got jurisdiction."

Jamie pulled his phone from his belt. "I'll take care of that."

Meaning, Jamie would call Dayne Andrews, a close friend of theirs and a top-notch FBI K-9 agent. Dayne and his fiancé, billionairess Katrina Vandenburg, lived in a castle—literally—just over an hour away. All Jamie had to do was say the word, and Dayne would be here in a heartbeat.

And in the meantime, Kade was seriously contemplating his backup plan—a little unexpected visit to Colon's house. Confronting a drug lord on his own turf and accusing him of kidnapping a little girl might not be the smartest move, and his agency would probably shoot him down, calling it *way* premature without any substantial evidence pointing directly at Colon. Kade didn't give a shit.

"Run me through your department's kidnapping protocol," he ordered.

Laia groaned. "More protocol."

Kade knew that law enforcement's reaction during the first four hours of a kidnapping were crucial and could make all the difference. Every agency, whether it was the FBI, state, or local police, had implemented fairly standardized kidnapping protocol, particularly where children were involved.

Sergeant Malloy opened his mouth when a phone rang.

Laia ran to the credenza and grabbed it. Her face fell as she looked at the screen. "It's my mother. I have to talk to her. I have to tell her what happened." She took the phone into the kitchen.

"Go on," Kade said to Malloy.

"I have units out looking for witnesses and leads. An Amber Alert has been initiated. We'll also spread word locally of the girl's disappearance. Using the photo Ms. Velez provided, we'll blanket the area with flyers. I'll put out an APB on the girl." Malloy paused, frowning. "But if you really think Fernando Colon took her, that's a whole different ball game because if that's the case, we know who we're looking for. Do you have any proof that he took the girl?"

"No." Not yet, anyway. The locals wouldn't act against a drug lord with a mountain of pricy lawyers on retainer 24/7 without a boatload of evidence to back them up. For that matter, neither would the DHS.

Malloy tapped his pen on the pad. "What does he want with a five-year-old girl?"

Kade wasn't prepared to tell anyone in the Manasquan PD exactly who Laia was or her connection to Colon. All they needed to know was that Rosa was missing, and while he was 99 percent certain Colon was behind this, he still couldn't be absolutely certain Rosa hadn't been taken by someone else. Which was equally disturbing.

"If it is Colon, he doesn't want the girl," Kade snarled. "He wants something in return for her." The ledger and the cool two million in cash that Josh stole from him.

The back door at the top of the steps opened, and a young officer came in holding a plastic evidence bag containing a slice of pizza with a small bite taken out of it.

"Found this on the other side of the dune," the cop said, holding up the bag.

Laia had returned from the kitchen and gasped. "Oh God. Pineapple. It's Rosa's favorite. When I got back to where I'd left her on the beach, I could swear I smelled pizza. I thought I was imagining it. How did they *know*?"

"Good question," Kade growled. "However they found out, they obviously used it to lure her from the beach. It could have been drugged."

A strangled sound bubbled up from Laia's throat, and she covered her mouth with her hand. Kade pulled her into his arms. Her body shook as she tried valiantly to hold it together. Rage, the likes of which he'd never experienced, pounded in his head.

Keep it together. For Laia and Rosa's sake. If he lost it, he'd be no good to them.

Smoke uttered a snort, then sat, looking up at Kade, waiting for orders. Smoke was feeding off sounds, body language, and the smell of Laia's fear. He sensed something was totally off, even if he didn't know what.

"Laia," he said softly, swiping away a tear with the pad of his thumb. "I need to get out there with Smoke. If anyone can find her, he can. Will you be okay here without me? I need to know you'll be okay."

She rolled her lips inward, jerkily nodding her head. Man, he admired her guts and her game.

"Atta girl." He tried giving her an encouraging smile. "Sergeant, can you or one of your officers stay with her?" Kade didn't want her to be alone, and if she received a call from the kidnappers—whoever they were—he wanted to make sure there was a law enforcement witness.

"You got it." Malloy pointed to the cop still holding the bagged slice of pizza. "Stay here with her, and make sure forensics gets that. Good find."

"Thank you, sergeant." The cop nodded.

Before heading out to the beach with Jamie and Smoke, Kade took the phone from Laia's hand. "People will be coming soon to set your phone up with a recording device and a tracing app. In the meantime, do you know how to record a conversation on your phone?"

"Yes." She nodded.

"If you do get a call, make sure this officer—what's your name?"

"Officer Gonzalez, sir."

"If you get a call, record it, and make sure Officer Gonzalez is here to listen in."

"Okay." Again, she nodded, and her forehead creased.

Kade kissed the top of her head, trying to offer reassurances that he didn't quite feel, then went to the sofa and picked up Rosa's pink sweatshirt for Smoke to get a scent from. "I'll be back. Jamie, you're with me."

"Copy that."

Jamie followed him and Smoke down the stairs to the beach and over to the taped-off blanket, beside which were the remains of Rosa's sandcastle. Smack dab in the middle of the sandcastle was a footprint, at least a men's size ten.

About a hundred yards offshore, a small Coast Guard vessel began cruising back and forth in a crisscrossing search pattern.

She's not there. She can't be. Kade couldn't allow himself to believe that Rosa was lying at the bottom of the ocean.

"You really think he has her?" Jamie asked.

"Well, I don't believe in coincidences, that a random kidnapper just happened to grab Rosa at the very same moment Colon is so hot to get his ledger and his money back. And where did that couple go?" He swept his arm to encompass the entire beach. "They didn't just vanish into thin air. I think they hauled ass the second their job was done—creating a diversion. So yeah. I think he has her."

And they had jack to prove it. Maybe that would change. Maybe not. If that was the case, he fully planned to take matters into his own hand.

Flashing blue-and-red strobes flickered just over the top of the dunes as more units arrived. Probably the PD's forensics team. Eventually, the FBI.

As if on cue, Jamie said, "Dayne is on his way with Remy." Dayne's German shepherd K-9 was well-known for being an amazing tracker. "He reached out to the closest CARD team. They're on their way, but they were down in DC, so they'll be a few hours."

Kade didn't doubt the FBI's Child Abduction Rapid Deployment teams' abilities. Deep down in his soul, he knew their efforts would be wasted. Fernando Colon would reach out to them when he was good and ready. Until then, they'd have no choice but to play the waiting game.

He snapped on Smoke's leash so he wouldn't disturb the taped-off area, then held Rosa's sweatshirt out for his dog to sniff. Soft huffing came from Smoke's snout as he drew in her scent. "Smoke, find Rosa."

Smoke put his head to the sand, sniffing and circling. There were plenty of other footprints in the sand, including those from himself, Jamie, and Deck from when they were all body surfing the other day. Narcotics was Smoke's specialty, but Kade was counting on the strong bond Rosa had forged with his dog.

After more circling and sniffing, Smoke picked up a track and led Kade and Jamie to a break in the dunes that opened to Stockton Beach Park. Smoke led them into the park where at least a dozen people were playing ball on the two baseball fields.

Smoke continued directly to the parking lot, which was mostly empty. He sniffed the ground then pulled Kade to an empty parking spot near the dunes. His dog circled again, always coming back to the same spot.

Kade's grip on the leash tightened, as did the pain in his chest. "She was here."

"No cameras facing inside the park but look." Jamie pointed to a pole at the edge of the dune. "A surf cam."

Pointed directly at the beach and in the general vicinity of where Laia and Rosa had been.

"I'll get with Sergeant Malloy and download the footage." Jamie started running back to the shack.

"C'mon, Smoke." Kade headed to the baseball fields. "Let's go meet some people."

Twenty minutes later, he'd interviewed every single man, woman, and child in the park. One kid vaguely recalled seeing two men walking with a little girl to a silver or gray car.

When Kade showed the kid a photo of Rosa on his phone, the boy couldn't say with any certainty if it was her he saw getting into the car.

His phone buzzed with an incoming call from Jamie. "What have you got?" Please, *please* let it be a neighbor saying they found Rosa wandering around or playing in their yard or—

"Haul ass back here," Jamie said in a hushed voice. "Laia just got the call."

Chapter Twenty-Five

"I want to talk to my daughter." Laia's belly quivered. Her panic had risen to hysteria. If it weren't for Jamie, she would have completely forgotten to hit the record button. She held her cell phone tighter to keep her hand from shaking, but it didn't work. "Put Rosa on the phone. I want to hear her voice."

"What *you* want is irrelevant," a computer-generated voice said. "Listen carefully. We want the book and we want the money. When we have them, you'll get your daughter back. Don't call the police. If you do, we'll kill her. Don't call the FBI. If you do, we'll kill her."

Laia's head nearly exploded. "Don't you *dare* hurt my baby. I'll give you anything you want. *Anything. Please* don't hurt her. She's only a child. She hasn't done anything to you."

The front door opened, then closed. A moment later, Smoke trotted into the living room. Then Kade was there, a large, reassuring presence by her side.

Jamie rotated his finger in the air, a silent message to keep the guy on the phone talking. Kade grabbed the pad and pen in Sergeant Malloy's hands and began scribbling something.

"Do exactly what I say, and you'll get your daughter back," the voice said.

Kade shoved the pad in front of her face.

Tell them you won't cooperate until you hear Rosa's voice. Be strong.

He was right. If she lost control, she might say the wrong thing. "I won't give you anything until you let me talk to my daughter." Her demand was met with a moment of silence, one that stretched into seconds so agonizing she had to roll her lips inward or scream. "Did you hear me?"

Shuffling sounds came through the speaker, then, "Mommy?"

"Oh, thank God." The relief coursing through her was so overwhelming she nearly passed out. Kade's arm around her shoulders was the only thing keeping her vertical. "Rosa? Sweetheart, it's Mommy. Are you all right? Tell me you're all right."

"I'm okay," came the sleepy, sweet little voice she'd recognize anywhere. "They gave me pizza. Pineapple, my favorite."

Laia looked at the plastic evidence bag the young cop had put on the credenza. "I know." *Bastards.* Again, begging the question: how had they known?

Again, Kade shoved the pad in front of her.

Keep Rosa talking.

"I'm coming to get you, baby. Be brave for me. Can you do—"

"That's enough," the computer voice said.

"I'll give you the book *and* the money," Laia cried. "Tell me where to bring them."

"We'll call you back tomorrow with a time and place. Remember what I said. No police, or she dies. No FBI, or she dies."

"No, wait!" But the call had ended.

Laia vacillated between numbness and a total and complete meltdown. She stared at the screen. This phone was the only lifeline to her daughter.

Kade took the phone from her trembling hand and touched his finger to the screen. "No caller ID." To Laia, he said softly, "You did good."

"*Good?*" she shrieked, jerking her phone back and pointing to it. "This is not *good*. This is anything *but* good. This is…"

A nightmare that could not *be happening. But it was.*

Vaguely, she registered Kade's arms coming around her, holding her tightly against his chest while her body began shaking violently first, then wracked with uncontrollable sobs.

"We'll get her back," he said firmly. "We *will* get her back."

She pushed away and sniffled, wiping the tears from her face. "Of *course*, we will. They said 'no police' and 'no FBI,' so all we have to do is get the ledger from the evidence room and the money from the bank box. As soon as they call me back with the time and place, I'll bring it to them, and they'll give me Rosa."

Kade's expression was grim. She turned to find Jamie with the same foreboding look. The two men were speaking to each other, communicating silently in some language only the two of them understood.

"What?" She grabbed Kade's arm. "*What* aren't you telling me?"

"Sweetheart." He touched two fingers to her cheek. "It's not that simple."

"Yes, it is." She swatted his hand away, not understanding why they weren't already halfway to the DHS office to retrieve the ledger and the key to the safe deposit box.

His jaw went hard. "We can't just hand over the ledger."

She shook her head, her disbelief growing by the second. "Why not?"

"It's original evidence," he said.

"Then make a copy, and give me the original."

He shook his head. "With Josh gone, there's no one to authenticate a copy. Even if we verify it's his handwriting, the AUSA will still demand we retain the original."

"Then can't you just go and arrest Fernando Colon? You *know* he's the one who took my daughter—your niece, by the way, in case you forgot."

"Laia," he said, stroking his hands up and down her arms in what was meant to be a consoling gesture, but which only enraged her further, "we don't actually have any evidence against Colon. Whoever made that call was careful not to use the word 'ledger,' and there's no solid evidence he's behind this."

"Are you *kidding*?" He had to be. Didn't he? "We *all* know he took Rosa. All we have to do is give him what he wants."

"Once we do that"—Kade's throat worked as he swallowed—"they'll kill her."

"You don't know that." She clenched her hands, welcoming the pain as her nails bit into her skin. "The only thing we know for certain is that they'll kill her if I *don't* give them what they want, and they'll kill her if we involve more feds and police."

"I know you don't want to hear this," Kade said as he tried clasping her shoulders, but she skirted away from his reach. "The only leverage we have over them is the ledger and the money. There's standard protocol to be followed in all kidnapping investigations. The key is to let the police, forensics, and the FBI help us find her. In the meantime, we come up with a plan to handle this when we *do* find her."

"*Protocol?*" Her jaw dropped. "Is that what you were following when you arrested Josh? *Protocol?* Look where that got him. *Dead.*"

It had been a low blow, but she couldn't help it. She was angry, distraught, and more scared than she'd ever been in her life.

"Laia." Again, he reached for her, and again, she backed away.

"No." She shook her head. "Just give me the ledger and the bank box key and I'll go get my daughter myself."

"I can't do that."

She parked her fists on her hips and glared up at him. "*Can't?* Or *won't?*"

He ground his sculpted jaw so hard she could practically hear his teeth squeak. "You have to trust me to find another way. First, I need to make some calls. To the prosecutor, to Manny Dominguez, we need to put together a plan that won't get Rosa hurt or..."

Killed was the word he didn't say again, and they both knew it. "Can't you just wire me up or whatever it is you do for undercover cops, then follow me to where Rosa is?"

"I'm not putting you in danger like that."

"That's *my* decision to make, *not* yours. Rosa comes first. If anything happens to her, my life is meaningless." And it was. Rosa was her entire life. She'd once hoped *Kade* would be part of her life, too, but that hope seemed to be slipping away by the second.

"No," he snapped. "We'll find another way. I know you want to rush out there and go get her, but the second he sees you, he'll take what he wants and kill you both." This time, he did manage to grab onto her forearms. "Please, Laia. Stand down and let me do my job. You have to trust me."

She stared into the depths of Kade's beautiful hazel eyes. At first, she'd taken comfort in him doing everything by the book. She understood it was his full nature, but now it was getting in the way.

Her stomach lurched, only a little at first, then it intensified into violent waves. She clapped a hand to her mouth, then ran past Jamie and Sergeant Malloy, directly to the powder room.

Barely making it in time, she slammed the door shut behind her, flipped up the toilet lid, then dropped to her knees and threw up. With her stomach nearly empty, not much came out, although her body shuddered with dry heaves.

The phone slipped from her hand and hit the tile with a thud. Tears streamed down her cheeks. Her baby was in the hands of a vicious drug dealer, one who'd already murdered her husband. Now he held the life of her precious daughter in his filthy, homicidal hands.

Sonofabitch! I will not let my baby die. I will not.

Slowly, she got to her feet, then washed her hands and splashed cold water on her face. For a long moment, she stared at her reflection in the mirror.

Her life was never supposed to turn out this way. Marrying Josh was supposed to make life easier. For her *and* her unborn child. Instead, it had only made things worse.

Laia dried her hands and face with a towel, then squeezed her eyes shut. Josh had given her Rosa, then turned her life into a soap opera that was still unfolding in horrific ways she'd never imagined possible. Would his secrets and betrayal never end?

For nearly six years, her entire life had been centered around Rosa. Falling in love had never been an option. In fact, she'd nearly given up on it. Then Kade had come back into her life, and she'd stupidly begun to hope that she could actually have the love she'd always dreamed of and that he would become part of hers and Rosa's lives. Now she knew that wasn't possible.

Last night, when they'd made love in the ocean, Kade had

said he'd do anything for her and Rosa. *Anything.* Apparently, that wasn't true. He couldn't break with his precious protocol to save his own niece. First Josh. Now Rosa. Duty, honor, and obligation came first for him, even before family.

A cry rose from the depths of her soul, and she clapped a hand over her mouth to stifle the sound. When she'd managed to get a grip on her emotions, she cracked the door open.

"Dayne is on his way with the FBI CARD team," Jamie said.

She couldn't see Jamie or Kade, just heard their voices. Only Sergeant Malloy was visible, standing in front of the picture window facing the ocean.

"Thanks. It's a start, but I honestly don't know if there's a way to find her," Kade said in a choked voice. "I'm calling Deck, Brett, and Evan. They're on shift right now, but if they can be here, they will be."

Laia couldn't believe the words she'd just overheard. She flung open the door and bore down on Kade. "What do you mean, you don't know if there's a way to find her? There *is* a way, but *you* won't do it. I've been patient, but you just keep going in circles around your precious 'book.' Every minute my daughter is out there, she's in even more danger. Tell me you'll keep your promise. *Tell* me you will get my daughter back. *Promise* me!"

Kade ground his jaw but remained silent, telling her all she needed to know. He wasn't answering her because he couldn't make promises that he felt he could no longer keep.

The ugly truth crashed over her. The Sampson brothers had been the best *and* the worst things to ever happen to her. She'd relied too much on both of them. Again, she fled to the powder room, slamming the door shut behind her.

"Laia," a deep voice—Kade's—came from the other side of the door. "Are you all right?"

Am I all right? Until she had Rosa back in her arms, she'd never be all right.

"Just leave me alone," she called out. Taking a deep breath, she stared once more at her reflection. No longer was she the same person she'd been six years ago. This woman was strong, independent. *This* woman didn't need the Sampson brothers.

A plan materialized in her head, and she knew what she had to do.

Laia picked up her phone, the only connection she had left to her daughter. She stuffed it in the pocket of her sundress, then opened the door. Kade was no longer there. She was about to leave the powder room when the doorbell rang, and Sergeant Malloy started walking through the living room, heading toward her.

Gently, trying not to call attention to herself, Laia pulled the powder room door closed, leaving it open just enough to see into the hallway. She heard the front door open. Voices and more footsteps filtered through as people came into the house. She didn't know if it was more police, forensic technicians, or the FBI. Half a dozen people, some wearing suits and carrying black plastic cases, walked past the powder room.

With her heart racing, she slipped out, then tiptoed quietly and quickly to the front door. Her purse sat on the small table in the hallway, and she threw it over her shoulder. A moment later, she was outside and down the steps.

As she speed-walked to the road, she glanced at the many police cars and dark sedans lining Second Avenue. Trying not to look suspicious, she nodded to one officer who stood by her patrol car, a cell phone pressed to her ear.

Her plan might not work, but she couldn't sit around on her ass and wait around a minute longer. If she died trying to get her daughter back, so be it. At least she'd die trying.

Chapter Twenty-Six

"She's gone." Sergeant Malloy was the last one to check in.

Kade swallowed every colorful expletive on the tip of his tongue, which meant he was about to choke on them.

They'd searched the entire house, garage, and adjacent beach, and no one could find Laia. She wasn't thinking clearly. Her daughter had been kidnapped, and he'd messed this whole thing up as royally as any human being possibly could have by driving her away. Now he worried for her just as much as for Rosa. In her irrational, grieved state, who knew what Laia would do.

Knowing she'd taken her phone with her, he tried calling her for the third time. When it went to voicemail, he left another message. After stuffing his phone back in his pocket, he let loose with some of those expletives he'd been holding in check.

The only thing keeping him grounded was Smoke, who'd sidled up to him and pressed his big head against his thigh, forcing him to reach down and pet his dog's head. The second his fingers touched the long, soft fur, an eerie calm settled around him.

Jamie came through the front door, watching and waiting, Kade knew, for whatever plan he came up with. No sense wasting time over what he *didn't* know, namely Rosa's location, so he focused on what he *did* know.

The long-distance video footage from the camera facing the beach showed two men walking with Rosa toward the dunes. Laia didn't have the ledger or the money, nor did she have any way of getting them. The ledger was secure in the evidence locker, along with the safe deposit box key. What she *did* have was her phone. Colon's goons would call her again, and when they did, Kade needed to be there to make sure she didn't do something stupid. Like go after Rosa alone.

To Malloy, he ordered, "Put out an APB on Laia Velez. If anyone finds her, take her into protective custody. She'll fight you. Do it anyway, then call me." To Jamie, he said, "Let's roll."

Kade and Smoke hopped into Kade's SUV, while Jamie followed in his black Interceptor. As soon as they hit the main drag in town, Kade punched it, heading north to Asbury Park and Laia's house. If she was even there. The way she'd snuck out of the shack told him she didn't want to be found. Not by him. He had no idea what he'd say to her at this point. What if he *couldn't* get Rosa back?

Don't even think it.

Words from one of his instructors at West Point came to mind.

Failure is nothing but the non-existence of success. Fiasco, on the other hand, is a failure of huge proportions.

By arresting Josh, perhaps he'd failed his brother as a human being and with the direst of consequences. No way would he make that mistake again.

He zigzagged through traffic, not bothering to check behind him to verify Jamie was there. His friend was a natural phenomenon behind the wheel. If Jamie had gone the NASCAR route, he'd have broken every record in the books.

Kade grabbed his phone and cued up Manny Dominguez, whom he'd called earlier to let him know about Rosa's kidnapping and to request the AUSA get them a search warrant for Colon's mother's house.

"I've got bad news," Manny began. "The AUSA says no dice. Unless you've got rock-solid proof that Fernando Colon had something to do with the girl's kidnapping, the U.S. Attorney won't authorize any warrants. They don't want to go up against Colon and his lawyers again without incontrovertible evidence."

"You're kidding." Kade pressed his lips together. He'd been sure that where a missing child was involved, the U.S. Attorney's Office would relax their standard of proof enough to get them a warrant.

"Wish I was, man. But hey, we should have the warrant for that bank box by mid-morning tomorrow."

Well, that was something. Kade only hoped it wouldn't be too little too late.

Smoke stuck his head through the kennel window, whining as he landed a few licks on the side of Kade's face. His dog didn't have to understand English to know Kade was royally pissed.

"Call every one of your informants. Tell them there's a $10,000 reward for any information leading to the safe return of Rosa Velez."

"I need to get that kind of cash approved, first."

"The money's coming from *my* pocket, so just do it!" A little girl's life was at stake, and every prosecutor in the U.S. Attorney's Office was too scared of Colon and his army of lawyers to do what had to be done. "While you're at it, run a FinCen check on Laia. Find out what credit cards she's got, then track them. If she makes any new purchases, call me with the location."

"You got it."

Kade ended the call as he came to a screeching stop in front of Laia's house. Since her Ford Escape was still locked in his garage in North Plainfield, she had no mode of transportation of her own. Chances were, she'd gotten an Uber or a Lift the second she'd slipped out of the shack. If she wasn't here, he'd initiate a track on her phone.

As Kade and Smoke charged up the walkway to Laia's side of the duplex, Jamie fell in step behind them. He tried the knob, but the door was locked. He didn't really think she was inside, but he pounded on the door anyway. "Laia! Open up."

"She's not there."

He whipped his head around to find Alvita standing just inside the duplex's other door. "Do you know where she is?"

Alvita shook her head. "No, but you just missed her. She asked to borrow my minivan for a day or two, then took off. I'm on vacation for the rest of the week, so I said 'sure.'"

Kade narrowed his eyes on the other woman. Why would Laia come back to the house only to leave again? "Do you know what she did inside the house? Did she take anything from inside?"

"She changed clothes," Alvita said, looking confused. "And she had a small suitcase with her when she left."

Then wherever she was going, she didn't plan on coming back soon. "Do you know where she went?"

"No. She looked upset, and when I asked her what was wrong, all she said was that she had a family emergency."

Kade tugged his creds from his back pocket, then pulled out a business card and handed it to her. "If you see or hear from her, call me right away."

She took the card, and a look of worry filled her eyes. "Is she in trouble? Is Rosa okay?"

"What's your license plate?"

She recited the tag. Before he'd even finished jotting the number onto another business card, he, Smoke, and Jamie were already halfway down the steps. "Just let me know if you hear from her," he threw over his shoulder. "It's important."

Great. Now Laia had wheels and could be anywhere.

He handed the business card with Alvita's tag written on it to Jamie. "Get Sergeant Malloy to add this to the APB out on Laia. And follow me."

"Where to next?"

Kade jerked open the door. He couldn't believe what he was about to do—bust through a thick wall of DHS protocol *without* authorization. "Fernando Colon's. We need to have a little chat."

...

Laia pushed through the heavy glass door at the Regional Bank & Trust, pulling the rolling suitcase she'd retrieved at her house behind her. She cast a wary glance at all the security cameras angled toward the door. What she was about to do was beyond illegal.

And she didn't give a crap.

Luckily, Li-Mei was in today. Laia could see her friend sitting at her usual desk. At her approach, the other woman looked up and smiled.

"Laia! It's good to see you again. Are you here to get into your box?"

"I am." She forced a smile, doing her best to hide the bevy of emotions churning inside her. Her hands were sweating buckets as it was. "But I have a bit of a problem." She sat in one of the chairs facing Li-Mei.

"Oh?" Li-Mei's brows rose.

"Yes." She cleared her throat. "You see, I've lost my key

to the box. Both of them, actually. But I'm willing to pay the drilling fee," she added quickly.

The one downside to her plan was that for every bank's safe deposit box, two keys were needed, and the keys weren't the same. The bank had a master key, while whoever rented the box was given two identical renter keys. For security, there were no other copies, and no reputable locksmith would ever make a copy of a bank box key. If both renter keys were lost, the only way to get into the box was to drill through the outer door at the renter's expense. Where Josh had stashed the spare key was anyone's guess.

Li-Mei looked at her watch. "Let me make a couple of calls."

Laia tugged her phone from her pocket to check the time. It was already three p.m. The chances of getting a locksmith on site today were slim to none, but she'd had to try.

She'd received no other calls from the kidnappers, just three from Kade, all of which she'd ignored. She swiped to delete the notifications of his calls and the voicemail messages he'd left for her. Listening to his voice would be enough to undermine her resolve. Talking to him would only shred her heart that much more.

She stuffed the phone back into the pocket of her capris, double-checking to make sure she hadn't inadvertently put it on vibrate. The only call she didn't want to miss was the one telling her where and when to bring the ledger and money.

Li-Mei sighed as she hung up the phone on her desk. "As I suspected, our contract locksmith won't be able to get here until tomorrow morning at the earliest, but he said he'd be here when the door opens. Can you come back tomorrow at nine? You can pay the fee then."

Again, Laia smiled. "Thank you, Li-Mei, and I'm sorry to put you to this trouble."

Li-Mei made a pooh-poohing gesture. "No worries. You

used to work here, so you know people lose these keys all the time."

"True," Laia agreed, standing. "I'm just so embarrassed because I *do* know that. I should have been more careful. I'll see you first thing in the morning."

"I'll be here. Right where I always am, in the lap of luxury."

With one final wave goodbye, Laia dragged her suitcase through the bank and out the door to Alvita's minivan.

Knowing how banks worked and given the time of day, the delay in her plan had pretty much been a foregone conclusion. But the night wouldn't go to waste.

She put the suitcase in the back of the minivan, then started the engine. Rather than driving off, she sat there a moment longer, wondering if she was stupid to try and do this alone. She wasn't a cop, wasn't a federal agent, and had zero hands-on experience dealing with homicidal, kidnapping drug cartels.

Shutting her eyes, she let her head fall back against the headrest. Behind her closed lids, Kade's handsome, worried face appeared, then just as quickly vanished. The urge to call him was a constant, nagging drumbeat in her head and worse…in her heart. But he'd shown his true colors—red, white, and military blue. Duty first and always, no matter the cost. The new-and-improved Laia would have to do this on her own.

With renewed resolve, she cranked the minivan's gearshift into drive and headed from the parking lot. When she was about to turn onto the road, a police car drove slowly past. She flicked the sun visor down, hoping it concealed her face.

Kade would try to find her. He knew she didn't have her Escape, but he'd go to the duplex, and when she wasn't there, he'd go next door to Alvita's. Her friend would tell him she'd borrowed the minivan. He'd stop at nothing to find her and keep her from going after Rosa alone. He'd—

My phone! How many cop movies had she watched in which people were tracked via their cell phones?

She glanced in her rearview mirror, checking to see if anyone was behind her. When she'd confirmed there wasn't, she shifted into reverse and backed into the same parking spot she'd been in.

With shaking hands, she removed the battery from her phone. The kidnappers said they wouldn't call until tomorrow. She could always turn her phone back on periodically to check for messages, just in case.

With her cell phone deactivated, her heart rate began to slow. Once again, she headed from the parking lot, looking left and right for more police cars. She prayed Kade and Manny didn't get the warrant for the bank box before she had the chance to empty it out.

She drove to a store she'd been to many times for office supplies. In truth, she had no idea what was in the box, but it stood to reason there was money inside. At least, she hoped there was. Because Rosa's life depended on that money.

Now to put the rest of her plan in motion.

Chapter Twenty-Seven

Kade parked in front of Cecelia Colon's house on Tyler Street in Trenton. Jamie pulled up behind him. Since Fernando Colon's compound had been seized years ago, this was the address of record he'd given when he was paroled two weeks ago. There were no vehicles parked in the immediate vicinity of the house.

That didn't mean Colon wasn't inside.

Like many of the old homes in New Jersey's capitol, the house was barely twenty feet wide and typical of Trenton's historic "skinny" homes. *Unlike* the other similar brick houses on the street, Cecelia Colon's had clapboard siding painted sky-blue with white trim and was the only house on the block—or within a square mile, most likely—that had white flowerpots brimming with red flowers flanking the front door, a black wrought iron and wood bench in the front yard, and a satellite dish attached to the siding. The tiny plot was also the only one with grass that wasn't dead.

Cecelia Colon's house was an oasis inside one of the most dangerous cities in the country. If the place had belonged to anyone other than the mother of New Jersey's most powerful drug lord, the flowerpots, bench, and dish would have been stolen long ago. A reminder of just how much influence and authority Fernando Colon had in the Garden State.

Before getting out of the SUV, Kade grabbed a handheld radio and shoved his phone in his back pocket. "Stay," he ordered Smoke, who'd been pacing in the kennel and now sat with a disappointed huff.

Jamie met him on the sidewalk. "This ought to be interesting."

"True that."

"What's the plan if he's not here?" Jamie asked.

During the forty-minute drive from Asbury Park to Trenton, Kade had given that possibility considerable thought.

Every law enforcement officer in the State of New Jersey knew how much Colon loved his mother. Word on the street was that when he'd tried to get her to move into his lavish compound, she'd refused. Her husband might be long dead, but Cecelia Colon would always be a cop's wife. She'd never condoned the life of crime her son had chosen. Nor would she ever provide any evidence against him.

"Then we'll talk to mommy dearest."

"You know if word gets back to your agency, you'll catch a lot of flack for this," Jamie warned.

"Yeah, no kidding." Accusing Colon face to face of kidnapping a little girl when he didn't have any proof other than gut instinct wouldn't go over well with his bosses. Approaching the guy's mother for information was about half a peg down from that on the how-to-get-your-ass-fired list. But he'd do anything to get Rosa back.

Including preying on a mother's love for her child.

As they walked to the house, Kade pointed to the camera attached to the lowest bracket on the satellite dish. Colon had no doubt installed that to keep his mother safe and to send a message to anyone stupid enough to trespass: *mess with my mother and you won't live to see the next sunrise.*

Kade knocked on the door while Jamie stood on the grass by the bottom step, looking up and down the street. In his peripheral vision, he caught the curtain at one of the ground-floor windows moving.

Someone was inside.

A few seconds later, a sharp click filtered through door as a deadbolt was thrown. Slowly, the door cracked open, although a brass security chain remained in place. A woman in her mid-sixties, about five-four, and with gray hair and gray eyes peered at him warily over the security chain. Kade recognized her.

Cecelia Colon. The mother of the man who murdered his brother.

"Ma'am." Kade held up his federal ID. "I'm Officer Sampson with the Department of Homeland Security. That's my partner." He nodded to Jamie, who still guarded Kade's six. "Sergeant Pataglio with the Port Authority. Is your son, Fernando, here?"

Cecelia made a *hmpfing* sound. "I figured you were police, and no. Fernando isn't here. I'm sorry, I can't help you." She began closing the door.

Kade stuck his foot in the space between the door and the jamb, preventing her from shutting it in his face. Her eyes flared with alarm. "Please, ma'am, wait. This is about a missing child, and you may be able to help."

The woman's gray eyes narrowed, but she didn't try closing the door again. "You came here asking for my son. How is it you think *I* can help?"

There was no beating around the bush. "A little girl has been kidnapped. I have reason to believe your son took her. If we can't find her, I think he'll kill her." Just saying the words made his blood run cold.

Cecelia's eyes widened again, but not from fear. When her lips pressed together, Kade expected her to tell him to pound sand, but she didn't. Nor did she tell him he was out of his mind and that her son wasn't capable of such a horrific crime. Meaning, she fully believed Fernando Colon *was* capable of kidnapping a child.

"Please," he added. "I'm not wrong about this. May we come in?" Taking a chance, he removed his boot from the threshold, then held his breath. He was giving her the opportunity to slam the door in his face.

Again, her lips pressed together, forming a thin, tight line.

The door closed. Kade hung his head and exhaled a frustrated breath. Coming here in the first place had been a Hail Mary. He hadn't really expected to get anywhere. He looked at Jamie and gave a quick shake of his head, but as he turned to leave, another sound stopped him—the soft rasp of metal sliding on metal.

The sound of the security chain being slid along its track. And opened.

Cecelia held out her hand, beckoning them inside. Quickly, he exchanged glances with Jamie, who hustled to join him. Kade hadn't really thought they'd get their feet in the door, but here they were. Walking inside the house Fernando Colon had grown up in.

"Thank you," Kade said as he went in.

"Ma'am," Jamie said as he followed.

They waited for Cecelia to close the door. She didn't bother reengaging the security chain and deadbolt. Guess she figured with two armed officers in her house, she was safe enough.

"This way." She led them down a narrow hallway, the walls of which were lined with framed photographs. The distinct smells of garlic and herbs permeated the air.

Cecelia walked slowly enough for Kade and Jamie to identify and catalogue as much information as possible.

There was a wedding photo of a younger Cecelia and her late husband. Family photos, including those of Fernando Colon as a boy with her other children, a younger son and daughter. Kade stared alternately at two photos in particular. A New Jersey State Police sergeant receiving a medal of honor. The next image was of the same man posing with a young boy—Fernando Colon.

"My husband, Miguel." Cecelia said, stopping to look at the photo. There was no hiding the pain in her voice.

"He was a legend in the state police," Kade said. He'd read that the man's UC exploits had been responsible for more narco busts than any other undercover in that agency.

"He's *still* a legend." Cecelia placed her hand over her heart. "Here. Always." She smiled, but there was an undeniable aura of sadness and loss in her expression. "Life didn't turn out the way either of us expected."

Join the club.

In that moment, Kade understood what she was silently telling him. Never in a million years would she or her husband have dreamed that their son would turn into a vicious criminal.

"I'm sorry for your loss," he said, his own heart aching for his brother and for the pain and suffering Laia had experienced and was *still* going through, not knowing whether she'd ever see Rosa again. "It's never easy to lose those we love."

Cecelia cocked her head. Gray eyes pinned him. "Spoken as if you, too, have experienced great loss."

"I have," he admitted, doing his best not to think about the additional losses that could very well be in his future.

Jamie sniffed. "Is that homemade marinara I smell?"

"Yes." Cecelia's face brightened. "Come. Have early supper with me. The pasta should be ready by now."

Jamie flashed the woman his trademark killer smile, one Kade hadn't seen since Jamie had returned from wherever he'd been for the last six months. "We'd be honored."

In truth, Kade was starving, but food was the last thing he wanted. Time was of the essence. Even though he knew who'd kidnapped Rosa, every hour that passed would make it more difficult to find her.

They followed her into the kitchen.

"Sit." She pointed to an old, scratched wood table in the corner.

When he and Jamie were seated, Kade tapped the fingers of one hand on his thigh. Getting straight to the point was more his style, but he understood that both he and Jamie had just established a fragile rapport with the woman who, Kade recalled from investigative reports, was actually of Italian descent, not Hispanic. Hospitality and food were at the core of her culture.

"My mother still makes homemade gravy for me every time I visit her." Jamie patted his stomach. "But it's been a while, and I'm looking forward to a good meal."

Over her shoulder, Cecelia smiled, then turned back to strain the pasta. She began dishing up plates of spaghetti piled high with "gravy," as Jamie had called it, and topped with sausage, meatballs, and some kind of rolled meat Kade couldn't identify.

"Ah, braciola." Again, Jamie flashed that grin he'd used to warm the hearts of women for as long as Kade had known him. "I haven't had good braciola since the last time I was home."

Man, Jamie was laying it on thick, but clearly, Cecelia was enjoying the praise. Getting—and *keeping*—her on their good side was all that mattered.

She put the plates on the table, followed by garlic bread and salad. Kade forced down the food and after ten minutes of eating was stuffed to the gills.

"That was delicious, Mrs. Colon. Thank you." Kade set down his fork. Interrogating the woman was what he should do, but she needed to be handled gently and with due deference to who she was.

A dead cop's wife. A family member of the thin blue line.

"Awesome, Mrs. C." Jamie grabbed another bite of garlic bread and bit into it.

Along with his driving skills, Jamie was known for having the innate ability to gain peoples' trust. That's what made him such a good undercover, which, Kade suspected, was what he'd been doing while he'd been MIA.

"Thank you. Call me Cecelia," she added, dabbing at her mouth with a napkin, then setting the napkin back on her lap. "Now, what is it that you think I can do to help you?"

Finally.

"What I'm going to tell you won't be easy to hear," Kade began.

"Son." She rested her hand on his shoulder. "I was married to a man who arrested criminals for a living. Criminals like my son. I will love Fernando until the day they bury me, but don't ever think that I don't know exactly who and *what* he is. It's highly unlikely you could say anything that would shock me."

Kade wasn't so sure about that. "The child is my niece, Rosa. She's the daughter of Josh Sampson, your son's former bookkeeper. And my brother," he added, then waited for that information to sink in.

Cecelia steepled her hands, her gray brows lowering. "The newspapers speculated that Fernando murdered your brother. He was never charged with that crime."

"No, he wasn't." With all the layers between Colon and

Josh, he probably never would be. Kade had been nothing but honest with Cecelia. That's what had gotten him and Jamie into the house in the first place, so he went with it. "I believe your son had my brother killed in prison so he couldn't testify against him. I can't lose—" His throat threatened to close up on him. "I can't lose another family member."

"If what you're saying is true, then Fernando wants something in exchange for the girl. Something *you* have."

Kade nodded.

"If you're right, and you find the girl, then my son will go to jail again." Cecelia blinked rapidly. "He was released from prison two weeks ago. If he goes back there, I'll probably lose him forever."

Kade appreciated Cecelia's impending loss, but what he had to say next was necessary. "And if I don't find Rosa, there's another woman out there who will lose her child forever."

There it was. They were at an impasse. If she dimed-out her son, he'd likely get put away for another twenty years. If she refused to help, Rosa would likely die. Perhaps Laia, too, if he couldn't get to her before she went after Rosa on her own.

"Do you know where Fernando is?" he asked softly, knowing just how thin the ice he was standing on actually was. "Cecelia, if you know where he is, please tell us." Going with the honesty thing, he added, "Bringing Rosa home safely is my goal, but I can't lie to you. I *will* arrest your son. There's no getting around that."

"I appreciate your honesty." A single tear leaked from each of Cecelia's eyes, and she picked up her napkin to wipe them away. "Now please leave."

He blew out a breath of disappointment, then pushed back his chair. He stood and pulled out one of his business cards. Handing it to her, he said, "If you change your mind…

if you can find out where he's holding my niece, please call me." When she didn't accept the card, he set it on the table next to her plate. "We'll let ourselves out."

The second Kade made it to his SUV, he pounded on the hood, eliciting a startled snort from Smoke. "Dammit! I thought we were getting through to her."

Jamie rested a hand on Kade's shoulder. "You *did* get through to her."

"Yeah," he growled. "Just not enough."

His phone vibrated with an incoming call, and he grabbed it from his pocket. "Dayne, what've you got?"

"Not much, unfortunately." Kade heard the frustration in his friend's voice. "We're still canvassing the neighborhood, but there are no witnesses. The PD's printing out flyers as we speak. The CARD team can't go up on Laia's phone without the phone, and that's a bust, too. We tried working with the cell carrier to track the phone, but there's no signal to track."

"She must have taken out the battery."

"That's what we're thinking, too. Until she turns it back on, we can't find her. Unless a patrol car spots that minivan, she's in the wind."

Kade let his head fall back. It felt as if it weighed a hundred pounds. If they didn't get a break and soon, Rosa *and* Laia would be lost to him. "Run a search on all of Colon's properties. Most of them were seized. Let me know if there's anything else listed for him besides his mother's house."

"Will do."

Kade cued up one of his informants. Someone had to know something. Even in criminal networks, gossip ran like molasses on a hot day. "Chico," he said when the man answered. "Have you heard anything about Colon kidnapping a little girl?"

"No, man. Nothing."

"You sure?"

"Yeah. Something like that, I woulda heard."

"Call me if you do."

Kade hung up. Everyone was doing everything possible that could be done, and it still wasn't enough. He stared through the windshield, analyzing the basic tenets of his entire life in a matter of seconds.

As a kid, he'd played by the rules, never once cheating and always being fair. In the military, he'd followed orders to the letter, something he'd continued straight into his law enforcement career. This strict adherence to policy had been so ingrained in him, he'd never imagined doing otherwise. Until now. Because there was only one option left.

For what he was about to do, he could lose his job. His career would be toast. If things went totally south, he could go to jail. If he lost Laia and Rosa, none of that would matter.

The time for playing by the rules—duty, honor, and all the red tape that went with it—was over.

He unlocked the SUV and yanked open the door.

"Wait." Jamie stepped in his way. "Where you headed, buddy?"

"The DHS office. I gotta get something." He made another move to get in, but Jamie didn't budge, telling Kade that Jamie knew exactly what was about to go down.

"You *sure* you want to do this?"

"More sure than I've been about anything in my entire life."

Jamie barked out a laugh. "We always knew you were in love with Laia."

"Yeah, well…" And this time, he *would* do anything for her.

Even if it killed him.

"In that case," Jamie said, heading to his vehicle, "I've got your back."

Chapter Twenty-Eight

Laia walked out of the office supply store, clutching the brown-and-black leather ledger book and other items she'd purchased tightly to her chest. From what she remembered of the one Kade had pulled from the hidden compartment in Rosa's dinghy, it was approximately the same size, shape, and color.

She continued into the parking lot, darting her gaze back and forth, looking for anyone watching her. Including the police.

Knowing Kade would keep trying to find her, she'd intentionally parked in the lot next door. If she saw anyone waiting for her, she'd have to abandon the minivan and rent a car, but then she'd have to use a credit card, creating a trail. Luckily, she'd had enough cash in her wallet to pay for the new ledger and fill up the minivan with gas.

She stepped over the concrete divider separating the parking lots of the two stores and headed to the minivan. Just before she would have opened the driver's side door, a young man walked toward her. When he began taking something from his pocket, she tensed, preparing to run. But the man kept walking past, then got into a pickup truck and drove away.

With her heart threatening to beat its way right out of her chest, Laia quickly got into the minivan and drove from the lot.

All she had to do now was find a place to stay for the night. A hotel would require her to show ID, and that was a chance she couldn't take.

She turned off the main road, meandering down the side streets, searching for just the right place that was close enough to the bank that she could quickly get there when it reopened in the morning.

Remembering what Kade had said about parking somewhere that didn't have a night crew on staff, she continued driving until she found what she was looking for, a recycling center just off Route 18. The front parking lot was empty. She drove around the side of the building, then turned into the rear lot. The only vehicles there were heavy-duty collection trucks. No personal vehicles that she could see.

She backed into a narrow spot in between two of the trucks parked against the side of the building and directly in front of a large, corrugated metal door at the loading bay. With her back to the wall, and the tall, vine-covered chain-link fence lining the opposite side of the lot, she'd be well-concealed for the night.

Before shutting off the engine, she cracked the windows to let some fresh air in. The stench of garbage filtered into the passenger compartment, and she wrinkled her nose. Here she was, wedged between two garbage trucks and hiding out like a wanted criminal. With a heavy sigh, she let her head fall into her hands.

What were they doing to Rosa, right now, right at this moment? They wouldn't really hurt a child. Would they?

Her body shook from the effort to keep from screaming at the top of her lungs. If they harmed Rosa in any way, she'd rip them to shreds with her bare hands. Somehow, she'd find a way.

For a moment, she wavered. Kade was the federal agent. He was the one trained to shoot, kill, and take no prisoners. His entire life had been spent defending this great nation abroad, then protecting its citizens back home. Should she call him?

The urge to fling herself into his arms...to feel his strength and warmth envelop her...to hold her and tell her everything was going to be okay...

An illusion. That's what he was. Part of a wishful dream, a life she'd secretly hoped for with someone she loved and who loved her back with the same passionate fervor. That wasn't meant to be.

It was time to harden her heart against the truth. Yet again, she was alone.

She drew in a series of calming breaths, then pulled her cell phone from her bag and snapped in the battery. The kidnappers had said they would call her tomorrow, but she couldn't take the chance of missing another call from them.

Once she hit the power button, it seemed like forever before the screen lit up. There was another message from Kade.

Tears threatened to destroy what little remained of her composure. Despite her earlier resolve, the need to hear his voice won out, and she cued up the message.

"Laia, it's Kade. I know I hurt you. I know you've lost faith in me, but you have to know...you and Rosa are everything to me. I don't want to lose you. I'm working on a plan to find Rosa. Don't put yourself in jeopardy. Do *not* go after her alone. I couldn't—" He broke off, his voice choked. "I couldn't take it if anything happened to you. Please, call me back right away."

Hearing his voice, absorbing the meaning of his heartfelt words, nearly took down the steel wall she'd erected around that special place in her heart reserved solely for Kade. She wanted to believe him, but there was too much at stake to change course now.

Taking another deep breath, she deleted the message, then popped out the battery. Next she emptied her bag of purchases on the seat. The ledger. Several blue and black pens. Whiteout. And three small flashlights. Tucked away as she was and shielded from what remained of the light of day, she'd soon need them.

Part one of her plan was to retrieve what she assumed was Fernando Colon's stolen cash. Creating a phony ledger—one good enough to pass muster, at least long enough to get to Rosa—was the second part.

With her knowledge of banking, plus whatever she could remember of the entries in Josh's ledger, she could do this. Not knowing what those two-letter codes were could be a problem. The main thing was that her version had to be an original, not a photocopy. Assuming, as Kade had said, the prosecutor would demand the original to press charges, then Colon would want the original, too.

Eventually, Colon would figure out everything in the book was phony. The only part of her plan yet to be written was that teensy-weensy part about how to get her and Rosa out of there safely.

Wherever *there* turned out to be.

・・・

Kade assumed the last message he'd left for Laia would go unanswered. Even if she did turn on her phone, he doubted she'd call him back.

Man, I messed up with her.

He might as well be wearing his ass on the top of his neck instead of his head, because that's what he'd been. An ass. But he could—and *would*—fix this.

Smoke whined, so as soon as he pulled into the DHS parking lot, he popped the rear door for Smoke to stretch his legs and relieve himself.

Most of the lot was empty. He recognized Manny Dominguez's G-ride, along with several other fed cars. Jamie pulled up next to him and rolled down the window. "At the risk of being a nag, are you sure this is the right course of action?"

"No, but right now it's the *only* course of action." And he was done waiting around for one of his or Manny's informants, or the FBI to call him with any concrete news.

"Okay then." Jamie shut off the engine and joined him outside.

Kade shook his head. "This is my fuck-up to un-fuck. I need to do this alone." He gave Jamie a meaningful look. He hadn't exactly lied to his friend, but the real reason he didn't want Jamie with him was because it would make him an accessory.

He went to the back of his vehicle, then flipped up the door and grabbed a dark-green backpack. After closing the door, he motioned for Smoke to follow him inside. He took the stairs two at a time. Smoke loped behind him, his nails clicking and echoing on the concrete. They hadn't even gone into the office yet, and already Kade was sweating. He was about to break every rule in the law enforcement handbook. Plus a few in the penal code.

Outside the agents' door, he paused, then swiped into the office. While it was late in the evening, seven thirty, there would always be someone working late on a big case.

Like Manny.

Somehow, he had to sneak in, grab what he came for, then haul ass before anyone got wind of what he'd done.

The heavy metal door clicked shut behind him and Smoke. After trekking up the stairs, his dog was panting.

He leaned down and held his finger in front of his mouth. "Shhh." Instantly, Smoke snapped his jaws closed. *Atta boy.*

Voices came from the end of the corridor in the vicinity of Manny's cubicle. He and the forensic accountants were probably still poring over Josh's ledger. He was counting on them having made a working copy and securing the original in the evidence room.

Moving as quietly as possible, he and Smoke continued down the corridor. Halfway there, he stopped and stared at the tag on the door.

Evidence/Tech Room.

Getting in was a longshot. Since this wasn't his official duty station, he wouldn't normally have access. But as recently as a month ago, he'd been assigned TDY—temporary duty—to a narcotics squad operating from this location. He and Smoke had been seizing so much narcotics, he'd been given access to log in all the seizures. He prayed it hadn't been rescinded yet.

He held his card up to the reader, wincing when the box beeped. His heart raced as he stole a glance down the corridor, but no one popped their head out.

Slowly, he twisted the knob and pushed open the door. He indicated for Smoke to go in first, then he followed and nudged the door shut behind them.

Rows and rows of metal shelving stared back at him. About two-thirds of the shelves were jam-packed with evidence, mostly cardboard boxes containing documents, or drugs, or…Josh's ledger. The other third contained tech equipment that was valuable enough to be locked up and also required a signature to sign out.

Kade pointed to a spot directly in front of the door,

whispering, "Guard."

Smoke sat next to the door. If anyone so much as twitched on the other side, Smoke was trained to notify Kade with a soft huffing sound.

The evidence log sat ominously on a desk just inside the door. Agency policy required anyone entering the evidence room to sign in, regardless of whether they actually removed anything.

Ignoring the logbook, Kade went directly to the black three-ring binder sitting next to it. The Evidence Inventory Sheets. Once evidence was formally logged in, it was given a location code, making it easy to find. Row, shelf, and position on the shelf.

Knowing the ledger had to be one of the most recent seizures, he flipped to the last page. There it was. Row 5, Shelf 3, Position C.

Kade easily found the ledger. It had been placed inside a large brown envelope with the DHS address in the upper left corner. A large white evidence label had been secured to the outside of the envelope.

He took the envelope, then unzipped his backpack and stuffed it inside. He'd thought his heart had been racing before. Now it was pounding like a jackhammer. He zipped up the backpack and slung it over his shoulder. Before opening the door, he took a deep breath, trying to calm his heartbeat.

Not working.

Smoke watched him, a worried canine expression on his furry face. Even his dog knew he was up to no good.

He put his hand on the knob, about to open the door, when another crazy-ass idea came to him. Releasing the knob, he went to the other side of the room, the one housing the tech equipment. It took him a few more precious minutes he didn't really have before finding what he was looking for—the box containing the brand-new micro-transmitter and receiver he'd seen on Manny's desk.

He reopened his backpack and stuffed that inside next to the ledger. Boy, when he broke the rules, he *more* than broke them. He shattered them into smithereens. After cracking the door open, he peered in the direction of Manny's cubicle. Voices still filtered to him, but the corridor was empty.

After he and Smoke stepped out, Kade eased the door shut. Thirty feet and he'd be home free. Until they realized what he'd done.

Eventually, they'd check the card reader record and see that he'd made entry without signing in. It wouldn't be long before they figured it out. After that, he'd be toast. But if his plan worked, at least Rosa would be safe.

Smoke followed him to the exit door. He grabbed the handle, about to pull it open, when Smoke snorted. Pounding footsteps came to his ears, the sound of someone running on carpet.

"Kade! What are you *doing*?"

He turned, his fingers tightening around the strap of his backpack. He was so fucked it wasn't funny.

"I didn't even know you were here," Manny said, a little out of breath. "You're not gonna believe what the money geeks found in the ledger."

"What?" Kade asked, his relief so great at realizing Manny was clueless as to what he'd just done, he nearly dropped the backpack on Smoke's head. That combined with the fact that Manny had already made a copy of the ledger might give him a couple of days before anyone realized he'd stolen the original.

Manny grinned. "We've got him. Almost. That ledger documents over a hundred million dollars of drug money flowing through Colon's hands. There's even one entry for $20 million that looks like it might not have been collected. It was made the day before your brother was killed."

"That could be another reason why Colon would be itching to get his hands on the ledger," Kade suggested. "Maybe Josh hadn't gotten around to transferring the funds yet." Which would explain why there was no check mark next to that entry.

"Exactly." Manny's grin broadened. "But we still can't figure out that two-letter abbreviation. We will, though, and when we do, we can trace it to all of Colon's shell company accounts. This is all fun and games for the money geeks. They live for that shit."

"That's good news." Just when Kade thought he was about to get out of there, Manny grabbed his arm.

"Wait. I need you to go to the Regional Bank & Trust tomorrow. The AUSA said she can get that warrant for the bank box signed first thing in the morning. I've got court, so you'll have to serve it without me. I'll call you when it's signed, then you can come pick it up."

"You've got it." Kade opened the door. *Now* he had the ledger. *Tomorrow*, he'd have his hands on Colon's money. Some of it, anyway.

He and Smoke headed down the stairs. Like Manny said, the forensic accountants would follow the rest of the money and track it through Colon's dirty hands. For them, it really was all fun and—

Games.

On the bottom step, Kade froze. Smoke looked up at him, waiting patiently.

"Games," he whispered to himself. It couldn't be. But it was.

He'd just cracked Josh's ledger code.

Chapter Twenty-Nine

Once she'd made the last entry in her phony ledger, Laia had done her best to scuff up the front and back covers and bend some of the pages so that it wouldn't look brand-new. Then she'd stretched out on the backseat of the minivan.

Sleep had been slow to come. The only reason she knew she'd slept at all was that she'd woken with a start when someone had rolled up the metal door to the loading bay. She'd scrambled into the driver's seat, turned on the engine, then driven off and parked in the employee lot. There she'd waited for nearly three hours.

The lot began filling up with employee vehicles starting around eight a.m. Now the sun had fully risen, and she was literally counting the minutes before the bank opened for business. Once again, she put the battery back into her phone and powered it up. There were no new messages, not even from Kade.

Kade. Just thinking his name made her heart ache with a fierce desperation. *Don't think about it. Don't think about him.* Pressing her lips together, she powered off the phone, then removed the battery.

When the digital clock on the dashboard hit nine a.m., Laia turned the key, then drove from the lot and began making her way back to the bank. At each intersection, she held her breath, praying there'd be no vigilant police officer waiting and watching and who would pull her over. Mercifully, she made it to the bank without incident. Still keeping with her plan, she parked outside the convenience store next to the bank.

There were already several employees' cars in the Regional Bank & Trust lot, including Li-Mei's white Prius that the woman had owned for years. Parked by the curb directly in front of the bank was a blue van with the words Marlboro Locksmith printed on the side panel.

Laia shut off the engine. Seconds later, she was rolling the suitcase into the bank. Beside Li-Mei's desk stood a short man holding a large toolbox.

"Your timing is perfect." Li-Mei stood and smiled. "This is Cal Morton, our contract locksmith. We were waiting on you."

"Good morning," Laia said, giving both Li-Mei and Cal Morton a perfunctory smile. "And thank you for doing this on such short notice."

"Not a problem," Cal said.

"It's $200 for the drilling service and lock replacement," Li-Mei said.

"Of course." Laia dug into her handbag for the checkbook she'd also retrieved from the duplex. She scribbled out a check and handed it to Li-Mei.

"Let's go." Li-Mei led the way to the vault and unlocked the outer gate first, then the heavy iron door. "It's box two thirty-nine, one of the big ones on the bottom." She pointed inside the vault, indicating the locksmith should get started. "You'll have to sign in again," she said to Laia, then pulled the Safe Deposit Box Admission card from the metal box and dated the next empty line with today's date.

While Laia signed the card, she couldn't help but notice that this was, to all outward appearances, the twenty-fourth time she'd signed into the box and that all the other signatures were a very close replica of her own. Josh had done an admirable job of forging her signature.

"There you go." She handed the card back to Li-Mei.

Cal—the locksmith—slipped on a pair of gloves, then got to work. The screeching of his powerful drill on the metal door forced Laia and Li-Mei to cover their ears. Finally, he flipped open the door. "You're all set, ladies." He stood and began packing up his drill. "Be careful, though. The metal will be hot for a few more minutes. I'll have to come back this afternoon to install the new door."

"Thanks, Cal." Li-Mei smiled as the locksmith grabbed his toolbox and left the vault.

"Thank you," Laia muttered, eager to get the box inside the private room and see what was inside. If it wasn't filled with cash, she couldn't exactly rob the bank.

Li-Mei opened one of the private rooms outside the vault. Laia rolled her empty piece of luggage into the room, then accompanied Li-Mei to the box.

"Do you need any help with that?" she asked.

"Maybe." Laia peered inside the open box compartment. At twelve inches wide, twelve inches tall, and another twenty-four inches deep, the green metal box staring back at her was one of the largest in the vault.

Careful not to touch the edges of the outer door, she tugged on the box's metal handle and pulled. Eventually, the front of the box hit the floor with a resounding *thud*. Whatever was inside was heavy. Laia had no idea how much cash a box this size could hold.

If there even *was* cash in the box. For all she knew, it

could be full of books. Or bricks. Or...anything.

She looked up at Li-Mei. "I've got it." After pulling the box out the rest of the way, she hefted it into her arms, then carried it into the small private room and set it on the desk. "Thanks, Li-Mei." She followed the other woman from the room and retrieved her suitcase.

"You're welcome. I'll be at my desk. Just swing by before you leave so I know you're done."

Laia nodded, then closed the door behind her. The moment of truth had arrived, and she was scared to death. What if what she hoped was in the box actually wasn't? *Only one way to find out.*

A quick glance at the cheap clock on the wall told her she didn't have time to waste worrying. It was already nine thirty, and the kidnappers said they would call half an hour from now.

Her palms were sweating as she undid the catch on the side of the box and flipped open the lid. Her jaw dropped. Inside the box was cash. *Lots* of it. Bundles held together by hundred-dollar denomination money wrappers.

Though she'd worked in a bank for most of her adult life, she'd never actually seen so much money in one place before. She picked up several bundles. Each stack was comprised of hundred-dollar bills. Judging by the weight of the box, and if she assumed that all the other bills were hundred-dollar ones, there had to be at least $2 million dollars here.

$2 million in filthy drug money that Josh skimmed from Fernando Colon.

Josh had intended this money for her and Rosa, but she could no sooner have kept it than she could have robbed the bank at gunpoint. She was certain that when Josh had begun stashing these bills in the box, he'd had no idea that it would turn out to be ransom money to get his own daughter back from the very same sonofabitch for whom he'd laundered money.

She picked up the luggage and set it on the desk beside the box. After unzipping it, she began transferring the money from the box to the suitcase, being careful to stack the bundles neatly so it would all fit. Ten minutes later, the job was done.

She slid the suitcase to the floor and pulled out the articulating handle. Just being near this money made her feel like a criminal.

Get over it and get the heck out of here.

With the suitcase behind her, she opened the door, searching what she could see of the inside of the bank before heading out. Only a few customers had come in and were waiting in line for a teller. Mustering a smile, she walked briskly, waving as she passed Li-Mei's desk. "I'm all set. I emptied out the box, and I won't be needing it anymore. Thanks again."

"Oh, that was fast." The other woman stood. "Would you like to grab lunch sometime?"

"Uh, sure." Laia threw back over her shoulder, appreciating the gesture but knowing she'd never have lunch with Li-Mei or anyone else who worked at this bank. Too many memories. "I'll call you."

Then she was out the door. Searching the parking lot, she maintained a wary eye for police cars and SUVs like the ones Kade and Jamie drove but saw none. Some inner sense warned her to walk faster.

The suitcase wheels clicked on the asphalt, then thumped when she dragged it over the cement barrier between the bank and the convenience store lots. A man and a woman came out of the store and looked at Laia. Her heart rate picked up, but the couple proceeded to their car, ignoring her.

Great. Now she was losing her marbles, paranoid to the point where it felt as if everyone knew what she'd done.

Stolen $2 million dollars of drug money from a bank box

that the federal government was, right at this very moment, getting a search warrant for.

She could already feel the cold metal handcuffs snapping onto her wrists just before being shoved into the backseat of a police car. She clicked the key fob and slid open the rear door of the minivan. With a grunt, she lifted the suitcase onto the seat and closed the door. She flung open the driver side door and got in, slamming the door shut.

I did it.

With the phony ledger she'd created and the cash she'd stolen, she was as ready as she could possibly be.

The digital dashboard clock read 9:55 a.m. She dug into her bag and reinserted the battery before powering up the phone. Pissing off the kidnappers by missing their call wouldn't help any. The only missed calls were from Kade, but he'd left no more messages.

As she started the minivan and turned back onto the road, her phone rang. Her already pounding heart did so even faster. She grabbed the phone, barely avoiding hitting the car in the next lane as she inadvertently swerved.

She pulled onto the shoulder and braked to a stop. "Hello?"

"Do you have them?" the same computer-generated voice asked.

"Yes, I-I have the ledger and the cash."

"Good. Drive to the address I'm about to give you. Remember, no police, or she dies. No FBI, or she dies."

Laia gritted her teeth. "I want to talk to my daughter first. Put her on the phone."

A moment later, she heard, "Mommy? I want to come home."

Laia hissed in a breath. At least Rosa was still alive. "Are you okay, baby? Mommy is coming to get you real soon. I love—"

"Copy down these directions."

Her hand shook as she scribbled the directions on a piece of paper.

"You've got two hours. Don't be late."

When the call disconnected, Laia squeezed her eyes shut for a moment, then opened them, blowing out short breaths to clear her mind before heading back onto the road.

If all went well, by tonight, Rosa would be watching a movie or reading *Cinderella* and eating pineapple pizza at Alvita's. Laia, on the other hand, would probably be in jail. As long as her baby was safe, she could live with that.

If things didn't go well, they would both be dead.

Because there was no way that she was returning home without her daughter.

Chapter Thirty

"Good morning," Laia's friend, Li-Mei, said to Kade when he and Jamie walked up to her desk. "What can I do for you, gentlemen?"

"We're federal agents," he replied, holding up his ID, then the warrant. "This is a search warrant for safe deposit box number two thirty-nine. I have the renter key," he added, wanting to get the box open ASAP.

The AUSA had made good on her promise to get the warrant signed that morning, but it had taken significantly longer than expected. Now it was pushing eleven, and the stolen ledger was burning a hole in the backpack slung over his shoulder. Laia would already have received the call from the kidnappers. She could be anywhere by now.

Li-Mei's dark brown eyes widened as she took the warrant but barely gave it a passing glance. The skin on her forehead creased. "I don't understand. Laia never said you were a federal agent."

"That doesn't matter. We need to get into that box immediately. Call your manager if you have to." In his experience, when an agent slapped a search warrant on a business, the first person on the receiving end usually scurried away to find the boss and let them take the hit for whatever came next.

Li-Mei didn't do that.

"I'm sorry, but you're too late." She handed him back the warrant. "Laia was here over an hour ago. She said she lost the key and would pay for the drilling charges to get into the box. The box is empty."

Kade stepped closer, narrowing his eyes as he towered over the woman's desk. "Are you sure?"

She nodded. "Yes. I put the box back into the vault myself. Laia told me to close out the account and said that she wouldn't be needing the box anymore."

"Show me." Not that he didn't believe the woman, but he had to see with his own eyes.

He and Jamie followed her into the vault. Box #239's silver door was open. The key casing had a gaping hole in the center from where a locksmith had drilled. He pulled out the large green metal box and undid the clasp. Sure enough, empty.

Kade snapped the lid shut and shoved the box back into its slot. He should have seen this coming. Laia had worked in banks her whole life, and she was smart. *Too* smart. Even though she didn't have the customer key, he should have figured she'd find a way into the box. "Did you see what was in there before she emptied it out?"

Li-Mei took a step back and placed a hand to her chest. "Of course not. That's a violation of client privacy. I put Laia in that room over there." She pointed to a door just outside the vault. "She took the box inside with her, and when she came out, that's when she said she wouldn't need it anymore."

"Was the box heavy?" Kade prodded. The box was large, at least two cubic feet. If the box had been completely packed with cash, it could weigh forty or fifty pounds.

"I think so, but I didn't carry it into the viewing room. Laia did."

"How did she get the contents out of here?" Jamie asked.

"She had a suitcase." Li-Mei's frown deepened. "Is Laia in some kind of trouble?"

Seriously? Kade wanted to shout but didn't.

When federal agents served a warrant, someone was *always* in trouble. At least now he knew why she'd grabbed a suitcase from the duplex.

"Did Laia say where she was going?" Kade asked, ignoring her question.

"No." Li-Mei shook her head. "But she seemed like she was in a hurry."

"Thank you," he said, then gave Jamie a look that said they were outta there.

They left Li-Mei standing in the middle of the vault, a bewildered expression on her face.

Back at their SUVs, Smoke's furry face appeared in the kennel window, his thick curled tail whipping back and forth as he caught sight of them. Kade opened the passenger door and threw the backpack on the seat.

"What next?" Jamie asked.

"I don't know." *He* had the ledger but not the money. *Laia* had the money but not the ledger. But the kidnappers didn't know that.

He planted his hands on his hips and stared at the asphalt. "What does she think she's going to do all alone? Storm in there like Rambo and demand they give Rosa back to her?"

Jamie gave a subtle shake of his head. "Don't know. But she's one smart cookie and has one heck of a motivation."

"That's exactly what worries me." Love was like that. He ought to know.

For nearly six years, he'd loved Laia Velez. He realized

that now as clearly as he'd known anything in his life. Hell, his friends had known it before he did. That love had morphed into something so powerful and all-consuming that he'd done things he never would have imagined doing.

Like stealing evidence. Like thinking about her and Rosa every minute of the last twenty-four hours.

Unable to sleep last night, he and Smoke had driven to the duplex, hoping she might have snuck back in and spent the night there, but she hadn't. She'd probably assumed he'd look for her there. He'd tried calling her several more times, also with no success.

Wherever she was now, she had over an hour head start.

Kade's phone buzzed, and he looked at the screen. *Dayne.* "What've you got?" he answered.

"Laia turned her phone back on. By the time we picked up on it, she was on I-80 heading west near Paterson. She turned it off again, but I put out a special alert on the minivan. If she's spotted, she'll be pulled over and detained until you get there."

"Thanks, man." With luck, a patrol car would spot her. If not, he had no idea where she was going. Only she did.

"We found a few properties we thought Colon might have been holed up at," Dayne said. "All negative."

Kade pressed two fingers to his temple, trying to massage away the pounding that had taken up residence inside his skull. Much as he'd been hoping otherwise, he hadn't really expected that lead to pan out.

"I called all the guys," Dayne added. "Eric's on his way. Matt would be here, but Trista's in the hospital about to give birth any second. Markus just left for his honeymoon, and Nick's out of the country with Andi. The rest of us are on standby. Me, Deck, Brett, Evan. Just let us know the place and the time."

Jamie was in deep enough with him as it was. Involving

the rest of his friends was selfish. But a child's life was at stake, and they all knew it.

"Thanks," he said. "I'll let you know." His friends were all the best a guy could ask for, but he had to keep a healthy distance between them and the crimes he'd likely be charged with when this was all over.

Over. How *would* this all end? He couldn't bear the thought of living the rest of his life without Laia and Rosa in it. What he needed most right now was an ace in the hole. Something, anything to give him a lead. Not knowing what was coming next made him feel helpless. One thing a military officer never did was leave things to chance. Every operation had a goal, and it was every officer's duty to find the most strategically sound path to obtain that goal. Every officer needed intel to work with. Right now, he had squat.

Again, his phone buzzed, and he tugged it from his pocket.

No caller ID.

"Sampson," he said, then stiffened as the caller identified themselves. "What can I do for you?"

Picking up on Kade's agitation, Jamie stepped closer.

For the next thirty seconds, Kade listened, his blood pumping faster. "No, that's not possible. Just tell me where they are." He frowned at what the caller said next. "Fine," he replied reluctantly. "I'll be there in forty minutes." He ended the call and rounded the hood. "Follow me," he said to Jamie.

"Who was that?" Jamie asked.

"*Maybe* my ace in the hole."

On the way to his destination, Kade made several calls.

Now that he was nearly 100 percent certain that he knew where Laia had gone, the plan had gelled in his head within seconds. Most of it anyway. The rest of it he'd have to wing. Not the most strategic approach, but it was the only one available to him. At least he and Jamie wouldn't walk into this alone.

He hit the exit for Route 195, then punched it, flipping on the strobes. Cars ahead of him moved over as he and Jamie whizzed past at over ninety miles an hour. There was no time to put together a formal ops plan or go through official channels within his own agency, but the FBI took point on kidnappings, so Dayne and his colleagues were totally on board.

Good thing, that. Because there was no way he was about to let protocol or procedure or any other obligation get in the way this time. This time, he'd go with his gut.

Dayne, Eric, and the Colorado boys were already on their way north to meet up with him and Jamie at a rest stop off I-80. Taking this detour to pick up his passenger was a risk, but one he'd begun to think was well worth it.

Laia might have had a head start, but she wouldn't want to attract attention and would probably be doing the speed limit. The FBI hadn't received any notifications from the state police that she'd been spotted. Unfortunately, it looked as if she'd slipped through their fingers.

Keeping one hand on the wheel, he made the next critical call in his plan. Figuring out Josh's code was one thing. Knowing what to do with that information hadn't become apparent until he'd received that unexpected call.

"Manny, it's Kade," he said without preamble because there wasn't time. "I have something to tell you, and you're not gonna like it. How do you feel about a quick trip to Atlantic City?"

Chapter Thirty-One

This is it.

Before turning onto the narrow dirt road, Laia loosened her cramped fingers from the wheel. After getting off the interstate, she'd headed north on Route 209 into the Poconos, past Marshalls Creek, and half a dozen signs for fishing and hunting clubs and vacation cabins.

Small towns had given way to agricultural fields and the occasional house. Eventually, the fields and houses had disappeared and the only things visible on either side of the narrow two-lane road were tall coniferous trees.

She turned onto the dirt road. There was no house number, no mailbox, no signage of any kind. If she hadn't been given precise mileage to follow, she would have missed the turnoff completely.

The minivan rocked back and forth, worrying her that she'd bottom out and get stuck. Proceeding at barely a crawl, she had no idea how far she'd driven. Low scrub and towering pine trees lined the twisting road, preventing her from seeing too far ahead. It was around noon and the sun was high in the sky, but the trees were so tall and thick, they shaded the area, giving the illusion that dusk was only moments away.

She took her foot off the gas. The dangerous reality of her situation settled around her shoulders like a dark shroud.

This location was barely two hours from the largest city in the United States, but if things went wrong and her plan didn't work, she'd be completely alone.

Whatever this place was, Fernando Colon had chosen it for a reason. The last house she'd passed had to have been over a mile before she'd turned off the road. Again she worried that she'd made a horrible mistake in thinking she could actually pull this off.

I can do this.

Still…it couldn't hurt to hedge her bets.

Working quickly, she grabbed her cell phone from her bag, snapped in the battery, and powered up the phone. Not waiting for the phone to come fully back on line, she reached over and pulled up the passenger seat's foot mat, then shoved the phone beneath it.

She stepped lightly on the gas, inching the minivan deeper into the thickly wooded forest. The vehicle rocked again, more forcefully this time, and some part of the undercarriage hit a rock. *Sorry, Alvita.*

Only now did she realize her thoughtlessness. She should have left a note for Alvita back at the duplex. If Laia didn't come out of this alive, her friend could have her Ford Escape.

A minute later, a rustic, one-story split-log cabin came into view. Two gleaming black Cadillac Escalades were parked beside the cabin, a stark contrast to their rugged surroundings and the log cabin that looked like it had been built over a hundred years ago.

Five men outside the cabin started walking toward the minivan, intercepting her and preventing her from parking directly next to the cabin. Handguns stuck out from their waistbands. One even had a rifle slung over his shoulder. The one with the rifle held up his hand, ordering her to stop as he came alongside her window.

"Get out," he said in an accented voice loud enough for her to hear through the closed window.

She did as he ordered. Compared to the hot, humid air of coastal New Jersey, the temperature here had to be at least ten degrees lower and with considerably less humidity.

He jerked her by the arm, pulling her away from the minivan while the other men opened all the doors and began searching the vehicle.

One of them took out the suitcase and her bogus ledger. Another dumped the contents of her shoulder bag onto the hood and began rifling through her belongings. Her sunglasses and wallet. A small folding mirror and zippered cosmetics bag.

"Put your hands on the car," the one with the rifle said.

Again she did as ordered, planting her hands on the hood of the minivan. As he began running his hands down her back to her waist and buttocks, she tensed. She knew he was only searching her for weapons or a hidden microphone, but the humiliation and fear that this would lead somewhere else had her heart pumping madly.

Finally, his hands moved to her breasts. Instinctively, she rammed her elbow into his chest. "That's enough! I'm *not* hiding a machine gun on me and I'm *not* wearing a microphone!"

He arched a dark eyebrow. "You'd better not be." He jerked his head to one of the other men, who handed him a plastic wand. "Don't move." He ran the wand up and down her body. Only when he stepped back did her heart stop feeling as if it would climb right out of her throat.

The other four men had stopped to watch the show and were now smirking and laughing. When she'd first been informed that Colon had probably ordered the hit on Josh in jail, she'd had no trouble finding images of the man online. None of these men were him, which shouldn't surprise her. Would a drug lord answer the door of his own house? Of course not, he'd have his butlers do it for him. Or in this case, armed thugs. She had no way of knowing if he was even here.

Mustering bravado she didn't actually feel, she planted her fists on her hips. Inside, her belly was quivering like a leaf in a tornado. "I want to see my daughter. *Now*."

Rifleman, as she'd dubbed him, pulled a small radio from behind his back, then clicked a button on the side of it. "She's here, and we're coming in." He grabbed her upper arm, propelling her toward the cabin. One of the other goons had her ledger tucked under his arm and began dragging the suitcase across the dirt.

Laia nearly stumbled at the top step, held upright only by Rifleman's big, beefy hand. The goon holding the ledger opened the door, and she was unceremoniously shoved inside the cabin.

The interior was musty, although fairly clean and with minimal wood furniture. Sitting at a large oak table in the center of the room were two more men. A man wearing glasses and another…

Fernando Colon.

The man whom every news outlet in the country had described as the driving force behind one of the largest and most powerful illegal drug operations in the country, a man suspected of either committing or ordering the murder of dozens of other people, was about five-foot-ten, average build, with dark brown hair and eyes, and what anyone who didn't know better would describe as a pleasant enough face. Ironically, he was just plain ordinary looking.

But behind that ordinary looking facade was a man so deadly it made her gut clench.

Colon raised his brows at Rifleman. "She alone?"

"Si."

"Send Juan down to the main road and tell him to stay there. If anyone else tries to drive up here, stop them and let me know."

"Si." With near-military precision, Rifleman about-faced and went out the door.

Unexpectedly, Colon stood, as if someone had instilled gentlemanly manners in the man. "Mrs. Sampson." He dipped his head slightly.

Laia clenched her jaw. "After you murdered my husband, I reverted to my maiden name. So it's Ms. Velez, now. Thanks to *you*." Something she guessed he was already fully aware of. Calling her by her married name was meant to remind her of Josh, and it did. "I want to see my daughter," she demanded through gritted teeth.

It was all she could do not to launch at Colon and scratch his eyes out. Through the haze of rage clouding her vision, she knew she wouldn't make it to within three feet of him. Not without the other goon shooting her full of holes.

Ignoring her homicidal dig, Colon snapped his fingers, holding out his hand to the goon with the ledger. "All in due time." He handed the ledger to the other man sitting at the table. "Put the case on the table." After the goon had complied, Colon unzipped the bag and began pulling out bundles of cash, flipping through them. He did this with three bundles sitting on the top, then dug down to the bottom of the suitcase and pulled out another. After inspecting it the same way, he rezipped the suitcase.

Without waiting for a verbal command, the goon lifted the case and rolled it to one side of the room against a wall beside one of two closed doors.

The other man at the table had opened the ledger and begun flipping pages. He opened up another ledger she hadn't noticed earlier and seemed to be comparing entries. It was anyone's guess as to how long it would take before they figured out her ledger was comprised of approximately twenty pages of meaningless numbers.

Which meant time was running out.

"I want to see my daughter. *Please*," she added. "You promised me that if I gave you the money and the ledger that you'd let her go."

Colon stared at her for a moment, his face completely bland. Then he hitched his head to one of the closed doors behind him. The goon grabbed her arm, dragging her to one of the doors. He opened it, then shoved her inside.

Laia gasped. Asleep on a bed and still wearing the same purple shorts and pink tank top she'd worn over her bathing suit yesterday was Rosa.

For a moment, she stared, holding her own breath until she confirmed that Rosa's chest was rising and falling steadily. Then she sat on the mattress and stroked a soft, shiny strand of hair from her daughter's eyes. She inspected Rosa's arms and legs for bruises or any other signs of abuse, but there were none. If they'd hurt one hair on her sweet little head, she'd have gone berserk and turned into a raving lunatic.

More than she already was.

"Rosa? Honey, it's Mommy. Can you wake up for me?" When she didn't respond, she pressed a hand to Rosa's cheek. It was cool to the touch. Had they drugged her? "Rosa?" she repeated, gently shaking her shoulder.

Rosa's lids fluttered, then opened, revealing sleepy green eyes. "Mommy," she said on a yawn. "You came."

"Of course I did." Unable not to, she lifted Rosa into her arms, cradling and rocking her against her chest. Her daughter was alive and seemingly unhurt. Trying not to cry, she sat there, continuing to hug her daughter.

"Mommy, you're squeezing me too hard."

"I'm sorry." She settled Rosa on her lap. "I'm just so happy to see you," she said, drinking in the healthy glow of her cheeks.

"I'm happy to see you, too." Rosa yawned again. "Can we go home now?"

"Yes, baby. We can go home now." She hoped.

But as she gathered Rosa in her arms and turned around, her hopes were dashed straight into the ground.

Fernando Colon stood in the open doorway holding the ledger. His eyes were cold, dead. "Did you really think I wouldn't figure it out?" He threw the ledger on the bed. "This is not your husband's ledger. Now where. Is. The ledger?"

"I don't have it," she cried, praying he'd believe her and take pity on her. *Not likely. He's a cold-blooded killer.* Pity wasn't in his repertoire. "You have to believe me. I don't care about the money or the ledger or anything. I just wanted my daughter back. If I could have given you the real ledger, I would have."

"Where *is* the real ledger?" he asked in a voice edged with anger.

"Mommy?" Rosa whispered, her eyes frightened as she clutched Laia's blouse.

"Shh, baby." She stroked Rosa's hair, wishing there was something she could do to take the fear from her eyes. "I don't know," she lied. If he killed her and Rosa, at least the federal government could still charge him with additional crimes. "And I don't understand why you ever thought I had it in the first place."

"That is of no consequence," Colon said. "What is of consequence is that I have no further use for you."

The other man who'd accompanied them inside pulled the gun from his waistband.

And pointed it directly at Laia's head.

Chapter Thirty-Two

"No!" Laia spun and tucked Rosa to her chest, as if that could actually protect her from a bullet.

"Idiot," Colon shouted. "Take them outside. I don't want any blood in the cabin."

"No, *please*," she cried over her shoulder.

"Mommy, I want to go home." Tears began streaming from Rosa's eyes.

It can't end this way. Not for her baby.

"Let Rosa go," she pleaded. "She's just a child. She doesn't understand any of this. She can't tell anyone anything. If you drop her off at a rest stop somewhere on the highway, I promise she won't say anything. She wouldn't even know *what* to say. Just let her go. *Please.*"

A quick glance over her shoulder, and she thought she might have gotten through to Colon. His face had softened. Some, anyway.

"I'm truly sorry, Mrs. Sampson. Children should never be separated from their parents. Sometimes, it's unavoidable. She is a precocious little girl. *Too* precocious." Colon's face returned to what she now understood was his typical look. Mean. Unfeeling. *Homicidal.* "I can't take the chance. I'm sorry."

When he turned to leave, any remaining hope died that at least Rosa would survive this.

She'd tried, *really* tried. And failed. At least they would die together.

Laia squeezed her eyes shut and began doing something she hadn't done in years.

She prayed to God.

Please, God. Don't let my daughter suffer. Let her feel no pain. Let her—

A radio crackled. "There's a fed here. He wants to see you."

"What?" Colon barked, echoing Laia's thoughts.

It can't be.

Still holding Rosa away from the goon with the gun, she glanced over her shoulder to see Colon grab the other man's radio.

"*What* fed?" Colon shouted into the radio.

"Kade Sampson," came the response. "Homeland Security."

Happiness and hope burst inside Laia's chest.

Kade is here. Actually *here.* He'd come for her.

Colon's eyes narrowed, on *her* this time. "You were told not to call the police or the FBI. Did you tell your brother-in-law where you were going?"

"I didn't. I swear it. I did exactly as you told me to." Well, aside from the tiny little thing about creating a phony ledger. "I came here alone and didn't tell *anyone* where I was going."

"Then how did he find this cabin?" Colon said through his clenched jaw.

"I don't know." Was it possible Kade had managed to track her phone from the brief moments she'd had it on earlier?

"Did you check her for devices?" he asked the goon, who

nodded. "What about her car?"

"Si." The goon nodded vigorously. "No tracking devices."

These idiots had missed her phone. Or they hadn't searched well enough and didn't want to admit their mistake. But she'd only just turned it back on, so that couldn't have been how Kade had found her so quickly.

Colon clicked a button on the side of the radio. "Is he alone?"

"Si."

"Are you sure?"

"Looks like it."

"What does he want?" Colon asked.

"Says he wants to talk to you and *only* you. He says he has the ledger, and he wants to make a trade."

Kade brought the ledger? He'd made it crystal clear that giving the ledger to Colon wasn't an option. Did his agency know he'd taken it? Had he stolen it? Was he lying?

Either way, he's here.

Colon's eyes narrowed to slits so thin they were barely open. He began tapping his finger on the side of the radio. "Search him, then bring him up here. Check him again for wires or guns. Comprendes?"

"Si."

"Diego, watch them," Colon said to the goon, then walked out.

Through the open door, she saw Colon talking to the man who'd gone through her ledger. She couldn't see them leave the cabin, but they both disappeared from view followed by the sound of a door squeaking open, then closing.

The goon closed the bedroom door, then stuffed the gun back inside his waistband and sat on the only other piece of furniture in the room, a simple wood chair next to the door.

Laia sat on the edge of the bed, still holding Rosa who, thankfully, had begun drifting off again, leading her to believe that they had indeed drugged her, and whatever they'd used was still in her system.

Outside the cabin, she heard a vehicle drive up. *Kade.* He was outside, less than thirty feet away. She couldn't begin to understand what his plan could be. All she knew was that just when she'd been about to lose all hope of her and Rosa getting out of this alive, he'd come for them.

Gently, she laid her now-sleeping daughter on the bed. If he'd really stolen the ledger…if he'd come here alone… how did he plan to take out Colon and his small army all by himself without getting them all killed?

She stole another glance at the armed man in the chair.

Kade might have come for them, but they might very well all die here. Together.

• • •

The moment Kade stepped out of the SUV, he was shoved roughly against the hood, then patted down yet again for weapons. Knowing he'd be thoroughly searched, he'd handed over his duty weapon to Jamie at the rest stop on I-80 just before they'd all exited the highway.

Handing over his weapon had been hard enough. Transferring Smoke to Jamie's care had been worse. Smoke had resisted, straining at the leash and whining as Jamie had loaded him into the other vehicle, but he wouldn't risk his dog getting hurt. Colon's men would rightly assume Smoke was a K-9—a weapon—and deal with him accordingly, something Kade wouldn't chance. Without a gun, most officers would feel powerless. Not Kade. But without his K-9 at his side, he *did* feel powerless.

During the pat down, he methodically and tactically assessed his surroundings and exactly what he was up against.

Two Escalades were parked in front of the cabin. Alvita's

green minivan was parked off to the side. Laia and Rosa were nowhere in sight, probably being held in the cabin.

If they weren't dead already.

Focus. They have *to be alive.*

If they weren't, he'd know it. He'd feel it in his gut.

The two men who'd escorted him up here were both armed, one with a handgun and the other with a rifle that was now aimed at Kade's head. Three other men surrounded him, all sporting Glocks. That made five armed assholes plus the two on the front porch, one of whom he'd ID'd as Colon. He had to assume everyone was armed.

One of the men pulled a device from his pocket—a bug-detection wand.

"Does it really take six of you to babysit one fed?" he asked, knowing it would piss the men off but doing it anyway so that his friends would hear what they were up against.

"Shut the fuck up, cop." The guy with the rifle raised the muzzle and held it two inches from Kade's head. "Hold out your arms."

"Copy that," came Jamie's voice in Kade's ear. "At least six yahoos."

Which was a good thing.

With Colon's resources, Kade had expected a small army, not half a dozen men. Which *could* explain why there'd been no gossip in the wind about a kidnapping. Wisely, Colon had kept the circle of his people in the know very tight, limiting the number of loose lips that could sink his ship.

Kade did as ordered, holding out his arms while the wand was run down his back then his legs. If the tiny transmitter/receiver in his ear wasn't up to spec, the detection instrument would beep and flash, a warning that he was wired.

Being several inches taller than the guy with the wand, the guy had to stand on his toes to run the device over and around Kade's head. No beeps that he could hear and no flashing lights that he could see.

"He's clean," the man shouted.

"Get the ledger," Colon called out. "Then search the truck. And tie him up, for fuck's sake."

One of the men opened the passenger door and retrieved the ledger, bringing it to Colon while two others began opening all the doors of Kade's SUV. One of them procured a thin piece of rope and tightly bound Kade's wrists behind his back.

That left three guns aimed at Kade.

"Where are Laia and Rosa?" he said loudly enough for Colon to hear. "I assume she brought you the money. I brought you the ledger, so you can let them go now." He knew Colon had no intention of letting *any* of them go free. That's why even his backup plan had a backup.

Colon handed the ledger to the man standing beside him—his new accountant?—who went back inside the cabin, taking the ledger with him. Whoever that was, Colon trusted him to verify the book's authenticity. Kade was counting on that man to figure out the ledger was worthless without the code.

The one that only Kade knew.

Colon stepped off the porch and strolled over. "You're either the bravest man I've ever met or the stupidest. Maybe both. You didn't really think I'd let them go, did you?"

Kade smiled, doing his best to mimic Colon's smirk when what he really wanted was to smash his fist into the guy's jaw and wipe it off for him. "I might not be the bravest, but I'm definitely not the stupidest. So no. I didn't think you'd let us go." *Especially not me.*

Colon held his arms wide. "Then what did you hope to accomplish here?"

Stalling for time, he needed Colon's new accountant to do his thing, and he also wanted to alert his friends to Laia and Rosa's general location. Until he knew where exactly they were and how many guns were guarding them, he couldn't risk sending his friends in and inadvertently getting them killed. "That's my sister-in-law and my niece you've got inside that cabin."

"Copy that," Jamie said. "We're in position. Waiting on your signal."

"I couldn't leave them here without at least trying." And getting a confession.

"Take him into the woods," Colon said. "Bury the body. Then do the same with the woman and child."

Colon's new accountant must not be the sharpest tool in the shed. He was taking too long.

"Kade?" came Jamie's worried voice.

Two of Colon's men grabbed his arms, then started to drag him away.

"If you want your money," Kade said over his shoulder, wincing as a shaft of pain shot up his arms, "you might want to hold off killing me."

"Wait!" Colon held up his hand to his men, who stopped. Wariness had crept into his dark eyes. "Why?"

The door to the cabin swung open, and the accountant hustled out, holding the ledger in his hand. "We have a problem. Based on the numbers and the dates they were transferred to your accounts, I can verify the ledger is authentic. What I *can't* verify is what bank the last $20 million is located in."

"Why the fuck not?" Colon growled.

Good. When people began losing control, they tended to say things without thinking, which was exactly what Kade was counting on. The more agitated he could make Colon, the better the evidence transmitted to the receiver in Jamie's SUV.

The accountant flipped open the ledger and began running his finger down the page. "These are account numbers that Sampson used to temporarily park the money before transferring it to your overseas accounts."

"I know that," Colon bit out.

"And these," the accountant continued, again running his finger down the page, "are the amounts of money that were *in* these accounts. That's how I verified the ledger is authentic. These numbers add up right down to the dollar with the list you gave me. But these…"

The accountant ran his finger down the page again. While Kade couldn't see exactly what the man was pointing to, he knew he'd discovered the two-letter codes.

"You see these two letters under the bank column? I don't know what they mean. These aren't abbreviations for any bank that I know of. We have no idea what banks Sampson was using to park the money in."

A muscle in Colon's cheek began twitching. "What about my $20 million?"

"That's what I'm trying to tell you." The man flipped to the final page of the ledger. "Here's the entry for the $20 million. See this column? There's a password for every account. But in the bank column, there's only a two-letter code. MA, OA, KA, IA, the list goes on. There's an account number for the $20 million and a bank code: OA. But I have no idea what that stands for or where it is. There's no way to *find* the money. It could be anywhere in the world."

Colon reached behind his back and pulled out a Glock. He stalked over and rammed it against Kade's forehead. "*Tell* me where it is."

Kade's heart jackhammered faster than an AK-47 spewing out rounds. "You want something from me…I want something from you. Looks like we're at an impasse."

He was playing a dangerous game of chicken with a man who might very well blast him full of lead. The only question was which of them would flinch first.

Chapter Thirty-Three

First, she had to get Rosa to safety. Then, she had to help Kade.

But how?

Even if she was correct, that Diego was the only one left in the cabin, he had a gun. Not only didn't *she* have one, but she had absolutely nothing available to her that might constitute a weapon. Except her body. And the element of surprise.

Sitting in the chair, Diego was barely six feet away from where she perched on the edge of the bed facing the window. She stood. As expected, the movement caught his attention.

"Sit down," he ordered.

"My leg is cramping." She shook her leg out, pretending to limp slightly as she started pacing back in forth in front of the window.

Diego leaned forward in the chair. "I said, sit *down*."

"Oh, come on." She stopped to massage her thigh. "It's really cramping. Besides, where would I go?"

Grumbling, he settled back in the chair and readjusted the butt of the gun sticking out from his waistband.

After shaking her leg out one more time, she resumed pacing again between the side of the bed and the window. With each circuit, she inched just a little closer to where Diego sat.

A dark shadow caught her eye outside the window, barely visible in the distance through the trees. Something black. A bear? *Wonderful.* If she could get herself and Rosa out that window, she might very well have to fight off a black bear.

By the time she'd made half a dozen circuits between the bed and the chair, Diego seemed to pay her less attention.

I can do this. I can.

Never in her life had she intentionally inflicted harm on another human being. But this sonofabitch sat between her and freedom.

She uttered a quick gasp and snapped her head up, pretending to hear something. "What was that?"

Wait for it.

"What?" Diego's eyes narrowed.

"Oh my God." She pointed to the door, hoping this guy fell for her lousy acting job. "It came from inside the cabin."

Wait for it.

Diego stood, then set the radio on the chair and pulled the gun out. He went to the door and placed his hand on the knob. When his back was completely to her, she dug deep and summoned up the courage she prayed was in there somewhere.

Now!

She raced forward, hurling her body against Diego's. His forehead crashed into the wood door with a loud *crack*. She jumped back, fisting her hands and readying to punch him in the face.

To her shock, he slid to the floor. Blood spurted from his nose, and there was a bloody gash in the middle of his forehead. The gun remained in his hand, but his fingers had loosened on the handle.

For a second, she stood there, breathing heavily. *I did it. I actually did it!*

He could wake up at any moment. Every second counted.

She pried the gun from his hand, grabbed the radio from the chair, then set them both on the floor in front of the window. Casting a quick glance over her shoulder to verify he was still out cold, she set to work on the old window latch. She pushed with her fingertips, ignoring the pain as the edge of the rusty latch bit into her skin. Eventually, it snapped open with a squeak.

The metal handles at the bottom of the window were equally old and rusty. She put her fingers beneath the handles and tugged upward, straining until it felt as if her shoulders would pop. "C'mon, open!"

But her hands were sweating too much. Her fingers slipped off, and she cried out.

A moan had her turning her head to see Diego's arm move.

"C'mon, c'mon!" She tugged again. The window started to move. She pulled it up as far as it would go, then went to the bed and picked Rosa up in her arms. "Wake up, sweetie. Wake up."

Her lids fluttered. "Are we going home now?" she asked sleepily.

"Yes." She glanced at Diego, who hadn't moved again, then sat Rosa on the window ledge so her legs dangled outside. "We're going for a walk in the woods first." Carefully, she eased Rosa off the ledge, then lowered her by her arms to the ground and plopped her on her bottom.

Another moan came from behind her, and she whipped around. Diego slid his hand along the floor, holding it to his nose.

Oh no. Her pulse galloped.

Not wanting to leave it behind for Diego to call for help, she twisted the knob on the radio, turning it off before dropping it on the ground outside the window. She grabbed the gun, then slipped her legs over the windowsill, grimacing as the sharp ledge scraped against the backs of her thighs, tearing her capris. The second her feet hit the soft ground next to where Rosa sat, still looking somewhat dazed, Laia turned to see if Diego had figured out they were gone.

So far, so good.

Except Rosa was still too out of it to walk. Unable to carry the gun, the radio, *and* Rosa, she hurled the gun and the radio as far away from the cabin as possible.

"C'mon, baby. Let's go." A moment later, Rosa was in her arms, and she was trekking up the wooded incline behind the cabin.

A hundred feet or so later, sweat trickled down her temples. The slope had grown steeper to the point where she could barely take another step. Every muscle in her arms, shoulders, and legs screamed in protest. She set Rosa down, steadying her when she wobbled on her feet.

"Mommy, I'm tired," she whined. "I want to take a nap."

"Not yet, baby. We need to keep going." She reached down, intending to pick Rosa up again, when shuffling sounds came from behind her.

Diego was charging up the hill behind them, close enough that she could see the blood from the damage she'd inflicted. His lips curled back, exposing his bloody teeth. If he caught up to them, there'd be no escaping his rage.

"Rosa, let's go! Wake up!" She grabbed Rosa's hand, knowing there was no way she could outrun Diego.

The shuffling sounds of him charging closer grew louder.

They wouldn't stand a chance.

A low growl came from up ahead, then a large black blur shot past them. That bear?

"Smoke!" Rosa pointed.

Smoke crashed into Diego's chest, sending the man flying backward and sliding down the slope on his back. The dog latched on to the man's arm, issuing another low growl from his throat.

More sounds, this time from ahead of her. Jamie charged down the hill, a gun in his hand. Behind him were Deck and his Belgian Malinois, Thor.

Laia knelt, tucking Rosa into her embrace.

"You okay?" Deck said quietly, holding his finger to his lips in a shushing gesture.

She nodded, trying to calm her racing heart and process the fact that Jamie and Deck were there, in the woods behind the cabin.

Kade hadn't come alone.

Jamie dragged a struggling Diego to his feet, keeping his hand securely over the guy's mouth.

"Wait here." Deck pulled out a small roll of duct tape from one of the large pockets on his vest, then walked down the hill. As Jamie removed his hand, Deck quickly strapped the duct tape over the man's mouth.

Jamie handcuffed Diego, then started pushing him up the hill. Smoke trotted over and licked Rosa's face, nuzzling her chin when she didn't respond with her usual excitement at seeing him.

"Wait!" Laia whispered as Jamie and Deck escorted Diego up the hill. "We can't leave. We have to help Kade."

"We will." Deck nodded, then pointed.

Laia followed the direction Deck indicated to see three more men—Evan with his dog and two other men she didn't recognize—taking cover behind the trees and facing the cabin.

"Why aren't they going down there to help him?" Laia looked from Jamie to Deck, not understanding how they could leave Kade alone.

"Because," Jamie said, "he's not ready."

"Not ready?" She shook her head. "I don't understand. What is he waiting for?"

Rather than address her concerns, Jamie looked straight at her and said, "Kade. We have Laia and Rosa. They escaped on their own. They're safe and unhurt. We're just waiting on your signal, buddy."

Chapter Thirty-Four

At hearing Jamie's words, a soothing balm settled over Kade's soul. He didn't know how Laia had managed to escape. The important thing was that she had, and she'd made his job a helluva lot easier.

No matter what happened next—if he didn't miraculously manage to get his ass out of this in one piece—Laia and Rosa were safe. They might wind up living their lives without him, but they'd be living them.

"Get the woman and the girl," Colon ordered Moises, who nodded, then headed into the cabin. Colon sneered, his upper lip curling back to reveal surprisingly even, white teeth. "We'll see how brave you are when I press a gun to *their* heads."

Rather than respond, Kade braced himself. When Colon realized his captives were gone, he'd throw a conniption.

Three. Two. One.

Moises stormed out of the cabin. "They're gone," he said, winded from running.

For a split second, Colon didn't react. Then his eyes

rounded wider than golf balls. "What do you mean, gone?"

"The woman, the girl, and Diego," Moises sputtered. "They're *all* gone. The bedroom window was open."

"Then go find them!" Colon shouted. "Take Juan, and don't come back until you do."

"Si." Moises practically bowed at the waist, as if Colon were his king.

Moises and Juan hustled to do their "king's" bidding and disappeared around the side of the cabin.

Little did Colon know that Moises and Juan would never return. They'd soon be in handcuffs, which also meant that now there were only four men left out front guarding Kade. Colon, the accountant, who may or may not be armed, plus two other men who *were* armed. Even tied up, those odds he could tackle. *Time to get down to business.*

"Now what were you saying about pressing a gun to their heads?" Knowing full well it would piss Colon off, which was part of his plan, Kade smiled. Not a grin but a full-blown smile, teeth and everything. Then for good measure, and to get Colon really riled up, he chuckled. "That's some crew you've got there. They can't even handle a defenseless woman and a little girl." Not that he'd ever thought Laia defenseless. Somehow, she'd managed to thwart Colon's men.

"Shut up! Shut up!" Colon tried getting in Kade's face, but at six-foot-three, he towered over the man by at least five inches. Colon raised his arm, then swung it, slamming the gun against the side of Kade's head.

Pain blasted through his skull. The ground moved, then completely fell out beneath him as his knees hit the dirt. He opened his eyes. At least, he thought he did, but all he saw were swirling shadows and tiny white lights dancing in his line of sight.

Again, Colon jammed the muzzle of his gun against Kade's forehead. "I can kill you any time I choose."

Kade grunted, shaking his head to clear it so he could really start to amp things up. "Yeah, but you won't. Without me, you'll never get your money."

Colon bent at the waist, so close to Kade's face he could easily head butt the guy in the forehead. "Give me the code," he said in a deadly voice, "or I'll shoot you anyway."

Kade doubted that. Colon could never walk away from $20 million dollars. "Okay," he said, affecting a defeated look on his face, while inside his guts clamored with the violent need to do Colon some serious bodily harm. "OA stands for Oriental Avenue. It's in Atlantic City, and there's only one bank on that street. That's where your money is."

"Check it out," he said to his accountant, who'd already pulled out a cell phone.

It was another minute before the man spoke. "There's a South Shore Bank on Oriental Avenue in Atlantic City. I'll try logging into the account."

"Well?" Using the muzzle of the gun, Colon indicated the ledger.

Kade's head pounded from the blow, but at least the gun was no longer rammed against the side of his head.

The accountant pressed his lips together. "The money's there. I can see it. Twenty million. But there's a problem."

"Just transfer it to the overseas account."

"I can't." The accountant held out the phone.

With his free hand, Colon grabbed it. "Unable to complete transaction at this time. What the fuck does that mean?"

"It means," Kade said, "you don't get your money." Thanks to the call he'd placed to Manny. By now, DHS agents stationed in Atlantic City had put a freeze on Colon's account. "The only place you're going is back to prison."

Colon spun, aiming the gun at Kade's face. His upper lip had begun twitching violently. "I don't *think* so."

Almost there.

Colon's fuse was lit, but the flame hadn't made it to the bunker yet. To get him to say the magic words, Kade needed to script this carefully. Only then would he signal his friends to move in because once they did, Colon would lawyer up and Josh's killer would go free.

Hopefully Colon would confess *before* he pulled the trigger.

"Remove the hold or die." Colon leaned in so close Kade could smell the man's fury. And see that he'd curled his finger fully around the trigger.

"Kade?" came Jamie's worried voice in Kade's ear.

"Not yet," he said, responding to both Colon *and* Jamie. "When you hired my brother to be your dirty accountant, you got the best. He was a whiz with numbers, and you knew it. That's why you hired him. That's also why you killed him. Isn't it?"

Colon's lip twitched faster. "Your brother stole from me."

"And he would have testified against you," Kade continued. "That's why you had him murdered in prison. But you had someone else do your dirty work for you, so you wouldn't get your precious little manicured hands dirty. Did I get that right?"

When Colon still didn't take the bait, but stood there, his chest rising and falling faster, Kade dug in for the coup de grace. One that might push Colon too far and make him pull that trigger.

"You're nothing but a coward." Kade spat on the ground, intentionally hitting Colon's shoes. "Say it. I'm. A. Coward."

"I am no coward." The man's jaw clenched, then he puffed up his chest. "What I am is powerful. More powerful than you could ever hope to be. All I had to do was snap my fingers, and a dozen inmates jumped at the chance to kill your brother for me. All it took was one. For him, it was a badge of honor. I was told your brother dropped like a stone."

Kade exhaled slowly.

Gotcha.

Not only was Jamie now a witness to Colon's confession, but thanks to the tiny transmitter in Kade's ear, the man's words were digitally recorded for posterity.

And a federal prosecutor.

The gun shook as Colon struggled not to pull the trigger. Kade's time was up.

"Monopoly," Kade snarled. Knowing what was about to happen, his muscles tightened.

"What?" Colon cocked his head in confusion.

"Monopoly," Kade repeated the signal, catching movement in the trees behind Colon. "You do *not* pass go. You do *not* collect $200, let alone $20 *million*. The game is up. You're going directly to jail."

"Federal agents! Put your guns on the ground and your hands in the air!"

Jamie and Smoke charged from the trees, followed closely by Deck, Dayne, Eric, and Evan, along with their dogs.

Startled, Colon spun. Kade jerked his head out from behind the muzzle of the gun, then shot to his feet and body slammed the man to his right. The guy stumbled, then began windmilling his arms before going down on his ass. The gun flew from his grip, and Kade dove for it, covering it with his body, then flipping onto his back to grab it in his tied hands.

Getting to his feet, the guy made a move toward Kade.

He twisted his arms around enough that he could aim the gun at the guy's chest. "I wouldn't. Face down. On the ground. *Now*!"

When the guy had complied, Kade got to his knees in time to see Smoke charge at Colon. Another of Colon's men pointed his gun at Kade's chest. *Not good.* With his hands still tied behind his back, Kade could never get aimed in before the guy blasted him full of lead.

The crack of a gunshot reverberated through the trees. The man who'd been about to shoot Kade staggered, then dropped to his knees. Then in slow motion, he fell face first on the ground.

Jamie had taken the kill shot, then covered off on Colon. But Kade had given strict instructions to take out Colon only in the event of a kill-or-be-killed scenario.

Smoke had quickly eaten up the distance and was preparing to launch at Colon. Right behind him was Thor.

Colon raised his gun, aiming it at Smoke.

Not in this lifetime, asshole.

With his hands still tied behind his back, Kade rammed his shoulder into Colon's back. The gun went off.

Kade's heart stopped. Had he hit Smoke?

Lying in the dirt, only a few feet from Colon, Kade twisted to see Smoke flying through the air, landing with his front paws on Colon's chest. Kade gritted his teeth, pulling at the ropes binding his wrists until he finally slipped free. All around him, his friends were busy subduing the rest of Colon's men.

"Fucking dog!" Colon wrestled with Smoke, pounding at his dog's head as he grappled for the gun that had fallen from his hand.

Kade lunged, wrenching the weapon away and bending Colon's wrist backward. The snap of bone came first, followed by a high-pitched scream. Kade straddled Colon's chest and smashed his fist into the man's face. More crunching as he broke Colon's nose. Blood spurted from his nostrils. Kade sent one final blow to the side of the man's skull, knocking him out cold.

Still straddling his chest, Kade wished he could hit him again and again for what he'd done to Josh, Laia, and Rosa… to Kade's entire family…but he wanted Colon alive to go to prison for the rest of his godforsaken life.

"Don't shoot! Don't shoot!" The accountant was on his knees, his arms stuck straight up in the air as high as he could possibly stretch them.

Kade had pegged the guy as a bookkeeper, not a fighter, and he was right.

Barking and growling drew his attention to where Deck's dog, Thor, guarded one of Colon's men on the ground. Dayne and Evan's dogs, Remy and Blue, stood with their heads down, panting as they eyed the men like they wanted to eat them for dinner.

"You good?" Jamie held out a set of handcuffs to Kade.

"Yeah. I'm good." As he accepted the cuffs, he gave his friend a curt nod of thanks. Jamie had fired the shot that had saved his life. "Release," he said to Smoke. When his dog unclamped his jaws from Colon's arm, Kade flipped the guy onto his belly and cuffed him, broken wrist and all.

Dayne did the same with the guy Kade had body slammed. Evan pressed two fingers to the other guy's carotid, then looked up and gave a quick shake of his head.

"Think you could have cut it a little closer?" Eric grinned at Kade as he made quick work of cuffing the accountant. Eric's Dutch shepherd, Tiger, stood off to the side, ready to launch, should the man rethink his surrender.

Evan snapped his fingers. His big German shepherd, Blue, trotted to his side and sat. "Gotta say, we all thought you were about to get that thick skull of yours aerated."

So did I. So. Did. I.

He *had* cut it close. *Crazy* close. It had been worth it.

With the additional charges they'd likely get from the information contained in the ledger, Colon would be going away for a long time. Added to that would be kidnapping charges. The icing on the cake was that no slimy defense attorney in the world was good enough to get Colon off a murder charge now. Not with a verbal confession and federal agents as witnesses. Once they knew the accessory charges they'd be facing, even Colon's men might turn on him.

Deck chuckled. "The things a guy will do to impress a woman." He grabbed the radio clipped to his belt and pressed the mic. "The coast is clear."

Kade turned at the sound of vehicles coming up the road behind him. Two SUVs, the first of which was Brett's. Brett's enormous golden Chesapeake Bay Retriever, Blaze, sat in the passenger seat, his big tongue lolling from the side of his mouth. Through the kennel bars behind them, he could just make out three heads. The rest of Colon's crew.

Now it was Kade's turn to chuckle. K-9 vehicles weren't designed for prisoner transport, but Brett had stuffed all three of them into Blaze's kennel anyway.

Jamie's SUV came next. Laia sat behind the wheel. The passenger Kade had been forced to pick up was in the passenger seat. Laia jumped out and ran toward him, her expression anxious as she checked him out from head to toe.

"I heard gunshots. Are you—"

"I'm fine," Kade managed, though his head was pounding like a rock concert. "Rosa?" He looked over her shoulder to Jamie's truck.

"She's okay. She's asleep. They must have drugged her to keep her quiet."

He closed his eyes and exhaled a serious breath of relief. When he opened them, he caught the glistening sunlight in the wetness on both her cheeks. He wanted to catch her up in his arms, to hold her and never let go again, but she hadn't made any move to come closer.

True, he'd stolen evidence. True, he'd told her he'd get Rosa back. But he'd failed her when she'd needed him most. The distance between them now was hers to close.

The passenger door to Jamie's vehicle opened. Cecelia

Colon got out and looked at her son's prostrate form. He was still out cold, handcuffed on his belly. The blood had stopped gushing from his nose where Kade had pummeled him, but his face was smeared with it, and his arm was a bloody mess from where Smoke's teeth had punctured his flesh.

Kade hadn't liked the idea of bringing a civilian into this mess, but Cecelia had given him no choice. When she'd called, she refused to give him the location of the cabin unless he took her with him. It had been a guess on her part that Colon would take Laia and Rosa there. Turned out the place was in Cecelia's father's name and still was. That was why it hadn't shown up on any property searches they'd run for Colon. When Laia's phone had pinged on I-80 heading westbound, it seemed like Cecelia had been right.

Colon groaned, then tried to roll over, a distinct impossibility, given that one of Deck's size-twelve shit-kickers was planted firmly on his back.

"May I talk to him?" Cecelia asked calmly as she looked at Kade from watery eyes.

He nodded, then watched her go to Colon and start to kneel beside him. When she struggled to maintain her balance, Kade rushed over and held out his arm for her to lean on. She gave him a grateful look, then knelt beside her son. The irony of the situation wasn't lost on him.

Fernando Colon was one of the most dangerous criminals on the planet, but his mother was a good woman, and Kade's heart went out to her. She'd known something like this was coming. Either Colon would wind up in handcuffs...or dead. Which brought up another problem.

Laia and Rosa were safe. For now. But Colon was still alive. In or out of prison, Kade knew firsthand how the long arm of Fernando Colon could reach out and do deadly damage. The man would still have enough contacts outside prison, ready and willing to do his bidding.

Making it that much more tempting to stomp his boot on the guy's neck and crush his trachea. Maybe he should have let Jamie drill him full of lead after all. But Cecelia had other plans. The *real* reason he'd brought her with him.

They'd struck a deal.

As Colon regained consciousness, she leaned down to brush the hair from his brow. Given the circumstances, the gesture was so gentle, loving.

"Nando," she said.

Colon blinked. "Mama?" He blinked again, as if not believing his mother was truly there.

"Si, Nando." The look she gave her son was so sad, so utterly filled with despair.

"*You* told them?" Realization dawned in Colon's widening eyes. "You told them where to find me?"

"Yes." Cecelia nodded, wiping at some of the blood on her son's face as if he were a small boy who'd fallen off his bike and cut himself.

"Why, Mama? *Why?*"

Cecelia's chest heaved. "For your entire life, I've turned a blind eye to what you were doing. Because I loved you, and still do. I can't look away any longer. You kidnapped a child. You would have killed her and her mother. I couldn't allow that. I have to accept what you've become, and you have to accept what's coming to *you*."

"To *me?*" Colon asked incredulously. "What about Papi? His own department abandoned him. The job killed him, and when it did, the state police abandoned us, too. All I did was take what he taught me and turn it into an empire. *That* was justice."

"No, Nando." Cecelia exhaled heavily, her shoulders sagging. "Your father would never have approved of the things you've done. *I* don't approve."

Colon glared up at Kade. "I'll kill you. I'll fucking kill

you, just like your brother." Spittle mixed with blood ran down his chin. "There's no place you can hide that I can't reach."

"This has to stop *now*!" Cecelia screamed. She slapped his face, her hand coming away with her son's blood on her palm. "I forbid it! You will not hurt this man." She pointed first to Kade, then swung her arm to Laia. "And you will not hurt that woman or her daughter. If you do, you will never see me again. I will never visit you in prison. Ever."

Colon's lips began trembling. Tears leaked from his eyes. "No, Mama. Please, don't say that. I can't lose you."

Cecelia stroked a lock of hair from Colon's eyes. "And I can't lose you. But you must promise me. Promise me you will not harm these people, and you won't order anyone else to harm them, either."

Reluctantly, he nodded.

Her hand stilled. "Say it. Speak the words. On your father's memory, say you swear it."

Colon swallowed, then he took a breath. "I swear it."

Jamie caught Kade's eye and cocked a brow.

Yeah. Who'da figured? Despite the evil flowing through Colon's veins, he truly loved his mother.

In exchange for Kade acquiescing to Cecelia's demands that she be here, she'd stuck to her part of the bargain, insisting that she could extract such a promise from her son. When she began sobbing silently, all Kade could do was rest his hand on the woman's shoulder.

It was over. It was finally over.

Chapter Thirty-Five

Unseasonably pleasant and dry early morning July air rolled through the open window of Jamie's SUV, blowing strands of hair into Laia's face.

She brushed them away, then counted all the K-9 SUVs angle-parked across the narrow lot with their engines running. Kade had retrieved his government-issued vehicle, and she could just make out the tips of Smoke's ears in the kennel. To the right of Kade's SUV were Dayne Andrews' and Eric Miller's K-9 Interceptors. She'd met both men that awful day in the Poconos. On the other side were Deck, Brett, and Evan's SUVs.

Laia looked up the concrete steps to the entrance of the Peter Rodino Federal Building in Newark. Somewhere inside that ominous, dark-windowed fourteen-story building, Kade and his friends were meeting with the federal prosecutor to go over everything that had happened over the last week.

The infamous ledger had been returned to the DHS evidence locker, and the digital recording of Colon's confession that Laia hadn't known until this morning had even existed had also been logged in as evidence, a copy of which was, at this very moment, being turned over to the U.S. Attorney's Office.

She dragged a hand down her face, then yawned. Not knowing whether Colon would keep the promise he'd made to his mother and not seek revenge against her, Rosa, and Kade had eaten at her throughout a very long, nearly sleepless night. That and worrying about Kade, who hadn't returned to sleep at the shack.

Jamie sat in the driver's seat, reading a text message he'd just received. Since he'd been the only other direct witness to Colon's confession, he'd already talked to the prosecutor yesterday. "He'll be down in a few minutes with the rest of the guys. You're up next."

"Thanks." Since leaving the Poconos two days ago, she hadn't seen or talked to Kade, though he'd been on her mind constantly.

Her first priority had been getting Rosa to a hospital to be checked out. A DHS agent she didn't know had shown up at the ER to drive her and Rosa back to Manasquan. It had been Deck who'd called her hours later to let her know they were all still in the Poconos securing the scene and answering questions.

The Pennsylvania State Police had arrived first to assist in transporting Colon's men to the nearest federal facility for processing. Colon had been taken to another hospital to have his broken nose set and his bite marks attended to. Then DHS agents had swarmed in to take control, including the Newark DHS Special Agent-in-Charge. It was anyone's guess what would happen to Kade for stealing the ledger.

"How's Rosa doing?" Jamie asked.

Laia smiled tiredly but honestly. That morning, she'd dropped Rosa off at Alvita's, along with the minivan. "She's doing great. The drugs are finally out of her system, and she's as hungry as a hippo. Think you're up for pineapple pizza tonight?"

"Sure." Jamie set down his phone. "Although I'm not sure I'll ever be able to think of pineapple pizza the same way."

"Me either."

As soon as Rosa had been coherent enough at the hospital to start remembering things, she'd asked for pineapple pizza. Again, begging the questions: how had Colon's people known that was Rosa's favorite food, and how had they found them at the shack in the first place?

Turned out the night Kade had caught Rosa playing on Laia's cell phone, she'd actually been talking to Colon's people. Their initial goal had been to scare Laia into turning over the ledger. It had been an unexpected boon for them that Rosa had answered. They'd taken total advantage of the situation by asking what her favorite food was, then telling her they could deliver it to the house. After more subtly probing questions that a five-year-old would never pick up on, Rosa had inadvertently given them their approximate location by describing the carousel at the nearby kiddie carnival. Enter the arguing couple on the beach.

The Manasquan police had done their due diligence but had never found the couple who'd most likely been paid to distract Laia while Colon's men had moved in and taken Rosa.

For the umpteenth time, she looked at the stairs, half expecting to see Kade dragged out in handcuffs. Not knowing what would happen to him was driving her absolutely crazy.

Jamie leaned over and rested his hands on top of hers. "He'll be okay."

"How can you know that?" The desperation that had been slowly building inside her finally cut loose. "How do you know they're not snapping handcuffs on him as we speak?

He's in a lot of trouble, and it's *my* fault."

"None of this is your fault." For emphasis, he squeezed her hands before releasing them. "All of this is Colon's fault. Don't ever doubt that. We make the best choices we can at the time we have to make them. Doesn't always work out, but that's all we can do."

A dark cloud seemed to pass over Jamie's eyes, as if he were talking more about his own choices than Kade's.

"Look," Jamie continued. "Best—and probable—case scenario, he'll only be suspended."

"*That's* a best-case scenario?" Not to her. Mostly because that meant there was also a *worst*-case scenario.

"Worst case, he'll be fired. Absolute worst case, criminal charges could be filed, but I don't think that would ever happen."

"Oh God." Her heart ached from thinking about all the horrible outcomes Kade might be facing. None of them good. It had already been decided that no charges would be filed against her, but Kade's situation was significantly more dire. He was an agent of the U.S. government and, as such, would be held to a much higher standard. "How can you be so sure? Deck said that when the Special Agent-in-Charge shows up on site, it either meant something very good happened, or something very bad."

"What they should do," Jamie said, "is give him a medal. He might have broken a few rules… Well, okay. A lot of rules. But he not only got evidence to charge Colon with more drug money laundering charges, but the guy confessed to murder."

Right. Murder. *Josh's* murder.

"What if they *don't* give him a medal?" Along with desperation, now guilt had begun to eat away at her. "He stole that ledger, then put his life in jeopardy for me and Rosa. You *all* did."

She fingered the strap of her bag, realizing just how much

Kade and his friends had put on the line for her. Their careers and their very lives. "I said some horrible things to him." Things she could never take back and wished that she could.

"I know. I was there."

She took a deep, unsteady breath, desperately trying not to lose control of her emotions. "I accused him of putting his job—honor and duty—before family. Then he went above and beyond to prove that for him, family *does* come first and always will."

Even then, she'd loved him. She didn't know when the full realization hit her, but there it was. She was crazy in love with Kade. But was it too late?

Jamie touched her shoulder, drawing her back to reality. "You and Rosa can stay at the shack for as long as you need to."

"Thanks, but we need to go home and start cleaning up the mess." Her side of the duplex was still in chaos.

"Maybe you and Rosa will be moving out soon." The way Jamie said it was more of a question.

"What do you mean?"

"Who knows? Maybe you'll be moving somewhere else." He hitched his head toward the stairs. "Talk to him. Tell him how you feel. Things might not be as dire as you think they are."

Kade and his friends now stood on the top step, deep in conversation. The gray suit he wore made his shoulders seem even broader. A crisp white dress shirt contrasted with his dark-blue tie and tanned face.

Slowly, he turned, and a huge lump formed in her throat. The love she could have had with him might very well now be forever beyond her reach.

"It's time." Jamie got out of the SUV and came around to her side just as she opened the door and stepped onto the curb.

Instead of her usual brightly colored sundresses, she'd managed a quick shopping expedition at one of the local malls in Manasquan. Kade's eyes lingered on her face before lowering to take in her conservative green sheath.

Emotionally, his clean-shaven face was a blank mask, revealing nothing, though the intensity of his stare made her body heat as if she were standing in the middle of the Sahara Desert. She could have imagined it, but for a moment she could swear there was unabashed longing in his eyes. Just as quickly, it was gone.

The sweet memories they'd made that night on the beach were ones she would cherish until the day she died. Getting back to her life without him would be difficult, but she could do it. Getting her veterinary degree would keep her busy. But there would never be another man for her like Kade. He was her true love, the kind books were written about.

If only she hadn't thrown that once-in-a-lifetime love away.

...

Beautiful.

Maybe one day his heart would stop pounding whenever he so much as looked at Laia Velez. Today wasn't the day.

The way that emerald-green dress hugged her waist and hips reminded him of just how stunning she was. Inside *and* out. And of her naked body beneath him as they'd made love under the stars.

A cell phone blared, tearing him out of his pathetic reverie.

"Decker." Deck's brows lowered as he listened to whatever the caller was saying.

The rest of Kade's friends stood nearby, scrolling through emails and text messages.

Kade took the stairs and met Laia and Jamie on the curb. A gust caught her hair, whipping it in front of her face. He'd been about to lift his hand to tuck it behind her ear but stopped. He'd never touch her again. Whatever they had was over before it had even truly begun.

"Laia."

"Kade."

So this was what it had come down to. Formalities. Guess he'd help her through this meeting with the prosecutor, then go back to what he did best, what he'd done for years. Stay out of her life. Taking a barrage of bullets to the chest would have been less painful.

"How is Rosa doing?" he asked, not knowing what else to say. He'd miss his niece's smiling face and watching her teach Smoke all kinds of crazy tricks.

"She's doing much better." Laia smiled, but he knew her well enough to see it was forced. She still hated him for not agreeing to turn over the ledger right away. Not that he could blame her.

"How's your head?" she asked.

"Better. Nothing a bottle of aspirin can't take care of." At least he hadn't gotten a concussion.

"Kade!" Deck shouted. The rest of his friends came down the stairs. "Gotta head west." Deck grabbed Kade in a bear hug and clapped him on the shoulder, as did Brett and Evan. "Denver's a beautiful place, but it's also a hotbed of crime. The Mile High city needs us."

"What would Colorado do without K-9 Special Ops?" Brett asked, although it was more of a statement.

"Hooyah!" Deck, Brett, and Evan said in unison, their hands meeting in a brief fist-bump.

"Laia," Deck said as he gave her a hug. "Glad you and Rosa are okay."

"Thank you." Laia kissed Deck on the cheek, then

proceeded to do the same with Brett and Evan. "Thank *all* of you."

As the Colorado guys hopped into their SUVs, Dayne shook his head. "Showboats. I think the lack of oxygen out there has gone to their heads."

Jamie had tugged his phone from his pocket. "Pataglio." He listened for a few seconds. "When?" He walked a few feet away.

Dayne frowned. "Something's up with him."

"And where's Jax?" Eric asked.

Kade shrugged. "Don't know. He wouldn't say." From the sudden stiffness in Jamie's posture, he worried this was "the call" his friend had been waiting for and that he was about to take off again.

"That sure isn't good," Dayne said, looking just as worried as Kade felt. "I've gotta go, too. Kat will ream me a new one if I don't take some annual leave."

"I'm outta here, too," Eric said.

"Thanks, guys." Kade shook Dayne and Eric's hands.

"Me, too." Laia gave both Dayne and Eric a quick hug. "Thank you."

"Anytime." Dayne looked to where Jamie stood ten feet away with the phone still pressed to his ear. "Keep us posted on what's going on with Romeo."

"Will do," Kade said.

Dayne and Eric strode to their SUVs.

"On my way." Jamie ended the call.

"Jamie?" When his friend didn't respond, the worry in Kade's gut worsened. "You good?"

"I will be. I've gotta go." He stuffed the phone into his pocket, then walked over. "Remember what I told you," he said to Laia.

Moments later, they watched the barricade drop, then Jamie's SUV roll past, followed closely by Dayne and Eric's.

"Will he be all right?" Laia asked softly.

"I don't know." Whatever Jamie was mixed up in left Kade with the feeling that he was on the verge of losing one of his best friends. Loss was something he'd gotten used to. First Josh and soon, Laia. Although he'd never really had her in the first place. "Are you ready?"

She nodded. "As I'll ever be."

He led the way into the federal building, then flashed his ID and escorted her to the front of the visitor's line where she put her purse and sweater on the conveyor belt. He waited on the other side for her to walk through the magnetometers.

At the bank of elevators, he pushed the up button. Voices echoed in the nearby corridors, but an awkward silence settled around them.

"I heard you figured out the code in Josh's ledger." Laia fidgeted with the green sweater draped over her arm. "What was it?"

"Monopoly." He chuckled. "Remember when I told you Josh and I used to play board games? Monopoly was one of them. Josh never lost. He always wound up with all the hotels on—"

"Park Place!" Laia's face brightened. "PP. All those two-letter codes stood for locations on a Monopoly board."

"Yeah. I should have figured it out sooner." The awkwardness returned, and he glanced up at the blinking numbers indicating the elevator was about to arrive. "I heard how you took out one of Colon's men so you and Rosa could escape out the window. You made things a lot easier for us." Although when Deck had described what had gone down in the cabin, Kade's gut had twisted at the danger she and Rosa had been facing.

Briefly, she smiled. "I never knew I had it in me."

The doors opened, and they waited for several people to get out of the elevator before stepping inside.

Kade indicated Laia should go first, then he pushed the button for the fourteenth floor. The elevator began an excruciatingly slow ascent.

With every second that ticked by, he wanted to pull Laia into his arms. *A supremely bad idea.* Though she'd been cordial, she probably still hated him for not turning over the ledger immediately the way she'd begged him to.

The elevator lurched, then slowed to a stop. Several more seconds passed before it started rising again.

"Kade, I—" She turned to face him. "I wanted to thank you for coming after us. For saving us."

He opened his mouth to say the first thing that came to mind: *I would have died to save you,* but she held up her hand, stopping him.

"Please, let me finish." She bit her lower lip. "I also need to apologize. I said some terrible things to you, and it was wrong. I guilted you into stealing the ledger, and you did. Now you're facing the horrible possibility of getting suspended, or fired, or maybe even going to jail."

"I don't think that will happen." Jail, that was. Suspension, probably. Getting fired, maybe. The only reason none of that had happened yet was because the U.S. Attorney's Office needed him in order to formally file new charges against Colon. So at the moment, the DHS was holding back canning Kade's career.

Laia shook her head sadly. "Rosa and I are a burden to you. I never should have called you. If I hadn't, none of this would have happened. But you don't have to worry any longer. As soon as I'm done here today, I'll pack our things and we'll go back to the duplex. Back to our own lives. You'll never have to see us again."

Kade couldn't believe what he was hearing. "Let's get something straight." He slammed his fist against the red emergency stop button. The elevator jerked to a stop, forcing them both to grab onto the silver railing. "You were *never* a burden to me. You and Rosa are a blessing. I didn't do any of this out of family obligation. I did it because I love you. I've *always* loved you. In fact, I'm pretty sure I've been in love with you since the day we met."

He hadn't meant to say it, but there it was. Whether he liked it or not, his heart had spoken the truth, and it was too late to take it back now.

"If you want to go back to that duplex and walk out of my life forever, I'll let you go." But inside, he'd be dying. A slow, painful death that would last him the rest of his life.

Instead of telling him to go to hell as he expected, she didn't. Her jaw dropped and her eyes widened. When he expected her to recoil and tell him to pound sand, she didn't do that, either.

The look of total and utter shock on her face morphed into something else. Her eyes softened, glistening as they filled with tears. A gentle smile turned up her mouth. "What did you say?" she whispered.

"I said, if you want to go back to the duplex—"

"No, not that part. The part about loving me."

Huh?

She crossed the distance between them, standing so close she could probably hear his heart hammering away. Slowly, she slid her hands up his chest, pressing her body to his and linking her hands behind his neck. "Say it again. Please?"

He swallowed, feeling as if he were in another dimension. Was she asking him to love her? He couldn't possibly be that lucky. "I love you."

The smile she gave him was brighter than the sun. Brighter than the brightest muzzle flash he'd ever seen. "I love you, too. I've *always* loved you. Please don't ever leave me again."

His heart nearly blew apart. Unable to speak, he wrapped

his arms around her waist, then captured her mouth and kissed her. She opened to him, and he deepened the kiss, tasting her essence, trying to breathe her very soul into his lungs.

He *was* that lucky. Because the only woman he'd ever loved was in his arms, kissing him back. As he continued kissing her, it occurred to him they'd come full circle. Because here they were again...

In love in an elevator.

Epilogue

Five months later

Moist, humid air surrounded them. Frogs croaked in the low scrub, and birds flitted in and out of the tall Sierra palms and guava trees.

Kade stepped over another root belonging to what looked like a three-hundred-year-old guava tree. Bamboo lined one side of the wet trail, lush green bushes the other. Sweat dripped down his temples and his back, and all he could do was smile like an idiot.

El Yunque Rainforest was even more beautiful than he remembered. Probably because this time, he was here with Laia and Rosa, taking that vacation to Puerto Rico he and Laia had talked about in the elevator that fateful day. Laia's mother, Millie, aka Mima, had been shocked when Kade had insisted she join them.

Mima tripped over a root but didn't go down. Kade took hold of her arm, steadying her while she regained her balance. "I'm fine," she reassured him, patting his arm.

Getting to know Mima had been awkward at first, but he'd had plenty of free time to break through her shell. Thirty days in fact, the length of time the DHS had suspended him without pay for all the rules he'd broken.

Shortly after that, Laia had been accepted for the winter term at UPenn's veterinary school in Philly. He'd put in for a transfer and was picked up almost immediately by the DHS at Philly Airport. Then he and Laia had declared that they were all moving to a suburb outside Philadelphia.

Rather than shrugging him off as he'd expected, Millie kept her hand on Kade's forearm, leaning on him as they continued walking.

Millie had taken the news that Laia and Rosa were leaving New Jersey with grace, but the minute Laia's back was turned, she'd glared silently at Kade. Until he'd suggested she relocate there with them. Since then, they'd formed a tentative truce.

"C'mon, Uncle Kade! C'mon, Mima!" Rosa waved her hand, urging them to keep up. "You're lollygagging."

"Lollygagging? Never!" he shouted back, unable to stop grinning. In truth, he'd never smiled more in his life since Laia and Rosa had moved in with him. That had been another bone of contention with Millie. Living in sin, unmarried, and with a child in the same house. The glaring had picked up again until Kade had shown Millie four plane tickets to San Juan, one of which was in her name.

Laia and Rosa stopped to look at a book Laia had purchased at a local bookstore on the rainforest's flora and fauna. They both wore matching khaki shorts, hiking boots, and sleeveless orange shirts.

"Thank goodness," Millie said as she sat on a fallen tree trunk. "I thought they'd never stop walking."

Kade sat beside her, leaning down and pretending to retie his boot lace. For a woman around seventy, Millie was in great shape, but he wanted to make sure she didn't overdo it.

"You know," she said, leaning in closer, "I never told you this…"

Uh-oh. Kade had no idea what bomb Millie was about to drop.

"When I met you the day of Laia's wedding to your brother, I thought to myself: my daughter is marrying the wrong man."

Kade's fingers froze on his boot. *Say what?* He straightened, thinking he must have misheard her.

She elbowed him in the arm and laughed. "Don't look so shocked. I saw you two together that day. It may not have been obvious to anyone else, but I know my daughter. She was in love with you even then."

Kade shook his head, trying to digest this revelation. "Then why did you—"

"Nudge her into Josh's arms?" Her brows rose. "Because she was carrying his child. Marrying him, not you, was the way things had to be at that time. Could you really have been with her when she was bearing your brother's child?"

"No," he admitted. He'd figured that out a long time ago.

"It would have torn your family apart," she continued. "While I never wished your brother any ill will, things are finally the way they were always meant to be."

"I thought you didn't like me." More like hated his guts.

"That was never the case. I was worried about the impact you would have on my daughter if you tried being a part of her life back then. But you did the right thing."

"By staying away." Even though it had killed him.

"Yes."

They watched Laia point to the book, then up at the trees. Rosa followed her gaze, also pointing.

"This is our last day here, so what are you waiting for?" Millie nudged his arm.

Since seeking and receiving Millie's blessing, Kade had been stalling. Not because he wasn't more and more in love with Laia every day but because he was scared shitless that the new and improved, independent Laia wouldn't want to go through the formalities again.

Millie held out her hand. "Help an old woman up. I want to hear this." Her eyes crinkled and her lips twitched. "Find your courage, young man."

Courage?

In his military and law enforcement careers, he'd faced more danger than most people, but he'd never been more scared than he was now. As he tugged the tiny box from his pocket, his hand shook. Millie hooked her hand into the crook of his arm as they joined Laia and Rosa, still looking up into the trees.

"Uh, Laia?" He cleared his throat.

"Uh-huh," she said, pointing to where a green bird was barely visible sitting on a limb over their heads. "See that bird, Rosa?" Laia redirected her daughter to the book in her hands. "It's not as rare as a Puerto Rican Parrot, but we won't see anything like that in Philadelphia."

"Laia!" he said louder than intended.

She snapped her head up. "What?"

Rosa gasped and smacked her hands to her cheeks. "Is it time?"

"Yeah, Cream Puff. It is."

Getting Millie to keep the secret that he was going to propose during their trip was easy. Getting a five-year-old to keep that secret had been a miracle, one that had involved promises of pineapple pizza every week for a month.

Kade got down on one knee and opened the green velvet box. "Laia Velez, you and Rosa are the center of my world. The hearts of my heart. My life is nothing without you in it. Will you marry me?"

Rosa began jumping up and down. "Say yes, Mommy! Say yes!"

Laia's eyes filled with tears. When she didn't say anything, Kade's heart about stopped. Then slowly, she nodded. "Yes," she whispered. "Yes!"

Still jumping up and down, Rosa threw her hands in the air. "Yay!"

Behind him, Millie started clapping.

Kade pulled out the ring and slid it on the ring finger of Laia's left hand. Then he stood and captured her mouth in a searing, heart-melting, soul-binding kiss, not caring that Millie was watching.

Fluttering directly over their heads brought their kiss to an end. A few leaves floated to the ground at their feet.

"Look!" Laia whispered, pointing.

A green bird about twelve inches long with blue wings and a distinctive red crown perched on a limb over their heads.

"A Puerto Rican Parrot," Millie murmured. "It's a sign of good luck."

"It *is* good luck." When Laia reached up to rest her hand on Kade's cheek, he clasped her hand, tenderly kissing her palm.

He had to agree. He'd never felt luckier in his life. And Millie was right.

As he stared into the eyes of the woman he loved, finally… this *was* the way things were always meant to be.

Acknowledgments

To all my friends in Tee O'Fallon's MarTeeni Room… Thanks for being there and for your encouraging messages clamoring for my next book! It means the world to me.

To Heather Howland, the best editor a writer could ever hope for. I'm grateful you're in my corner. Your amazing editing skills and insight continue to elevate my writing higher and higher with every book.

To my longtime friends, Kayla Gray and Cheyenne McCray, for never saying no to my requests for manuscript critiques.

To James Borchers, U.S. Customs Service Special Agent (retired), for your invaluable assistance with the world of money laundering and drug smuggling.

To Rebecca Pappalardo and Milagros Grovas, for giving me a glimpse of your Puerto Rican heritage and for sharing your family experiences.

To Lisa Dente, VP Community Branch Manager, M&T Bank, for setting me straight on bank protocol and safe deposit boxes.

To the entire Entangled team for doing what you do behind the scenes. Special thanks to Bree Archer, Jessica Turner, and LJ Anderson for getting this cover just right!

About the Author

Tee O'Fallon is the award-winning author of the K-9 Special Ops, Federal K-9, and NYPD Blue & Gold Series. Tee spent twenty-three years as a federal agent conducting complex, long- and short-term criminal investigations, especially undercover operations, across many agencies at the federal level, and multi-state investigations as a police investigator. It felt only natural to combine her hands-on experience in the field with her love of romantic suspense. Tee has lived in New York State most of her life with a five-year stop in Colorado. When not writing, Tee enjoys cooking, gardening, chocolate, lychee martinis, and kicking back with her Belgian Sheepdogs, Loki and Kyrie. Tee loves hearing from readers and can be contacted via her website https://teeofallon.com where you can also sign up for Tee's newsletters.

Don't miss the Federal K-9 series...

Lock 'n' Load

Armed 'n' Ready

Dark 'n' Deadly

Trap 'n' Trace

Serve 'N' Protect

Also by Tee O'Fallon...

Tough Justice

Burnout

Blood Money

Disavowed

Discover more romance from Entangled...

HELL & BACK
an Outbreak Task Force novel by Julie Rowe

Racing to lock down the CDC's deadly virus samples, ex-Special Forces medic Henry Lee enlists smart, sassy microbiologist Ruby Toth's help. And then realizes she's hiding something. Terrorists have kidnapped Ruby Toth's brother and demand a vial of Small Pox in exchange for his life. Her prickly—and hot—boss, Henry could help, but she's undercover to root out those plotting to unleash a bio-engineered pandemic, and she can't trust anyone. Not even Henry.

HONOR AVENGED
a HORNET novel by Tonya Burrows

Leah Giancarelli would have crumbled if not for her late husband's best friend, Marcus. She has her issues with his team, though—after all, Danny would still be alive if he'd never accompanied them on their last mission—but Marcus has always been by her side...until after one impulsive kiss, he becomes so much more. But Danny's death was only the beginning. Whoever hired the hitman is looking for something, and they think Leah knows where it is...

ZONE OF ACTION
a novel by Cathy Skendrovich

When former terror cell expert Audrey Jenkins uncovers her ex selling military secrets, she turns him in and returns to civilian life. CID Special Agent Cam Harris knows his former teammate will resurface in Audrey's town. She may not want anything to do with hunting down her ex, but when a terror cell she's all-too-familiar with launches a deadly attack on army intelligence soldiers and officers, she has no choice. Helping Cam is the right thing to do, but the attraction between them may be the mistake that gets her and Cam killed…

A SURREALIST AFFAIR
a novel by Jacqueline Corcoran

Elle Dakin, an Art History doctoral student, is in Paris to attribute a newly discovered painting but finds herself neck deep in a murder. Handsome art exporter Ryan is protecting her from the dangerous side of Paris—or so she thinks… Undercover FBI agent Ryan DeLong is stuck in Paris chasing down art thieves when he meets enchanting but shy Elle, who seems to know more than she's telling and he's determined to learn her secrets.

Printed in Great Britain
by Amazon